COLD STARS MIDNIGHT GLOW

THE GODKISSED BRIDE
BOOK FOUR

EVIE MARCEAU

Cover Designer: Trif Design trifbookdesign.com

Content Note:

The Godkissed Bride series is a fantasy romance with sexually explicit scenes, violence, trauma, and adult language.

Are you new to the Godkissed Bride series? *Cold Stars Midnight Glow* is Book 4, and for it all to make sense, I recommend starting with Book 1, *White Horse Black Nights*!

THE ANCIENT IMMORTAL COURT

Vale the Warrior, *King of Fae*
Iyre the Maiden, *Goddess of Virtue*
Artain the Archer, *God of the Hunt*
Solene the Wilderwoman, *Goddess of Nature*
Popelin the Trickster, *God of Pleasure*
Meric the Punisher, *God of Order*
Samaur the Sunbringer, *God of Day*
Thracia the Stargazer, *Goddess of Night*
Alyssantha the Lover, *Goddess of Sex*
Woudix the Ender, *God of Death*

PRONUNCIATION GUIDE

HOUSE DARROW

Sabine Darrow: sah-BEEN DAIR-oh

Lord Charlin Darrow: CHAR-lin DAIR-oh

Lady Suri Darrow: SOO-ree DAIR-oh

HOUSE VALVERE

Lord Rian Valvere: REE-an val-VAIR-ay

Lord Berolt Valvere: BEH-rohlt val-VAIR-ay

Lady Runa Valvere: ROO-nuh val-VAIR-ay

THE IMMORTAL FAE COURT

Vale: vayl

Iyre: EYE-ur

Artain: ar-TAYNE

Solene: soh-LEN

Popelin: POH-peh-lin

Meric: MAIR-ick

Thracia: THRA-see-uh

Alyssantha: ah-liss-AN-tha

Woudix: WOO-diks
Samaur: sah-MAR

OTHER NAMES
Basten: BASS-ten
Folke: FOHLK-uh
King Rachillon: RAH-shee-yon
Captain Tatarin: Ta-TAR-en

PLACES & VOCABULARY
Astagnon: AH-stag-non
Volkany: VOHL-kah-nee
Monoceros: mon-oh-SAIR-ous
Tamarac: tam-UH-rak

CHAPTER 1
SABINE

This is what it feels like to die.

I never imagined it—how could I? Who would dare? To feel darkness creeping around the edges of my mind, folding in around me like dirt closing in on my grave.

I feel the life draining out of me onto the punishingly cold stone floor, and no matter how I scramble, I can't hold it in. Can't catch it up in my fists.

And, gods, it *burns*.

Ice-cold lightning rips through my heart's center, shooting into my bones, until I'm sure they'll splinter from the pain. Bursts of light flash behind my closed eyes, lighting up the spider-web veins in my eyelids.

With all my strength, I try to breathe. But I'm a sieve now, so full of holes that I can't capture a single gasp.

Panic crawls over my skin.

It's getting dark.

Darker.

And I'm fighting, gods, how I'm fighting. I'm fighting

with every human ounce of flesh, scrambling to cling to that tiny slip of light I see cracked beneath my eyelids.

I have reasons to live. People who need me. Someone I love more than life itself.

And yet no matter how I try, my fingers turn colder by the second. I try to wiggle my bare toes, but they feel stiff as a cadaver's.

How...how did this even happen?

I remember leaning in to hug my father one final time. My birth father, who I didn't know existed until a few days ago. It didn't matter to me that he was Immortal Vale, King of Fae. The most powerful god to walk the ten realms. Because for once in my life, I had a family.

And then?

Oh, right.

He stabbed the Serpent Knife in my back.

For a brief moment, I manage to scrape together enough strength to focus my energy. It's anger. White-hot and boiling. Fury that I was betrayed by a man I thought loved me as a daughter.

I was so, so wrong. There's only ever been one man who loved me.

Basten.

I try to part my lips so I can murmur his name. He's here. I can sense him, somewhere close by. He was with me only a moment ago, our hands clasped, our eyes full of love, as we finally were about to get the happy ending promised to us.

But even the thought of Basten slowly bleeds away.

Basten, I'm....sorry.

And just like that, my mind empties.

My heart thumps one final time. Spent, finished,

drained. Slowly, coldness seeps in, frosty as the stone beneath me, frigid as the blood in my veins, icy as my lips.

My soul's final scream comes out hollow.

Then, there's nothing.

Nothing.

Nothing.

Nothing.

Nothing.

Nothing.

Nothing.

～

And then?

Something stirs.

It begins soft as a mothwing flutter, the faintest tickle in the back of my skull. I can't be sure how much time has passed. Maybe a second. Maybe a thousand years. But a spark—faint but determined—glows in the shadows shrouding me.

My lips tingle with the memory of breath.

Until—

With a jolt, my heart gasps back to action.

And it *hurts*.

My body remains still, but somewhere deep inside, something is sprouting. Pain ricochets through my chest with all the force of a hundred lightning bolts, but this time, I welcome it.

Because I *feel* something again.

It's enough to nudge my waking mind back into the present. All my hopes and dreams chase after that tiny spark of light. It burrows into my body until the shadows are pushed to the edges, and in the semi-dark, one thought surfaces:

I'm...alive!

Vaguely, my ears pick up on voices outside of my body.

Yes—there.

People are talking. At first, their voices bleed together into one blurred orchestra, but slowly, one voice stands out. Deep and rasping.

"Kill him."

Suddenly, as though I've been doused with ice water, I snap back into my memories.

I remember where I am: *Drahallen Hall's throne room. Basten and I were leaving. Saying our goodbyes and heading to Astagnon to confront Rian. My father betrayed me with a knife to my heart...*

And now?

The back-stabbing bastard is going to kill Basten, next.

A bitter tang spreads down my tongue. Energy builds beneath my skin in a way that's somehow cold and bright and deadly all at once. A thousand wasps thrash inside me, buzzing and fiercely territorial, ready to explode in defense of the man I love.

I will not let Basten die.

My body might remain a tomb, but I don't need my body, I realize—I've done this before.

I did it when I possessed the tigers in Duren's arena.

I did it when I took control of the cloudfox, Plume.

I did it when I synced my mind with Tòrr and decimated hundreds of Volkish raiders.

Before I can truly process what's happening, that long-buried second self roars into control. It's like shedding a snakeskin. Casting away the tender-hearted little girl they tried to break.

A part of me wants to cling to that previous self like an old, threadbare coat that's kept me warm for years. But the light thrums beneath my limbs, buzzing and hot, pushing at the inside of my skin with the force of nature itself.

A gasp hisses between my teeth. Bitter, biting rage drips thickly down my throat.

I—*erupt.*

Light tears out of me in a hundred directions at once. It blisters down the length of my arms and my legs. It bursts from my temples, down the sides of my blood-spattered face, shooting out of the corded lines down my neck. It's cold and terrible, blinding and seismic.

Come to me, creatures of the skies! I command.

From a million places at once, I feel them respond. Birds from across the castle gardens and deep into Vallen Forest. They pinwheel toward the Aurora Tower unquestioningly, as surely as I were pulling them on kite strings.

My eyes remain closed, but my ears are open. I hear wings pounding at the locked glass windows. Caws sharper than blades. Talons scratching at the latches.

Come to me, creatures of the land! I beckon.

The ground rumbles as my call is answered by an army of mice, cats, foxes, beavers.

I call to the yellowjackets. To the goldenclaws in the stable. To Plume.

And I don't stop there.

I summon forth the creatures of the waters—fish and eels and salamanders—which means raising the very waters of the raging Ramvik River right here to this throne room.

The ground rumbles beneath me, vibrations rattling the windowpanes.

Wind, I command. ***Thunder. Quakes. Everything. Come to me!***

The floor trembles harder, and I hear the gasps of people around me as they try to process the impossible happening. My summoned creatures burst through the windows and door, flooding the throne room with claws and stingers and sharp beaks.

Screams ring out.

The stone tiles crack and break apart as the Ramvik River rushes upward.

Pins twist in my stomach. It's exhilarating, this power.

It's wild.

It's—

"Sabine?" Basten's velvet-deep voice calls in my ear, and it's so shockingly familiar that it tugs me like a rein, tethering me back to myself.

My eyelids flutter open, slowly, as my spirit swims up from the blindingly bright depths of endless light.

There—I can see him. He's a hazy outline against the brightness. Even blurred, I know the shape of him the way I know my own breath. The flow of his raven hair. The softness hiding in his lips. The way his eyes drown in mine.

My lips purse to call his name, but a different voice interrupts my attempts.

"No." Vale's voice is stern yet rings with a strange note of pride. "That isn't her name. Not anymore. That isn't *what* she is."

"I know who she is!" Basten bites out, fierce and sharp. "She's the only thing in this damn world worth the gods' wrath!"

At his words, my eyes snap fully open, and I stare up at the beautiful chaos I've called to me.

There's Basten, so handsome it hurts, his eyes bleeding out every fear in the world as he gazes down at me.

Just over his head, more birds than I can count sweep through the arched chamber with deafening caws like shattering glass. Wind and rain roar through the open windows, and thunder rumbles so close that the chandelier sways.

"Basten?" I whisper on cracked lips.

His eyes widen for a fearful, awe-filled moment, like he's watching a star being born. But the shock is short-lived. He blinks, then grips his powerful hands around my shoulders so tightly it hurts.

"Sabine?" he croaks. "You're—you're really alive?"

I gaze up at him as if seeing him for the first time. My eyes have changed, somehow. Now, I see all the little details I was too blurry-eyed to take in before. How could I have never noticed the dozens of shades of auburn in his hair? The pinprick scar just under his bottom lip?

I shift my gaze to Immortal Vale, standing behind Basten with the Serpent Knife still in hand.

All my love twists sharp as a needle.

I hiss aloud, "I'll break the world before I let them hurt you, Basten."

My jaw clenches iron-tight, the burn of my light blazing even brighter.

Heat builds in my palms, a power I don't even understand beginning to spark.

Artain's voice suddenly rises, high-pitched and sharp. "Brother Vale—look at her fey lines! She's going to blast the fucking castle apart!"

My attention hooks on him. My eyes narrow. *This golden*

bastard staged the Night Hunt so he could kill Basten and claim me as his own. Now, it's his turn to be afraid.

I let out an exhale, and as though I'd spoken aloud, a swarm of yellowjackets swerves straight for him. He yelps as dozens of stringers batter every inch of his exposed skin. Angry welts rise on his sinewed forearms.

He flicks them away with zaps of his own flame-orange fey, but hundreds more swarm in to take their places.

"Fuck this! *I'll* make her stop." Grimacing under the wasps' onslaught, Artain swings his bow around, knocking a golden-tipped arrow that he aims at Basten's chest.

"No!" I scream.

Roots tear out of the river-soaked floor, twisting up from between shattered stone tiles and weaving themselves around Basten and me. Thorns jut out on the opposite side from us. Leaves unfurl to hide us from sight, forming a living barricade to keep any arrows or blades away from Basten.

"Sabine!" Vale shouts over the roaring wind and churning waters. "As your father and your god, I command you to end this!"

But he might as well be speaking to the storm itself. His words glide right off me.

He might be a god...but I'm starting to understand that *I'm* something else, too.

As a ferocious cry tears from my lips, I twist my fingers in the air. More roots burst out from the floor to wrap around Vale's legs, weaving into his armor to drag him down to his knees, the river waters rapidly rising up around his waist.

I throw out my hands to send a dozen hawks swooping toward his eyes. Their talons catch the candlelight, sharp as razors.

The Serpent Knife clatters out of his hand and skids across the floor.

Any human would duck to protect themselves from the onslaught, but Vale?

He smiles up at the hawks grimly as he unhooks the battle axe from its harness on his back, and sweeps in a vicious arc that slices every bird clean in half the second that it attacks.

Blood-stained feathers rain to the floor.

Anger coils hotly inside me, and before I realize what I'm doing, I weave my fingers in the air again.

The rushing Ramvik River bubbles up faster from the floorboards and builds with the force of a tidal wave, headed straight for Vale and the other fae near the head table.

At my side, Basten watches with a mixture of horror and awe.

A flicker of doubt runs through my belly.

Does he fear me like...this? What I've become?

But that worry is swallowed by the memory of my father ordering his death, and I shove my hands to command the wave to rise even higher.

Then, the air splits.

A flash of golden light blasts from the window—it's Samaur, God of Day. He wields his sunlit fey to blind me, trying to break my focus.

But I summon thick clouds to block him and his sunlight.

When both Artain and Samaur's attempts to subdue me fail, Iyre growls, reaching her fingertip toward my temple. In a flash, I know what she's trying to do. Steal my memories. Scramble my brain until I don't remember who I am.

I command the water to blast straight at her instead.

She's slapped backward, drenched down to her prim white boots.

Woudix—cold, patient Woudix—raises his palms toward the flock of ravens overhead. Black fey sparks from his palms, but before he can release the charge, I sweep my hands together. Wind crashes in from both directions, extinguishing the spark.

Wild with power, I throw up my arms. Thunder crashes against the tower walls, raining dust down from the ceiling joists, splintering the three-thousand-year-old head table.

"Enough!" Vale shouts, his voice clapping like a massive bell.

He frees himself of my vines and steps forward, towering over where Basten and I crouch in our shelter of vines, by all appearances ready to smite us both to ash. And yet, there's the slightest waver in his eyes.

A flash of uncertainty.

Fear, I realize—of *me*.

For a heavy moment, everything quiets. The wind. The shrieking hawks.

Even the five gods.

"You claw your way back from death itself," my father snarls, "you split the sky with storms, and all for what? To save a mortal?"

I lift my chin and seethe, "You started this when you gave his death order."

"He's human! He's so much *less* than you."

I bristle, cheeks reddening with building fury. My voice drops. "You have no idea the lengths I'll go to keep him safe. I'll open the earth. Bury the five of you so deep you'll never rise again."

Vale's laughter booms through the shattered hall, but

there's a nervousness to the way he paces. "You're unstable. Not yet practiced. Stop your histrionics, and I will strike a bargain."

My heart—my cold, ice-block heart—slams in my chest. Anger makes my limbs quake with tightly coiled power. "Why would I bargain with you? You stabbed me!"

Vale picks up a handful of soil thrust up from between the floorboards by my earthquake. "A fae bargain," he spits out. "Unbreakable. Stop this, and Lord Basten will remain safe from me for as long as he is in my kingdom."

My vision is starting to blur at the edges. Exhaustion is rapidly overtaking me. I burned too bright, too hard. My dress is stained with crimson blood, but when I touch my hand to my chest wound now, quicksilver spills out instead.

My ears suddenly tune into the distant screams of the castle servants. Are people hurt? Did...did *I* hurt them?

"Sabine." Basten wraps his arms around me. "He's right —you have to stop this or you'll kill everyone in the castle."

"Basten," I choke. "I don't...I didn't mean to..."

"End this," he urges in a low murmur.

My words fall away. I don't know what's happening. Where I went...how I'm back.

But I trust in Basten.

"A pinch of earth to close the deal," Vale recites the fae bargain phrasing. "What's given now, the ground will seal."

With a shaky hand, I reach through my fortress of vines and clasp a fistful of dirt, letting it sift through my fingers. I repeat the bargain's wording on broken lips.

"It's a bargain," I say.

In that instant, all the strength goes out of me.

There's nothing left in me but hollow veins and a

strange hunger that shreds its way through my insides, demanding sustenance that I can't put a name to.

As soon as the last few clods of soil fall from my fingertips, my body gives out. I slump onto the floor, half-tangled in the vines I brought forth from deep underground. I stare dimly up at the ceiling, crawling with spiders who answered my call.

And in the chandelier?

My mirrored image winks back at me, fractured into a hundred quivering reflections. Not the girl who was locked away in a convent for twelve years. Not the woman paraded bare across half of Astagnon, either.

Something *else*.

Fey lines burst with silvery light from my temples and down my limbs. The shells of my ears rise to faint points, matching the upward lilt to my eyebrows.

Sharpened incisors wink from my parted lips.

Not painted.

Not costumed.

Ancient.

Real.

Whatever I am now...

it's not what I was.

CHAPTER 2
BASTEN

"Sabine!"

I drop to my knees, catching her hand before it falls. Her skin burns against mine, but I force myself to hold on through the pain.

The ground shakes. The walls groan. Vines continue to thrust up through the floor, tearing apart stone like paper. The raging Ramvik River churns through the room, drenching everyone up to our knees.

"Stop," I beg, though I'm not sure if I'm speaking to her or whatever's inside her. "Please, you have to stop. You're hurting people."

Her head jerks, eyes flashing—but I don't recognize the look in them.

Fear crawls through my chest so fast I choke on it.

Gods help me, this is the woman I love. Even like this. But love feels small against the force she's become.

From the corner of my eye, I see the protective fortress of vines around us draw back, slowly slinking down into the floorboards until they've all but vanished.

Beyond, the five fae gods rise slowly to their full heights, brushing wrinkles from their clothes, tucking their hair back into place. I pick up on a few quickened heartbeats among the lot, but those soon return to a steady, if not also wary, patter.

Sabine's show of power rattled them—but maybe it wasn't entirely a surprise.

"Little violet." I clasp Sabine in my arms, smoothing the sweat-soaked hair off her forehead. "I'm here. You're going to be okay."

She murmurs something that not even my ears can pick up on.

I brush my lips against her ear and breathe, "Hold on, little violet."

At the same time that I'm smoothing blood flecks off her cheek, I'm all too aware of the panic spreading through the castle.

My godkissed hearing picked up on the servants' terrified screams as soon as Sabine unleashed her earthquake. Someone on the first floor now cries out in pain, pinned by a falling ceiling joist. A gaggle of maids cluster in the Twilight Garden outside, frightened words spilling from their lips as they try to understand what has happened.

I mean, I get it.

Nature just came fucking *undone.*

My gaze shifts to Sabine, carefully studying the contours of her face. There's a part of her that is—and always will be —my perfect violet. I feel it in my gut, missing memories be damned. That tender curve of her mouth, the readiness to smile at any passing nuthatch. There's a brightness in her eyes—still hopeful, somehow, even though they're unfocused.

And yet.

Silver fey lines cut down her smooth temples, running down her neck to disappear under her traveling clothes. Her incisors have grown, flashing like a predator's.

I have to admit it: She's not just a girl who sings with spiders anymore.

She's as dangerous as any fae god.

Because...fuck, I can hardly say it.

She's one of them.

Heavy footsteps approach, and the flutter of unsureness in my chest tucks itself away, replaced by a protective roar.

Immortal Vale's iron-tipped boots come into view. Anger tightens like a fist in my gut as I glare up at him.

"What's happening to her?" I bark. "She came alive— only to weaken again."

"The Gloaming." Vale speaks with irritating calmness as he strokes a hand down his silver beard, seemingly unbothered by the decimated throne room. "It happens whenever a god is awakened from their human body. The transition is not gentle. It's violent, it's painful. We all went through it."

He lifts a hand toward the other fae. Now that the river has drained back through the floor cracks, Samaur is righting one of the toppled wooden chairs. Iyre hunts through the overturned wine bottles for one with a few sips remaining. She finds one, and Artain tries to swipe it from her, but she bares her teeth at him like a snake.

"It's always hardest on her, however." Vale's voice hitches as he gazes, softer now, on his daughter. "On Solene."

I wince at the name.

So, there it is.

Immortal Solene, the Wilderwoman, Goddess of Nature.

The muscles along my shoulders pull tight, wanting to resist the reality in front of me. But what's the point of fighting it? The bitter truth is out, now, and there's no going back to the way things were.

"You made her into Solene?"

Vale scoffs. "She always *was* Solene. I merely awakened her true self." He draws a step closer. "Give her to me, Lord Basten. She's more special than you know."

I snatch the Serpent Knife off the floor and brandish it with white knuckles. "Not another fucking step forward."

Vale stops, eyes on me instead of the blade in my hand, a curl of condescension riding the corner of his mouth. "There is no need for a blade, Lord Basten. You are protected. My daughter and I sealed a fae bargain that cannot be broken. For better or worse, all of our fates are bound, now."

I shove to my feet, raking the hair off my forehead.

"It's *her* neck I'm defending, you ass. Not mine."

His right eye twitches at the brazen insult. I can smell the fury radiating off him, and for a second, I'm sure the only thing keeping my head on my shoulders is that very bargain he mentioned.

Finally, he explains in strained patience, "The Gloaming drains an awakening fae of their power."

Though his words are slow and calm, I can pick up on the waver of urgency behind them. His eyes flick to the window, then back. The side of his jaw twitches.

He continues, "Her strength isn't waning. It's simply *hungry*. If she doesn't replenish her spent fey, then she'll spiral further out of control until her earthquakes bring the entire kingdom to the ground."

At my feet, Sabine whimpers. I drop to my knees, hugging her close as she moans through the pain. By the gods, I want to tell Vale to fuck off straight to the underworld.

But for Sabine, I rein in my temper.

I ask warily, "Hungry for what?"

"Offerings," Vale spits, rising impatience rushing his words. "From her altar. So, surrender my daughter to me, and I will get her the sustenance she requires."

He stretches out a claw-like hand. I pin Sabine tighter to my chest, a growl ripping from my throat, as I bite out, "Like hell. *I'll* take her."

I hoist Sabine in my arms. Her eyelids flutter up at me as her pupils swim back and forth, disoriented. A groan rumbles from deep within her chest.

In the distance, a rumble of thunder answers her in a preternatural echo.

"Basten," she whispers. "I'm *hungry*."

There's a feral snarl to the way she says the word that sends a lick of unease crawling up my spine. Just for a moment, I'm not sure who I hold in my arms—if it's Sabine, or something ancient wearing her skin.

But just as fast, that worry disappears.

What am I thinking? She'll always be my violet.

"I've got you," I murmur against her sweat-soaked temple. "Always. Through any storm."

More thunder rumbles, closer this time.

Even ones of your own making, I think with a twist in my gut.

"Open the gods-damn doors," I bark at Captain Tatarin, who stands closest to the exit.

The door hinges are broken, but the captain manages to push one side open. As I head into the hall, my heart bucks. Sabine feels dangerously light in my arms. The tang of her spilled blood clogs my nose and mouth, turning my stomach. Her heartbeat is sluggish. Faint. Not like the other fae, whose hearts clap strong as iron bells.

A headache throbs behind my right eye as I stride down the maze-like hallways. At least these passages are undamaged; Sabine's ire was limited to the throne room.

A creeping daze hits me with every step. I've always been cool-headed in a crisis. Hell, I can't count how many battles I've been in. But this time, I don't know what I'm facing.

I don't know who my opponent is—if I should fear her as well as protect her.

Wide-eyed servants hurry out of my way. I can hear each of their breathless whispers to one another, threaded through with fearful awe.

The rumors are true, a lady's maid says. *It's Immortal Solene!*

She raised the very Ramvik River from its bed, a sentry answers. *Three people were swept out the window—they're lucky to still be alive.*

A half dozen more are with the castle healers from falling debris.

There are always sacrifices with the fae. It will be worth it in the end, you'll see. The sixth fae has awakened from slumber— only four more still sleep!

I tuck their gossip into a pocket of my mind to process later, focused only on the weakened girl in my arms. With every step, it's like she's evaporating before my eyes.

I clutch her harder, speeding my steps.

"Hold on, Sabine. Hold on, sweetheart."

The servants, wary and frightened, are hesitant to open the exterior door, so I kick it the rest of the way open, slamming it back against the wall, and stride across the pathway to the Garden of Ten Gods.

From this angle, the ten gods' statues seem to loom higher than the Vallen Mountains in the distance. Townspeople who have come to present their offerings cower, gasping as they part to make room for me to pass. A million scents assault me from gifts spread on the altars. Sticky bowls of wildflower honey. Over-ripe pomegranates. Scented rosewood beads. A raw lamb haunch. Spiced wine by the barrel.

I swallow back the bile rising in my throat as I shove my way past wide-eyed onlookers, straight to the altar resting at the base of Immortal Solene's statue.

My hand falls on the closest edible object—a pomegranate.

I break the thick peel with my thumb, then nudge the fruit toward her lips. "Sabine, here. Eat."

As soon as the dark red juice drips onto her lips, her bleary eyes focus pinprick-sharp. Her tongue darts out to taste the drop.

She gasps as if lightning has struck her core.

She wriggles out of my arms like a spitfire cat, and I barely manage to set her bare feet on the ground before she's clawing at the broken fruit.

"Give it to me." Greedy, she rips the pomegranate out of my hand, prying it open with her fingers, then tearing into its flesh with her sharp incisors. Bloodred juice pours down her chin to dribble onto her already ruined gown. There's a feverishness to her energy. A frenzy that sets my nerves on alert.

She tosses aside the spent rind and motions to a ceramic bowl. "The milk. Now."

As soon as I pick up the bowl of still-warm sheep's milk, she snatches it out of my hands and guzzles it down. I lean back, muscles primed, observing with a soldier's keen eye. I've seen Sabine eat and drink countless times, though I lost my memories of most. Even at her most famished, I can't imagine it's ever looked like *this*.

All around the Garden of Ten Gods, pilgrims laden with offerings stare in rapture at the newly awakened fae goddess.

Already, I can hear the rumors spreading from person to person. Traveling like an infection from the garden, to the castle gates, and out into the streets of Norhelm.

Vale and the other fae approach, stopping at the highest level of the sunken amphitheater, the weight of their presence bending the air itself.

The ceramic bowl shatters behind me as Sabine drops it, careless, to move onto a bunch of grapes on a bronze platter.

She stuffs a handful in her mouth, but her eyes dart needily over the altar's other offerings. Oven-warm loaves of dark bread. Carved wooden figurines. Vegetable-dyed wool skeins. She pounces on a cured lamb haunch and sinks her teeth straight into the salted flesh.

After a few bites, she comes up for air, wiping her glistening mouth with the back of her hand. Her fingers are shaking. Eyes glassy, distant.

I gently touch the small of her back, and she jumps, whirling on me.

She blinks, trying to focus. "Basten." Her voice comes out like a gasp for help. "I don't know what's happening... Everything inside me is too loud, too bright. Too hungry. I— I can't turn it off."

Her voice breaks into a sob, and with it, the last of my hesitation shatters.

I tighten my fingers on the back of her gown. How could I ever doubt her? She's no monster like the others.

She's still my little violet.

"I've got you." I pull her into my arms, letting her hot tears stain my shirt. "I'm with you."

"I didn't know, I promise," she chokes out. "I would have told you that I was—was—" She briefly turns her head to gaze up fearfully at the fae at the top of the stairs. A hiccup makes her jump. She whispers, "I don't want to be like them."

She suddenly breaks eye contact and begins to shake.

Her eyes are rolling again, wide like a raging horse. I cup her chin in my hand and gently guide her attention back to me. "Hey. Eyes on me, sweetheart. Listen, human or not, you aren't like them. I *know* you."

Her hands twist in my shirt. "How can you? I don't know myself! I don't recognize who I am like—like this."

She swipes the back of her hand again on her cheek, brushing away a slather of greasy lamb's meat. Her stomach groans, followed by her eyes darting back to the altar.

A deep, distant clap of thunder rolls across the horizon.

"Don't fight the hunger," I urge her, giving a worried glance at the sky. "You have to get through this. Your father called it a Gloaming. You need to—" I look doubtingly over the altar offerings, none of which seemed to make a dent in her appetite. "—to build back your strength."

Her throat bobs in a hard swallow, but her will is no match for her insatiable appetite.

She grabs an oat roll and tears into it. She relaxes, but after only a few bites, her face twists into another scowl. She throws aside the half-eaten roll and grabs a wine bottle instead, tipping it up to guzzle straight from the source. Her throat bobs until the entire bottle is empty.

She throws it down, where it shatters.

A woman nearby shrieks and shies away. Sabine briefly comes back to herself, eyes widening at the woman's fear, but then her stomach growls again, and she pivots sharply back to her altar.

Her fingers tear anxiously over bolts of woven cloth, golden coins, tapered candles. Nothing she touches seems to satisfy the frenzy in her eyes.

All around us, townspeople stand rooted to the stone steps, their offerings nearly forgotten in their arms. The air in the amphitheater feels like it's holding its breath. Hardly anyone moves, except to lean forward, straining to make sense of the sight.

At the top of the stairs, Vale watches with a hooded expression. Iyre smirks as she packs a plug of Wicked Weed into a long-handled pipe.

The only people not focused on Sabine are the redheaded human twins who serve Samaur as his acolytes. They saunter up to him and try to loop their arms through his, but he swats them away.

"Not now," he chides.

A memory shoots back to me: watching his lips latched to their necks one at a time, teeth to their jugulars, throat bobbing as he took turns drinking down their freely offered blood.

Is that what Sabine needs? A blood sacrifice?

It's so damn twisted.

Wicked.

Positively fucking obscene.

Hesitant, I rub my palm over the rough scars on my left forearm where, weeks ago, I carved Sabine's name into my flesh. The bottom loop of the "e" skims over my wrist's thick blue vein, almost like a map.

A drip of sweat slides down my temple.

"Sabine." I roll my sleeve cuff back to my elbow, fully exposing my forearm. "Sabine. Hey—look at me. Try this."

She's so busy tearing into a greasy pork chop that I have to grip her by the chin and force her attention on me. Her eyes are wild, frenzied. The sharp points of her new incisors dig into her bottom lip, pricking silver blood.

I draw my hunting knife with my opposite hand.

"Look," I prompt her. "Here. I think this is what you need."

I set the blade's tip against my throbbing blue vein. Realization of what I'm about to do hits her, and Sabine's eyes suddenly snap into focus.

She pounces on the knife in my hand.

"Basten, stop! What are you doing? Have you gone mad?"

"Sweetheart, you're changing. Gloaming—whatever it's called. Wine and bread aren't going to get you through this." I drop my voice. "You know the stories, just as I do."

For the span of a long breath, she stares at me, wide-eyed as a doe. Her bottom lip trembles. I can see the indecision in her gaze as it bounces back and forth between my face and my wrist.

Fuck it.

I make the cut. It's a small but deep gash. Dark red blood spills out.

I growl softly, "Use me, little violet."

Something shifts in her face. The doe disappears, overtaken by a predator. Her pink tongue snakes out to lick the drop of silver blood off her lips. Her eyes lock onto my wrist. She takes a hesitant, jerky step toward me, dropping her lip to hover over the wound but holding back.

Warring with herself.

I flinch, struck by an electric shiver. *She did this before,* I realize. *She told me about it. We were in the woods outside Duren. She said she sucked on my cut thumb on impulse, no idea why.*

But now I'm wondering if this was why. Maybe it's more than a coincidence. It could be a pattern, history looping back on itself like a snake eating its tail.

How many times has she drunk someone's blood?

That line of thought vanishes, however, as Sabine's tongue darts over my bloodstained wrist. The cut stings, but to help her? That kind of pain I'd drink for days.

A moan rattles out of her chest, and with just that one lick, all her inhibitions disappear. She seizes my wrist, fingernails digging in like claws. Her tongue and lips punish my skin as she feverishly laps at the blood.

"That's it," I murmur, though my heart slams against my ribs—unsteady, uncertain—as she grows wilder in her need. "Take what you need."

For a few frenzied moments, she sucks and claws and kisses at my wrist until my blood drips down her chin.

"Yes," I hiss as she grows almost feral. "Drink me down to the dregs, if that's what you need."

At this, she comes up for air and blinks, almost as if seeing me for the first time. Her pupils are round as buttons.

Her gaze moves to my lips. I hear her pulse suddenly speed in her veins.

"I want...something *else.*"

Like an animal, she pounces on me. Her small arms pull tight around my neck, straining on tiptoe, trying to climb me like a tree with no branches.

"Kiss me, Basten," she gasps.

"Gods, little violet."

She's getting blood all over both our mouths—tangy on my tongue like metal. She's so frantic that it's all I can do to scoop her up around the waist, bring her closer, one hand supporting her ass.

She locks her legs around my waist, fingernails twisting in my hair as she thrusts her tongue between my teeth.

I pick up on murmurs in the crowd as the townspeople's mood shifts—from fascination to something more uncomfortable. Embarrassment. Like they're witnesses to something too intimate and don't know where to look now.

Gently, I try to break the kiss. We can continue this in her bedroom.

But she meets my attempt with a growl as her arms latch tighter around my neck, thighs squeezing my hips. My lungs constrict. I don't think a monoceros could drag her away from me.

Oblivious to the shocked onlookers, she rolls her hips against mine, needy and demanding. An indecent moan rolls off her lips.

"Fuck me right here," she begs, so loud that people a hundred paces away could hear. "Hard. I need your cock in me now."

My jaw unhinges. Her father is twenty paces away. The rest of the fae, too. As well as a hell of a lot of little old ladies carrying sweet, embroidered quilts to lay on Vale's altar. With their wide-eyed grandchildren in tow.

Sabine nips at my jaw, hot breath full of lust. And just like that, I realize she isn't going to make it to the bedroom.

"Everyone," I shout in a hoarse voice. "Get the fuck out right now."

A handful of onlookers quickly shuffle away, cheeks burning red, but uncertain murmurs find their way to my ears as some people linger, too caught up in wonder to tear themselves away from Sabine's transformation.

I crane my neck back toward Vale and shout, "Tell them to fucking *go!*"

The other fae flinch at my tone, but Vale remains stoney-faced. However, he unclenches his arms and slowly raises one hand toward the gate.

"Leave us, everyone," he commands.

His voice is deep enough to shake the earth itself. Shrieking, people in the amphitheater scramble up the stairs toward the exits, flowing like water from the Garden of Ten Gods until the only thing remaining is someone's still-bleating goat.

Sabine lunges at my shirt, ripping off the buttons like it's the last barrier between her and salvation, and tugs it free of my arms.

Bare-chested, I throw a glare toward the five gods. "You, too, fuckers."

Vale growls with that earth-shaking voice, "She needs guidance."

"From who?" I snap. "You? You tried to kill her."

Vale nods toward the others. "Any of us is capable of giving her the instruction she needs."

Iyre picks her nails, uninterested. The three Blades speak low amongst themselves, slapping each other on the shoulder, cruel smirks on their faces. I can only imagine what kind of "instruction" those assholes would like to give her.

"I'll guide her," I'm quick to answer, as Sabine shimmies out of my arms and starts to tear at my belt. A gust of hot wind suddenly blasts from the east, blowing my shirt a few feet away. "This path? It's mine to take her down, not yours."

Artain lets out a rip of laughter. "You might amuse her for the time being, human, but if you're speaking of fate, then you should know that she's mine. She's always *been* mine."

"Maybe that was true once," Vale answers Artain, "but you fucked up this time, didn't you?" Vale grabs the prissy god by his vest's leather ties and sends him toward the exit with a hard shove. "The rest of you, too. Leave them. Let Lord Basten realize for himself that he isn't up to the task."

Iyre gives me a smirking wave with red-tipped fingers as she saunters away.

Once I hear their footsteps return to Drahallen Hall, every ounce of my attention whips back to Sabine.

We're truly alone now.

On her knees, she jerks my belt free, the leather snapping clean as a bone break.

Overhead, a shower of acorns suddenly rains down everywhere but directly on us, like the trees can't control themselves.

"Easy," I coax her, but she doesn't seem to hear. Her lips are all over my bare navel, teeth sliding over the hard cut of muscle at my waist. "Sabine. Eyes on me."

I capture her small, pointed jaw in one palm and force her head up. But her eyes dart between the scattered offerings, my bare chest, and the falling acorns.

I chit to get her attention. "*Only* on me."

The command manages to cut through her haze. She lifts pleading eyes to me that waver with confusion.

"I need—" Her voice shakes too much to finish. The hot wind shifts direction, this time turning so icy cold it might as well come from the frosted North. "I need..."

My voice softens. "I know, little violet."

I lightly grip her wrists, tugging her to her feet, and press my lips to hers before she can utter another word.

Look—sex with Sabine is always transcendent. But this moment? It isn't about my pleasure. I don't even think it's about hers.

It's about steadiness.

She doesn't need a lover—she needs grounding.

"Sabine." I call her name as clear as a ringing bell, cupping her chin so our gazes connect. Echoing her trembles, the stones rumble underfoot. I can feel even deeper tremors far below, ready to burst forth if I don't find a way to tether her to reality.

I claim her lips again.

She opens her mouth willingly to me, so eager that her incisors clatter against my bottom teeth.

When she realizes she nearly bit me, she jerks as if to pull away, but I press a firm hand around the small of her back, rooting our bodies together.

Her shaking hands twist in my open shirt, barely holding on. Thunder cracks overhead, followed by a rash of icy frozen rain pelting us. A crack opens in the amphitheater floor in front of her statue, snaking its way between our feet, shifting the earth.

By the gods, I think, pulling back for a breath. *She could tear open the world.*

"Basten, don't stop!" She clings to my bare shoulders, fingernails digging into my skin, sending pain rocketing down my back muscles.

A vine tears out of the ground with enough force—moving like a snake, *possessed*—to slam into my chest, knocking the breath out of me.

I stumble back, letting go of Sabine. Before I can recover my balance, the vine wraps around my ankle and yanks my foot out from under me.

I tumble backward, tailbone jarring painfully against the ground.

Sabine growls and throws herself on top of me like this was the plan all along. Her lithe body writhes against mine as she shucks my pants down my hips.

There's no tenderness here. Not this time.

Only hunger.

A drip of crimson blood runs down her chin and patters against my bare chest.

"Easy, little violet," I coax. Once, I'd have met her bite for bite. I've always loved the violent clash of our want. Hell, the thought of my palm cracking across her bare ass is enough to stir me even now.

But this time?

This time, I keep still. She's the waves and I'm the rock to break herself against.

"Basten, I can't stop myself," she pants.

"So don't." I trap her hands on my chest, holding them there. "Let it out. Let it come. I can take it. You're not going to break me."

Another vine rips out of the ground, sliding around my left ankle and pulling tight enough to nearly pull the bone out of the socket.

Sabine grips the vine as an anchor, rocking back and forth while straddling me, her hair loose and tangled in the wind that blows at her command. Her thighs tremble around my hips.

She's trying to hold herself back.

But the vines don't listen to the last whisper of her human restraint. They're commanded by something ancient in her, driven by pure, wicked desire. Another vine loops around my chest and pins me down, chaining me at her will.

She grips this one even harder.

I grimace at the pressure but don't let her see a bit of my pain.

With my free hand, I grab her chin and drag my thumb against her bottom lip. "Don't fight it, Sabine. You think I can't handle you in this form? I've seen you bare. I've seen you in a crown. I fell in love with each person you've shown me. I want *every* version of you. Each terrible and beautiful part. You won't scare me away. You could break the world in half, and I'd still be at your side."

The storm clouds clear in her eyes, leaving them wide and open as the sea.

"That's it," I offer gently.

Unsure at first, she rocks her hips against mine, still clinging for dear life to the vines. She moves slower this time. More in control. With her vines holding me down, there isn't a place I could go to escape her—but I don't want to.

Her head lolls backward, her windblown hair cascading down her shoulders. She's so wet between her legs that she's soaking through her dress. The sharp scent of her need is like a drug to my groin.

I want to stay in control, to lead us—but gods, she makes it hard.

"Take what you need from me," I groan.

I drive my hips upward as far as the vines allow, and she gasps and arches her back. Her beautiful breasts strain at her dress's fabric, her nipples so hard I can feel their ache.

"Take that dress off," I command.

She runs her hands down her curves, and more vines snake over to peel her out of her dress, pulling it down her hips like a moth emerging from a cocoon, darkly beautiful and new.

And then she's bare to me. No holding back. It's different this time—I see the goddess and the girl, wrapped up in that perfect body I'd go to hell and back for.

Her hands on my bare chest are feverish, uncontrolled. She grinds mindlessly against me, purely driven by adrenaline. I shift my position to give her the friction she's seeking. As my cock lines up with her swollen heat, a gasp tears from her lips.

"Yes, Basten!"

My free hand holds firm to her waist as I rock my hips up, sinking my cock in deep. Finally giving her the sustenance she needs. This isn't sex; it's desperation. It's her way of surviving the enormity inside her. Each roll of her hips is a demand as she works through the need gushing through her.

I hold fast, guiding her so that she can find her way back to me.

"Do you feel that?" I pant between thrusts. "How connected we are?"

Her muscles tremble. Her eyes roll back in her head.

I keep my eyes on her. Reading her face as she rocks up

and down to meet my thrusts. Gauging her need as I angle my hips to slide even deeper inside her.

The moment before she comes, a flock of blackbirds alight. Mist pours into the amphitheater basin. The trees groan and bend, their roots writhing underground. Lightning forks across the sky to illuminate roiling black clouds.

Every shudder of her body is echoed by the land and weather and creatures around us.

Her pulse shallows, and it's all I can do to hold myself back, to let her ride out her release instead of letting my own need loose.

I clamp my molars, grimacing to hold back.

The sky opens, and snow falls around us, gentle and silent, but heavy as a goose-down blanket. It lands on her brow, her hair, her eyelashes. She might be oblivious to the way she's tearing apart the land with fistfuls of emotion, but I'm not. Everywhere snow touches, my nerves spark.

The snow thickens, falling faster, harder.

She's so damn close. I rock my hips with her, guiding her toward the release she needs to survive—to transform into whatever she's supposed to be.

Vines squeeze tighter around my chest until I see stars. Her fingernails dig against my scalp. The earth shakes, and another crack opens near my head. Steam hisses out from the fissure, soaking my brow.

The snow turns to hail.

It falls so damn hard against my face, it'll leave bruises.

That's when Sabine comes.

She comes harder than ever before. Her breath is as quick as butterfly wings. Her fingers twisted painfully in my hair, holding on hard. Shivers of adrenaline course through me as I find my own release.

Gradually, the fight pours out of her.

The earthquake that shattered half the amphitheater subsides into nothing more than slight tremors. The snow stops, the last flake catching on her cheek. The wind fades to a whisper. And at last, those damn vines let go of their death grip on me.

And she lets go of her death-grip on my hair.

But her eyes are glassy.

"Breathe with me," I murmur, not wanting to lose her now. "Focus on me."

I guide her lips back to mine. As I lead the kiss, melding my lips to hers, tracing my tongue over the seam of her mouth, her heartbeat slows to normal.

I look up at her straddling me, her statue looming over *her*. Like that, I see the two souls in her at once. Human and fae. Goddess and girl.

For a brief flicker, I mourn the mortal life I thought we'd have. A future together, growing old and gray, living a simple life.

But that's not her anymore—and I make a vow to fight to the ends of the known world to defend both sides.

As though an invisible cord has been cut, she slumps over my body, my cock still buried deep inside her, and with a final sharp exhale, she passes out.

Satiated.

Spent.

At long last, nature itself shudders to rest, and one final snowflake settles at my feet.

CHAPTER 3

SABINE

I *broke the natural world.*

It's the first thought that comes to me when I'm able to find words. Has it been minutes? Weeks? Time feels like a slippery thing. Flashes of memory come to me in bursts. Falling snow, despite the warm sunshine. Vines thrusting up from the earth.

Slowly, I swim up through my mind's haziness until I blink my eyes open.

The light around me is dim, orange. *Candlelight.*

Soft feather pillows hold me upright in a bed carved from a single tree trunk. Warm reindeer pelts drape over my bruised knees.

At the foot of the bed?

It's the delicious weight of the man I'd recognize through any haze.

"Basten," I gasp through cracked lips, sitting upright and reaching out for him.

My father stands near my bedroom's arched window, speaking in a low rumble to Basten, but at the sound of his name, Basten whips toward me with a hunter's instinct. His eyes spring wide. Before a sob can rise up my throat, he wraps his arms fiercely around me.

"Sabine. Sweetheart. I've got you—you're okay now."

He smooths his hands over my shoulders, then down the length of my arms. Where my shift's capped sleeves end, there's only warm peach skin. No fey lines blister along the length of my arms.

I feel my teeth with my tongue—no sharp incisors press back.

The tight knot in my chest works free, and I collapse against Basten's chest, burying my face in the solid, sturdy rock of his shoulder.

From the corner of my eye, I glimpse stars winking beyond the bedroom window.

It's nighttime—and we're still in Drahallen Hall.

No, no, no, I think weakly, too spent to feel much of anything but Basten's steady breathing beneath my cheek. *We're supposed to be halfway to the border wall by now.*

"How do you feel, Solene?" Vale asks, coarse and clinical.

I flinch as though he's struck me, and Basten instantly folds me tighter in his protective hold.

"That name..." I start, but choke it off.

Hearing that name stirs a tangle of long-buried memories, emotions, images. Most I don't even recognize, as though they belong to a stranger. They press behind my ribs, sharp and demanding, like a swallowed fish bone.

"Call her Sabine," Basten barks. "At least, until she decides for herself how she wants to be called."

Vale's nostrils flare with impatience, but he nods. Relenting on this one battle.

"What…happened?" I manage to utter. "I only remember pieces."

Vale looks out the window at his kingdom rolled out far below. As though reporting the weather, he explains calmly, "It all comes from a mistranslation, really. In the Book of the Immortals, the ancient scribes wrote that between the First and Second Return, the gods *'slumbrian o tornn'*. That phrase was interpreted to mean "slumbered underground," when it truly meant "slumbered under *skin*". It led to the long-running rumor that fae rest in underground tombs between our Returns. While it's true that we go dormant, it does not happen in tombs. Rather, we lose our mortal bodies; only our souls remain. Our resting places are within godkissed bloodlines, remaining hidden through generation after generation, until something triggers an Awakening."

"You." I press a hand against the base of my raw throat and rasp, "You triggered it this time."

The hint of a smile touches Vale's lips as he rests a hand on the window's latch. "Yes. The Third Return is now upon us. We have the potential to rise during any generation, but as King of Fae, I am always the first to awaken. You see, S-- Sabine,"—he stumbles a little over the name, "For generation after generation, I slumber until one of my human selves is strong enough to Awaken. Then, I search for the other nine gods. I find them one by one. Not in buried tombs. In *people*. It can take months. Years, even. To follow rumors of godkissed people throughout the kingdoms and determine if they are one of us."

"Sabine is your biological daughter." Basten's hand falls on my knee, holding tight. "Not that hard to find."

Vale moves to the bedroom dresser, where he digs through the jewelry box until he finds a garnet ring. He cups it in his palm like it means something to him—like the weight is heavy with memories.

"Yes," he says, voice distant. "It is no coincidence. In every Return, there are patterns. Solene is always intimately connected to me, in the form of a daughter or sister or niece. I believe it is because Solene commands nature, and nature cannot be separated from the core of our power—which resides in me."

He hesitates as if unsure whether to share more, rubbing his oversized thumb on the small ring, and ultimately lets the jewel fall back into the box. A heavy stretch fills the room, and I can't shake the niggling itch in the back of my head that there's more than the version he's giving me.

I twist my hand in the bedsheet. "You aren't telling me everything."

He barks a laugh. "Four thousand years of history can't be explained in the span of one evening."

"It's more than that." My voice cuts, jagged, and a flare of anger ripples under my skin that feels cold and wrong. "You're keeping secrets on purpose. What don't you want me to know?"

At my side, Basten rubs a steadying hand down my back. His head cocks as though he's using his godkiss to listen to my pulse, my breathing, my scent, my temperature.

"Easy, wildcat," he murmurs, and I have to wonder if I registered as human to his senses...or something else. "You're still weak."

Vale moves back to the window with a grunt that I'm not sure signals approval or scorn. "Your man is right."

"No, *I'm* right." I throw off the sheet, swinging my bare feet off the bed. I marshal my strength to push to my feet, holding onto the bedpost for support. "I'm strong enough. Now, tell me."

Vale peruses the orange-pink blossoms growing on the vines climbing my bedroom wall, as though searching for something.

Finally, he plucks one.

He spins the blossom in his finger slowly as he explains, "Every fae must undergo a process called the Gloaming upon waking to their true self. It is not easy on any of us. However, after sating their hunger, the other nine gods have always readily embraced their true divine identities. Solene has always been an outlier among us. In both the Beginning, as well as the First and Second Returns, she has...resisted her Awakening."

He presses his thumb into the flower's center, splintering the delicate petals. A dissection. "She's the Goddess of Nature, and nature is in opposition to divinity. It's more akin to the wild, barbaric realm of humanity. In the previous Returns, her Awakening has proven contentious. That is why, this time, I decided to attempt a different approach."

Strange energy rustles up my spine, kicking my heartbeat up a notch. I rub my thumb over the bedpost's natural bark exterior. In a way, I feel like I've been here before, many years ago. Felt this same rough bark against my skin. And the flicker of ancient life that's still buried deep in the wood's core.

Basten stands up and tugs a velvet dressing gown out of the dresser, draping it over my thin cotton shift. His hands close protectively around my shoulders, tethering me back to the present.

"Maybe you should rest more," he murmurs.

I shrug off his suggestion, clutching the bedpost harder

as I ask my father, "Shouldn't I remember? The times when I was Solene before?"

Vale folds his fingers over the blossom, crushing it like a mosquito. "Memory is like mist. The more you chase it, the farther away it drifts. All you can do is simply wait for it to come."

He opens his hand and lets the crushed petals waft to the tufted rug.

Outside, a hawk caws sharply.

I glance out the window. The bird soars past, its course dangerously close to the castle tower. It falters before regaining its flight. As broken and unsteady as my mind.

"This whole 'different approach' plan," Basten asks, his voice laced with poison. "Did it always involve stabbing your daughter in the heart?"

Vale scowls. He lets his heavy boot fall on the plucked petals, grinding them into the floor. "That's on you, human. For trying to take her away from Volkany."

Basten laughs darkly as he rakes a hand back through his hair. "Sabine won the Night Hunt, fair and square. The prize was our freedom. Just because that ass, Artain, didn't come crawling to you for permission first—"

"Raise your voice to me, mortal, and—"

"Stop it!" I throw out my hands between them, my head aching. I glance at my father. "Basten asked a good question."

Vale prowls over the rug, further tromping the flower petals. "The truth is, the Serpent Knife is indeed the key to awakening. The human soul must die for the fae inside to arise. But it wasn't supposed to happen as it did. There is usually a ceremony. An agreement. It is meant to be a beautiful, holy process. Not..." he scowls, hand flexing. "Violence."

My hand drifts to the place between my breasts, just reachable between the string ties of my shift, where he plunged the Serpent Knife into my heart.

The skin is smooth now. No wound. Not even a scar.

Vale clears his throat. "I had hoped to bring you slowly to awareness of your true self. To first introduce you, in your human form, to the Fae Court. I thought if you met your brothers and sisters, learned our ways, saw our world, then the transition would be more seamless this time. That you would *choose* to undergo the Gloaming, eagerly, as the others do. Instead of having it forced upon you." He lets out a long breath, heavy with the trace of myrrh and Wicked Weed. He mutters almost to himself, "But it seems history has a way of repeating itself."

I rub my finger over the place where a scar should be, wondering how many times the skin has been torn, ribs broken, by the knife blade.

"A word of advice?" Basten says tightly, baring his teeth at my father. "A thousand years from now, at the next Awakening, maybe give a word of fucking warning before stabbing your daughter."

Vale huffs in mild amusement, as though even as a human king, Basten is as simple-minded as a lapdog.

Vale turns to me, instead—his focus always circling back on me, like orbiting planets. "You are immortal, Sabine. Nothing can permanently maim you. Not even Woudix himself is capable of harvesting a fae's soul for his underrealm. The sooner you shed your former human habits, the more easily you'll embrace your powers and your memories. What happened at the Garden of Ten Gods was a showcase of your raw, untamed fey. You'll need to harness it. To tame it. To remember how to bend your power to your will until every human before you cowers."

Beside me, Basten rolls back his shoulders, tense for battle.

A trace of a smirk twists Vale's cheek as he faces Basten, looking him slowly up and down. He wrinkles his nose at what he sees. "You preferred her in her human form, didn't you?"

Basten presses his hands together, drawing in a tight breath. "Listen close, King of Fae. I don't give a fuck about your fae-human squabbles. I don't kneel to gods, and I sure as hell don't kneel to men. The only king I ever bent a knee to fucking burned me for it. So hear me now: the only loyalty left in my bones is to the woman at my side."

A thread of warmth finds its way into my cold center, and I toy with the twine ring on my fourth finger that Basten gave me, wishing for an instant it was only the two of us. That the bed's canopy of sewn fabric leaves was real, that the rugs underfoot were swishing grass, that the window was open to the stars.

Like our early days together.

"She isn't yours, human," Vale growls.

"I am his, and he is mine," I interject before Basten can answer. A clap of anger beats alongside my heart. Outside, thunder suddenly cracks, though there's no sign of a storm. "You could stab me in a thousand places, and each one will bleed for him."

Wind rattles the window panes, sending a tree branch outside snapping at the glass.

"Easy, wildcat." Basten's steady voice in my ear calms the storm inside me.

I blink, swallowing back my anger, and the wind outside dies down.

Basten drapes his arm around my waist, low and intimate. "Try to tear us apart again, Vale, and you'll see history repeat itself in blood. Sabine and I are a package deal. I'm the one who got her through the Gloaming at the Garden of Ten Gods. Not you. Not Artain. Not fucking Iyre. Sabine drank my blood, carved her need into my skin, broke her pleasure on my cock. That bond isn't something you can break."

I preen with pride, leaning into his promises.

Vale plucks a piece of dust off his shirt, unbothered. "To what length would you go for her?"

Basten's back jerks upright. "What?"

"You heard me."

"Any length." His fingers curve possessively around my hipbone, pulling me closer. "Isn't that clear?"

"Would you give *all* your blood?"

There's a catch in his voice—a trap. My stomach pulls in tight, and immediately, I think of how Basten found Paz's pale, dead body in Iyre's cabinet. Drained of memories, prayers, and most of all, blood.

"She'll need a mortal acolyte." Vale rubs his fingers, lets the imaginary dust fall to the ground. "I suppose that's *one* thing you could be useful for."

A warning beat picks up in my chest, but as soon as I turn toward Basten, he cups my jaw and says without hesitation, "I'll be whatever she needs—it isn't even a question. Wildcat, you know I exist to serve you. I'll be your acolyte. Companion. Worshipper."

I grab his shirt collar, the metal buttons cutting into my palm. "No. You're a king, not a throat just waiting to be opened."

He snorts as though I've made a joke. "Look, I don't want to agree with your father on anything, but he's right in this. You need someone to satiate you. Breathe, blood, sex, worship, prayer. You think I'd let any other man on this earth give that to you, instead of me?"

I open my mouth to protest, but the rush of words poised on my tongue fades. I close my mouth and swallow hard. Like it or not, I have to admit he has a point. I don't *want* to need that from someone. But even now, the hunger is returning to my core, hot and demanding.

"You're sure?" I ask.

He laughs softly—leaving no room for doubt.

My breath catches, unsure how to find the words to tell him what this means to me. I'm about to lean in to kiss him instead when Vale's heavy voice cuts the moment. "It isn't quite that simple."

My mouth goes dry. "What do you mean?"

"It's a commitment to become an acolyte. A *lifelong* commitment."

The tone in Vale's voice sends prickles running down my limbs over the now-hidden fey lines, and I smooth a hand over my forearm, a wrinkle forming on my brow.

"Not a problem," Basten responds easily.

"Wait," I say with a hitch in my voice, as the hidden lines resting just below my skin burn colder. "What do you mean, Father?"

Vale saunters to my dressing table. His fingers close around a small, sharp pair of embroidery scissors.

I suck in a breath, stepping in front of Basten and stretching out my arms. A crackle creeps over the room's windows, where frost crystals have suddenly spread like a defensive barricade.

"Ease your fears, Daughter." Vale turns on us with the tiny, decorated brass scissors dwarfed by his massive palm.

Really, it's only a seamstress's tool—hardly the Serpent Knife. Still, in Vale's hand, even a maid's implement feels like it could be an executioner's axe.

"When I say lifelong," he says slowly, "I do not mean twenty or forty or sixty more years. Acolytes' average lifespans, once they commit, is counted in *months*. None have lasted a full year. Our fae needs are too great; and once we get a taste for blood, it only gets harder to stop."

I shake my head fiercely. "I wouldn't do that. I'd stop before I took his life."

"You say that now," Vale explains in stark, matter-of-fact words. "When you are still deeply connected to your humanity. The longer you're fae, the less you will care about preserving his life."

"But you swore a fae bargain that Basten would be safe."

"While he resides in Volkany, yes. He is safe from me. Not from *you*."

My stomach hollows out.

To my surprise, Vale hands the scissors to me. "To become your acolyte, Lord Basten must freely drink of *your* blood."

My lips part in soft uncertainty as I spin to face Basten, our bodies only inches apart, searching his velvet-brown eyes. "I would never hurt you, but if it's too risky..."

His answer to my silent question is to cup my face, grazing his rough thumb over my cheek. He murmurs, "You and me, little violet. How many times have we defied the odds? We can with this, too."

A thread pulls taut in my stomach, and my fingers curl over the scissors. "No—I'll find another acolyte."

But as soon as I speak the words, I know they're false. In good conscience, I can't lay a death sentence on any strangers who worship at my alter. Besides, every fiber in my body loves and wants to protect Basten. Maybe, with a stranger, I'd go too far—but with Basten, I'll always be able to control myself.

The cold under my skin burns harder, and I can almost remember something. The shadows of people on their knees, backs bent in prayer. Primitive robes fastened around their waists with twine. Chants pour out in a long-lost language.

I've done this before—Basten isn't my first acolyte.

"Gods, Sabine. What are you waiting for? There's nothing to debate." Before I can stop him, Basten steals the scissors from me, takes my hand in his forcefully, and jabs the needle-fine point in my index finger.

I flinch more with surprise than pain.

A tiny drop of red blood wells, but right behind it rises a bead of pure silver. Stronger, pushing out the old remnants of my human blood.

My heart hammers so damn hard I can practically feel the bedposts shake with it. I flinch with the urge to pull my hand free—but then relent.

What choice do we have? Better it be Basten, and our own choice, than whatever tricks the fae may think of next.

Slowly, I nod.

Basten lowers his mouth to my finger, taking the full length in his mouth. He sucks gently in a way that stirs something deep and hot in my belly. Pleasure flows from the sensation of Basten's lips on me. It makes me acutely aware of the fact that my father is three paces away, staring at my blazing red cheeks.

This act shouldn't be sexual, but gods, it's close.

Basten sits up, dragging his tongue over his bottom lip to lap up any silver remnants, and for a second, the room is so quiet I can hear all three of our breaths. I wait, unsure what I should be experiencing. But Basten and I are already bound by something stronger than blood—by choice.

"It's done," Vale says. "Daughter, your only task now is to survive the next few days, until the fever of the Gloaming breaks." His eyes shift to Basten, the corner of his mouth curling with disdain. "Keep her alive—then, we'll see how long you can manage to keep yourself out of the grave, too."

Gods, that word clings to me like sweat.

The *grave*.

For the next week, I hardly leave my bed—not because I'm sick or weak, but the opposite. My new body is intimidatingly strong—every step I take ripples in outward quakes. If I so much as stand, pinecones clatter against the windows in sudden volleys. Shutters burst open, curtains billowing. This is no peaceful partnership with nature—it's a battle raging between me and the elements.

And my *hunger*.

Servants can't bring trays of honeycakes fast enough to satisfy my roaring belly—I drain the wine goblets, lick the plates, and still crave more. Priests cart in overflowing baskets of offerings from my devotees, anxious to win my favor. I roll every string of rosewood beads between my fingers, breathe in every bundle of rosemary, rub every silk scarf over my shoulders, my thighs, my breasts. I want to devour every texture, every taste, every scent.

Each time I touch an offering, the chaos inside me eases. The punishing wind down the chimney fades into a breeze. For a moment, I can breathe.

And sex. Gods, the *sex*.

Basten and I hardly come up for air. It's been a constant tangle of limbs, stroking and squeezing, a collision of hips only broken to throw a reindeer pelt blanket over our naked bodies when the blushing maid brings in our breakfast trays. Deep claw marks run down every inch of his back. His neck is bruised from my kissing.

His wrist is marred by my teeth marks.

It...gnaws at me. My father's warning that acolytes don't live longer than a few months. I try not to drink from Basten, and push for sex or prayer instead, but every little flash of his tanned skin only makes me more ravenous. Here and there, I can't help but take a few deep sips.

He begs me to use him and swears I won't hurt him— but he's human, and I know his strength is no match for the hunger inside me. Yet still, he offers himself. Again and again. Until I'm terrified I'll break him.

Somehow, night after night, he proves even stronger than I knew.

And that gives me hope that we *will* defy the odds.

Over the days, something shifts. Each night, the Gloaming fever burns a little less. The frenzied wind loses its edge. The floorboards no longer quake with every step. I begin to feel...not myself, exactly. But as though the clouds have lifted.

And then one morning, I blink awake with Basten's slumbering arm thrown over me, and for the first time, I'm not famished. No restless wind whips the trees outside. The hawks circle smoothly.

With this new stillness, a strange power raps at my pulse.

Basten snores in my ear, worn out from last night's exertions. I rub my bleary eyes and get out of bed, then slide on a robe and open the door.

I step into the hall for the first time in days.

To my surprise, overflowing piles of offerings fill the hallway. There are flower bouquets. Brown loaves of bread by the dozen. Fragrant bundles of fresh-cut lavender.

The heavyset, grizzly-bearded captain posted outside my door straightens in surprise before quickly dropping to one knee.

He lowers his head to me in a rush. "Lady Solene."

I stare, blinking a few times before I realize he's speaking to *me*.

It's...going to take a while before I get used to that name.

And all the bowing.

And the offerings.

"I—wanted some fresh air," I say, my throat raspy and unused. "I thought I'd go for a short walk. Just in the gardens."

Without lifting his head, his eyes shift nervously to the left, and before I can ask what the problem is, voices rise from around the corner.

"*Lady Solene? Is she awake?*"

"*Is that her?*"

"*Is she here? Lady Solene! Goddess of Nature, gift us with your presence!*"

Eager feet scuff, and more voices rise and fall, and before

I know it, a practical battalion of worshippers storms around the corner.

Their eyes are wide, adoring. They clutch their hands to their chest in prayer. Worn, wrinkled clothes hang off their frames, and they carry blankets and baskets of food slung over their arms, which makes me realize they've been here for days. Camped out in the hall.

Waiting for me.

I retreat a step into my bedroom, hand flying to tighten the folds of my dressing gown. The army captain bolts his feet and pivots hard on the devotees, drawing his sword with a metallic ring.

"Back!" he commands. "You heard Immortal Vale's command. All pilgrims seeking an audience with Immortal Solene must wait in the second-floor library, outside the boundary of the royal residential hallway."

But a bright-eyed young mother, cradling her infant in a woolen sling, wags her finger at me. "It's really her! Look at her ears, it's true!"

My face blanches. I clap my hand over the shell of my ear, eyes widening to find that it does, indeed, rise to a soft point. When I drag my tongue across my teeth, they snag on incisors. But my skin? It's pale. Still in human form. No glowing lines to blind them with.

By the gods, I'm only half in human glamour, still groggy from sleep and the Gloaming.

I might as well be half-dressed.

"Umm..." I squeeze my ear, not sure how to banish the point.

"Lady Solene!" A lanky man with a limp hobbles forward, swiping off his woolen cap and clutching it in his calloused hands. A spiral tattoo, reminiscent of swirling water, marks his chin. "Give us your favor, my lady. It's a blessing from Vale himself that you're waking exactly when we need you most."

As the worshipper approaches, the army captain thrusts his sword forward as a warning. "You've already cluttered the hallways with your damn offerings, now get back before I have to clear you out of the way, too!"

He raises the sword, taking a menacing step forward, and the crowd's worshiping rumble rolls into uncertainty. Still, the rag-tag pilgrims' eyes gleam with determination. I spy more of the same spiral chin tattoo among the crowd— it must be their people's mark.

The limping man dares another step forward, even with the guard's sword aimed at his chest.

"Damn you," the captain caws, "I said stay back!"

"Wait!" My feet sweep me forward, my hand falling away from my ear. "Stop, don't hurt them!"

I'm too short to reach the guard's raised sword, but on impulse, I lift my palm. I don't even know what I'm doing. Just following some deep river of knowledge in my bones.

My palm tingles like frostbite.

The guard's steel glove suddenly frosts over from the base to the fingers, an icy coating spreading up his sword blade in snowflake patterns.

He yelps, stumbling backward, tugging desperately to get the gauntlet off. It falls to the floor with a hiss of ice. Beneath, his bare hand is red, chapped. Nearly frostbitten.

A hush falls over the hallway.

As though one, all eyes turn to my raised palm.

"The Wilderwoman," a gap-toothed woman utters as if in a trance, speaking Immortal Solene's moniker.

The air begins to spark with renewed eagerness, and I

can feel it—the coming storm. My heart pounds as I step forward with a hand tentatively raised, afraid to rest it on the guard's shoulder to check on him, in case I turn him to pure ice.

"I'm…sorry," I gasp, bending down to grab a pair of woolen mittens from among the offerings. "I—I just didn't want anyone to be hurt."

As if a peace offering, I offer the captain the mittens.

His breath is quick, like he's facing off against an enemy army. Even though it's only *me*.

He bows his head again.

"They've been here for days," he explains, sliding on one of the mittens with a nod of gratitude. "Immortal Vale consented to them leaving offerings—" he nods to the piles overflowing outside my door. "—but it's an audience with you they want. Say they won't return home without one."

"We've no place to return to!" the lanky man cries, clutching his woolen cap harder. "No home, not anymore, thanks to King Rian Valvere!"

My spine pulls straight at this, the other mitten slack and forgotten in my hand. I feel it slip from my fingers and fall with a whisper.

The hallway lanterns flicker unnaturally.

"*What* about Rian Valvere?" I demand, my soft voice suddenly bladed.

The captain falls back, eyes darting between me and the pilgrims. Most of them are eyeing the oddly-behaving lanterns apprehensively, but the man with a limp steps forward.

"My lady, we're from the Lunden River valley." He motions to the dozen or so pilgrims behind him. "King Rian poisoned the river that flows across the border into our lands. The fish are all dead. The wildlife sickened. The forests are dying. Entire crops have turned black, leaving us with nothing. We traveled a week with only the clothes on our backs and what meager offerings we had, when we heard the rumors you'd Risen. It's divine fate. Our river is poisoned, and a day later, the Goddess of Nature rises. The only person who can heal our river!"

One by one, the pilgrims drop to their knees and bow their heads.

I gape at them openly. From their strained but shining eyes, I can tell that hope is the only thing that's gotten them this far. My eyes fall to the baskets of dried trout, the mended nets. Every scrap of value these people have, they laid at my feet.

My palms tingle, fey energy prickling beneath my skin, gently asking me to be set free.

I want to help these people, I think. *Right Rian's wrong.*

Yet, as soon as I have that thought, I think of when my powers decimated the great hall.

I squeeze my fists tight to silence the fey.

"I can't," I blurt out, as a wave of panic crashes over me. Before I know it, I'm stumbling back to the safety of the bedroom. "I'm so sorry. I want to help you, but I...I..."

I might raise the river to drown you instead.

The worshippers push forward despite the captain's attempts to hold them at bay, pleading voices like nails down my back.

"I'm so sorry," I choke.

I slam the door behind me, back pressed against the wood like a cornered animal, breath so fast and thin that I'm afraid I'll pass out.

At the sound of the slamming door, Basten jerks awake. Groggy. Exhausted. He rubs his bleary eyes.

"Sabine?"

There. My name. My *real* name. It's like music to my ears that someone still sees the girl in me.

With a broken gasp, I stumble toward the bed. "Basten, I can't do it. They ask too much. I want to help, but I'm afraid I'll destroy everything. I...I don't know how to do what they need me to do."

He sits up in bed, raking back his tousled hair, then throws off the covers and swings his legs out so he can pull me into his arms. "Hey. Easy, violet. We'll find the answer. Get someone who can help. Even if we—" he grimaces, "—have to ask one of the fae to train you."

I collapse against him, my fingers twist the bedsheet like a lifeline. "So many people were hurt when I made the Ramvik River rise. People nearly drowned. What if I hurt someone again?"

He cups my face gently. "You saved my life."

I still. Slowly, I hiccup. "What?"

"Your father would have slaughtered me if you hadn't cracked open the earth with your fury. The river came alive for you. You made roots burst through stone and drag him to his knees. You forced him into a bargain for my life."

I blink, lips parted, robbed of words.

"You think you don't know what you're doing," Basten continues, smoothing his hand down my wild hair, "but even without your control, your power chose life. It chose *me*. That kind of instinct? That's not destruction. That's mercy, Sabine. That's love."

I burst into tears, the ground softly rumbling underfoot,

and fall into the arms of the only person who still sees me as human.

CHAPTER 4

BASTEN

"There's a reason the commonfolk have long used the term 'Heaven's Fire' to describe the natural phenomenon of lightning," Woudix explains in a blistering monotone. "Bolts of lightning and the fey that gods wield are similar in scientific structure; the key difference is that lightning cannot be tamed. We *can* learn to command our fey, however. Bend it to our will like a broken horse."

The damn God of Death stands in a grassy patch in the Twilight Garden, that walking carcass of a guide dog lying at his feet, pouring his attention all over Sabine like sun-warmed honey.

I don't like it. Hell, I fucking hate it.

I chew on the side of my cheek while I slump on a wooden bench fifty paces away, at the garden's edge, arms crossed so tightly I'm cutting off my own damn blood flow. Ever since Sabine's Gloaming reached its fever pitch and broke, she's been the picture of health. Physically, I mean.

She literally radiates—especially when she isn't paying attention—with a divine glow.

But her soul?

Her soul is in fucking tatters. Apparently, I'm the only one who can see it. The other gods treat her like she's already seated on one of their ten thrones, guzzling from a golden goblet.

Since I drank her blood, I can sense things about her, more and more each day. How heavy each step feels across the throne room floor. How each smile pains her. She can't even bear to look at her offerings, though they'd give her strength—all she can see is suffering people who need her for a power she can't yet wield.

And so here we are. *Someone* had to help her. Train her. Teach her how the fuck to be a goddess.

I'd have dragged myself to hell by the fingernails before I'd let Artain, that deceitful bastard, teach her a damn thing. Same goes for Iyre. She might be the Goddess of Chastity, but seriously, she's the biggest bitch I've ever crossed. I'll admit that the God of Day, Samaur, doesn't grate quite as much on my nerves, but I still don't like the way he eyes Sabine like a midnight snack. And Vale? That asshole is the one who put her in this mess with a blade in her heart.

Which leaves only one god.

Immortal Woudix.

He's the only one out of their vicious so-called family I grudgingly approve of to help Sabine, despite every voice of common sense in me screaming that this is a bad idea. Every woman in the castle drools after Woudix's tall, dark, silent self, never mind that he could kill them with a single touch.

"*I* can tame lightning," Sabine counters Woudix, holding up her palms.

I smirk to myself as I listen in. *You tell him, little violet.*

"Solene could tame lightning," Woudix corrects. "You are not Solene. Not yet. Lightning may respond in unpredictable ways to your wildest impulses, but you will not be able to summon it at will until you've mastered your fey."

Sabine huffs a long breath, leaning back on the blanket she's sitting on at his feet. "Go ahead."

"Fae bloodlines," Woudix continues in his flat affect, "are not linear. They fork and spiral. It's why locating the correct godkissed people can be a challenge for Immortal Vale. Also, why it is not a quick process. During the Second Return, it took one hundred godkissed searchers twelve years to find Alyssantha. Her resting place was discovered to be within the body of a young whore in the southern Golath hills."

Sabine leans forward, her legs crossed in the tall grass, hanging on his words. I can pick up on the wariness in her breath—she doesn't trust Woudix an ounce more than I do —but her rabid hunger extends to knowledge, too.

If she could, I think she'd drink down all the facts Woudix is spewing like wine.

Gods help me, *weeks* pass like this. Hours upon hours of Woudix and her seated in the grass, with me watching from a distant bench, as he dulls my mind with such achingly boring lectures that I want to punch holes in my ears.

Me? I only care about fae lore enough to help Sabine through the worst of her changes. And to know my enemy. At least my time with Rian taught me that.

I assumed Sabine would be in lock-step with me. Sure, she still curses out Iyre whenever their paths cross, and she refuses to so much as speak to Artain, but each day she leans a little closer to Woudix. Her questions to him used to hang heavy with suspicion. Now, all I hear is curiosity. Yesterday, she *laughed* at something he said.

And that motherfucker's sense of humor is dull as a wooden axe.

I understand why she's interested in fae history. She needs to know these things—what came before, what built this world, and what broke it. She's trying to find her place in it.

But while she's learning the past, I can't stop thinking about the future. That itch between my shoulder blades is getting louder. The one that won't let me forget the map of Lunden Valley. The rumored movement of Rian's troops. Astagnon's encroaching battalions along the southern wall. The itch that whispers what I keep trying not to say aloud:

You're a king, whether you want the crown or not.

So fucking act like it.

"Lord Basten." A castle messenger addresses me from a few steps away, and I jump.

Gods, I didn't even hear his footsteps approaching. I'm off my game. Distracted. *I blame Woudix and his sinful smile.*

"What is it?" I snap.

Bowing his head, he says, "As you requested, the Luden River Valley refugees have gathered. They are waiting for you in Hailstrom Tower's second-floor chamber." He averts his eyes when he addresses me. It plucks an errant chord in my gut. He might as well have addressed me as *Your Highness.*

I sigh. Life was a hell of a lot easier when I was just *Wolf.*

"Right." I groan as I push to my feet, sliding a growlesome look toward Woudix, who is currently cuddled up next to Sabine on their blanket, showing her illustrations from a dusty, leather-bound manuscript. He's rattling on now about some fae tribunal eight hundred years ago.

It grates at me, walking away from Sabine. Leaving her alone with the Ender. I don't think he can kill her, but he can do worse: Seduce her with his dark charm.

I'll admit that I've eyed him like a hawk, but in the weeks they've worked together, Woudix hasn't once tried anything. No lingering looks, no flirtations, no fae bullshit. Just those droning, endless lectures. Which—fuck me sideways—seem to actually be working. Day by day, Sabine is... different. She's steadier now. Her heartbeat more regular. Her eyes clearer.

I just wish it wasn't *him* helping her.

"Hey. Deathbringer." I stride up to interrupt their conversation—moved on now to the fascinating topic of seasonal court decorations—and lower my voice to its deepest growl. "I have somewhere to be. While I'm gone, if you lay one glowy finger on this woman, I swear by gods greater than you that I'll hollow out your skull and use it as a piss bucket."

Immortal Woudix calmly tilts his head toward the sound of my voice, blinking at the threat as if I'm nothing more than a warm breeze. He's in his human glamour now, but even like this, he gives off such otherworldly energy that it gives me fucking chills.

"Where are you going?" Sabine asks, looking up at me so sweetly it aches.

"Nowhere." I soften my voice for her. "You just study. Take your time. I'm proud of how hard you're working."

The question remains in her eyes.

"Truly," I insist. "I'm a paltry human doing paltry human things."

She snorts but turns back to the illustration of themed seasonal garlands.

As I follow the messenger across the Twilight Garden, I roll my shoulders back. Trying to work out kinks from the old injury that still pains me, though recently, the ache has settled in my shoulder blades more by the day.

Shadows swallow us as we enter the Hailstrom Tower and make our way to a spartan meeting room on the second floor, with a single leather chair and a yew desk as the only furniture to speak of. A gathering of a dozen road-weary peasants, their backs slumped with exhaustion, clusters in the room's center. Almost all of them bear the spiral tattoo on their chins.

When I appear in the doorway, the menfolk remove their woolen caps and duck their heads. "Lord Basten."

Dammit—that ache in my shoulders is back, worse than ever.

Every throb reminding me I'm not a commoner like them anymore.

"Can't we get these people some damn benches?" I bark at the messenger. His head cocks like a bird, puzzled by the request. I stare him down until he scurries off, and soon, a few wooden benches are carted in.

Once the villagers are seated, I circle the heavy yew desk and—after a deep breath—settle into the leather chair that reeks of privilege.

"Right. Thanks for coming." I pick up the desk's dagger-like letter opener without thinking, then realize I'm basically brandishing a knife. I set it down and awkwardly adjust my position in the chair. "I—I summoned you because I wanted you to know that your pleas to Lady Sab—to Lady *Solene*—haven't fallen on deaf ears."

"We tried to make our case to Immortal Vale, as well," a red-nosed woman in a tattered shawl says. "To all the woken fae. None of them listened."

And you're surprised? I think wryly.

I clear my throat. "Times are tense. Vale is intently focused on locating and waking the remaining fae. It's all part of preparing for an inevitable war with King Rian's forces in Astagnon. For her part, Lady Solene is anxious to provide you with aid. And she will—as soon as she's able. She has a long journey ahead before she can harness her powers without, you know, blasting half a mountain apart."

Nervous looks answer me.

I quickly add, "As a figure of speech, of course. In any case, I'm here. So, say what you need. Tell me what issues you're facing, and I'll do what I can. No promises, but I'm listening."

Stunned, uncertain silence bounces off the chamber walls. I get the overwhelming sense that no one with an ounce of power has ever spared ten minutes to listen to their problems.

The rail-thin man limps forward. He seems to be their spokesperson.

"Thank you, Lord Basten," he says, working his jaw. "We're from the lower Lunden River valley, just north of the border wall. What's left of the valley, that is. Lord Rian's poison decimated the area. Everything is gone. There was no choice for us but to leave and follow the rumors that Immortal Solene had awoken. We hoped that she could repair our lands." He pauses, head bowed in thought. "If that isn't possible...well, there's land upriver that is still workable. If Immortal Vale could spare seed, tools, and maybe a few tents, we could rebuild. We're not asking for charity—we'll earn it. Pay his generosity back with offerings."

I shift again, the leather groaning under my weight. See, this is what royal-born pricks like Rian and Berolt and even Vale himself never understand. They think peasants are simpletons desperate for their favor; but I grew up on the streets. Surrounded by these same people. They don't need rescuing—they only need the damn royal boot lifted off their necks.

I pivot slightly to look out the window. They're far, but I can see Sabine and Woudix in the garden, still flipping through that dusty old book. Her hair glints like sparks in the sunlight. From this distance, her words are hard to make out, but I can pick up the lilting rise and fall of her voice. It's light. Curious.

I feel a tug in my chest. A tether between us. The bond tells me, *she's all right for now.*

The refugee leader watches me. Waiting.

"You've done the difficult part already," I say, bouncing my foot under the desk. "You kept your people alive. You didn't give up even when the fae refused help. That tells me everything I need to know. You'll have what you need to start over. I'll speak to the castle steward today."

I nod to dismiss them.

They leave holding their heads a little higher—and damn, if my own doesn't feel a little lighter, too.

Maybe, just maybe, I can do this whole run-a-kingdom thing after all.

～

Each night, Sabine and I tumble beneath the sheets, making love and clinging to one another in our sleep until dawn. But during the days, we're apart. A space stretches between us the more she trains, and I work with the river valley refugees. I reassure myself it isn't a growing crack between us. Hell, she still drinks my blood for breakfast. Falls asleep with my cock inside her.

But I can't shake the way Woudix looks at her.

Hungry, plotting.

For more than just her body.

He hovers too closely during lessons, smirks too easily when she missteps. And she—gods, she laughs, too. As if she's forgotten what we both know.

The fae are fucking liars.

Before the Gloaming, Sabine used to say the same. She would spit the word "fae" like it burned her tongue. But now, she makes excuses for them, says that Woudix has shown her amazing sides to their powers that could help people.

It frightens me how easily her doubt is slipping through her fingers. I try to remind her of everything we've seen: the bodies, the betrayals, the knife in her own chest. But she only sighs and cups my face and says I'm tired.

So, while she's training with Woudix, I start to walk the castle halls and listen at keyholes. After all, someone has to figure out what's really happening in Volkany, and I seem to be the only candidate. I want to know the *real* facts about the fae, not the cleaned-up myths they spoon-feed to Sabine like honeyed milk.

Unsurprisingly, the damn castle is locked down like a prison.

Fortunately, I know a lock-picker.

Getting help from the forest mouse is a slow, maddening process. I can't talk to animals like Sabine, not even with our acolyte bond. Still, that hasn't stopped them from *trying* to communicate with me ever since her Awakening. Nuthatches dive bomb my head. Caterpillars fall from their silken threads to land on my shoulder. Like they fear how Sabine is changing—like they want *me* to do something.

In an attempt to communicate with the forest mouse, I draw questions in the dust, pantomime like a lunatic, and all the while the damn furball just twists her head and stares.

But after days of this, the mouse finally scurries to the door, then pauses to look back at me as if to say, *"Coming or not, asshole?"*

"Coming," I mumble.

She leads me through a first-floor hallway in the Stormwatch Tower wing, whose dusty floor appears to have been long overlooked by the maids. We pass through archways thick with cobwebs. At an iron door, the mouse climbs thick bolts to reach the lock. A few quick maneuvers with her deft paw, and the latch clicks.

The door groans open, breathing out a gust of ancient air.

We descend uneven stairs lit by a single candle flickering in a wall sconce, burned so low it's nearly dead.

The air is stale down here. Cold in a heavy, still way, as though it hasn't felt a breeze in a hundred years. Down, down, down I follow the mouse. Fuck, how deep do these stairs go? Finally, the mouse reaches the bottom and disappears down a lightless hallway, vanishing into shadows.

I toy with the idea of going back for the candle, but I

don't want dripping candle wax marking my path, giving away the fact that someone was down here.

Fortunately, my night vision gradually adjusts until the shadows are clear but drained of color.

Impossibly, we head even *deeper* through the tunnel, until I can hear the Ramvik River rushing outside the heavy walls. Moisture drips down the ancient stones. There are no more bricks here. This passage is hewn directly into river-rock, strange blast marks that couldn't have come from any human pickaxes.

Fey carved this, I think.

This must be the castle's original foundation. Thousands of years old, if I had to guess.

The mouse stops and loops back, circling me urgently.

"What are you trying to say, huh? Oh...Oh. I see." My voice fades as I take in dark paint marks, almost like writing, on the stone walls. They're covered by a half inch of dust, like everything else down here.

Making a fist, I brush the dust away, coughing as it clouds the air. I shake it from my hair, raking the strands back, and study the walls.

At first glimpse, it's just nonsense paint streaks. I lean close and sniff. Actually, it isn't paint. It's lampblack, which I haven't heard being used as paint since ancient history. But the brush strokes—faint though they are—don't lie. Someone smoothed chalky lampblack over this wall in only this one section.

Strange.

With a shiver, I think back on when I left Duren in Rian's entourage, on our way to Old Coros. We passed a warehouse with a large mural of Sabine on the side, but someone had painted over it as a protest against her Volkish heritage.

I lean forward, picking at the flicking lampblack with a grubby fingernail. As a shard flecks off and falls at my feet, it reveals a faint—but unmistakable—painted eye underneath.

Unnerved, I step back, only to trip over the dusty rubble at my feet, nearly stomping on the forest mouse.

I bark a quick, "Sorry."

It tears my fingernails to the quick, but I claw away flecks of rotting lampblack until I can make out more of the original painting beneath. If someone went to the trouble of covering this up, deep in this ancient basement, it must be for a reason.

Finally, I step back.

I regret not bringing the candle with me. My night vision is keen, but lacking in color, and I can only imagine this mural once glowed in iridescent hues of ground red ochre, azurite, gypsum powder.

"Fuck me," I breathe.

It's a portrait of the Immortal Court. All ten of the fancy fae bastards in their greatest finery, seated at a rough-hewn stone table in the middle of the woods. Their reddened cheeks, rumpled robes, and wine-stained lips hint at a debaucherous tale. Their clothes are simple and primitive, the style of thousands of years ago, though they're bedecked in rough-hewn jewels.

The faces are different than they wear now. Immortal Vale is completely white-haired, though the exact same Battle Helm Crown rests on his head. Iyre has long, black hair in bouncy waves down to her waist. Artain is still a blond, preening bastard, but this version of him has a squared-off jaw. It's easy enough to recognize him by the bow at his feet, though.

And—gods damn it—the woman at Artain's side, his hand resting possessively over hers, is a beauty with curly mahogany hair woven into an Immortal Crown. A wren perches on the woman's left shoulder. A snake coils like a bangle around one wrist. Behind her, a buck bows his antlers.

"Sabine," I whisper, the breath ripped from my lungs.

It isn't her. Not *my* little violet. The face is wrong. The posture, too, leaning toward Artain with her tits practically shoved up in his face, and something almost sinister about her smile as she gazes over her shoulder at the buck.

But the way those animals flock to her?

Yeah. *That* I recognize.

A nasty scar in my mind flares with old pain. I should remember so much more about Sabine than just the way nature fawns at her footsteps.

It's Iyre's fault. Stealing my memories.

For so long, I chased that void like a bloodthirsty hound. *My* memories might be gone, but this? Communal memories, long buried? That someone clearly wanted to keep secret?

Well, I'm a hunter. If I can't get my own memories back, maybe I can stalk *these*.

I step closer to the ancient painting, fingers hovering over the few flecks of lampblack I couldn't scratch off. The ache inside me doesn't fade—it sharpens. My whole life, I instinctively knew the fae gods were full of shit. Not worth the incense the holy temples burned through by the barrel in their honor.

Here's my chance to prove it.

I step backward to scan the dark hall ahead. There's no telling where such an ancient tunnel leads. I sniff. There—at the far end, before the hallway turns a sharp corner, there's the scent of more smoky lampblack.

The mouse scampers at my heels as I locate another blacked-out mural, and tear at this one with already shredded fingernails. Slowly, streaks of the mural reveal themselves. This one shows a wizened old man with a twisted-oak staff and long gray robes, holding court over a maze with willow-reed walls.

Immortal Meric, I think. *God of Order.*

With a growl, I turn the hallway's corner, stalking through the muted darkness on the prowl for anything else that can tell me about Sabine. I find more painted-over murals. One of Immortal Alyssantha, mid-coitus with a pair of naked milkmaids. Another of Immortal Samaur and Immortal Thracia, wearing primitive masks of the sun and moon.

Then—finally. Another mural featuring Solene. This time, she stands before an ancient city composed of a giant temple surrounded by obelisks. I can only imagine it's Calisyrune—a fabled city that was supposedly razed to its foundation three thousand years ago, during the fae's Beginning. No one knows if the mythical city ever actually existed. If it did, its location must have been long since over-grown by forests.

But here it is.

Solene is on her knees in the foreground, weeping into her hands, surrounded by birds drawn to her obvious pain. In the distance in front of her, Calisyrune pumps out smoke from countless clay chimneys, kilns, and blacksmith forges, darkening the sky, causing birds to fall to their death. The river is dammed, and dead fish wallow in the dry bed along with the bones of otters and beavers. A fleet of woodcutters axes the forest apart, decimating every living thing in their path.

My stomach sours.

There's another mural next to it, almost a mirror image. Most of the lampblack has already worn away, though I smooth my hands over it anyway, hungry for every detail. Anything could be a clue.

In this second scene, Solene towers upright as an oak, arms outstretched, hair cast back in a wild gust of wind. A flock of starleons drops poison dust over the ancient city. Thorny vines as thick as barrels smash into the obelisks. Roots burst from the dirt pathways, causing rifts in the earth large enough to swallow a horse. Goldenclaws slam into the dam to break it down.

As the city turns to rubble, the look on Solene's face is unforgiving.

I stumble back, dragging a shaking hand over my face. That look? I've seen that *exact* look before. The first time was when Sabine took possession of the tiger in Duren's arena. I saw it again when she commanded Tòrr.

Like an obsessed man, I prowl every hall in the basement, ducking through every iron gate the mouse unlocks for me. Searching for more. More answers. More ancient memories—though I'm afraid of what they'll mean.

"Hey—no one is permitted down here!"

The sharp bark of a castle sentry pulls me from my hunt. The lantern in his hand burns so bright it nearly blinds me until my day vision switches back on.

I shade my face, grimacing.

The forest mouse vanishes into the shadows with barely a whisper of little feet on rubble.

"Lord Basten." The sentry's posture shifts, his head

bowing, though his eyes dart nervously to the pitch-black hallway. "Forgive me, I didn't know it was you."

I roll my shoulders back, trying to look kingly instead of like a desperate man.

"Leave me," I command in a deep voice. "I'm looking for supplies for the Lunden Valley refugees. Any old tools or bedrolls that might have been left down here."

The sentry hesitates, well-trained eye flicking to my broken and bleeding fingernails. He clears his throat. "Understood, however, I'm afraid even you are forbidden from wandering these hallways, by order of Immortal Vale himself. The foundation isn't sound. Rubble could fall. It's dangerous."

I fight the urge to snort. *Sure.*

For a brief moment, I consider simply ignoring the sentry's command. But a quick assessment shows that despite his humility, he's a beast. He rivals my size, and the sword at his side gives him an advantage.

"Right," I mutter, and drag my feet after him.

Only a temporary setback, I tell myself as I follow him through the maze of hallways. The forest mouse can always lead me back here once I can get some gods-damned privacy.

On the way out, we pass the first mural I came to, the one of the ten fae seated in their primitive woodland court, golden and glowing beneath pine boughs. But in the sentry's orange lantern light, my eyes catch what I missed before.

When my night vision only let me see grayscale.

That cherry-red sneer on Solene's face? Artain wears it too, as if they share some dark joke.

My gaze moves to the giant buck behind her. Now, it's

clear that he isn't simply gazing at her beauty. A crushed human body lies under his hooves, bloodied and stabbed through by antlers that are stained red from blood. Another corpse lies beneath tall grass, nearly hidden, eyes pecked out by hawks.

I didn't notice the bright red stain of blood before.

And it changes everything.

In the Beginning, Solene didn't just govern creatures of air, earth, and water.

She weaponized them.

CHAPTER 5

SABINE

Thick hemlock boughs shade us from the midday sun, but more than that, they hide us from the world. Under these branches, Woudix and I have spent weeks poring over tottering stacks of leather-bound books, some hundreds of years old, with yellowed pages and moth-eaten spines.

And oh, the things I've learned here in our private world beneath the branches.

Things like how Vale first became a god by drinking sacrificial blood. How, one by one, each of the ten fae drank after him and uncovered their unique affinities. Couples in the street fell in love as Alyssantha passed—Goddess of Sex. Card players suddenly hit a good luck streak when Popelin —God of Pleasure—winked at them. One after another, they rose in power until the fae court dominated the human and fae realms.

I can't flip through the pages fast enough. This terrible hunger inside me craves more than peasants' offerings of chicken eggs or woven flower crowns. It wants blood. It wants sex. It wants *truth*. To drink the past down like wine straight from the bottle, until my stomach is sickly and sated and I collapse in a dizzy mess.

Before the Gloaming, I couldn't tell you five facts about the Beginning or the First or Second Returns. To me, the fae gods were as distant as the high, snow-capped Darmarnach Mountains, and certainly just as harsh.

Take Immortal Iyre.

Late at night, I've woken more than once in cold sweat, thrashing in Basten's arms, violently jolted from nightmares of being back in the Convent, a Sister shoving my face in the ground at the goddess's statue's feet, mouth rubbed in dirt until I kissed her stone toes. Basten holds me, planting soft kisses along my temples, murmuring reassurances that it was only a nightmare.

Fair to say, a year ago, I wasn't exactly devout.

Now? What does one do when one *is* the very type of goddess one once loathed? There are moments when panic sets in. I think of that hateful stone statue of Iyre, and how the real Iyre is no less cruel. And Artain—what an *ass*. Being fae like him makes me want to claw into my flesh, dig the glowing fey lines out like ripping apart a doll's seams.

On days like that, I hide behind my human glamour, stay in bed all day, sobbing into my feather pillow, wishing away the silver in my blood.

But not every day is so troubled. The truth I never would have guessed is that being fae feels, well, *electric*. All my life, I never knew what it felt like to fully stand up straight instead of hunching over a mop and bucket. To fill my lungs with cool winter air to their fullest, without the pinch of frostbite. To marvel at a body so alive that I feel as bright and new every morning as the rising sun.

I wish on every damn star that I could gift this feeling—this lightness—to everyone. If I could only show Basten what it was like, I know he'd tip back his head and laugh in awe. He'd be happy, for once.

The clouds shift overhead, bringing me back into the present.

Woudix sits at my side, leaning toward me so he can flip the pages of the book in my lap while he explains the meaning of the architectural renderings of the ancient city of Calisyrune.

A fledgling sparrow lands on a branch above us, its newly grown feathers sticking out at awkward angles.

Hello, little one, I murmur. *Still learning to fly?*

It chirps indignantly. *I can fly!*

I smile. *Of course you can. My mistake.*

Woudix glances up. "What's it saying?" His tone is dry but amused.

"It says...that you seem to have overlooked a comb this morning." I teasingly flick an errant lock off his forehead.

"Mmm," Woudix purrs, smooth and devious. "Is that so? Tell it that if it shits on this book, I'll give it instant passage to the underrealm."

I feign indignation. "Rude!"

The sparrow flies off, equally offended.

Just then, a shape moves in the trees. Through the gap where the bird had perched, Basten stomps into view in the distance.

My breath stills, lips parting slightly. It's rare to get to watch him when he doesn't know he's being observed. His godkiss means he's always ten steps ahead, even of the fae. But now, he strains under a wheelbarrow full of steel tools fresh from the blacksmith's. He's so intent on not dropping his load that he isn't paying attention to the sights and sounds of his surroundings.

Gods, I could watch him all day.

Sweaty-soaked, messy, muscles straining—he's so handsome it hurts.

The tools, I'm certain, are for the river valley refugees. Basten has never been one for words, but at night, when we lock my bedroom door and it's just us, I manage to corkscrew out of him the details of his days: that he's been busy meeting with the refugees, gathering tools, seeds, cloth—whatever he can scrounge—for them to start afresh.

He'd snort if I said it out loud, but it's plain as day: This is what a *king* does.

He's ridiculous, really—this growlsome brute prowling around like a bull with a wheelbarrow, trying to help people. He embodies the beautiful, maddening contradiction of being human. He's broken but trying. Caring and gruff.

Cold, pale fingers snap in front of my face, making me jump.

I jerk around to meet black storm cloud eyes.

"Lady Sabine." Woudix's voice rolls like rough velvet as he says my human name, which I've asked to be used in private. "Your attention isn't on Calisyrune, is it?"

"Oh—no."

Softly, teasingly, his lips purse in a scolding *tsk-tsk-tsk.*

I blush, a guilty smile tugging at my lips, as I obediently return to the book's architectural renderings. "Sorry—I don't know what's going on with me today. It's harder to focus. I want to be here, I promise. I can't tell you what it's meant to me to learn about the fae world."

Woudix drapes a long arm over his bent knee. His blind

eyes are always distant, and yet, somehow, I get the sense he can see me clear as day.

"It's the weather," he says with certainty, lifting his face toward the highest tree boughs. "Do you feel that? This morning, the grass was covered in frost. Now, one could bake bread beneath that sun. The wind comes from the east, then the west. The world is restless. The seasons are changing. They're affecting your focus. You're letting yourself be shaped by nature, instead of shaping it yourself."

I run my fingers over the book's stiff pages, marinating in his words.

On impulse, I sneak another glimpse through the branches at Basten, but Woudix must sense the tilt of my chin, because he leans over to flip the page.

"Like *she* did," he murmurs, tapping the open book to get my attention.

I marvel down at the book's full-spread illustration rendered in sepia ink. I don't understand how Woudix knows the contents of each page by memory, but it's Immortal Solene in full fae splendor. She stands naked in a pond. Her gown is made from living river reeds that wind around her limbs to cover her nude body. Flower blossoms spill out of her hair, and in her extended palm sits a lime-green toad.

I'm so struck by the sheer power of this goddess, captured in ink, that it takes me a moment to notice the more minor details: actually, those aren't reeds. It's a rice field, and on the nearby shore, rail-thin villagers with hollow, hungry eyes kneel to her, hands clasped in supplication.

"This was the great winter famine of Western Golath," Woudix explains. "Thousands were at risk of starvation.

Immortal Solene thawed the frozen fields and sprouted a bounty of rice that matured within a single day. She fed a kingdom of hungry bellies."

My fingers rub over the illustration, trying to grab it and make it real. A hunger pang thrums in my belly. It aches, how badly I want this. To help the river valley refugees just as Immortal Solene helped during the winter famine.

It's like a splinter I can't unearth. The urge—no, the need—to let my fey flow.

Tears sting my eyes as something dark and mean suddenly twists inside me. I slam the book shut, turning sharply away. I hug my knees to my chest.

"People need her now, like they did then," I spit out. "And I can't do anything but *read* about how powerful I was in the past."

A sob catches in my throat. No matter how quickly I wipe tears off my cheeks, the warble in my throat gives me away. The next time I go to brush away a tear, Woudix grabs my wrist, tight like a shackle.

I freeze.

He's...touching me. He's never touched me.

I pause, breath held, eyes wide and wary of the god who commands death itself.

Slowly, he draws my arm toward him, gently but forcibly unfurling my tightly held fist until my palm is open to him.

Like a map of my secrets.

He drags one cold finger down the line of my inner wrist. Following the fey line that's resting just beneath my human-glamoured skin. Wherever he touches, my body responds on its own, erupting in glowing silver light that I can't tuck away again.

My heart slams against my ribs, quick and painful.

I feel more exposed—just from an open palm—than I did riding across half of Duren naked.

"You see?" Woudix says as the glowing lines appear. "She's here. She's always been here. Waiting for you to find her."

One by one, he ignites the lines that run along each of my fingers. Thumb. Index. Middle. Ring. Little finger.

When I finally catch my breath, it's to realize he's placed a tiny brown seed in my palm.

A rice seed, gods knows where he got it.

He presses his thumb over the seed in my palm, securing it, before guiding my hand to the earth beneath us, where he plants my palm firmly against the soil.

I tug slightly, testing, but his grip is unyielding.

"What are you doing?" I breathe, not sure if I should be frightened.

"Not all knowledge comes from books."

He finally removes his hand, and somehow, the world feels wrong without his touch—like I'm all on my own.

I shift, thighs keenly sore from hours of sitting cross-legged. I swallow and blurt out, "I don't understand. This isn't talking to animals. What am I supposed to do?"

"Sprout the rice the same as you did three thousand years ago."

I nearly laugh with the impossibility of it, but Woudix's stony expression makes the breath die on my lips.

I clear my throat. My eyes sink closed. The tiny, hard seed bites into my palm, dry and lifeless. The fey lines glow along my hand, urging to be set free.

I concentrate.

And...nothing stirs.

"I can't," I admit, shame pinching my throat.

"Solene didn't *try*," Woudix murmurs. Not unkindly—simply a fact. "She listened. To the seed. To the soil. To the breath of the earth beneath her. She *made* it respond."

My fingers tremble. "I don't know how to be her."

"You don't have to be her—that's what you aren't understanding. Three thousand years ago, one version of Solene walked through primitive villages and temples. Two thousand years ago, a different Solene woke. A thousand years later, yet another, different Solene emerged. And now? You are her, but you are also *you*. Sabine Darrow."

He taps the book in my lap and continues, "These history books record events, but not what it means to be fae. We're more connected to our mortal selves than Vale and the others like to admit. Thus, we both are and are not the same in every Return. In each iteration, our physical bodies are different. Our temperaments, too. As are our relationships. Sometimes, you and Vale are siblings. Sometimes father and daughter. It changes, whether the ten fae gods are lovers, family, rivals, enemies. We call ourselves brothers and sisters, but that is a moniker only. You get to choose, do you feel that? Who you want to be *this* time."

I run a hand up my bare arm, over the icy-hot fey line hiding beneath my skin.

"You must remember who you are," he continues. "Not with your mind, but with your body. It already knows what to do—you proved that on the night of the Gloaming, when you called the Ramvik River from its bed."

He presses his hand against mine again, anchoring my palm—the seed trapped beneath—to the soil.

"Remember," he urges.

I lick my lips, suddenly dry, bloodless. A cold burn tingles in my palm, and for a second, I'm frightened. I feel transported back to that awful day of the Gloaming, when I unleashed nature in all its ferocious chaos upon Drahallen Hall, destroying everything that threatened to keep Basten and me apart.

Woudix leans in, his voice so low it might as well be whispered in a dream. "Master this," he murmurs, "and anything you desire is yours. The world." His voice catches. "Maybe...the underworld, too."

A shiver runs through me that isn't altogether unpleasant. Something about this—being here with him, his hand over mine—feels deep and inevitable, like bedrock undisturbed by eons of tremors.

It sparks something.

A memory, maybe. Or a long-buried feeling.

"You and I," I blurt out before I even realize what I'm saying. "Were we ever..." I stop short, suddenly doubting myself, feeling like a fool for even thinking it. I blush and look away. "Never mind."

"What were you going to say?"

"Nothing. It was a foolish notion."

In the awkward silence that stretches, my insides twist up so hard I regret eating so much greasy chicken for lunch.

His jaw parts. "You want to know if we've ever been lovers."

"No," I say in a rush, instantly mortified down to my toes. I glance through the branches, praying Basten—with his superior hearing—isn't within miles. "No, that isn't it at all."

Woudix only smirks like he can see into my heart. "The answer is no. It was always you and Artain. It's *always* been you and Artain. Some patterns in our fates repeat themselves. Thracia always pairs with Samaur. Popelin and Meric are always at odds—sometimes to the point of blades. And of course, you and Artain."

His words linger as if there's more there, but I can't even pretend to guess what it is. A cloud shifts overhead, plunging the hemlock grove into shadows.

I clear my throat and look down at my hands. Gods, the tension is thick as fog.

"I can't see how I was *ever* with that ass," I joke.

Woudix—always so stoic—almost smiles in return. "Let's just say it was always a love-and-hate relationship between you two. And..." He reaches out to catch one of the loose curls cascading down my shoulder, working it softly between his fingers like corn silk. "You're different this time."

The pit of my stomach tightens, though I'm not sure why. He isn't just talking about the color and texture of my hair.

I'm so damn hopeful that I *am* different this time.

"You and I," he continues, "have always treated one another more as true siblings. As...equals."

My chest sinks with relief. Yes. Yes, that's it. The connection I feel. How I can tolerate him more than the other fae. He isn't my brother, not by blood.

But it feels right.

Family.

The word hums in my chest, alive, like something I'd forgotten but never really lost. My pulse snaps—not with fear, but wonder.

My palm suddenly tingles with pins and needles.

As a faint tremor shakes the ground, a tendril of greenery thrusts out from beneath my hand. More tendrils weave between my fingers, growing up toward the light with astonishing speed, twisting and dancing with life.

A shriek slips out of my mouth. I clap a trembling hand—fey lines blazing silver—over my mouth, gazing in awe at the rice seedling that's rising from the ground. Tiny threads of roots bury themselves deeper in the soil. Inch by inch, the seedling unfurls until it's waist high.

Without meaning to, my human glamour melts away to reveal my fae self. All dazzling bright lines, pointed ears, and pin-sharp teeth.

"It grew," I gasp. "*I* made it sprout."

Woudix gives a nod that could almost be considered proud, as he lets my lock of hair slip from his fingers. "Of course you did."

Before I know what I'm doing, I throw my arms around him with such vigor that he has to lean back, catching himself with one hand planted behind him.

I laugh and cry and sniffle against the hard leather of his doublet, shaped to look like a corpse's ribs. For once, he doesn't feel like a cold, distant god.

I feel his breath, feel his chest rise and fall.

Something is returning. Maybe not memories—not yet—but old impulses. Instincts. Habits. Something has shifted here, beneath the boughs, under Woudix's deft hand. Just look at the rice seedling twisting toward the sun.

Deep in my bones, a quiet thrill thrums.

If this is what is awakening in me...maybe I don't have to fear the stirring.

CHAPTER 6

BASTEN

"Basten!" A honeyed voice snags my attention, and I whip my head toward the golden-haired girl sprinting across the grass. "Basten—I did it!"

I slide the 100-lb bag of seed off my shoulder just in time for Sabine to leap into my arms, her legs closing around my waist. I cup one hand over her ass, holding her up, but I hardly need to—she's clinging to me like moss on bark.

She's beaming, cheeks flushed in a fresh-faced smile that shows none of the sharp-edged rage she always seemed to wear under Rian's control. Her gown is robin-blue velvet over a chemise with lace sleeves that fall to her wrists. Soft as a cloud.

Amused, I let myself smile, too. Not something I plan to do often, mind you, but her grins are so damn contagious. "What is it, little violet?"

Her hands twist excited knots in the hair at my nape. For a minute, with her bright face shining on me, I could almost forget that we're at the brink of war.

She gushes, "I sprouted a rice seed with my fey. It wasn't

like before, during the Gloaming. There was nothing scary about using my power this time. I felt in control. Even at peace, I'd say. Like I was working *with* the seed. Oh—" She glances down at the fallen bag of corn kernels, where a handful is spilling out of a split seam. "I'll show you!"

She wiggles her perfect ass until I set her down.

She drops to her knees in the tall grass, scooping a handful of corn kernel seeds, then presses them into the soil, holding them there like trapped ants under her palm.

There's a lightness to her movements. A raw vigor I've only seen in her when she rides Myst, wild and free.

At the same time, though, my godkiss picks up on something that gives me pause. Her enthusiasm is hot and fast—almost manic. Her pulse is rushed, even for a fae.

"Woudix told me that my body remembers how to do this. It's just my mind that needs to catch up," she rattles.

Her fey lines break out across the back of her hands, snaking up her wrists, where they disappear under her lace sleeves, only to blaze again with full force as they reach her neckline and spread to her temples. Her attention is so riveted to the seeds that I don't think she's even noticed how her ears have grown points.

And, I'm not the only one watching.

Throughout the garden, a chorus of awe-filled gasps spreads as she slips into her otherworldly fae body. Hedge-trimmers and kitchen girls stare. Courtesans and cooks stop in their tracks to watch. That bastard, Woudix, is crouched down to stroke Hawk's back, but he doesn't fool me—his attention is on her, too.

I clock each onlooker, as protective over Sabine as a wolf with its mate. I can't begrudge some gangly young soldiers their adoration. No matter how many times I've seen Sabine drop her human glamour, I lose my damn voice for a minute too.

She isn't just beautiful—she's mythic.

From the moment I saw Sabine Darrow, I thought of her as a goddess. Now, she simply reflects the way I always saw her. *Utterly fucking divine.*

But something's wrong.

Her eyebrows draw together to form a thick line of worry. Her hand shakes. When I sink into a crouch next to her, resting one hand on her shoulder, her eyes are still feverish-bright, but there are deep hollows around them.

"You're exhausted," I say softly. "You need a break. You used up all your fey sprouting the rice."

"No!" She turns sharply back toward the soil, knocking my palm off her shoulder in the process, but doesn't seem to take notice. "I—I can do it again. I know I can."

Her eyes glaze over the same way they did during the Gloaming.

"I want to show you what I can do—" she insists.

She closes her eyes, wrinkles deepening as she concentrates. And, it happens. A tiny, weak green shoot breaks through the loamy soil to curl around her cupped palm.

She lets out a small cry of satisfaction, but it's immediately overshadowed by her flickering fey lines, which dim to a barely-there flutter.

She moans as she slumps forward, her hair cascading forward over her bowed head.

That's all I fucking need to see.

"Yeah—you're coming with me," I mutter. "You need rest."

Every protective instinct roars in me as I scoop her up in my arms, throwing her weak, too-light body over my shoulder. Damn, but she feels even lighter than the seed sack, like she might float away on the next breeze.

"Wait," she protests, wriggling her pretty hips on my shoulder, but there's no real fight in her. She used up every ounce of her energy on that tiny sprout. "Wait, I can do it. I promise."

"Little violet, trust me, I've seen you do the impossible. I know you can sprout a damn seed. But right now, I need to take care of you."

I scan the garden. A cluster of pit diggers toils near the entrance—I'd rather not have them see Sabine up close like this, vulnerable and in desperate need of sustenance. I could carry her beneath the giant hemlock where the branches form a natural tent, but Woudix is only paces away. And I don't like that dark smirk on his lips, the way he's rolling a plucked rice shoot between his fingers.

I pivot sharply the other way, swallowing a bite of jealousy, and spot a greenhouse nestled near the garden wall.

Inside, it's hot and bright—but maybe that's what Sabine needs to balance her silver blood. Potted ferns seem to turn our way as I push past them, as drawn to Sabine as every eye was in the courtyard. A showy orchid bursting with blooms bends forward to brush her cheek, but I swat it away.

"Thanks, but I've got her."

Gods—talking to plants now, Basten?

With every minute, Sabine's pulse grows more erratic, and in my urgency, I shove a stack of clay pots off a table to make room for her. They crash to the ground as I set Sabine's ass on the table.

Her eyes are frenzied as they roll around in her head. I

don't think she even notices how the potted vines strain toward her with a preternatural life of their own.

She chatters, voice falling in and out from exhaustion, "Woudix said that it was time to move on from the research books…"

"That right?" I mutter, utterly uninterested in anything to do with Woudix, as I start to unroll my sleeve back over the scars that spell out her name on my wrist.

"Yes," she gulps, "and he also said… He said—"

"Hey," I cut her off gently, offering her my bare wrist. "You need me. Drink."

Her eyes dart briefly to the throbbing vein beneath my wrist, her irises tightening for a second like a predator's, but then her feverish excitement returns.

She grabs my shirt collar, pulling me close.

"Basten, it was like nothing I've ever felt. True connection. Like the seed and I were speaking a language no one else knows."

"That's great, sweetheart." I know I might sound like a dismissive ass, but I *do* mean it. I'm proud as hell of her, but the thing is, I never felt a second of doubt that she could tap into her powers. "Now, drink."

I wiggle my wrist temptingly, and it's enough for her incisors to lengthen and gleam in the sunlight filtering through the greenhouse windows. She grabs my wrist lightly, distractedly.

But doesn't bite.

She continues, "It was all just theory until Woudix put his hand over mine. When I felt his fey against my own, it awakened something."

Immediately, my muscles pull tight as bowstrings.

Hold on. He *touched* her?

I flex, ready to slam my fist into whatever clay pot around here most resembles the God of Death's face.

Through the glass windows, I'm very aware that we still have an audience. Gardeners, pit diggers, and, sure enough —the damn miracle man himself.

Staring straight at the greenhouse as if his blind eyes can somehow see every move we make.

It stokes the huntsman in me. But Sabine seems oblivious to my growing jealousy as she rattles on about the seed's call to her and how Woudix made it all possible.

That God of Death and I? Yeah, we're going to have words.

"Woudix says...he says that with the right guidance, I might soon sprout...entire fields!" she continues, energy fading fast.

"Mmmhhmm," I mutter, wriggling my wrist.

Instead, she tightens her hold on my shirt collar until it digs into the back of my neck. "With Woudix's help, I could...answer the refugees' prayers, Basten. You wouldn't have to...help them all on your own. I could fix everything."

There's such hope in her exhausted voice that it nearly breaks.

A tenderness catches me off guard, like a hand around my throat—gentle, not choking. The bowstrings in my chest loosen.

It's a relief to hear her talking about using her powers for good. Not that I ever truly doubted her...but ever since uncovering the old pictograms in Drahallen Hall's foundation, I haven't been able to stop thinking about Immortal Solene with that devious smirk, the wreckage of an entire city behind her.

I'm loyal to her—no fucking question.

Then again, what good is loyalty from a man like me? I was loyal to Rian, too. Look at how that turned out.

Gritting my teeth, I unsheathe the knife at my side and slit my wrist. A line of blood spills down my skin, dropping thickly onto my boot.

The smell of iron blasts through the greenhouse.

Her words vanish as the scent hits her like a drug. She pounces on my arm, eyes shining like a night creature's, lips latching hungrily over my wound. She sucks, drinks, tastes. A groan rolls out of me. It does something to me, giving her my blood. Having her use me. Knowing I—*only I*—can do this for her.

"That's it," I groan between clenched teeth, grabbing the sloped wooden rafter overhead to steady myself. "Take it. Take what you need."

The more her soft lips hunt and suck at my skin, the more her sweet torture drives me crazy.

Her pulse steadies, alive now not with jitters but with the heady drive of hunger. I can see the change in her eyes, her skin—her cheeks pinken and fill out, and I swear that her hair shines bright as sun-touched silk.

She breaks away roughly, touches her lips and looks at the blood on her fingers with both horror and fascination. Her fingers begin to tremble. "Basten. I don't want to hurt you."

"Hurt me," I order gently.

Her eyes snap to me, slightly more focused, as she gulps in air. "You don't understand. It's hard to stop. I'm scared of losing myself—taking too much blood."

Her pupils are so blown they're like round black buttons. The glow radiating from her fey lines burns so bright now that it must look from the outside like I've trapped a shard of sunlight in the greenhouse.

The cut on my wrist closes up in seconds, healed by her saliva.

I grip the back of her neck, lowering my voice. "Then take something else."

Her hips begin to wiggle on the gardening table with a different kind of need.

"Basten." Her voice is husky, brimming with power. "I want you."

She leans back, spreading her knees, knocking over another clay pot that goes crashing to the floor. She doesn't flinch at the sound. With one fist, she balls her velvet skirt up around her hips, sliding her ass to the table's edge like the damn little temptress she is.

She wasn't lying—she's *ready*.

The greenhouse plants are writhing. Flowers blooming, vines twisting, condensation dripping onto the back of my neck. The scents are dizzying, thick. Heady pollen, sticky sap, stamens trembling like they're about to come undone. The whole damn garden is in heat.

And the perfume—fuck, the flowers' perfume. It gets to my head. To my blood. To my cock.

Yes, please.

My hand falls on my belt, wrenching it free, but I can't help but flick an irritated look out the crystal-clear windows. We still have an awe-struck audience, and it's about to get a hell of an eyeful.

"Wildcat," I purr, "how about you use your newfound bond with nature to fog up the glass so we don't have an audience?"

She blinks, slow and lazy like a cat in heat. I can see it in her eyes—she doesn't give a fuck about being on display for watching eyes.

And yet, curiosity sparks in her gaze. She wants to know if she *can*. Testingly, she reaches back to press her hand to the nearest window pane, palm flat and fingers splayed.

Now, with her strength replenished by my blood, her fey practically ignites. A miniature cloud forms in the pitched greenhouse ceiling, complete with tiny bolts of lightning. A few fat water drops fall on me—more condensation from the greenhouse boiler, or is it now rain from Sabine's storm?

Sure enough, the air grows thick with moisture, and my breath fogs. Muggy, hot fog creeps over the window panes until we're sheltered from prying eyes.

Satisfied, she leans forward. "I told you I could do it."

My eyes lock onto the glimpse of creamy breasts above her neckline. "Sweetheart, if you think I ever doubted you, you haven't been listening to my prayers."

I grab her hips, dragging her to the edge of the table, slamming her groin against mine. A pent-up gasp rattles up her throat, her breath fogging the steamy air. I finally free my belt with a sharp *snap* that makes her moan with desire.

She runs her hand up her velvet bodice, toying with the lace neckline, dragging her fingernails feather-soft over the rise and fall of each perfect breast.

"Fuck me," she commands softly, her eyelids half-lowered.

Ready and willing, little violet. But, as I grip her thighs, a muscle twitches around my eye. This time, something feels different. I've always been the dominant one when it comes to sex, bending her to my submission with bound hands or sharp commands she doesn't dare disobey. She's always liked it. Begged me for it, even. But that look in her eye now?

She's taking charge.

Not that I mind, exactly. Hell, she could command me to crawl after her on my hands and knees like a dog, and I'd thank her for the pleasure. But...that gleam in her eye is a power play I don't recognize.

During the Gloaming, I gave her everything—followed her lead, moved at her rhythm, let her hunger set the pace. But now, I'm starting to wonder if what she needs isn't just blind submission. If I submit, it might stoke the darker fae tendencies in her that crave power.

So, I purposefully slow the pace, taking my time unbuttoning my pants, drawing myself to my full height, towering above her. An anchor, grounding her before she drifts too far. *She's* still what matters here—her need. But maybe I can keep her from burning too bright.

She huffs, impatient, hips wiggling as she reaches for my pants buttons.

I cuff her wrist, *tsk-tsk*ing. "Such a hurry?"

In response, she rolls her hips against my groin with nothing but pure sin on her mind. "Don't tease me, Basten. *Touch* me."

"You're getting bolder, little violet," I say deeply. "But you're still *mine*. You haven't forgotten that, have you?"

She narrows her eyes, sly and sexy.

Slowly—testingly—I give her what she wants. A hand curled around the back of her neck, fingers twisting ever so slightly in her hair. My other hand drops between her legs, stroking her through the soaked fabric of her panties.

A moan tears out of her. She bucks against me, searching for more friction, and I test how much I can hold her back.

"Beg me for it," I say softly.

Her eyes flash, her tongue snaking out in a way that

shows her incisors. Sharp. Dangerous. "What if I don't want to beg anymore?"

My heartbeat kicks up a warning.

I lean in close to her ear, plunging my thumb under her panties to tease the hot, slippery button there, and from the way her eyes roll back, I know I've brought her back to *this*. This moment.

I growl, "Then I'll fuck that pretty throat until you forget how to speak entirely."

Her thighs tighten around my hips, as she runs her palms over my shirt, fingers twisting in the fabric, ready to rip it off. Buttons snap free under her newfound strength. It isn't long before the shirt is forgotten on the floor.

Her fingers curl around my bare shoulders, her grip growing more possessive as it moves down my body to the bulge in my pants. Locking her eyes to mine, she unbuttons my pants and takes out my heavy cock.

She rocks her hips to line up with mine.

"I'm begging, Basten Bowborn," she says, eyes locked on me. "For you to make me scream so damn loud every bird in the kingdom takes flight."

A ripple of pleasure—and a twinge of surprise—rolls through me. Fuck, I've never heard such words on my little violet's lips before. Filthy. Sinful. I can't believe this is the same innocent virgin I took behind a waterfall, at least at first blush—but I'm not fooled. Even then, I saw the wildness in her.

I anchor one hand on her hip to hold her steady, still stroking and teasing her wet cunt with my knuckle. I keep at it, punishing her until her little whimpers are *real* begging.

As a reward, I take her in one thrust.

My cock slams deep inside her—and fuck, it feels amazing. Her head falls back, a gasp escaping her lips. With her hair loose down her back, I can't stop myself from wrapping it around my fist, guiding her to arch her back more.

I pull out, only to slam in again.

She angles her hips, matching my thrusts, panting through it, and commands, "*Harder*."

I hesitate, unsure about her raw, wicked tone—but there's a real need in her voice, too, that has nothing to do with control.

So, I tug down her lace neckline, freeing her breasts. I squeeze and cradle and toy with the right one, then take the left nipple in my mouth.

She bucks against me, hissing with pleasure, as the miniature cloud overhead lets out a tiny bolt of lightning. The orchids strain toward us, splashing their scent all over the greenhouse.

"Blessed be these perfect fucking breasts," I murmur in her ear. Blood, sex, prayer—it all sates her. Everything I have to give. "Blessed be your mouth, gasping my name."

"*More*, Basten."

"You want a fucking litany? Will that get you going? How about I worship you until you come undone on every saintly fucking inch of my cock?"

With each uttered prayer, her fey lines glow brighter, pulsing with her building passion.

"Basten—don't stop. I want to feel *everything*."

She's so needy. So insatiable. Even with her pointed ears, there's still something so innocent about her that it makes my cock rock hard.

I trace a hand down the curve of her back, planting a firm palm against the small of her back, letting her know I'm not going anywhere. I drag my lips up from her nipple over the throbbing fey line on her throat, then settle them on her lips.

She sighs against my mouth, nudging my lips open so she can slip her tongue inside. Our tongues war with each other, in rhythm with our frantic thrusts. More condensation drips from the ceiling. The glass is fogged, but I'm well aware that while her storm might hide us from prying eyes, we're making enough noise that they can hear us even in the stables.

Deep inside, I smirk to myself, almost hoping Woudix is still nearby.

Let the God of Death get an earful.

Her cunt tightens around me, and I know she's close. Her power is snapping and popping, making the plants go haywire around us. My balls ache and tighten. I'm close, too, but I want to give her pleasure first.

When she comes, she makes such noises—sweet and sinful at the same time. Her fingernails dig into my back, tearing open wounds barely healed from our last bout of lovemaking. The sweet bite of pain shoots straight to my cock, swelling it even more.

I come a second after her, burying my cock root-deep, practically bending her over the table as my cum empties inside her.

Fat, warm raindrops fall on my bare shoulders, rolling down my sweat-soaked back.

I press my forehead against Sabine's as we both catch our breath, bodies trembling from the aftershocks. Her fey lines glow steadily now, bright as a freshly filled lantern.

"That's it," I praise her, smoothing a sweat-soaked strand of hair off her forehead. "You take everything I give you so well."

It swells in my chest. Raw, blistering, masculine satisfaction that I was able to ground her when she started to spiral. I tamed her storm, made her choose me instead of chaos.

She won't be lost to me—not like Solene in those paintings.

I step back, still riding the high, until I feel a tug around my ankle.

Frowning, my gaze drops.

A vine is coiled half a dozen times around my left ankle, with inch-long thorns stabbing outward like a warning: Move, and *bleed.*

Sabine is oblivious to the vine—I'm sure she didn't consciously ask it to trap me here.

Regardless, it's there. Fierce and possessive.

My stomach tightens. A ripple of concern crawls back into my mind—that maybe the ancient part of her that I saw in the foundation pictograms was the one holding the reins all along.

Sabine, however, merely sits upright, eyelids heavy and sated, a cat-like smile on her lips. She adjusts her dress back over her breasts.

"Tonight," she breathes, her eyes glowing with hopeful excitement, "I'll take a pot of soil to the throne room and show my father how I can sprout a seed. Show him what Woudix helped me unlock."

I flinch, forcing down a growl at the god's name. And discreetly free myself from the last of the vines.

"You sure you're ready for that?" Quickly, I give her a reassuring smile. "I know you're more than capable—but once your father sees your ability, what will he make you do? Let's not forget he tried to kill us both. The man is ruthless."

She cups a soft hand around my tight jaw. "I haven't

forgotten. But this is about helping the river valley refugees."

"You think Vale gives a fuck about the refugees?"

She slides her arms around my neck. "I'm not as naive as you think I am. I know Vale has greater priorities—and that those are almost always selfish. But that isn't what I meant. I don't want to show Vale my power for his approval—it's for his *intimidation*. So he knows he can't ever force you or me to his will."

Oh.

I'm speechless for a minute, berating myself for thinking of her as soft when I've known from the start her core is pure steel.

"Then show him," I murmur in agreement. "Show everyone—we'll summon the entire court."

In the back of my mind, I'm thinking that this show of Sabine's powers could be the perfect distraction for me to sneak back into the basement. With everyone rapt by her display—and let's be real, drunk out of their minds, like always—no one will notice if I slip downstairs to search for more murals. More secrets.

As I start to button my pants, her heartbeat kicks up again. She bites her lips in that telltale way, thighs drifting apart again.

"Gods, wildcat," I say in wonder. "*Again?*"

She gives a cat-like smile.

A knock at the greenhouse door rattles us both. She slides to her feet so fast she knocks over a potted fern.

A year ago, I would have yelled for whoever it is to fuck off. Back then, I was just a huntsman. A lone wolf. Now? I don't have that kind of luxury. Not when gods-damned royal blood flows in my veins and an entire kingdom is looking to me for guidance.

Sighing, I give Sabine a deep kiss before buttoning my pants and grabbing my belt. As I thread it through the loops, I stride over to the door and wipe my fist against the condensation.

Whoever it is had better have a damn good reason for the interruption.

But once I squint through the streaky glass, my irritation crystallizes into something uglier.

The brutish face staring back at me belongs to an old, cantankerous warhorse of a soldier I could happily go my whole life without seeing again.

Maximan—Rian's longtime bodyguard.

Behind me, Sabine comes to my side, eyes wide as my own as she stares at the old soldier.

"Basten—" she whispers but doesn't finish.

I only grunt in response. I know we're thinking the same thing.

It's not just that Maximan and I don't get along—granted, we *don't*. It's because of what his presence here must mean. Sabine knows it, too. Maximan wouldn't have left Old Coros, crossed the border wall, and ventured all the way across enemy territory to Norhelm—on the brink of war—without a good fucking reason.

It's about Rian.

The man I tried to forget.

The person I *wish* I'd lost my memories of.

CHAPTER 7
SABINE

Facing Maximan through the fogged glass is like seeing a ghost.

For weeks, that stern old guard was my shadow in Sorsha Hall, silently tailing me through the Valvere's lavish parties, watching me while I rode Myst, serving as prison guard at my bedroom door. Seeing him now—here—breaks the delicate spell I've fallen into since entering Volkany. Sure, it hasn't been all sunshine—I did *die*, after all—but at least Basten and I are together.

Now, I feel jolted back to the stark reality that these fragile few days of peace were never meant to last. War has always loomed on the horizon.

My reflection catches on the polished metal frame of the greenhouse, flashing my own glowing fey lines back at me. Quickly, I smooth a sweat-soaked hand over my face and down my arms, willing away the fae until only human skin shows.

Maximan doesn't know I'm fae, I remind myself. *Or that any of the fae court is awake.*

Basten wrenches open the greenhouse door, scowling at the old Astagnonian soldier. "Old man, how the fuck did you get all the way to Norhelm without getting yourself butchered?"

Maximan is no fan of Basten's, either, but when he doesn't match Basten's sneer—or even throw off a rude comment about Basten's bare chest—a spike of fear digs into my chest.

Maximan wipes his thinning gray hair off his forehead and says sternly, "I came to deliver a message. We encountered King Rachillon's forces north of the border and surrendered. We need to talk, Lord Basten." His once-blue eyes, now foggy with cataracts, shift to me. "And you, Lady Sabine."

A painful silence falls around us like snow.

I can feel it. Our beautiful time here breaking, breaking, breaking like ice. Basten and I—we're finally free. For once, I'm no one's prisoner. Or pawn. Or bargaining chip. Especially not a naked bride on horseback.

So, of course, Rian would find a way to destroy everything.

I see that the gates of the Twilight Garden are open, and a regiment of twenty Astagnonian royal soldiers stand at attention behind Maximan, along with two enclosed wagons. One looks to be for supplies. The other, however, is the iron-reinforced wagon that Rian used to transport Tòrr.

Except, of course, Tòrr is *here*.

Which means something else now prowls in that locked cage.

Curious Volkish sentries watch from their posts at the castle gates, along with gardeners who don't even pretend to be pruning dead branches. Woudix is among our audience, too, and seeing him makes a shiver travel down my arms, reminding me of his touch that unlocked so much.

I rub my bare shoulders, covered only by thin ribbon straps holding up my gown, which only seconds ago was shoved down to my waist.

"So, talk," Basten barks.

Maximan clears his throat, a strange waver in his eyes that I've never seen before. If I didn't know better, I'd say the old soldier was *afraid.*

"King Rachillon should be in attendance to hear my message," Maximan says, eyes sliding to the caged wagon. "It would be against diplomatic policy not to include him."

"He's with his generals," Woudix says smoothly, sauntering up with Hawk pressed to one leg. Like me, both he and his dog wear their mortal glamour. Only, now that I know the truth, it looks wrong on them, like an ill-fitting suit. I can't believe I didn't see the truth the first time I saw him.

Luckily, I don't think Maximan has the eye to spot magic.

"I can speak for the king," Woudix adds, reaching into his pocket to remove a solid gold calling coin studded with gemstones, the mark of the king's favor. "I'm one of his three Blades, trusted with every royal secret."

Maximan's eyes narrow, ever skeptical. He gives Woudix a once-over, from his dark chin-length locks to the thin metal armor pieces that curve over his chest like rib bones. He might appear human, but the chill rolling off him—laced with the scent of myrrh—makes Maximan flinch back.

"It's true," I confirm, tipping up my chin. "And, as the king's daughter, I give you permission to speak freely."

Maximan lets out a tense exhale before pointing to two

of the royal soldiers. "Private Hammon. Private Flynn. Unlock the cage door. The rest of you, at attention. Secure the chains."

Basten's nostrils flare—he scents something with his godkiss that makes his hand fall smoothly on the knife sheathed at his side. Always a huntsman.

Maximan signals to the soldiers. "Open the cage."

Private Hammon shuffles forward, trying to hide his shaking fingers as he pulls out a heavy keyring.

Basten slips his hand into mine, gives a grounding squeeze. "Little violet," he murmurs. "Check yourself."

That's when I realize that I've let my glamour slip—the fey lines on my hands are glowing. Quickly, I summon my disguise back.

Fortunately, no one's eyes were on me except for Basten's.

Private Hammon swings the door open and jumps back, gripping a thick chain threaded through the cage's port-holes. It pulls taut, and for a heavy second, we all stare at the dark interior of the wagon. From this angle, I doubt even Basten, with his night vision, can make out what's inside.

A wheezing, deathly exhale rolls out like fog. Shuffling footsteps scuff the cage's steel floor. Chains drag. I brace myself, brimming with pent-up fey, ready to step in and cast a punishing ice storm on whatever might emerge from that cage.

Another monoceros?

A mutilated, feral cloud fox?

I can't stop a jolt of surprise when what steps down instead of a monster is...a boot. Slow. Measured.

It's a...person?

The crimson robes of a Red Priest settle around the prisoner's legs as he sways—moving in odd twitches—out of the cage.

Finally, he shuffles into the sunlight.

Every person in the Twilight Garden lets out a gasp, but none is as great as my own. Because the person *isn't* a person—at least not anymore.

The man's skin is gray, his cheek rotten out to show broken teeth beneath. His eyes are as glassy as a dead bird's. A gash across his throat nearly separates his head from his body.

A fatal wound.

Yet he's *walking*.

That's when I recognize the white streak in his otherwise blood-stained hair.

I rear back, heart hammering. "It's Beneveto!"

The Grand Cleric of Astagnon.

The last time I saw Beneveto, my father was sending him to Old Coros to help with the coup. Until then, he'd been a source of comfort in Volkany. Not an ally exactly, but a fellow human. Someone who understood the fae ways and helped me come to terms with their world, before I even knew I was one of them.

Basten's hand closes like a vice around mine, as in one swift movement, he draws his hunting knife and steps in front of me.

Beneveto—or rather, his corpse—steps jerkily down the wagon's steps as strange gurgles reeking of decayed, fermented bile bubble up his throat. The chains fastened to his wrists pull taut as the royal soldiers hold him like a cross-tied stallion.

A brief worry spikes through my head. A walking corpse is terrifying, yes—but why the iron chains? What exactly, besides shuffling and gurgling, do walking corpses do that's so dangerous?

Basten spins on Maximan, voice rising in disbelief. "What the fuck is this?"

"It's the work of a godkissed Deathraiser." Woudix's voice, calm and confident, cuts in and ripples like a deep undercurrent through the nervous crowd. He steps closer with the unbothered confidence of a creature who's never had to run from anything. Hawk pads along at his heels, silent as ever. "This cadaver is not alive. His body is merely animated like a puppet, commanded by godkissed magic." He lifts his chin. "The soul belongs in the underrealm, but it is only halfway there."

The royal soldiers eye Woudix with suspicion. He never revealed that he was the God of Death—would they have believed him if he had?—but his easy calm radiates a wrongness that screams there's more magic here than they ever imagined.

"I don't understand," I blurt out, clenching my fists, the fey in my veins surging hot and wild. "Why would Rian do this? Is this a declaration of war? Did he find out the Grand Cleric was a spy for Volkany, send him like this as a warning?"

Maximan, who's been staring at the reeling undead thing with barely veiled disgust, jerks his head toward me. Gruff, he barks, "Beneveto was a spy?"

I blink, taken aback. "You didn't know?"

His brow caves inward, the line between his eyes deepening to a chasm. Clearly, he did not. "You're certain of this, Lady Sabine?"

I nod.

Maximan mutters under his breath, eyeing the cadaver with renewed disgust. "No, my lady. King Rian didn't know. None of us did."

My voice drops, a chill slipping into it. "Then why kill him?"

Maximan shifts his stance. "Grand Cleric Beneveto and Lord Kendan, with the help of Folke Bladeborn, attempted a coup upon the Astagnonian throne two weeks ago. They tried to murder King Rian while he was sedated, being worked on by a healer."

The words fall like bricks.

For one breathless second, all I feel is panic. Rian was attacked? It wasn't long ago that I explained to Kendan Valvere that Rian had an old back injury that required sedation and a healer's touch the first of every month.

Is he alive?

I might as well have held the killing blade myself.

The guilt rises fast—but just as quick, it crashes. Why should I feel guilty for aiding the coup? Rian may have laughed with me once, touched me like I mattered—but underneath it all, he's still the same bastard who earned the name Lord of Liars.

You don't get a title like that by being kind.

"Their attempt failed," Maximan explains, and gods help me, I feel a wild surge of relief before my better senses kick in. Maximan gestures to the half-rotten cadaver wheezing at the end of the chains. "In the skirmish, Rian killed the Grand Cleric, then was able to escape. No one knows his current location. At present, the Kingdom of Astagnon is without a ruler. The throne stands empty. I don't have to explain what danger that puts Astagnonians in."

Basten paces, his face pale, his stance tense as a bowstring.

It's a lot to process for me, too, but one question lodges in my mind like an arrow. "Wait—if Rian is a fugitive, how could he order a Deathraiser to resurrect the body and send it here as a message?"

"You misunderstand, Lady Sabine," Maximan says gravely. "*Rian* didn't send the cleric. Lord Kendan was the one who had the Grand Cleric's body raised in an attempt to hold the throne, at least temporarily. After Rian, Beneveto had the greatest claim to the throne out of anyone in Astagnon. We thought he'd be more-or-less comatose. Easily manipulated, like a child's doll. None of us expected..." he motions to the corpse, "...*this* would be the result. Consider him evidence, from Lord Kendan. Of the coup. And how dire our situation is."

The air seems to go still around me. I lightly drag my fingers over the godkissed mark on my breastbone, thinking of the poor Deathraiser who was forced to create this undead abomination.

"Kendan needs someone on the throne," I say, finally understanding. "Someone alive."

At my side, Basten stiffens.

Until this moment, I don't think he fully grasped what this entire horror show was about. That, for the first time since we set foot in Volkany, this isn't about me.

It's about *him*.

Maximan lowers himself to a knee, his old bones cracking, and dips his head to Basten. The royal soldiers follow suit behind him, and the ones holding the chains bow their heads.

I know it must kill Maximan to have to bend the knee to Basten—the scofflaw he knew as Wolf—but Maximan is nothing if not loyal to the crown.

"Lord Basten," Maximan says. "I've been commanded to bring you back to Astagnon to assume the throne. Immediately. At any cost."

CHAPTER 8
BASTEN

Drahallen Hall's great room reeks of last night's feast, though all signs of merriment have long been swept away. Everyone else has planted their asses in their seats—Immortal Vale at the place of honor, Iyre, Artain, Samaur, Woudix lined up beside him, Sabine opposite. Maximan sits, too—we had no choice but to tell him about the woken fae, and he still looks shellshocked.

I can't sit. My boots scuff the stone as I prowl behind them, shoulder tight, jaw grinding. Because the one thing in this room that rattles me isn't the gods.

It's that empty chair facing Vale. A throne, just like his. A king's place. Waiting. Daring me to claim it.

It took half a day to summon the rest of the fae here, from whatever bullshit they were up to, as well as the most influential human leaders, who stand around the edges.

Captain Tatarin, head of Volkany's mage army. Captain Vallois, the elderly yet graceful female leader of the archers. Captain Perrin, a block of a man who oversees the infantry. And the stoic Captain Huntill of the cavalry.

"Lord Basten, if you continue to avoid sitting in your seat, we'll never get on with the day." Artain circles his long fingers methodically on his wine goblet's base like setting a snare.

Sabine nudges my heavy chair out an inch with her foot.

It still grates my nerves to take a throne—let's face it, I'm not anyone's first choice for leadership material—but when she sets those soft eyes on me, beckoning with a pat on the chair's armrests, my coiled muscles slacken.

I sink down, growling my unease.

"Now," Vale starts, ignoring my grumbles, hunching forward over an unrolled map of the Near World. "Maximan says that King Rian was last seen—"

"*Uhhhnnhnnn.*" A groan rolls out from the south-eastern corner of the great hall, where Grand Cleric Beneveto's cadaver is strapped to a chair with leather binds.

Vale's jaw snaps shut, frustration sparking in his icy blue eyes. He draws in a long breath to find his patience. "As I was saying, if we are to take—"

"*Uhhnnhhhnnnnhn.*"

His words halt. again. He grimaces. "If we—"

"*Huuhhhnnhhuhh.*"

Vale tosses up his hands, sitting back with his own groan. "Can't someone shut up that fucking cadaver?"

Immortal Samaur leans forward, showing off a flash of his golden front tooth. "How exactly do you propose it, brother? Slit his throat? The man is already dead."

Another moan rattles out of Beneveto's body, this time punctuated with some phlegm-filled gagging, then a loud hiss of gas from somewhere I'd prefer to remain a mystery.

Captain Tatarin hides her snicker behind her hand,

turning toward the window as though something has suddenly caught her eye.

"Then get a damn Deathraiser in here," Vale demands, "and find out how to kill an already dead man!"

"I can silence him," Woudix utters, resting his hands flat on the table.

I fight the urge to roll my eyes. Oh, fantastic. Woudix is the last person I want to hear from. I fight the urge to tighten my fists on the table as I imagine how good it would feel to slam them into his pale face.

It's a toss up, really. Which one I hate most.

Immortal Iyre stole my memories.

Immortal Artain tried to kill me.

Immortal Vale *also* tried to kill me.

Apparently, it's open hunting season on Basten Bowborn.

But right now, my ire fixes on the handsome God of Death who just *has* to put his hands all over Sabine to unlock her powers.

"Do it," Vale mutters, massaging the bridge of his nose.

Woudix pushes back his chair, scraping the hard stone, and stalks toward Beneveto like a wolf. The cadaver's jaw snaps hard, his broken and bloodied teeth glistening, like he wants to take a bite out of the god.

Fuck.

I recoil, leaning back in the throne. No wonder he was brought to Volkany in chains.

The woken dead have a taste for...flesh?

Woudix approaches in deathly-calm steps, circling the bound and chained cleric. Slowly, his human glamour falls away. Black fey lines break out on his exposed wrists and neck, climbing up his pale temples. His eyes turn entirely black, like window glass at night.

Beneveto snaps his jaw, almost biting Woudix's outstretched hand.

Woudix doesn't fucking blink.

He whispers low, in a language that doesn't seem a part of this world, and sparking black fey shoots out from his fingertips straight into Beneveto's gaping mouth.

Beneveto's body goes rigid, then jerks wildly as if fey is bouncing around inside him from throat to belly, dissolving his guts from the inside out. The cadaver begins to weep thick, gelatinous tears. More of the clear substance, swirling with faint pearlescent sheen, drips from his ears, nose, and mouth.

Whatever the thick substance is continues to ooze out of his pores until his rotting skin gleams and his clothes are soaked.

Woudix snaps, and the substance begins to boil right there on the cadaver's skin. Wisps of vapor rise into the air to disappear into nothing.

The cadaver shakes violently one final time, a hoarse groan on his lips, and then slumps backward.

No one speaks.

Everyone waits to see if Beneveto will move again.

There isn't a face in the great hall—human or otherwise—that isn't pale as a fucking sheet. That goes for my own, too. Because it's one thing to see the gods spark fey at their fingertips to heat their lukewarm cup of wassail. Another thing entirely to watch a soul bleed out of its casing.

"So that's how we go in the end?" I mutter, reaching for my wine goblet. "I'd better drink deep and live harder."

Woudix slowly circles toward me with a face as stolid as fucking granite. "If you'd rather, I could harvest your soul now, Lord Basten. Save you the torment of decades of human suffering."

His black fey sparks at his pale fingertips.

I lean forward. "Try it—I dare you."

Sabine presses her foot against mine under the table, sliding me a warning look.

Woudix smirks softly as he slides back into his chair at the table, folding his hands as if he didn't just suck a spirit out of Beneveto's body.

Discreetly, I wipe away a bead of sweat on my temple. For all my jokes, a part of me does wonder if that ass, Beneveto, is at peace now. It was a hell of a thing to watch, but I have to admit, there's a lightness to the room now that he's gone.

The cadaver is still, finally. Beneveto's soul peacefully ushered to the Underrealm.

Clean and final—an easy end. Unlike the absolute fuckery of the future *I'm* facing down.

But I get a whiff of violets as Sabine leans toward me, placing her hand over mine, and I snap back into reality. Sure, death might bring a certain calm—but what use do I have for peace if Sabine isn't there?

"As I was attempting to explain," Vale continues, tapping a heavy finger on the map. "If we consider Maximan's information and that of our own spies—" he gestures to Captain Perrin, "—it's likely that King Rian will attempt to flee to his family's hometown of Duren. Unfortunately, we do not know how much progress he's made, or what course he might have taken."

He drags his finger over various inked pathways from Old Coros to Duren.

Captain Tatarin toys with the dangling timepiece around her neck, nimble fingers plucking at the chain. "What are the chances the Golden Sentinels will remain loyal to the Valvere family if Rian attempts to reassert his power from Duren?"

"It's almost a certainty," Maximan utters bleakly. "The Golden Sentinels have overtaken most of Old Coros and driven the royal army and Rian's opposition to within the gates of Hekkelveld Castle. The Sentinel army is ten thousand strong. The Valvere family well paid them. Privileged them with wine and women. Since being incorporated into the royal Astagnonian army, they've had their pay cut in half and their workload doubled. Many—if not most—were more than happy to rise up against the opposition. They want Rian back in power. In Rian's absence, his generals, called the Cold Coins, are in charge."

"And the royal army?" Artain asks, flicking a speck of dust off his leather tunic.

"They remain loyal to the throne, and whoever sits in it," Maximan answers. "But there are half as many of them as Sentinels. Many are advanced in age and untested. For the last fifty years, the previous king relied on the Valveres' Sentinels as mercenaries to do the kingdom's fighting. The royal army was ceremonial."

"Lord Kendan," he continues, "was the one who captured a sentinel and learned of Rian's escape plan." He drags a hand over his rough beard. "Called it some maneuver, something like, Tamarind..."

A shard of ice buries itself in my belly. In a hollow voice, I ask, "Tamarac?"

Maximan bows his head to me. "That was it. The Tamarac Maneuver."

I sit back, reeling. It feels like a damn storm is stirring in my gut.

Tamarac—that was our private word for complete honesty with one another. It meant trust. Bound us closer than brothers. And now Rian uses it as the name for his coup? He might as well be reaching across the border wall to stab me in the back. Either he's mocking me, or sending a message.

What kind of man has the balls to betray Sabine, lie to me, and still dare to whisper "tamarac" across the wind?

Sabine's fingernails curl over the map, shredding it until all that's left of the illustration of Duren are some surrounding barley fields. A chill radiates from her stiff posture, as though she's ready for war.

Her incisors are out—flashing in the candlelight. She practically hisses, "Rian poisoned the Lunden River valley— why don't we repay his kindness? Send a flock of starleons to rain plague on his precious city?"

"There are civilians to consider," Captain Tatarin chimes in, measured and reasonable. "Tens of thousands in Duren might die. Women and children, too."

Sabine's lip curls in frustration, and I half expect her to snarl that it's their fault for living within Valvere territory. I shift in my seat, unable to look at her. It wasn't so long ago that her father made the same devil's bargain, letting starleons loose upon the innocent people in Duren's arena. At the time, Sabine did the impossible—rode a damn monoceros—to save them.

Now she wants to snuff those same lives out?

I clear my throat, and something about the sound makes her blink like she's been shaken from slumber.

She sits upright, smoothing back the torn paper scraps of the map. "R—right. Yes, I understand that. Of course, we don't want anyone hurt. But there still must be something we can do. We have a monoceros. Goldenclaws. Starleons. Gods who can turn day into night and banish souls to the Underrealm." She pushes out her chair to pivot toward Woudix. "Claim Rian's soul, as you did just now with Beneveto, and let's be done with it."

I flinch. Rian is a bastard—absolutely. And he'll pay for his betrayal. But her anger, her brutality...it's like I don't recognize her.

"I could," Woudix explains, sinking back into his chair and resting one hand casually on his dinner knife. "But claiming a soul before its time upsets the balance of the Underrealm. There have been instances, in the past, where it's caused...problems."

A chill bites at my ankles, and I drag my feet further under the table's shelter. I can't help but think of Beneveto's corpse snapping its undead jaw. Hungry for flesh.

"Then we'll go." Sabine turns to me with fever-bright eyes, picking up her own knife and dragging the pointed end across the map from Norhelm to Old Coros. "Rian wronged us as much as anyone, and now that I have the power to make him pay, nothing would please me more."

I don't think she notices how hard she's digging the knife's point into the map.

I shift in my chair, keeping the corner of one eye locked to that knife in her hand.

"What about your training?" I press my hands flat to the

table, steadying my voice. "You've come a long way, but even you said you're not in full control yet. Burying Rian in a rock-slide is one thing—but what happens if you lose control again? If it's another Garden of Ten Gods moment, only this time it's not just one man, it's a city?" I hold her gaze. "Maybe we stay. Just a little longer. Give you time to work more with...Woudix. Get your bearings before we push forward."

I practically have to vomit the god's name out. It's repulsive, the idea that I'm advocating for her to spend more time with that graveyard-loving asshole. But it's the only card I can think to play now.

Sabine's fingers slacken on the knife as she twists toward the window. Outside, storm clouds churn—thick, dark, and wrong. I don't think she called them with intention, but they're here all the same.

"She's ready," Woudix says, low and certain.

I don't care *at all* for his tone.

Vale stands, towering over the rest of us, and rests his fists with a finality on the table. "My interests are larger than who sits on a mortal throne. I care not for such petty squabbles—soon enough, we'll rule over all mankind."

Sabine folds her hands on the table and says measuredly, "That's true, Father. But wouldn't you say a kingdom at peace would be far more welcoming to fae rule than one at war? With Basten and I on the throne, we can ensure the public will embrace you with overflowing offerings, instead of putting up a resistance."

I bristle, hiding my emotion by tapping my heel on the floor. If you ask me, unleashing Sabine on the outside world still falls in the risky-as-fuck camp.

Vale considers this. "You can open Old Coros to me?"

I shift in my chair, biting back objections.

Sabine nods eagerly, sure. "The people will bow down at first sight of you."

He taps his finger on the map, considering, and then stands. "It's decided, then. Lord Basten, you and my daughter will return to Old Coros as soon as supplies can be readied. You'll take the throne. Prepare the public for our arrival. We will enter the town gates on the Blood Moon, and accept a devoted reception."

Sabine's eyes go wide. "The Blood Moon? That isn't much time. Only weeks. And the rest of the fae aren't awake—"

"The Blood Moon." His tone is final as he signals to Captain Tatarin, who begins to roll up the map.

Sabine looks down at her hands, steadies her feelings, and then looks back up with resolve. She nods. "We'll take Myst and Tòrr."

"Tòrr remains here." There's no crack in the foundation of Vale's voice. He offers no explanation, but I recognize a hostage when I see it. He's afraid that if Sabine has Tòrr, she might not fall in line with his plan. That we could rebel, turn against him.

Personally? I'm relieved—I'll say it. It'll be hard enough keeping Sabine tame during the journey, let alone a fucking monoceros.

"We'll take Myst and Ranger," I tell her. "Regular horses won't draw as much attention, anyway. We don't have Ferra to change Tòrr's appearance again—and the people of Astagnon don't know that you're Immortal Solene. Let's save that information for when it's most strategic to reveal, not when marching into the city on a monoceros."

Maximan says, "I'll leave as well straight after this meeting. Ride ahead of you to Old Coros to alert Lord Kendan of your arrival. He'll have the King's Council prepared for your coronation soon after you set foot in Hekkelveld Castle."

"Great." I slump over my dinner plate, my appetite fled, as though the weight of that damn golden circle is already making my neck ache.

Most of all, I'm worried about that vengeful glint in Sabine's eye. Since the Gloaming, she's been unpredictable. A different version of herself. I keep her satiated as much as I can, but what if she slides so far that I can't follow her?

No acolyte has lived more than a few months.

A soft hand falls on my shoulder, and I flinch. Always a soldier's instincts. But it's only Sabine, her big eyes so blue I could drown in them, her lips parted enough that I can see no sign of elongated incisors. I could almost pretend I imagined her feverish eyes earlier.

She tucks her head close to my ear.

"Volkany is my birthright," she murmurs low, knowing my godkiss will pick it up, "but Astagnon is my home. It's yours, too. So many good people there who don't deserve to be crushed under the wheels of war. If we can stop it, we have to try."

I scold myself for doubting her. My little violet is hardly a monster. She's still the same girl who won over all of Astagnon as the Winged Lady, fierce and forgiving at the same time.

Able to rein in her own worst tendencies.

And as her acolyte, I'll pray on my knees that she'll stay that way.

"Okay," I answer. "We'll leave at dawn."

And then, it's a feverdream of motion—packing foodstuffs and supplies for the journey, oiling the horses' tack, checking and rechecking that I've packed every knife I can strap onto my body.

The entire castle echoes with preparations, and in every raised voice and stomping boot, I can feel the restless shifting of people who don't need a godkiss to know that something is coming.

Like we're all trying to close a door against a storm we can't yet see.

CHAPTER 9
SABINE

Fae, I'm learning, are not sentimental.

There are no prolonged goodbyes when Basten and I mount our horses in the morning, as first light breaks over the distant Vallen Mountains. No embraces. No tearful farewells or even well wishes for our travel.

In fact, Iyre doesn't even bother to get out of bed.

So, it's my father and the three Blades who stand in Drahallen Hall's entry courtyard, wearing basic breastplates over their simple human glamour, not even bothering to change into full fae regalia.

But honestly? I prefer it like this. I came to Drahallen Hall as a messy-haired human girl, no pomp or parades, and that's how I want to leave.

Well—maybe the human part isn't accurate anymore. Not entirely. But sitting on my sweet Myst, with Basten at my side with his hair loose and wild, his skin ruddy from the early morning chill, I don't feel that far at all from the same fierce-hearted girl who arrived here atop of goldenclaw, in chains.

And it gives me hope. Maybe—just maybe—I can find a balance between my selves.

Clusters of pilgrims line the road out of Norhelm, laying offerings of flower chains and honey wine by the road as we pass, but once we're outside of the city gates, it's soon just us and the road.

The morning fog burns off, revealing a clear blue sky, and with the steady, familiar clomp of the horses' hooves underfoot, I take a deep breath for what feels like the first time in weeks.

Breathe in fresh, crisp air.

Breathe out all the tightness that's crackled in my chest since the Gloaming.

A squirrel suddenly darts across the road, right in Basten's path, causing his horse, Ranger, to spook. Once Basten has the horse calmed, he slides me a teasing look. "Was that you?"

I smirk and jest, "I don't always throw squirrels in your way. Only when you're being grumpy."

He grins with his eyes, and it's contagious—I can't help but smile back.

Just like that, we aren't Immortal Solene, Goddess of Nature, and the heir to the Astagnonian throne. We're simply Sabine and Basten.

My heart stirs, warming my cold fae blood.

"We'll be at the border wall in three days." Basten points to the southern peaks, then his hand falls on his pocket, where he taps it as though feeling for something, reassuring himself whatever it is, is there. "From there, it will be fastest if we head west."

"Why?" I ask. "Old Coros is southeast of Norhelm."

I think back on the maps I studied with Woudix. For the first time in my life, thanks to the God of Death's tutelage, I know something of geography. How to read a map. Even how to tell the direction by the sun.

"That's true," Basten explains, "but the Blackened Forest stretches to the east. Cutting through it without a road would add days to the journey, not to mention putting the horses at a greater risk of injury. If we skirt around the forest instead, the distance is longer but the path is more passable. Then, we'll cut south across the Arthurette Valley until we reach the Innis River, staying on back roads. We can follow that path to Old Coros. Maximan said only the southern gate is operational at the moment—the northern gate is permanently sealed. According to him, guards will be waiting there to help us enter the city without incident."

Mentally, I trace the path he's describing over what I know of Astagnon's topography. "That won't place us far from Bremcote," I say in surprise, then feel a twist in my belly. "And the Convent of Immortal Iyre."

Basten nods, his attention on the road ahead, though he flicks me a glance. "Bad memories?"

I sit back in the saddle, letting Myst take the lead so that I can fall into my thoughts. "Not...entirely. After all, Bremcote is where I became friends with Suri." I flash him a smile that I only have to force a little. "And where I met a brooding guard who wanted nothing to do with his master's headstrong new bride."

He chuckles, but I can see some pain in his eyes.

My smile falls. "Oh—you don't remember." I swallow down a lump. "Right. Sometimes, I still forget." I sigh. "Well, it's okay if we take that path. As long as we don't actually go to the town itself."

A cloud rolls in to block the sun, plunging us into an uncomfortable shadow—and I'm not sure if the weather is responding to my mood or simply doing what weather does.

I scramble for something else to say to fill the awkward silence, but Basten beats me to it.

"Tell me about it. The first time we met." His tone is velvet-soft and inviting, so different from the bitterness he used to use when speaking about his lost memories.

He's trying.

I brighten a little—and that pesky cloud blows away from the sun. "Well," I sit up straight in the sunlight. "You certainly *acted* like you weren't staring at my naked body."

He snorts. "Guarantee you that I was. I'm a hunter, sweetheart. I know how to hide where I focus my attention."

Wistfully, I touch my fine silken riding dress with golden threads in the shape of monoceroses. "The first night, you gave me your shirt to wear. It was filthy. Stank of your sweat. But, I cherished it because it was the first kindness you did for me. The first time you bent your loyalty to Rian."

At the mention of Rian's name, we both fall silent again.

Nice going, Sabine, I tell myself. I might as well have invoked the devil.

"When we find him..." I start again, my voice scraping this time, "...are you going to hold the knife, or am I?"

I meant it as a joke, to lighten the mood—but it came out raw.

For a few moments, there's only the sound of the horses' hooves on the dirt path. Finally, Basten takes a deep breath. "Rian should be thrown in the dungeon like any other prisoner to await sentencing from the justice tribunal."

I twist in my saddle, jaw hanging open as I stare to see if he's fallen and hit his head. "Justice tribunal? Basten, Rian *knew* Iyre was coming for me and practically threw me into her arms."

He shifts in his stirrups, keeping his gaze on the road. "Oh, he'll be punished."

I sputter, "That's it? Punished? I thought you'd pledge to rip his head off with your own two hands."

Maybe Basten hears the slight break in my voice, because he nudges Ranger closer to Myst and takes my hand. "Little violet, I'm not going to let him get away with what he did to you. I'll make sure he spends the rest of his life regretting he ever knew your name. But the old Basten? Wolf, the hunter, who only cared about himself? I have to leave that brute behind—at least, try to. If our plan works, I'm going to sit on a throne. Rule a kingdom. Have hundreds of thousands of people's safety in my hands. I can't go around slitting throats anymore."

There's a rare vulnerability in his voice, and it gives me pause. I realize, maybe for the first time, that I'm not the only one struggling to balance two different identities. Basten's world has turned upside down, too. Can I blame him for trying to find a way to navigate both?

After all, he became my acolyte. Even at the risk of his own death, he freely gives me his blood, his breath. Gods, his patience most of all.

I suppose I can try to be patient for Basten, too.

"I—I understand." I squeeze his hand, hold it as long as I can before the road forces our horses too far apart. My hand falls at my side, my palm cold without Basten's warmth. I slide him a mischievous wink to break the tension. "*I'll* slit his throat, then."

He laughs, but there's a ripple of concern in his eyes that I might not be joking. Which, honestly, is keen of him. Because I'm not sure I'm *not*.

The further we get into the journey, winding through the dramatic scenery of the Vallen Mountains, it's easier to leave all the stress of Norhelm behind. Myst prances beneath me, happy to be together again, like we were for so many years.

Are you sorry we had to leave Tòrr behind? I ask her.

She snorts. ***Not in the slightest. His ego left no room in the stall for me.***

I grin, scratching her neck fondly. Still, I know she feels a deep love for the grumpy monoceros...even if the part about his oversized ego is true.

When the sun dips behind the horizon, we make camp off the road, in the ruins of an abandoned old shrine to Immortal Alyssantha. It's barely more than a few moss-covered marble blocks, now, the wooden roof long ago rotten out and overtaken by nature. A weather-worn stone statue of the goddess herself is half-buried under creeping phlox.

"Does it bother you?" Basten jerks his head toward the statue. "We could camp somewhere else. Somewhere without a whiff of your family."

I smile gently. "This is fine—after all, I haven't met Alyssantha yet. Maybe she isn't as odious as the others. There's always hope, right?"

He snorts as he drags over a fallen log to make a fire. "So far, the odds aren't good. Six fae awake, only one tolerable. *You.*"

I laugh as I gather kindling from around the clearing. "Woudix isn't that bad."

Basten growls deep in his throat, heavy with distaste. He drops the log into the middle of the clearing and then comes over to sweep me up in his arms instead, like laying claim. "If I don't ever see that damn coffin-peddler again, I'll die happy."

I rest a staying hand on his chest, gazing up at him through my lashes. "He only wants to help me."

"He wants to *fuck* you."

"Easy, wild stallion," I tease, twirling my finger around the laces at his shirt collar. "Not every person walking around with a dick thinks about sex as much as you do."

"*Mmm-hmm*," he grunts doubtfully. "And you have a lot to learn about men, little violet. Same goes for gods."

His gaze locks to mine, and his hands come to cup my jaw. I can feel the heat of him, smell the faint trace of leather and salt on his skin.

He kisses me—softly at first and then positively sinfully—and the world disappears.

When he pulls back, just barely, his lips hover above mine. "Alyssantha must still have some hold over this place," he murmurs. "No other goddess than the one of sex could dare stir this much want."

I let out a breath heavy with desire. "Then let her spirit watch," I whisper, pulling him back down.

When we finally break the kiss, breathless and spent, he heads to the edge of the clearing. "I'll take the horses to the stream to drink, then hunt us something to eat."

He disappears with Ranger and Myst into the leafy underbrush, where a burst of iridescent dragonflies rise into the sky in his wake. They're so beautiful they make my heart ache—but it's also a stark reminder that we aren't simply Basten and Sabine on the road to Duren, like before.

We're in Volkany. A land where the plants gleam and the insects glow.

I settle near the overgrown statue of Alyssantha, arranging the kindling like Basten taught me so long ago. The wood does something to my palms, spurs a strange, feverish tickle across my skin, like it's calling to me.

I glance in the direction where Basten disappeared. I can barely hear him and the horses at the distant stream. They won't be back for a few minutes.

"Okay, you can do this," I tell myself, crouching in front of the log pile. Fire, after all, is pure nature, right? And nature is my domain.

"No Woudix? No problem." I cup my hands around the dry kindling, and after a deep inhale, slowly let my human glamour fade away like shaking off raindrops.

I think about Woudix's words, how he pressed his hand over mine, and how my fey responded to his own.

Around me, the wind dies down, and the air grows warmer on my palms, even though the sun has sunk behind the horizon.

Something shifts inside me. It's as though my attention moves from my head—my ever-messy swirl of human thoughts—to my chest. No, even lower. My belly. As if I'm living truly in my body now, not my mind.

When I breathe out, it's with sparks at my fingertips.

There's a crackle. A burn.

My eyes shoot open to stare in disbelief at the small flame flickering on the kindling, which quickly grows into a tidy fire. I let out an excited shriek and look around at the darkening forest, wanting verification from the nearby birds and insects that I really did this—hell, from Basten, too, but he's too far away.

I lean back, away from the heat, letting the flames paint my face orange.

Marveling at what I've done.

All on my own, this time. And it makes me wonder— *what else can I do?*

The statue of Alyssantha catches my eye, and I hold up my glowing palm in its direction. *Breathe in, breathe out.*

It takes a few minutes of concentration, during which my stomach grumbles distractingly with hunger. But as I continue to steady my breath, the vines tangled around the statue's neck begin to ruffle in the breeze—except there is no wind.

Then, they curl back, rippling slowly as they draw away from the worn grooves in the stone, slink earthward until they've tucked themselves into a tidy wreath at the statue's base.

"I did that," I whisper like a girl learning to bake her first pie. "Me!"

What else, what else? My attention drags over the clearing, briefly touching on the high pine branches, a copse of bioluminescent mushroom caps glowing a dark indigo, a wasp's nest three trees over.

The ground beneath me is awfully hard—uneven from twisted roots and bare patches of soil that will be painful to sleep on, even with the saddle blankets we packed.

I scramble to my knees, running my hands over the ground, feeling a coil of warmth build in my palms.

Help me, I speak in my godkiss voice, only this time, I talk to the entire natural world, the trees and the stones and the rain, not just any nearby animals. ***Sense my need. Come to my call.***

Everywhere I move my hands over the earth, springy

moss sprouts and fills in to make a natural mattress for Basten and me. Soft clumps blossom for our pillows, and that's not all—the pine branches overhead lean in, sheltering us from a few sparse raindrops dripping from an earlier storm. A *crack* sounds nearby, and a small sapling falls right on my kindling pile—offering itself as wood to keep me warm.

I shiver, not from the cold.

I didn't specifically call the pines or the sapling.

But they still answered: *Sense my need.*

As goosebumps crop up on my arms, the fire swells to throw out more heat, as if it, too, feels my shiver and rushes to respond to my need.

I'm so awe-struck at how new this is, how wildly different, for nature to respond to me like this, that I don't even take note of the small, soft creature moving through the grass until out of the corner of my eye, I see the rabbit.

It's a big one. A buck. Fur a pure white, a color that Astagnonian rabbits never turn. Here, maybe they have to adapt to the more prevalent snow. The rabbit hops forward, unafraid, nose twitching as its glossy black eyes fix on me.

Hello, friend, I say. ***Aren't you a pretty thing?***

I reach out to pet its white fur, wondering if it's as soft as it looks, and there's a moment when my hand connects and I can feel its little heart beating so, so fast.

I've only touched it for a second when the rabbit takes one more leap—

—*into* the fire.

Flames immediately catch on its fur, but it doesn't scramble or jump away. It lies its body right on the hot coals, breathing in smoke, its eyes slowly dimming, muscles twitching until, within seconds, it stops moving.

It happens so suddenly that I shriek.

Immediately, I reach for it, trying to pull it out—but it's too late.

Fingers singed, I scramble backward from the fire, my own heart thumping far too fast now, and stare at the little body in the coals.

And it comes to me: *I asked nature to respond to my need—and I'm hungry.*

"No, no," I whisper, as I snatch up a stick and try to fish the rabbit's body out of the flames before it chars to ash. "This isn't what I meant! I didn't mean for you to sacrifice yourself!"

I get the rabbit's body close enough that I can grab a crisp paw, pull it out onto the grass. Its white fur is already burned off, its flesh smelling of Drahallen Hall's roasting kitchen.

My eyes fill, and a tear breaks to roll down my cheek. It lands on the rabbit's flank. And then, more tears burst free, a whole waterfall of them, and I bury my face in my hands and sob.

"Sabine?" Basten's worried voice cuts across the clearing, as he stomps toward me with the horses in tow. He quickly loops their leads on a branch and kneels at my side. "What is it? What happened?"

It's a while before I can even manage to point a shaky finger at the rabbit.

"You—you hunted our dinner?" he asks, confused, because I usually sing to the animals, not spear them.

My head drags back and forth, face still hidden in my palms, shame burning through me. "It came on its own, killed itself so I'd have something to eat."

I shatter into sobs again, wishing I could burrow deep

into the ground, away from all the watching little eyes of the forest.

Basten is quiet for a while. "Ah."

He gathers me in his arms, holding me in a steady embrace, letting me sob until the worst of my sorrow has dripped into a puddle in my lap.

"We would have killed a rabbit for dinner, regardless," he gently reminds me. "Whether with my arrow or your power, does it make a difference?"

"It isn't that." I wipe my damp nose. "I eat meat—I know the reality of what that means. But Basten, I was so swept up in my powers...I grew this moss bed...lit the fire... always, animals have listened to my voice in their head, but I didn't mean to call for its death."

He rubs my back, placing soft kisses on my temple.

I hiccup out, "This much power makes me afraid. I don't know how the world will respond. What if I shiver in my sleep tonight and the entire forest sets itself on fire to warm me?"

"You'll learn," he reassures me. "You'll find the difference between unbridled need and a controlled response. And I'll be there to make damn sure nature listens."

I gaze at him, feeling more hopeful.

It nearly turns my stomach to eat the rabbit that Basten finishes roasting on a spit, choking it down where it sits heavy in the pit of my stomach, but his words bring me a little comfort.

That night, we lay together on the moss bed beneath our saddle blankets. He holds me close, his forehead pressed against my own as though he knows that the only way I can fall asleep these days is to the rhythmic sound of his breathing.

Slowly, sleep comes.

I feel myself twitch, legs kicking out.

I'm dreaming of the rabbit.

It's strange—I feel both in the dream and out of it. A part of me, twitching and turning, is vaguely aware that I'm in the clearing with a snoring Basten, our legs tangled together, as the moon rises high.

At some point, however, the dream shifts. Now, there are many rabbits. Dozens of them, all snow-white, all full of life as they fill the clearing. Their twitching whiskers are a reminder that when one life goes, another comes to take its place. The old buck didn't just die for our supper—he left behind his legacy, filled this forest with his children, and his children's children.

In the dream, I sit up—my own ghost—and begin to walk through the forest. There, Alyssantha is more than a hunk of weather-worn stone. The statue's flowing locks, carved of granite, now ripple with soft life, her skin warm and peachy.

She stands by her temple, its walls freshly built, laughing as she smokes a long Wicked Weed pipe. She's speaking to a male I don't recognize, with ruddy tan skin and flowing curls down to his shoulders, his cheeks telltale pink from too much wine, his cackling laugh too loud.

When I pass, he pauses his conversation long enough to tip his wine glass my way, and I see the flash of a golden coin glinting as a single earring in his right ear.

It's Immortal Popelin, I realize. *God of Pleasure.*

Like this, he seems so real—so much more than any illustrated version I've seen of him, any artist's guess as to what he might have looked like in the beginning, or the First, or the Second Return.

I'm struck by something—how *familiar* they both feel to me.

I continue walking, and slowly, the forest changes—the towering, ancient oaks are now barely saplings, as though I've slipped backward in time, a thousand years or more. The undergrowth thickens with lush, unfamiliar ferns. Every leaf glistens with an iridescent sheen—greens and purples and silvers sliding over their surfaces like oil skimming water. Even the stones beneath my feet seem lit from within.

I reach out to move a low-hanging branch, and the moment I brush it aside, I freeze.

A river babbles ahead, weaving its way over smooth rocks, but in the water, the magic ends.

Fish float belly-up. Dozens of them. Pale and lifeless.

A preternatural tickle settles in my stomach. It doesn't feel sorrowful like earlier in the night—back in my real world—when the rabbit sacrificed himself. This feels more like...an inevitability. Like something that happened long ago.

I follow the poisoned stream to a clearing where a pile of dead crows rises taller than my own head. Circling it slowly, I watch with strange detachment as another crow falls on top, its wings giving their last flutter of life, as it exhales thick, black smoke.

A smolder of rage burns in my chest, but like this dream, it feels odd—distant.

The memory of an old feeling.

There's a break in the trees ahead, and I find myself stepping out onto a rocky overlook. A valley stretches below me, and while I don't recognize the forest, the mountains themselves haven't changed. It's the Vallen Mountains. Below, the Ramvik River churns through the valley where Norhelm should rest on that promontory.

But I don't see the dark spires of Drahallen Hall now. Or the gray slate, pitched rooftops of houses.

There's a different city here, now.

The name comes to me as a whisper: *Calisyrune.*

The city itself is a marvel—a primitive but megalithic collection of sun-baked brick houses, all circular like beehives. They spiral outward from an imposing stone temple made of polished limestone, guarded by twenty-foot obelisks lit from below by fires.

It isn't the striking architecture that captures my attention, though. It's the hundreds of pillars of black smoke rising high from cooking fires, blacksmith huts, burn pits— enough to blot out the sky. A heavy, poisonous haze hangs over the city.

Another crow flies out of it, faltering, coughing out smoke as it flies overhead toward the death-pyre of its companions.

The Ramvik River doesn't look crisp, now. It's clogged with the city's waste—human and animal refuse, livestock carcasses gone bad with disease, cast-off building materials, broken buckets, stained cloths. One of the creeks leading out of the city center runs pure red, coming from the butcher district.

I think of the dead fish, the coughing crows, the stunted trees.

Rage builds in me, thrumming and pulsing—but that's not what makes me take action. It's the *heartbreak.* I feel such a deep well of sadness, to be so connected to death and hurt in the natural world, that I'll break the world itself to heal it.

My body lengthens, seems to rise on the wind as though I'm almost hovering above the soil. Strange words slide from my lips. Power builds in my core, shooting down my fey lines to blast from my fingertips.

Everywhere the silver light strikes—the beehive homes, the obelisks, the temple itself—cracks open in the earth. A quake tears through the glorious city. Stones fall. Walls collapse. Screams are smothered under rubble.

Slowly, the earth stills.

As soon as the dust clears, my heart swells with hope. All the poison black smoke fades away, its fires' embers snuffed out and buried under the city's rubble. The sky clears, sunlight beaming down on the valley once more. The creek stops bleeding red with no more animals' blood poured from the slaughtering fields, and my beautiful Ramvik River flows clear.

I feel it—all of nature, the fish and the crows, singing with my heart, rejoicing in a world I healed.

It wasn't a dream, but a memory.

That's the first thought that fills my skull when I blink my eyes open, staring at the pine boughs overhead.

I'm absolutely certain of it.

The Alyssantha and Popelin I saw were the real fae, from thousands of years ago. The version of them from an earlier Return. I read about it in Woudix's book—*The Fall of Calisyrune*, though in the text, it said nothing of how Immortal Solene stopped the poison flowing out of the city to save the entire valley ecosystem.

I sit up, dizzy with the memory, trying to capture every detail in my mind's notebook before it all slips away.

"It's coming back to me, Basten," I say, shaking him awake.

Groggy, he groans as he flops over and rubs the sleep off his face. "What's that, wildcat?"

"I remembered something." I practically pounce on him in my excitement. "A memory from long ago. It was a beautiful one—one where I saved the lives of so many creatures. I reset the balance of nature. And I saw the other fae in their previous versions. And—and—"

The strange look in his eye stills my words.

I follow his gaze to the clear's edge and flinch.

When we fell asleep last night, the clearing was like so many others—pine boughs, doghobble, mossy stones.

Not so this morning.

Vines have woven themselves into fanciful arches and loops at the clearing's edge. Some knots resemble antlers, others spiral into whorls like dust devils. Stones lie stacked in improbable arrangements: boulders piled into precariously balanced stacks. From one angle, the stacked rocks take on the shapes of badgers rearing on hind legs. Mounds of dirt rise in playful postures reminiscent of dancing horses.

"Did you do that?" Basten asks, his awe edging into worry.

"*Did* I do that?" I echo, looking down at my hands. My fingertips pulse with dwindled fey, as though I've spent all night depleting my energy. I blink, flushed, and huff an incredulous laugh. "I think I did."

Basten rakes the hair back off his face, taking in each

beautiful but strange sculpture. He murmurs, "Gods, Sabine. It's art."

My chest softens to know he *sees* me—what I'm capable of.

A ray of light cuts through the branches overhead and starts to burn off the morning fog.

Myst snorts, ***Um...where is my breakfast?***

I laugh softly at her impatience. She doesn't care about my late-night artistic accomplishments, only her belly.

I rake my own hair into place, wrapping the blanket tighter around my shoulders.

"We should get an early start," I say. "Maybe we can even make it to the border wall by nightfall. Be in Astagnon tomorrow."

Basten looks to the south—toward the kingdom we both call home—with an odd expression. He's wary, but there's something else there.

Something softer. Something not all sharp and sparking.

"We'll get on the road soon," he says. "But there's one more thing we need to do before we reach Astagnon." His voice catches, a strange glint in his eye, like a secret. "I'll need some water to bathe—and I need you to tell that damn forest mouse that it's time I call in another favor."

I tilt my head, curious, but he only offers me a cryptic smile in return.

CHAPTER 10
BASTEN

This gods-damn comb.

Standing waist-deep in the stream, naked as the day I was born, I drag a silver comb I pilfered from Drahallen Hall through my dripping hair, where it catches on a snag, and no matter how I tug, won't work itself free.

I'm not one for combs in general—let's be clear. But I have plans for today. Big plans. And it won't do to have pine sap tangling my hair in filthy knots, my usual look.

I left Sabine back at the clearing to groom Myst, who decided straight after tromping through the stream that was the perfect time to roll in a patch of dirt.

Sabine will be busy for a while.

Water runs down my bare torso, frigid as glacier ice, finding the valley between my muscles. Winter is coming to Volkany, and it won't be that much longer before it reaches Astagnon, too—trailing our heels on this journey like a silent hunter.

But I clamp my jaw against the chill. It keeps me alert—

not that my nerves need any more stoking today. I'm practically jumpy as a baby goat.

"Come…*on*." I tug the comb once more, and it finally pulls free.

I toss the comb on the riverbank, next to my open knapsack. The bar of lye soap, too. It's done as much damage as it can. I've scrubbed every damn inch from my scalp to my toenails, until my skin is raw, and I smell fresh as a damn chambermaid.

As I grab my towel from a tree branch, the forest mouse scampers onto a river rock near the bank, wiggling her whiskers at me.

"Yeah, yeah," I mutter. "I'm hurrying."

Truth be told, it wasn't easy to set up my plans for today with a mouse. I don't have Sabine's godkiss; I can't understand its squeaks, and it can't make sense of my barked curses. I was hopeful that we'd manage, since we reached a tentative way to communicate while exploring the murals in Drahallen Hall's basement.

Turns out we were back at square one. Before I left Norhelm, the mouse and I spent a few frustrating days pointing at book illustrations to one another and trying—uselessly—to reach an understanding. If it hadn't been for Captain Tatarin's intervention, we'd be sunk.

One of her spies reported seeing me in the library with a mouse on my shoulder. She came to me, suspicious at first, until I explained my plan. She stared at me like I'd sprouted a second nose, then burst into laughter.

"Oh, *men*," she chuckled.

She sent for a member of the army's mage division who was godkissed with the ability to communicate through art across any language. Apparently, that even goes for *squeaks*.

The young man pulled out a slate tile and a horsehair brush. He dipped the tip in water, then painted on the slate in quick strokes that soon evaporated, leaving room for another set—but his skill was so keen that within merely a few gestures he could convey an entire scene.

The mouse dipped her paw in his water pot, then swept it over the slate, communicating back to him in a way that made no damn sense to me. But the artist could read pages in those paw prints.

Luckily, Captain Tatarin and her mage also understood the word "discrete."

So, here I am in the middle of the Volkish woods, about to do the craziest thing of my life.

But, fuck it.

There isn't a crumb of doubt in my heart. I've wanted to marry Sabine since the first time I saw her. Or, rather, the first—*new*—time seeing her. When I entered Drahallen Hall in chains, and she had her lips all over that bastard Artain's navel, and she looked at me with those big sea-blue eyes so full of surprise.

I fell for her all over again.

Hard.

So hard I haven't recovered from the fall.

I wade to the bank, scrubbing the towel over my hair, and then climb out and wrap it around my waist. The mouse bobs on the river rock, knitting her little paws together in excitement.

"Moving as fast as I can here, furball."

I throw the towel aside, naked to the world, and take a deep breath.

My last breath as a bachelor—if fate is kind to me today.

As I reach for my trousers, a pair of goldfinches land on

my knapsack, inspect the silver comb, and then fly off as if on a mission. I dry my ass and pull on the trousers, doing up my belt. Then, I tug on the fancy embroidered cotton shirt Captain Tatarin insisted I pack instead of the loose linen ones I've worn forever. It's not my style—black with golden threads woven in the shape of antlers over the shoulders—but I suppose I can be uncomfortable for a few minutes.

The mouse watches as I button up the shirt, wrinkling her nose as her head turns this way and that. As soon as I reach the top button, she leaps onto my trousers, digs in her tiny claws, and crawls right up the fabric.

"Hey! What the hell?" I hop from one foot to the other, tickled by the pinprick claws poking through my clothes.

She finally settles on my left shoulder, then begins combing her tiny paws through my hair. I flinch and grumble, but she seems determined to fix what the comb could not.

The goldfinches return with a stem that they unceremoniously drop on my head. I duck from the floral assault, snatching the stem. It's a thistle. So dark purple it's nearly black, wild, and as coarse as me.

"Sure, sure, I'll admit it," I mutter aloud. "Good choice."

How wildlife knows that I've planned today as our wedding, I have no fucking idea—but I've learned to shut up and accept the impossible whenever Sabine is around.

So, I slip the thistle stem into my upper buttonhole, twisting it about a dozen times to get the best side showing.

The mouse's claws still pluck at my hair, and I grumble, my voice rattling with nerves, "Done yet?"

Fuck me sideways. Between flower-delivering birds and a mouse's preening, I'm like a gods-damned storybook princess.

My chest rattles like a dice cup. I've never felt nerves like this, not even on the battlefield. I tell myself to calm the hell down. Sabine said she'd marry me. We're engaged. She still wears that frayed bit of twine like it's gold and diamonds.

Which ought to reassure me.

Except I don't remember giving it to her.

It was before.

Before Iyre stole my memories, before her father drove the Serpent Knife into her chest, and a slumbering goddess awoke in her skin. In so many ways, Sabine is the same girl she used to be—the one who warms my heart and makes my blood hot. But even with all my heightened senses, I can't see what's going on inside her head.

Gods help me, I don't know if one of the ten rulers of the known world will still accept a brute like me.

Well, you bastard, gotta try.

I throw my shoulders back, smoothing a wrinkle from my shirt, nudging away the birds trying to adjust my boot laces. "That's enough, ladies."

With my heart practically lodged in my throat, I make my way back to the clearing on shaky legs, clearing my throat about a thousand times.

I stop at the edge of the clearing, hanging back behind a cluster of holly. I want to simply look at her for a moment.

Sabine has her back to me, hands resting on her hips, horse brush dangling from one finger, head cocked at a curious angle.

I don't know what has her attention, but I'm struck speechless. Because there's a chance—if she says yes, which let's be honest, is more than my grumpy ass deserves—that this honest-to-fuck goddess will be mine forever.

I muster my courage and step forward, a twig snapping under my boot.

Sabine's head jerks at the sound, but she keeps her eyes on Myst. "Basten, come look at this. It's the most peculiar thing. These chipmunks appeared out of nowhere to crawl all over Myst's mane and tail. I thought they must be hunting up nesting materials, but no—they're braiding her hair! They even tried to braid mine, but I told them it tickled too much. Isn't that strange? They won't tell me why, sneaky little things. And a whole flock of blackbirds has been dropping wild gorse and heather blossoms all over the clearing. I didn't call them, I promise—"

A soft laugh huffs on my lips, because that little forest mouse has worked a gods-damned miracle. Somehow, even though, according to Sabine, most creatures can't communicate across species, the furry wonder has set up a wedding party complete with flower garlands.

At my silence, Sabine looks over her shoulder, eyes still bright with wonder from the animal activity. But then she sees me—in this ridiculous fancy shirt, hair combed for the first time in weeks—and her expression shifts.

The amusement fades.

Her mouth parts slightly, eyes going wide again, but not with charm this time. More like disbelief.

The thistle in my buttonhole, the flowers blanketing the clearing, the braids in Myst's hair.

"O—oh," she says softly.

A moment of terror slams into me. Fuck, is that a good "oh" or a bad "oh"? Until I hear the sweet little hitch in her breath, the soft flutter of her pulse that I recognize as joy.

Thank the fucking gods.

She continues to stare at me like I'm a painting come to

life as I approach slowly, rubbing my hands together as I give a nervous chuckle.

"Sabine," I start, stopping awkwardly a few feet in front of her, then have to clear my damn throat once more. "We've both known each other by so many names. But, to me, across lost memories and ones made anew, you'll always be my violet. The sweetest damn thing I've ever tasted. Better than candied blossoms. Better than anything."

I swallow hard, heart pounding.

"If you'll have me now, I'd like to make you my wife."

I've never seen bigger eyes, even on a doe with her sights set on my arrow.

"B—Basten," she sputters, and as though jolting from a spell, starts combing through the tangled curls of her hair, suddenly aware of the dust on her travel clothes. "I—I don't know what to say. How did you— I don't see how you— And here? Now?"

She sweeps her arms wide to gesture to the clearing.

Heat prickles under my collarbone. I rub my chin and admit, "I know it's no great hall, laden with a feast for a queen. That's what you deserve, but this is the best we can do now. When we left Astagnon, public sentiment had turned against you. They called you a traitor. Daughter of the enemy. Painted slurs over your murals. If you'd stayed, there's a chance you'd have been imprisoned. Or worse, attacked. I can't take the risk of bringing you back into the kingdom without protection. If you're married to the rightful heir to the throne, no one will dare to lay so much as an unkind eye on you."

She blinks a few times, starts and stops a thought, and then runs her hands over her face to start afresh. "No—no, that isn't what I meant. This place. This clearing. I mean that this is more perfect than you could ever know. I don't want a wedding of thousands. Or parades. Or banquets. This is *exactly* what I want." She toys with the twine ring on her finger. "You just caught me by surprise, is all."

She comes forward, cheeks flushed the most delicious pink, and holds out her hands for mine. I stumble forward like a schoolboy to clasp hers.

"How did you do all this?" she breathes in an awe-filled whisper.

I grin, scoffing. "With help, that's for sure. Captain Tatarin found a godkissed mage who could tell the forest mouse what I wanted, and that little fleabag took it from there. She even combed my damn hair into place."

"The mouse?" Sabine's eyebrows raise in delighted surprise. Still clasping my hands, she looks around in the grass. "Where is she?"

She falls silent for a moment, the type of pause I know means she's using her godkiss. A second later, she laughs.

"She says she's getting herself ready by the stream— bathing before the ceremony because it took so long to get *you* in shape."

I roll my eyes, but there's a chuckle on my lips, too. I squeeze Sabine's hands, drawing in a breath to fill every bit of my lungs.

"Are you sure this is what you still want?" I ask, running my thumb over her twine ring. "Marriage, I mean? A lot has changed."

She lets go of my hands and toys thoughtfully with the twine ring. "When you gave me this makeshift ring, it was in a forest like this. You asked me to be yours forever, and I said yes, as long as you agreed to be my forever, too."

I smile, but the word she used catches on a fear tucked

away so low I'd hoped it would never emerge. "Forever," I repeat, staring down at my boots. "Yeah. About that. This mortal body of mine won't live thousands of years, not like yours—"

"Stop that." She grabs my hands again, harder this time, lacing her fingers with mine like a vice. "The future—however long or in whatever form that might take for both of us—is far away. Right now, it's just you and me. For as many years as we have together. I'm ready to commit *all* those years to you."

I shift my stance. "Yeah?"

She grins and echoes my gruff, "*Yeah.*"

So, I take her hand and lead her to the circle of wildflower blossoms the birds have dropped in the center of the clearing. Fuck, but I feel like I'm fifteen years old again. Nervous as the first time I kissed a girl—only worse, because this isn't some awkward brush of lips in an alley. This is real. This is *her*.

My palms are sweating. I keep my grip light, terrified she'll feel the tremor in my fingers. Gods, she's so radiant.

And she's about to be mine.

I duck my head, swallowing hard. I'm half convinced someone is going to burst through the trees and shout that it's all been a mistake—that she was never meant for me. That a man like me doesn't get a happy ending.

But she's still holding my hand—with love in her eyes.

"I still don't understand how you made all this happen," she confesses, her hand trembling sweetly from her own nerves. "Even with the mouse's help."

"I can't take credit. It's these damn animals. They want you to be a perfect bride." And she is, even dressed in her dusty riding clothes with her hair windblown and tangled.

Then, I toe one of the blossoms. "Is it enough? You could use your power, you know. Grow a ring of rosebushes around us. Summon the stones to rise as an altar."

"No." Her head sweeps back and forth. Quick, certain. "No, I want it just like this. For us to marry simply, no temples, no altars, no *gods*. As plain and wild as when we first fell in love. Because no matter what comes next for us, our start was always simple."

I can only marvel at her. Gods, this woman. This perfect, beautiful woman.

Sabine suddenly perks up, cocking her head as though listening. "Oh—the mouse is back. She says we should stand next to that stump over there."

Sabine looks amused to be taking orders from a mouse, but we humor the pipsqueak and go to stand by a waist-high chestnut stump, the broken top worn smooth by time, blanketed with moss so vibrant green it nearly glows.

Myst whinnies from the other side of the clearing, stamping a foot. Sabine turns to her for a moment, exchanging silent words. Then, she laughs again. "One minute."

She slips her hand from mine and goes to untie the horse. Myst falls into step beside her, trailing close. When they return to the stump, the mare plants herself squarely behind Sabine, ears forward, head held high.

"She insisted," Sabine explains, nodding back at Myst. "Not that she has any concept of what a bridesmaid is, but she knows something special is happening and wants a proper look at the action. Claims her old eyes aren't what they used to be."

Myst steps forward just enough to press her nose into my shoulder. As if to say—*you'd better take care of her.*

"Yeah, yeah, crazy mare." I scratch her forehead fondly. "I've got your girl."

The forest mouse—looking exceptionally well-groomed for a pantry pest, I'll give her that—scampers up onto the stump.

A ruffle in the branches catches my ear. My attention is on Sabine, our hands clasped, but my godkissed senses are picking up a litany of tiny footsteps, ruffling wings, even soft hooves approaching from all corners of the forest.

From the corner of my eye, I see owls settling into the high branches. Scent the musky fur of a beaver. Glimpse the warm brown nose of a fawn.

Sabine bends toward the mouse, nodding as she listens, then straightens.

"She says that she once lived in the foundation of a village chapel and saw humans coming together like this. Says it always started with nervous humans holding hands and someone standing before them, telling them what to do. She wants to be that person." She gives me a puzzled look. "Did you—did you ask her to *officiate*?"

I lift a shoulder. "Someone had to."

Sabine's face twists in wry disbelief. "You're okay with a *mouse* officiating our wedding? Never mind that there was a time you wanted nothing more than to stomp her." She leans in and whispers, "You know this won't be binding in the slightest, right?"

"You know I don't give a damn about the Red Church, right?" I echo, teasing. "This is for us, little violet. I'll arrange official marriage documents when we get to Old Coros. Folke knows an excellent forger. We'll claim a village priest married us, if they ask his name, we'll pay off some record-keeper to say it checks out."

She grins—because *here's* the sneaky bastard she knows.

"Don't worry, sweetheart." I gently cup her cheek. "I've thought this through. Hell, I've been plotting something like this since the day I set foot in Drahallen Hall and laid eyes on you for the first—new first—time." I shift, plunging one hand in my pocket. "Captain Tatarin also got me this, though I owe her a king's ransom in gold once I have access to the royal coffers and can repay her."

I wrap my fingers around the small scrap of metal, then pull it out and open my palm.

The ring is small in size, but its decoration makes up for it. A gold circle made of woven metal strands made to look like vines, inlaid with pale emeralds as tiny leaves, all surrounding an amethyst-violet diamond cut like a blossom.

Look, I don't know jewelry. But this? I know this is *exceptional.*

Her fingers hover a few inches over the ring, as though she's afraid to touch it, like if she does, it might give a soap bubble's pop. She whispers, "Where in the world...?"

"A spoil of war. Captain Tatarin's great-great-grandfather took it off a fallen general during an ancient battle, and it's been passed down since. She was all too happy to sell it. Says that side of her family disowned her years ago when she left their farm to join the army. Her loss is our gain."

"Oh, Basten. It's *beautiful.*"

From the corner of my eye, I catch a flicker of movement. The mouse is on her hind legs, paws waving like she's calling court to order.

I arch a brow at the whiskered drama. "I think she wants our attention."

Sabine tilts her head to listen, then bites back a laugh.

"She's not actually sure what to say. She couldn't understand what the reverend used to tell the newlyweds back in the village chapel. You should hear what she thinks wedding vows are supposed to sound like. There's a lot about promising not to steal each other's seed stores."

"And here I thought the furry wonder could do all."

Sabine humors the mouse with a serious nod, then whispers to me, "I'll fill in her gaps." She straightens, clearing her voice. "Do you, Basten Valvere, heir to the Astagnonian throne, take me as your wife?"

"With every fucking piece of me."

Sabine gently nudges my arm, but there's a smile on her lips for my grumpiness. "And do I, Sabine Rachillon, princess of Volkany, take you as my husband?" She pauses for dramatic effect, seeming to revel in the torturous pause, before leaning in and purring, "With every *fucking* piece of me, too."

I moan to hear the delicious filth on her lips. "Good gods, little violet."

But Sabine listens to the mouse again, her face brightening. "Oh, here's one part the mouse got right. She says now is the time when we should kis—"

She hasn't even gotten the word out before I sweep her up in my arms, crushing her to me, my lips on hers. I wrap my palm around her back, anchoring her to me. We're bonded, now. Tied together forever. And, gods, I could stay like this until the end of time. With her sweet lips moving under mine.

All around us, birds flap their wings, squirrels chitter, and deer bow their antlers.

It really is a gods-damn fairy tale, I think to myself without a trace of sarcasm. *Every day with Sabine is.*

I finally set her down, still kissing the hell out of her, wanting every last taste of my wife's sweetness. Fuck, my *wife*. I could say that a million times over and it will never not make me marvel.

I let her go only enough to slide the ring on her finger.

She gazes down at it, such a perfect fit, like it was made for her. When she looks back up at me, there are tears in her eyes.

"I'm...a little scared, Basten. That this is a dream. That the moment we leave this clearing, it will be with a storm at our backs, walking into fire."

"Then let's stay here a little longer," I murmur, sweeping an arm around her shoulders, holding her head tightly to my chest. I lean down to kiss her hair, fighting the urge to hold her so hard she can't breathe, wanting to never let her go.

She exhales like she's been holding that breath for years, melting into me with all the weight of someone who's finally safe. My other hand finds hers, fingers weaving together so that I can't tell where mine end and hers begin.

She tilts her face up to mine, and when I kiss her this time—slow, aching, reverent—it feels like a vow.

Let the world burn.

Right now, I have everything I need in my arms.

CHAPTER 11
SABINE

When we cross the tunnel beneath the border wall into Astagnon, it's as husband and wife.

The next few days pass like a dream. Just us, the horses, and the forest—I feel transported back to the ride to Duren when Basten and I fell in love.

He might not remember it, but I'll never forget.

I remember every stolen glance. Every brush of his skin on mine. How, over the weeks, I went from loathing the sight of him to waking every morning famished for just a few of his words. In the days after our wedding, Basten asks me to recount every single story, over and over, as if he hears them often enough, they'll become the next best thing to his own memories.

In the evenings, when we stop to make camp, I practice using my affinity. It isn't always easy going. There are as many setbacks as there are advancements. Sometimes, I'm able to spark a controlled fire to cook our dinner, but the next attempt, I strike myself with lightning and pass out for a full day. When I wake, watched over by a distraught

Basten, it's covered in a blanket of living, woven vines of my own making.

Afterward, I drank so much of his blood to renew my strength that I berated myself for hours—I *have* to control myself so I don't hurt him.

Or worse.

But I feel heartwarmed, in part, as we finally reach mountain ranges I recognize, and berries and mushrooms I picked when I was a little girl. This region is where my mother's grave rests. It's where Myst and I forged a friendship for the ages.

But it's also where the darkest days of my life happened.

We're about three days from Old Coros, according to Basten, when we reach a fork in the road that's marked with a directional sign. An arrow to the left points the way to the small hamlet of Marblenz. The one to the right...

I draw Myst to a halt.

"Bremcote," I murmur.

Basten shifts in Ranger's saddle, his eyes on me instead of the forked path. "We can go east, toward Marblenz," he says. "It'll add half a day, but if you've changed your mind about passing near Bremcote..."

"No." I try to sound confident. I spur Myst to the right, ignoring the ache that suddenly spreads up my spine as soon as we set foot in the direction of my childhood trauma. "I can handle it. We're behind schedule anyway, after we lost that day near the Innis River."

Basten hesitates, and I can feel the questions on his lips. "Sabine..."

I twist in the saddle to shoot him a stare. "What?"

He rubs the back of his neck. Finally, he lets out a sigh. "As soon as we crossed into Astagnon, your heart rate increased. The further south we go—closer to your childhood home—the more it skyrockets."

"I'm worried there's a chance we'll run into Rian," I snap.

He pauses. "There are other signs. You sweat more."

"It's hot!"

He nudges Ranger alongside Myst and drops his voice, though it's only the two of us for miles. "During sex last night, a rain storm came out of nowhere and drenched us both."

I press my lips tightly, holding in the urge to defend myself. "What are you suggesting?"

"Look." He breathes in deeply, lets it out slowly. "Let's not pretend as if we both haven't noticed it. Nature has become more unpredictable the closer we get to Bremcote. Not just last night's sudden downpour. There was that frozen stretch of the Innis River, never mind that it's sixty degrees. Those vines that wove around my boots when I started across the footbridge, holding me back. The sudden herd of caribou that parked themselves in the road for half a day and wouldn't budge to let us pass."

I flick him a reluctant look. "You think I'm keeping us from Bremcote on purpose?"

"No." He tugs at his breastplate as though it's uncomfortably tight. "That's the problem. If you were doing it on purpose, I'd understand. Terrible things happened to you in Bremcote. Unjust things a young girl should never have to endure. But it's because you *aren't* wreaking havoc intentionally that has me worried. Some deep part of you—a piece you can't control—is making these things happen."

I spent a few minutes fiddling with Myst's reins. "I'm trying as hard as I can, Basten."

When my voice breaks, he spurs Ranger close enough to tip up my chin, making my eyes meet his. "Of course you are. You're doing great. You're so damn strong, Sabine, that in those moments, it frightens me. To see what you're capable of without even meaning to." He turns to look back in the direction of Volkany, a muscle pulsing in his jaw. "In Drahallen Hall, I found something. Murals. They showed the ancient fae court. And...they showed Immortal Solene..."

His eyes slide to me, watching closely. When I sniffle, holding back tears, he closes his jaw. His resolve seems to change.

"What did the mural show?" I ask.

He flicks his hand. "Nothing—it was nothing. Forget I said anything."

I study him, wondering if I should press. But then I jerk the reins, turning Myst onto the path to Bremcote. After a moment, I hear Ranger's hooves behind me.

I don't know what Basten thinks he's protecting me from. If anything, I should be protecting *him*. And it's not just about keeping him alive as my acolyte. Since gaining my affinity, I'm stronger than any human, godkissed or otherwise. With one spark of my fey, I could open the earth to swallow our enemies.

Well—once I can *control* my fey.

We wind up a jagged path to the top of a hill, and at a break in the trees at the top, the Bremcote valley stretches out into the distance. Sheep farms roll out for miles and miles.

Somewhere out there, the Convent of Immortal Iyre crouches like a cockroach.

When we make camp for the night, the silence between us is thick and hot. A summer fog rolls in, much too sweltering for this time of year, but I don't bother to try to control whatever part of me is calling to it. I'm relieved, in a way, to have some space between the two of us. There's enough on my mind to fill a church hall.

"Saw a female grouse a ways back," Basten says quietly. "I'll find its trail, see if I can get a clutch of eggs for supper."

He disappears through the unseasonable fog, and once I'm alone with the horses, I push to my feet. It's hard to sit still, this close to home. A familiar scent hangs in the air.

Can you smell that? I ask Myst.

Smell what? She asks, swishing her tail.

Sheep dung and peat fires. We're almost home.

She flicks her tail again, unbothered, and continues munching the tall grass with Ranger. It stirs something bitter inside me.

Home? I prod her. *Don't you know what I mean by that? I mean that we're close to the Convent.*

Her head jerks up, ears twirling forward on alert. She stares at me for a long time—maybe she's remembering all the pain both of us suffered at the Sisters' hands. My poor girl had it just as bad as I did. After we left, it took weeks for her harness sores to heal, for her skeletal ribcage to fill back out.

But she only returns to her grass.

I nearly hiss with frustration. *Myst! Don't you care?*

She flicks her tail, the horse equivalent of a shrug. I turn tightly away, sucking my teeth, flexing my hands to try to keep my blood flowing—because right now, it all wants to pour straight to my hot, angry brain.

A part of me knows I shouldn't be cross with Myst for not feeling the same anger I do. Horses, like most mortal animals, don't hold grudges the way people do. They only care about what's in front of them—grass, a mate, a predator.

Fae animals, on the other hand? If I've learned anything from Tòrr and Plume, it's that they hold grudges worse than anyone. I'm pretty sure Tòrr's vindictiveness stretches back *millennia.*

And me?

I guess that makes me a fae animal, because when I think of how wronged I was at the convent, I burn through and through with a grudge.

I swallow back the howl of rage that wants to tear from my throat, because Basten isn't far away in these woods. His godkissed ears would hear my cry, he'd come running, ask questions about things I'd rather keep to myself.

But my muscles are tight enough to snap, and I have to do something, have to—to—

I lift my hands to release a charge of fey at the nearest tree. Silver-hot sparks shoot out. The air smells crisp and off, like after a lightning strike.

When the smoke clears, a burned gash cuts the tree in two.

And someone behind me starts a slow clap.

Catching a gasp behind my teeth, I spin around.

Woudix leans against a river birch, still clapping, a slight curve to his lips. "You've been practicing."

An exhale shudders from my lungs as I rest a hand on my chest, sinking back against the singed tree, our postures mirroring one another. "What are you doing here?"

"I told you I'd find a way to continue your training on your journey."

"I thought you meant by lending me *books*."

He rumbles a low laugh, and I feel like a fool. "Have you spent enough days playing at being human that you've forgotten we're gods? We go where we like."

He holds up the fae needle with a smirk.

In the fading twilight, I scrutinize the God of Death from his raven hair, pulled back now, to the tips of his black leather boots.

"Of course I haven't forgotten. My blood won't *let* me forget." I swallow, flexing my sweaty palms, doing a quick scan of the woods.

Woudix puts away the fae needle and tuts knowingly. "Lord Basten can't perceive us, if that's what has you so attentive. Not even with his superior senses."

I narrow my eyes. "How?"

"Once you've mastered your powers, you, too, will be able to hide anything you wish from human perception. We can walk amongst them completely undetectable, if we so desire. As for your lover, I cast a—a shield, if you will—around us." He lifts an eyebrow. "I can lower it, if you'd prefer my visit not to be secret."

My throat tightens, and I find myself chewing on my bottom lip.

The last thing I want is to keep secrets from Basten, but he's made his feelings about Woudix more than clear. Besides, I can read the worry in Basten's eyes. He fears that my transformation means I'm becoming less human.

The thing he doesn't understand is that, like in my dream, if I want to save the world, I *have* to embrace my fae side.

"Well, love?"

I let my hands fall. "Do it—the shield."

He smiles in quiet triumph and draws a lazy finger through the air, as if marking an invisible wall around us.

Then, he pushes off from the tree and stalks toward me. My heartbeat kicks up, beating a steady warning. I can't help but take a step back—but the burned tree blocks me in.

He stops a breath in front of me. For a heavy pause, he seems to study me with a perception beyond vision.

Then, he grabs my hand.

I jump, instinct telling me to pull back, but I force myself to remain still.

He runs his hands down mine until he reaches the thick ring on my fourth finger. A dark glow fills his eyes.

"So. You bound yourself to the human."

"It's been done before." I snatch my hand back defensively, cradling it against my chest. "My father married a human—my mother."

"Before he awoke to become Immortal Vale."

I narrow my eyes. "According to the historical records *you* shared with me, Immortal Meric wed a human mage in the Beginning, and again in the First Return."

I ready a self-satisfied smirk, feeling I've won, but Woudix only laughs. "Exactly—by the Second Return, he'd learned his lesson. Yes, we fae consort with humans. We fuck them. We even bear children with them. But the only ones we bind ourselves with are our own kind."

My face flushes as if I've been schooled, and I force my chin high. "I suppose that's one more way I'm different from the other fae. Just like Immortal Solene always is. Closer to nature—to humans—than the rest of you."

He leans over me, resting one hand above my head on the tree, so close I can smell a trace of sage smoke in his hair.

"Make it snow," he orders.

My head jerks, eyes blinking hard. "What?"

"You've been practicing, haven't you? So, show me what you can do. Make it snow right here, only over the two of us."

I clear my throat and lift my palms skyward, marshalling the fey in my veins as I've practiced a dozen times. But this time, my hands tremble. Only a cold gust of air blows down on us.

He shakes his head, tutting. "You're a long way from facing King Rian's forces on your own."

It feels like a sting, but I keep my head up. I don't want him to sense for a second that he intimidates the hell out of me.

"I'm not on my own. I have Basten. The true king. We came to Astagnon so he could take the throne and stop this—" I struggle for the right word. "—this spiral of bloodshed. More senseless death."

His eyebrows lift. "*Senseless* death?"

I swallow hard, cheeks burning. Maybe that wasn't the best thing to say to the god of death. "I only meant that I don't want thousands of people to die."

He pushes off from the tree, and I let out a breath, feeling like a weight lifts off me. He paces to the campfire Basten left flickering, reaching out to catch a rising piece of ash between his fingertips.

"Personally," he says, "I see death as meaningful artistry. But if you don't wish for so many innocent souls to pass to my realm before their time, then you are missing the true war at question. It isn't between King Rian and his opposition. It's between fae and humans. Give it five years. Ten, at most. People worship us, but they fear us, too. They blame us for loss, for tragedy—anything they don't understand. If that fear isn't turned, armies will march against us."

"That's why we're going to Astagnon. To convince the people to embrace them. To hold off *war*."

Woudix saunters back over, slowly removing his black glove, lifting a hand toward my face, hovering a moment before making contact.

"May I?"

I nod, and he grazes his fingertips, somehow both soft and rough at the same time, along the rounded point of my left ear. "As I suspected." He makes a disappointed noise in his throat and puts his glove back on. "You might start by embracing your fae appearance. If you can't accept the wonder within your own body, it will be a challenge to make the public do so."

He slides his gloves back on, then removes the fae needle from his pocket. I can sense that he's about to leave.

I push off from the tree before I know what I'm doing.

"How did you know?" I blurt out.

He cocks his head; eyebrow raised in question.

"How did you know I'm in my human glamour even before you touched me?"

His only answer is the shake of his head, like I'm a child. "You still don't understand that we're *gods*. A piece of advice? I can feel your rage at the Sisters who wronged you. It burns like hot coals. It won't go out, no matter how much you play-act at being human. It will continue to demand an answer. So, *answer* the anger."

My cheeks warm, and I look down at my hands,

studying the all-too-human lines in my palm that I know as well as a map to my heart.

I take a deep breath, and slowly will away the wrinkles, the freckles, the old scar on my thumb, letting the fey line break out in my palm.

As if sensing the energy change in the clearing, Woudix stops. He turns his head back my way.

I close my eyes, steadying my breath, and extend my reach past the boundaries of my own skin and out into the trees. Then, even beyond. The tree tops. The clouds overhead.

Snow, I command.

The air ripples with a breeze that chills the inch of exposed skin on my ankles. It starts with only a few flakes. They could easily be mistaken for falling ashes from the fire—but more come. Falling thick over the clearing—in a circle eight feet wide—to blanket the confused insects crawling through the grass.

Woudix touches a snowflake on his cheek, turns around, and smiles.

"Snow is easy, love. Next, try brimfire."

My attention slams back into my own body, and the snowfall stops abruptly.

I say defensively, "I can spark a flame."

"I didn't say a spark. I didn't say a flame. I said *brimfire*."

Without further explanation, he jabs the fae needle into thin air, ripping the fabric of space itself. Warm lantern light spills out of the crack as he continues to unstitch a portal. He disappears into a low-lit stone room, then seals the portal behind him.

I'm left in the clearing, snow rapidly melting, confused

grasshoppers flinging themselves at my feet—as if begging
their god for an answer.

CHAPTER 12
BASTEN

Two more days until we reach Old Coros.

The closer we get, the more the old injury in my shoulder hurts. Sure, any soldier's body is a smorgasbord of old aches and pains, but this feels different. It's as if with every one of Ranger's steps, my body tries to tighten like rusty armor. Like I'm headed straight into war, and it's shouting at me through the pain: *Remember how much this hurt? Why do this again?*

There's a part of me that would love to jerk the reins to a sharp left, get the hell off this route, and ride straight to Salensa with Sabine. See the ocean, like she always wanted. Hunt for damn seashells. Eat oysters until we burst. Say fuck it to the world of gods and men alike and dive through the waves.

But I'm going to be king.

King, like in a fucking fairy tale.

The sun is painting the back of my neck red, burning deep into my aching muscles, and if it's possible to sweat on the insides, I would be.

I glance at Sabine. "There's an inn a quarter mile ahead, if I remember right. We can stop for lunch."

Her head bobs in a nod that feels automatic, like she's a million miles away.

I try again. "I'd kill for something other than hard tack."

"Mmm," she agrees vaguely, distracted.

I give her a closer look. The wedding was damn blissful perfection, but in the days after, we've both fallen silent. I've been mired in my own thoughts—worried with every step toward Old Coros about what it will mean to wear a crown.

Of course, it makes sense she's a mess of fears, too.

I give my senses free rein to inspect her, pick up her little tells. Her stomach is grumbling—she's ignored her hunger pangs. She's worked her wedding ring so much that it's worn a groove in her skin. She's squeezing her legs too hard around Myst.

I start, "Anything on your mind?"

Her lips twitch as if unsure what—or how much—she wants to say. The sun disappears as we plunge deep within a copse of black walnuts, working a chill into my limbs. A part of me wonders if the trees stretched extra tall, just now, so the shadows would match their goddess's mood.

My attention snags on her veins, pulsing beneath her skin with something thicker than blood. She's fighting an urge. Something dark.

For what? For...my blood?

"I want to go to Bremcote," she says suddenly in a deep voice I barely recognize as her own.

Oh.

I swallow, telling myself to keep a steady breath, but even Ranger beneath me picks up on the shift in my nerves. He flicks his ears back in alertness.

"Into the actual town?" I clarify. "There's a path around it. We needn't go directly through it."

"*Into* town," she says.

My wildcat is flashing her claws.

"As you wish." I keep my voice neutral, giving her restlessness nothing to rebel against. "After lunch, we'll take the road south and be there by this evening. You can visit with your old servants over some pints."

A light flashes, like sunlight glinting off Myst's polished saddle buckles—but then I feel an odd chill and realize Sabine's fey lines are breaking out on the exposed skin beneath her dress sleeve, creeping up along her neck above her neckline.

She doesn't seem to realize she's dropping her glamour.

"Not the manor house." She speaks in that deeper, *older* voice that sets my damn nerves jangling like an alarm bell. "We can bypass the village of Bremcote entirely, in fact. There's nothing for me there. The only person who was kind to me was Suri, and she's in Old Coros. I bear no ill will toward the servants—they had to obey my father's commands. As for him, I can't get revenge on a corpse."

I choke a little on the word. *Revenge*? Who said anything about revenge?

"That's one good deed to thank Rian for," I jest, still trying to break the tension. "Killing the old bastard."

It's dark humor, but still lighter than her mood.

She doesn't laugh. In fact, she doesn't seem to hear me at all.

"It's the Convent I want." Her eyes are wild, glowing softly. "Matron White and the Sisters."

With every word, her fey lines pulse brighter. Sabine is blazing now, lighting up the darkened shadows in place of the sun. Ranger tries to shy away. Even Myst is flicking her ears, on extra alert.

I mutter, "Going to rot all their apples on the branch?"

Her eyelids lower, a hint of a vicious smile on her lips. But then she seems to snap out of her dark mood and says in her normal voice, "Good plan."

We ride on. Lunch is a quiet affair. We're the only ones at the ramshackle little inn, and Sabine seems distracted, plucking at her travel cloak. My hoped-for beef stew is a long-lost fantasy. All we're offered is rock-hard bread and boiled turnips.

When we reach the next fork in the road, I stop at the directional sign.

Every voice in me screams to keep riding, to follow the road straight to Old Coros. Gods only know what's happening behind those walls—cloaked priests conspiring, Golden Sentinels smuggling Rian in through a bread wagon. The need to be there claws at me.

But the quieter Sabine gets, the more I feel her slipping away. And that terrifies me more than anything behind city gates. I need to talk to Folke once we get to the city. Gather my allies around me. Start making contingencies—not just in preparations against Rian.

Maybe—gods help me—against Sabine, too.

Sabine stares at the directional sign, chewing on her bottom lip. When I ride up beside her, she flicks me a smile that feels a little forced. She tries for a joke. "Prepare to rot apples."

I smile back, relieved—but it doesn't reach my eyes.

We pass a sprawling sheep farm dotted with windmills. It's familiar. This is the same route I took when Rian first sent me to pick up Sabine to escort her to Duren. I might have lost my memories of her, but I remember my feelings before I arrived at Bremcote. Before I met her. I was furious to be sent to a backwater village after some pretty girl—I wanted to be at Rian's side. Protecting him from enemies. Trying to get back in his good graces.

We pass through the few roads that make up Bremcote village, but all the shepherds are out with their flocks. The only people we cross paths with are a pack of children in burlap clothes, who chase after a wooden hoop with such glee that we're ignored. Once, a merchant steps out to stretch on his general store's front steps, and he takes one look at Sabine—even in her human glamour—and pivots back inside to shut the door.

Chances are good he recognizes her. By now, surely gossip has spread about King Rian's former fiancée, the godkissed girl from Bremcote who turned out to be a Volkish traitor.

There's a chance he'll send a message to Old Coros, but then again, we've passed dozens of travelers on this journey who have slid Sabine a wary look. Besides, Rian's forces have to know it's only a matter of time before we return.

Sabine takes the lead now that we're on her home turf. She leans forward on Myst, eyes hungry as she scans the rolling hills outside of the village.

"It's pretty here," I observe. "Like a painting. Ponds and sheep. Willows."

"I guess," she agrees.

After the next rise, I try a more direct approach. "Want to talk about it? The Convent?"

Her lips press tightly together. She gives a sharp shake of her head.

I sigh inwardly. *Great work, Basten.* Like always, I'm not

the best with words. Or feelings. Or especially putting them together. This is so far out of my wheelhouse I might as well be two kingdoms over.

But I try again.

"Let's remember, no one knows you're fae. Not yet. We're saving that secret until the right time."

"I remember," she reassures me.

I flick my eyes to the road ahead. "Why not let me deal with the Sisters. I have no qualms about rubbing old ladies' faces in goat shit. I'll tell them you sent a message—me, with a wooden baton to break down the damn cell they used to lock you in."

She flicks me a grateful glance but shakes her head. "Thanks, but I need to see their faces myself. I want them to see *me*. Think hard about how much they wronged me and Myst and—"

We crest the hill, and I see it before she does.

But only by a split second.

Sun-bleached stone walls ten feet high, surrounding several acres, with a heavy oak gate. The only thing visible above the wall is a church spire.

Out here in the middle of nowhere, it can only be one thing.

Sabine settles back in the saddle as if struck. Myst stops short, too, her tail swishing in irritation.

I rub my shoulder—that damn old ache is going to kill me. "So that's it?" I ask.

"That's it." Her voice is distant.

I'd clung to a small hope that maybe the Convent had been shut down, or the old Sisters inside had all died from some plague. But even from here, I can smell a cookfire burning. Hear the bleating of goats, followed by a woman's sharp scold to them.

Sabine nudges Myst forward with a heaviness like they're both somewhere I can't reach them.

"Fuck their apples, right?" I say.

And get no response. As far as Sabine is concerned, I don't think anything exists anymore beyond her and the Convent.

We're twenty feet from the gate when the hinges suddenly groan, and a bent-over woman shuffles out, dragging a sack of apple mash with bees buzzing around it, muttering curses under her breath.

She stops short when she sees us.

She's younger than I expected. Maybe late forties. The only Sister I've met before was the ancient and wizened Matron White, when she came to Hekkelveld Castle for Rian's coronation. But despite this Sister's relative youth, the deep sags at the corners of her mouth speak of decades of scowls, frowns, and sneers.

Her eyes scan over me—a ripple of licentious interest entirely unsuitable for a nun—but then land on Sabine.

Recognition fills her eyes. She positively *yelps* in surprise.

I see Sabine straighten, hear her pull in a clean breath.

Damn right, I think to myself, because a part of me will always want to see Sabine's enemies bow to her. *You fucked with the wrong little violet.*

"Sabine!" the woman cries, one hand on her unkempt red robes, a filthy apron thrown over top. "What are you doing back here, girl?"

I wince at that. *Girl*. As if she's still the servant who scrubbed their floors. Surely—surely—rumors have reached them that their former ward is no one to trifle with now.

"Sister Rose," Sabine says, drawing herself up to her full height like a queen about to lay down a pronouncement. "It's been a long—"

Sister Rose suddenly bursts into laughter, cutting her off. The crone doubles over, gripping her belly to hold in her cruel taunts. "By the gods, am I looking at that same old nag? Myst, was it? Lords above! How is it still standing? We all thought it would collapse on the road to Duren, all bones and sinew. Not enough meat for the coyotes."

Sabine's lips hang open in shock. She looks frozen—except for her rapidly reddening cheeks.

I shift on Ranger, snapping to alert.

The Sister doesn't seem to notice Sabine's growing anger—or care. "Oh, that fine lord who bought you didn't keep you long, did he? Must have seen how much trouble you were, just like we knew he would. Threw you out, eh?" She ducks her head back through the gate. "Sister Ruby! Sister Scarlet! Come see the latest riffraff to blow up to our doorstep!"

No, I think to myself sharply. *No, lady. Shut up.*

In fact, I swing off Ranger and stride toward her, rage burning me up like a candle. I grab the woman by her shoulder, fisting her filthy robes in my hand. "You seem to forget your place. You're speaking to a princess."

The woman's sneer falters to find a six-foot-six-inch beast hulking over her, but she must think her saintly robes will shelter her from violence, because she tries to pull away indignantly.

Another woman pokes her head out of the gates and bursts into laughter. "Princess of what," she sneers, "the land of filth?"

These. Fucking. Women.

Oh, little violet, I think. *I'm sorry I doubted you.*

"I knew Sabine's time here was bad," I mutter. "I didn't realize what *bitches* you are." Still gripping the woman by her robe, I tilt my head back toward Sabine. "Wildcat, you want me to lock them in the cellar and throw away the key?"

But there's no answer behind me.

Sister Rose's face changes. Her tight wrinkles sag, jowls loose as she stares behind me. The other women fall silent, too. One of them drops to her knees, hands clasped in supplication.

"Immortal Iyre, help us!"

Then, I see it. A reflection in the watery mirrors of Sister Rose's eyes. It's Sabine, still atop Myst, only she's dropped her human appearance and now burns like cold, silver fire.

I let go of the nun, and she falls onto her knees with the others, immediately dropping her head in prayer.

"Please," Sister Rose begs. "Please. Immortal Iyre, hear our prayers—"

"Iyre won't save you," Sabine snaps, her voice like flint striking stone. "Believe me, I know her. She's not your savior. Still, it's fitting you pray to her—because she's every bit as cold and cruel-hearted as the lot of you. You want virtue? You want grace? Then you've chosen the wrong Immortal. Iyre doesn't care who you are or how hard you pray. She taught me that herself."

One of the women starts sobbing. The third scrambles to her feet and runs back into the Convent.

Sabine opens her palm, fey sparking, and pebbles from the wall loosen in a gust of wind, raining down on the other two women.

She warns, "You'd best run back inside, too."

The women don't hesitate. They push hastily to their

feet, turn, and stumble over each other to scramble back into the safety of those stone walls.

Sabine throws open her arms, and a gust of wind throws open the enormous, heavy oak gates.

Her eyes are silver mirrors, pooled with her fey blood.

When the doors slam open, the Sisters inside shriek. Two of the three from outside run straight for the chapel, throwing themselves against the door, pounding on it with their fists.

"Matron! Matron, come at once!"

The third Sister falls to her knees in front of a stone statue of Immortal Iyre, choking on her own prayers as she garbles them out between kisses laid at the statue's feet.

With a hiss, Sabine lifts her hand, and a vine bursts from the floor, knocking the woman backward, away from the statue.

The rest of the convent's population—maybe a dozen red-robed women—are still at their work tasks, only now catching onto the disturbance. One leads a goat by a rope toward a pile of rotting vegetables. Another hauls a wooden wheelbarrow laden with a cider barrel.

The chapel door opens, and that old bitch, Matron White, strides out.

"What is the meaning of this?" she demands, only to drift to a stop when she sees Sabine in her full fae splendor, blazing as deadly and bright as a star fallen to earth.

"S—Sabine Darrow?" she stutters.

Her eyes flicker to me, but if she recognizes me, it's dim in comparison to her shock.

The other Sisters wail and fall to their knees. The one with the apple cart cries out, "Sabine, forgive us! We did not know what you were!"

This causes the Matron to snap back to her senses with a deep scowl. "And what is that?" she sneers, her words directed at the Sister, but her eyes on Sabine.

"She is fae!" another wails.

My heart's clawing at my ribs. The soldier in me is braced for a fight—but I can't tell where to point the blade. Sabine sits on Myst like a storm barely tethered, and I don't know if I'm supposed to help her or stop her...or if I even can.

"She's not fae," the Matron sneers. "The fae still slumber underground in their dirt tombs. This is some trick. She's charmed some godkissed mage—this brute here, no doubt." She jerks a finger at me. "It's a trick."

I step forward, placing myself between Sabine and the Matron, heart pounding as I scramble to diffuse the tension. But before I can speak, Sabine dismounts from Myst.

"You pray to the fae," Sabine says, the ground rumbling underfoot in a way that makes me shut my mouth. "And yet you do not recognize one standing before you."

I groan inwardly. *So much for keeping her fae nature a secret.*

"You?" the Matron sneers, and I have to admit, the woman might be dumb but has balls of steel. "You're just a traitor, flesh and blood, no more fae than that goat."

Sabine stretches out a long finger. "*That* goat?"

Oh, fuck.

Sabine presses her hands together, and the goat lowers his head like a puppet, then charges the Matron. He's no ram, but his horns are powerful enough to slam into the old woman's frail hips and knock her to the ground.

She cries out weakly, waving a gnarled hand in the air. "Sister Rose—help me up! Fetch my prayer stick. This wicked girl isn't so big now that I can't still beat her into submission!"

The other Sister doesn't move a muscle, but the Matron manages to push to her feet regardless. She shuffles over to snatch up a wooden staff and raises it high toward Sabine—but then smiles darkly.

She turns instead and slams it over the goat, who lets out a pained cry.

Oh, lady. *That was a mistake.*

I whirl on Sabine, gripping her shoulders, using my body to block her direct sight of the Matron. "Hey. Wildcat. Stay with me."

Sabine's lips peel back in a hiss like a beast, her head twisting to try to see around me.

"Eyes on me," I urge. "Remember?"

"Basten," she growls. "Let me go."

"Let me deal with them. I'll fucking make them rue the day they ever raised a hand to you. You don't want to do this, Sabine. Your powers...you could destroy half of Astagnon."

"No." Her voice is dangerously deep. "Only the part within these walls."

She sweeps her hands out, and hot bursts of fey blister from her palms. The bolts shoot out to the rooftops, where the dry, aged thatch catches fire immediately. This fire isn't like anything I've seen before. It burns a cobalt blue. Blue-tinted pillars of smoke, reeking of sulfur, rise into the night.

I stumble back, heart thrashing.

This...this isn't natural. At least it's no fucking part of nature I've seen.

In seconds, the bunk houses, the storerooms, and the goat barn go up in flames.

As the Sisters scream, Sabine continues to steadily pluck her fingers in the air. The barn door swings open on its own, and the goat herd suddenly bursts out, running straight for the convent gate as if herded there. Two tired old horses break free from the barn, stampeding out of the convent's walls. Rabbits scamper out, too, along with a whole family of mice. Insects wriggle up from below ground and fly or crawl through the gate.

So much for rotten apples, I think. She's about to wither *everything* within sight.

Sabine slams her hands closed, and a gust of wind closes the gate again behind the animals. She crooks her finger, and the deadbolt lock falls closed.

"Don't do this." I grab her arm, forcing her to face me, gripping her chin in my hands. My mind is racing. I haven't seen her like this since the Gloaming. "Me. Focus on me. Like we do when I'm fucking you."

"Let go, Basten!" She makes a fist in the air, and a vine bursts out of the ground to wrap around my boot.

I don't know what to do.

I can't stop her.

She's so much stronger than me—she's stronger than anything beneath the clouds.

She lifts her hands, fingers oddly angled downward. Her hair writhes around her like living creatures. A circle of swallows from the chapel steeple circles overhead, like a crown of feathers, before flying over the wall, away from the cobalt smoke.

A cold jolt lances through my chest—not pain, exactly, but something worse. The moment my eyes lock on her, I know. That pose, the animals—it's the exact image etched into the foundation stones of Drahallen Hall.

Immortal Solene, poised above burning Calisyrune.

"Little violet—" I try, but the vine curls up around my chest, continuing up to my neck, and squeezes just enough that I can't speak.

"You prayed to the wrong fucking goddess," she says to the weeping women.

And brings her hands down.

The ground tears open, the reek of sulfur gas pouring up. Matron White is swallowed whole. Not even her screams escape the pit. The other Sisters run for the gate, clawing at it, but Sabine sweeps her hands wide, and the blazes of blue fire streak across the courtyard.

Smoke fills the courtyard, so thick and blue that all I can make out of the women are their falling corpses.

"Sabine..." I choke out, but the vine tightens on my throat.

I know she means to keep me quiet. To keep me restrained so I won't get hurt by her blue fire. But she doesn't realize...

She doesn't know...

She's killing me.

CHAPTER 13

SABINE

Night slinks in as I crouch in the ruins of an abandoned old sheep barn somewhere deep in the woods, stacking firewood with trembling fingers.

The scent of sulfurous smoke still clings to my hair—a heady reminder of what happened.

Basten lies across from me, his head cushioned by a few handfuls of hay. He's still unconscious. How many hours has it been? Three? Four?

Myst and Ranger stand partway in a dilapidated stall, half open to the outside, swishing their tails. They don't eat the hay in front of them. They're still jittery. Anxious. Stomping their feet.

I lay another few twigs, then snap my fingers for a spark.

Damn. Doesn't work. My fingers are weak, shaking.

I grit my teeth and concentrate, pushing past the exhaustion that digs all the way to my bones, and snap again.

This time, fey sparks a tiny flame.

I sag in relief, but it took the last ounce of my strength. I sit back on my heels, dig through Basten's knapsack at my side, and pull out his iron pot. I pour in the last of our water canteen, then crush a handful of beautyberries and pine needles into it.

Wiping my tired eyes, I give a nod of dismissal to the chipmunks. ***Thank you for gathering these for me, friends.***

They scamper back into the barn's rafters, where they have babies to care for.

I stir the brew with a stick, willing the water to boil faster. If I had more strength, I'd make the fire burn hotter. Hell, I could probably even boil the water without a flame. But after what happened at the convent, I'm barely able to keep my eyes open.

I chew on my lip. Twist my hair in knots. Keep crossing and uncrossing my legs.

From across the fire, a weak groan sounds. I perk up so fast I forget to breathe, then scramble over to Basten's side. He moans again, reaching up to the angry red bruise stretching across his neck.

"Basten?" I shake him with eggshell gentleness.

Suddenly, he awakens with a jolt. He sits up fast enough to kick over my knapsack, his hand flying to his neck. His breath comes fast and hard.

"Sabine?"

"Shh, it's okay." I rest a calming hand on his shoulder. "You're all right. We're safe. We're in the ruins of an old barn I found. I brought you here with the horses' help."

His eyes—wild like an animal's—lock onto me. He still has his hand clutched around his throat. He swallows hard and winces, like it pains him.

I flinch with guilt.

"I'm making pine needle tea," I rattle out fast, moving back to stir the pot to busy myself. "I added some berries for taste. There's wild bergamot, too. It'll ease your sore throat."

He takes a moment to look around the old sheep barn, reassure himself that both horses are here and safe, and only then slides his feet under him and sits up.

He sniffs the air. "Sulfur."

I bite my lip, stirring the pot. Willing it to bubble faster.

"Sabine." His voice is so hoarse he can barely speak. "What...what was that back there?"

"Blue smoke exists in nature," I explain, wincing as my voice comes out sounding defensive. "I read about it in one of Woudix's books. When a crack opens in the earth, sulfurous gas can rise, and when it's ignited, it burns blue and hot. It's called brimfire."

He watches me for a minute like a hawk. "I wasn't talking about the fire's damn *color*."

I clear my throat, digging in his knapsack for a tin cup.

"Are they all dead?" he asks, voice hollow.

A stitch in my stomach tightens. I busy my hands by wrapping a towel around the pot so I can move it off the fire. As an afterthought, I flick my fingers, and the fire snuffs itself out.

"They were always so cruel to the goats." I explain, not looking at him. "They'd separate the newborn kids from their mothers within days, so they'd produce more milk, and have me feed the babies watered-down gruel mixed with egg yolk instead. Those two workhorses you saw are named Mayflower and Bluebell. Once, Sister Ruby whipped Bluebell hard enough to break the skin. An infection set in. Bluebell fell lame, but they only whipped her harder."

His voice is hard, uncompromising. "Sabine—are they all *dead?*"

I pour him the pine needle tea with badly trembling hands, sloshing half of it onto the dirt floor, pretending he hasn't spoken. As if tea can make everything bad go away. "The land the convent was built on was once a beautiful glen, did you know that? An old turtle told me, who'd lived long enough to see it. The Red Church cut all the trees. Tore up the earth for stone. Built that abomination instead. Here —tea."

I pass it to him, not meeting his eyes.

Finally, he takes it. He says flatly, "So they're dead."

"I...assume so." I quickly turn to smooth the wrinkles from my saddle blanket. "You were never in danger, though. I want you to know that. I knew what I was doing with the vine. Just trying to keep you from getting hurt. It was better if you were unconscious—I could keep you away from the smoke. I promise, I was in control, even though it might not have looked like it. It wasn't like during the Gloaming. And see?" I stretch out my hands toward the fields beyond the barn ruins. "Bremcote, the fields, everything is safe. I didn't singe so much as a blade of grass beyond the convent walls."

Finally, there are no more wrinkles to smooth. No more hay to pick out of my hair. No more pots to fiddle with.

I rub the back of my neck as I kneel next to where Basten sits, and for a long time, silence stretches between us.

I find the strength to look him in his bloodshot eyes. "You know I'd never hurt you, right?"

My voice comes out in a whisper, breaking just like my strength.

Somewhere far off, a coyote howls.

I can feel the ghost of my father's words. *Acolytes count their lifespan in months, not years.*

Basten sighs deeply, scrubbing his hands over his face as if he's as exhausted as I am. When he finally looks up, the wariness has eased into concern. "It isn't my place to scold you, Sabine. It's to support you. Hell, I gave myself to you. I *do* let you hurt me—willingly. You can bleed me. You can break me. I'd give my life to you, if you asked it. The thing is, I don't want you to take it on a lark."

The reek of smoke clots in my mouth. "What happened in the convent wasn't a *lark.*"

He leans forward, muscles tensing. "Look, those sancti-monious bitches had it coming. If it had been me, I'd have put them in the grave, too. There was a time in my life when I *did* kill my enemies—and worse. But...we both know it's different with you. You aren't some vengeful street boy. You command nature itself. That much power comes with duty."

I bristle, arching back from him. "Why do you get to make mistakes, and I don't?"

This catches him by surprise. He doesn't have an answer right away.

"There was no sorrow in your eyes when Jocki died," I continue.

"*I* didn't kill Jocki."

I press, "You told me once that you tried to, as a boy. So why is it wrong when I'm not sorry my tormentors are dead? Why can't I be petty? Vindictive?"

Finally, his hand falls away from the back of his neck. "Because, little violet, one petty word from you could break the world."

Somehow, last light has come and gone, and without the fire, it's completely dark now. I stand, muscles jittery and slack, adrenaline from earlier still punishing me, no place to go. I settle on grabbing a brush from my knapsack and moving to clean the road dust from Myst's back.

As I rub the brush over her, she side-eyes me closely.

Sharp words between you and him, she observes.

I brush her a little harder without meaning to, and when she flinches, I ease up. I sigh. ***Do you think it was wrong of me to have killed the Sisters? They would have kept hurting Mayflower and Bluebell, just as they hurt us.***

She leans into my brush, finding an itchy spot, as she considers this. ***No***, she says eventually. ***But I don't like the look in your eyes when you shine. I don't recognize you.***

My hand pauses.

I lean my head against Myst's shoulder, breathing in her musty scent beneath the reek of brimfire—the scent I know in my bones—and sigh.

I assured Basten I was in control, but was I?

The memory rises unbidden, curling like smoke through my mind. The convent walls cracking with heat, stones breaking loose. The earth itself groaning, opened up to swallow the Matron whole. Spit out sulfurous gas in its wake, which sparked and caught fire. Blue flames rising high on the thatched rooftops, jumping from one to another.

The only thought in my head was: *Good. Let it all burn.*

Now, Woudix's words echo at the back of my skull.

My advice? he said. *Answer the anger.*

The God of Death wouldn't judge me, I feel certain— he'd applaud me. Even now, he's probably ushering the Sisters' cursed souls into the underrealm. More citizens for his dead kingdom.

And—maybe he's not wrong. Some things need to end for others to begin.

But Basten...

Basten, with his steady gaze and calloused hands, and my name carved into his skin. I don't know where Basten's true feelings lie. If he fears me or understands me.

I'm not sure *he* knows, either.

I finish up with Myst and then sink into a cross-legged position on my unrolled saddle blanket, listening to the crickets outside.

"So," I start, testingly, trying to make peace. "Tomorrow we'll reach Old Coros?"

There's a moment when I'm not sure if Basten will press our earlier conversation. He sips the pine needle tea, and slowly, the tight set to his shoulders eases. He runs a hand through his hair, shaking out the last ashes.

"We should arrive mid-morning at the city's southern gate. You revealed yourself as fae, but all our witnesses are dead now. So, we still have that card up our sleeve. We'll disguise ourselves as commoners and meet with Lord Kendan's loyal guards who are watching for us at the southern gate. They'll get us into Hekkelveld Castle safely. Once we're crowned, we'll make a formal announcement. With you as my wife, no one will be able to arrest you for treason. As queen, you'll have royal protection."

I turn my hands over, study the lines in my palm. Caked now with dirt from grooming Myst. "When do I show them what I am?"

He digs in his bag for a hunk of bread, which he tears in half for me. He pauses, considering this. "We'll tell Folke first. That old bastard has seen it all—nothing flusters him. Which means telling it to Ferra, too, as long as they aren't on the outs again. Then, we'll reveal the truth to Lord Kendan, privately, and see how he reacts. We'll figure out how to get the populace to welcome the fae when they arrive on the Blood Moon."

I yawn, my eyelids so heavy they sit like bricks.

"Don't worry about what happens when we reach Old Coros," he says more tenderly. "Right now, you're depleted. You can barely hold your head up." He rolls back his sleeve. "You need to drink."

I shake my head, Vale's warning stabbing into me again. "I'm fine."

"Little violet, I can hear your stomach louder than the crickets."

I flick a piece of ash off my dress. True, the hunk of bread did almost nothing for my hunger. A few sips of pine needle tea aren't going to slake the thirst inside me, either.

The last thing I want to do now is take from him, but I have no choice.

I kneel next to him, unbuttoning his tattered shirt, stained with soot and soil, and peel it off his body. My breath hitches at the sight of him in the moonlight—his body bare to the waist, skin damp with sweat and smeared with ash.

As I settle beside him, he reaches up with a tenderness that steals my breath, brushing a dirty strand of hair from my brow with the back of his fingers.

"Take it," he murmurs, voice still rasping.

I lean in. My hand loosely circles his wrist as I bring his forearm to my lips and plant a soft kiss on the skin. His breath hitches—he'd expected the bite of pain. I run a line of tender kisses down his scarred forearm before finally easing my incisors into the flesh above his vein.

His warm blood floods my mouth. I swallow the iron taste, eyes fluttering as heat rolls through me.

My own silver blood responds to his like answering a song. My heartbeat quickens. The base of my belly roars.

Gods—has it always been *this* good?

I drink and drink, giving myself over to the flood of pleasure, the never-ending hunger.

Basten groans—a deep rumble that vibrates from his chest to mine. I can feel his gaze on me, heavy-lidded and dark, drinking in the sight of me as I suck at his wrist.

"You're so fucking beautiful like this," he says, almost to himself. "Hungry. Dangerous. Mine."

His words jolt me out of my trance, and I pull back sharply, licking the last of his blood from my lips. Immediately, my hunger seizes control, demanding I return to that beautiful fountain of blood rolling down his wrist.

My hands shake—I can barely force myself to let go of his wrist.

Keep drinking keep drinking keep drinking.

"Sabine?" he asks, unsure.

I let him go, breathing hard, though it takes every ounce of my strength.

The wound on his wrist closes up seamlessly—except for that scar he'll wear forever, the one that reads my name.

We stare at each other in the broken moonlight. Traces of soot line his face, but the bones beneath are strong. A king's build. *You didn't hurt him*, I reassure myself.

"It's...getting harder to stop," I admit, voice breaking.

He stares at me.

He pulls in a deep breath, tilting his head to draw in my scent, just like I did with Myst. Searching beyond the facade of brimfire smoke for something sweeter, more familiar.

Then, he kisses me. The rasp of his stubble rubs my jaw, anchoring me in the here and now—this moment. I slide my arms around his neck to deepen the kiss. His hand finds the small of my back, and I shift my hips until I'm in his lap, straddling him.

His thumb slides my sleeve off my shoulder, and he lays kisses on the curve of my skin. I lean into his touch like a cat, not realizing how starved I was for this connection between us. For days, there's been a...distance. His other hand fumbles on my skirt, bunching it up around my waist. As he undoes his pants, I coil my fingers in the hair at his nape and press kisses on that throbbing vein in his corded neck.

His skin still holds the sun's earlier warmth. I only realize now how much I've missed that, too. Warmth in the veins. I've felt so cold for weeks.

He takes me slowly tonight. Rocking his hips in measured, steady thrusts. I hold onto his shoulders and move with him, letting my head fall back and my eyes sink closed. Like we're on a boat together, rocking in the Panopis Sea.

Our desire builds and breaks together—at least in this, we are in sync. After the climax, Basten holds me in his strong arms, his head resting on my shoulder.

There's so much to say.

About the changes happening inside my body. My mind, too. Woudix's words keep circling my head, about how I'm only play-acting at being human.

We have Rian to find and bring to justice—whether at the end of a sword or in a cell.

We have his ruined Lunden Valley to heal.

We have fae to tame.

We have humans to lead.

We have a fragile peace to maintain before the kingdom shatters into war.

But right now, all I want in the world is to stay in Basten's arms, in this old sheep barn in a forgotten corner of the world, where no one cares what sparks at my fingers, whose blood flows in his veins.

Eventually, I pull back, running my fingers over his face.

"I worship at your feet, too, you know," I speak as quietly as a prayer. "You say that you'd burn the world for me. For you, I'd gather the ashes, shape them into something beautiful. Remake the world anew—just for you. One where your shoulder never aches, your hands never bruise, and you're honored as the king I know you are."

CHAPTER 14

BASTEN

The southern gate of Old Coros is a marvel of ancient engineering: a twenty-foot archway, the word "WISDOM" chiseled on the curved marble block, columns meant to stand as proud and tall as eternal oaks.

But today? All I can think is: *What a fucking dump.*

Tattered banners hang limp and soiled from either side of the open gate. A line of bruised criminals sits against the wall in chains. Dozens of travelers have set up a temporary encampment of pitiful campfires and strung-up tarps, awaiting entry into the city. They're blocked by a fleet of Golden Sentinels. All their fine brass armor—the gleaming color giving them their name—can't mask the filth they truly are.

Mercenaries.

Hang on. Scratch that. They're worse, if that's possible—they're *Rian's* mercenaries.

I know, because I was once among their midst.

Next to me, sitting on Myst, Sabine moves her cloak's woolen hood back enough so I can see her nose wrinkle. She whispers, "It smells like cow piss."

We're on the horses, in the long line of people awaiting entry into the city. Sabine wears a threadbare farm wife's dress with a soiled cloak, the hem ripped and dragging in the mud. I'm no prize, either, dressed as her potato-digging husband, complete with too-big boots and a ridiculously tattered straw hat.

I adjust the sack of potatoes over my shoulder—borrowed from a lakeside farm we passed this morning, along with the clothing—and mutter, "I wish it were *only* cow piss."

If I could turn off my damn godkiss, now would be the time. The smells wafting from Old Coros are an assault to the senses. Moldy cheese. Rotting fish. Piss and shit from everything that walks on two feet or four.

"I thought Old Coros was supposed to be a model city of law and order," she leans in to murmur, eyeing a sentinel as he ransacks through a woman's purse for "entry taxes" as she sobs that she won't have enough coins left to feed her children.

"Last time I was here," I reply, keeping my voice low, "it was. Streets so clean you could eat off them. Not so much as a stray dog. As for the royal army, they had soldiers in spotless armor stationed at every street corner, holding banners that proclaimed the virtues of the city. Wisdom, Honor, you know the litany. This..." I motion to the filth and disorder, "... is all new."

The sentinel finally allows the woman entry after he tucks her entire purse into his vest. He calls for another sentinel to confiscate her horse.

Sabine clutches a handful of Myst's mane defensively.

"When we get to the front of the line," I murmur, "tell the horses to limp as if they're on death's door. We don't want the sentinels looking too closely at their manicured hooves."

Finally, we're next in line. Sabine draws her cloak's hood higher, covering her hair, completely casting her face in shadows. She hangs back on Myst, shoulders slumped. If I didn't know better, I'd think she was identical to every other beaten-down farmer's wife in line.

She *did* tell me her mother was an actress.

"Next. You there." A heavyset sentinel in armor a few sizes too small beckons to me like calling cattle. He tugs on his breastplate uncomfortably, glancing at my sack of potatoes. "There's a fifty coin tax to enter, and we'll need to search your—"

"Barthy, Barthy, ho there! I've got this one." Another sentinel cuts in smoothly. "The Captain wants me to evaluate all horses coming into the city. You take that family with the ducks." He gestures to the farmer behind us with his daughters straining under wooden cages full of ducks.

The pot-bellied Barthy looks like he might object if it weren't for the three attractive, if painfully thin, teenage daughters. He shifts from one foot to the other, hands resting on his too-small belt, and signals for the duck farmer to step forward.

The swarthy sentinel faces us, scratches his ass, and then raises his helmet's visor an inch.

Well, well.

I grin.

Folke. The old bastard in the flesh.

I mask any recognition on my face by wiping away

phantom sweat, and keep my head bowed as a humble farmer.

"Potatoes!" Folke makes a show of digging through my bag, tossing a rotten one on the ground. "We have root vegetables aplenty! And what's this? A knife!"

With his deft hands, he draws his *own* hidden knife from the scabbard tucked into his waistband, flourishing it for all to see. "No weapons allowed—the punishment is imprisonment!"

I roll my eyes at his theatrics, wondering if this is necessary. But the other sentinels are watching, so I bow my head. "A thousand apologies. I only use it for potato peeling."

"Off those horses!" Folke commands, grabbing Myst's reins with a heavy hand. She jerks her head up, indignant, but she seems to recognize him enough not to bite his finger off. "I'm conscripting them into King Rian's sentinel army. As for you and your wife, into the prison wagon with you!"

He jabs his elbow toward an enclosed wagon with barred windows. Another sentinel, this one young and slight, silently opens the wagon door for us.

Sabine raises her eyebrows toward me, and I nod for her to obey.

Folke roughs us up a little as we dismount, herding us at the knife's point toward the wagon. Its two benches are empty—we're the only prisoners. As I pass the slight soldier, something oddly familiar rings about him. A scent in the air, delicate and spicy. I hold my gaze an extra beat, but the man scowls at me and gestures inside, remaining quiet.

Folke ties the horses' leads to the rear of the wagon, then climbs in himself and swings the door shut. He gives a quick sweep of the street before knocking twice on the roof.

The quiet young soldier climbs into the driver's seat, and the wagon rolls forward through the city gates.

Once cobblestone rumbles under the wheels, Folke tears off his helmet and tosses back his messy, gray-threaded curls.

"Here you are at last, you beast," he exclaims. "We expected you two days ago! I've had to pretend to be one of those piss-stinking sentinels for far too long!"

He breaks into a grin and leans forward to grasp my hand in his, a brotherly handshake that feels like putting on a well-worn glove.

I give a half-grin in return.

"We had...delays." I glance at Sabine. "There was a...fire outside of Bremcote. But anyway, what the fuck happened here?"

I gesture beyond the barred windows to the once-orderly city, where a pack of feral children runs wild.

Folke snorts. "Didn't Maximan tell you everything's gone to hell since our coup failed? Rian's disappeared. No one knows who to take orders from. Half the city still obeys our royal soldiers. Half obey the Golden Sentinels, run in Rian's absence by a gang of criminals calling themselves the Cold Coins. Hell, half the people are still listening to the fucking Red Church preaching the fae's return, even after Beneveto's corpse marched dead through the streets."

"That's three halves," I point out.

He groans. "Smartass." He turns to Sabine instead, flashing that smile that dazzles the ladies and won Ferra's heart. "Gods, is it ever good to see the face of someone reasonable."

Sabine smiles, amused, though she keeps glancing out

the rear door at Myst and Ranger in tow. "It's good to see you again, too, Folke."

He pauses, his keen eyes taking in the plump swell of her cheeks, the spark of light in her eyes. "Something different about you."

I go rigid, forgetting to breathe for a moment—but her human glamour is still raised.

She clears her throat, waving away his words. "How is Ferra?"

"Ah!" His eyes light up. "You didn't recognize my jewel outside?"

Sabine's head cocks.

Folke points in the direction of the carriage driver outside—the quiet, slight soldier.

Sabine gasps. "I thought that soldier looked familiar!"

He grins wider. "She hates using her godkiss to make herself look like a man. Says we're the lesser half of the species. Can't say she's wrong, either."

Sabine hides a giggle behind her hand, and Folke rears back at the sight of her ring.

"Gods alive! Look at that rock! Are you crazy, entering the city with that jewel on your finger?"

Sabine quickly covers the ring with her other hand. "I forgot to take it off—it already feels like it's a part of me."

Folke leans back, pulling out a fat Wicked Weed cigar from his pocket. He lights the cigar, then motions it between the two of us. "So, you got hitched, eh?"

My chest swells a few inches. I nod. "A, uh, village preacher up north performed the honors."

He snorts. "Sure, sure. One of those famous forest-wandering officiants. Don't worry, I'll tie up all the loose ends. This is good—it saves us a step. Planning a coronation and a wedding would have wreaked havoc on the poor archivists' fingers."

He takes a long inhale of the cigar, then offers it to me.

I shake my head.

"I'd congratulate you," he says, "but we have a kingdom to keep from sliding straight into hell. With some luck, we can get this prison wagon through the gates into Hekkelveld Castle. Lord Kendan and the royal army still hold control of the castle—for now."

Sabine peers through the window bars, studying the grimy streets. We pass a market with meager fare of rotted turnips. The pubs are packed with riffraff and those down on their luck, drinking down ale to numb themselves.

It's still all new to her, I have to remind myself. After being locked away for twelve years, there's still so much of the world she's experiencing for the first time.

I feel a wave of tenderness—followed by protectiveness that burns like a brimfire.

Sabine could summon the ocean from its bed, but there's still a part of her that's my sheltered violet. Soft. Unweathered. And gods help anyone who tries to crush her under their boot.

"What news is there of Rian?" I ask.

Folke lets out a long line of smoke before replying bitterly, "We scoured the city for him. Every pub and warehouse and ditch. Best we can tell, he's gone. Probably slunk through the sewers like the rat he is. We have reason to believe he's headed for Duren. We've already sent spies there and posted more along the road, but they've reported no sightings as of yet. The plan is to get the crown on your head soon. With plenty of witnesses. We could do it as early as Friday."

The prison wagon rumbles across a bridge, the river below reeking of human waste, and through the barred window I can make out the spires of Hekkelveld Castle high over the city's rooftops.

"This whole area used to be a forest," Sabine says suddenly, staring out the window with slightly glazed eyes, as if she's a million miles away. "Alders, ash, silver birches. Once, there were warring packs of cloudfoxes here."

The wagon falls into a heavy silence as Folke eyes her oddly. His gaze flicks to me. An eyebrow rises.

I give a nervous laugh. "Sabine's been studying ancient history…hey, darling, can you try asking the city's animals if they know of Rian's whereabouts?"

It takes a moment for her attention to shift back to the here and now—to me. She blinks, seemingly unaware of her odd statement.

"What? Oh—of course, let me ask." She goes studiously quiet, and after a moment, shakes her head. "Not according to the birds. So, Rian probably escaped through the tunnels, as you said, Folke. Once we're in the castle, I'll try asking the worms."

We continue traveling through the city, uphill toward Hekkelveld Castle. From the driver's seat, Ferra lets out a muttered curse, "Oh, hell in a wash basin!"

She can mask her appearance, but not her voice. No wonder she was so quiet.

"Ah." Folke clenches the cigar between his teeth as he draws a miniature crossbow from a hidden compartment in the bench seat. "Careful, now. Might want to put your head down, Lady Sabine. We're approaching Hekkelveld Castle and it's a bit of a battle zone."

Most of my weapons are hidden away back in Ranger's

saddlebag, but I draw the small knife I keep holstered in my boot.

Tall iron spires rise surrounding the castle's courtyard. Inside the fence, royal soldiers have their swords at the ready. Their heartbeats are fast, clothes pungent from days-old sweat. A bite of adrenaline hangs in the air.

Outside the gates, Golden Sentinels flank the fence to prevent anyone from entering. It's a battle line drawn in cobblestone and iron. Even before we pull up, curses are volleyed back and forth between the two armies like cannon fodder.

"My jewel!" Folke calls to Ferra outside. "Keep that pretty head of yours down!"

She yells back, "I know how to keep my head on my shoulders, Folke—do you?"

He chuckles. "What a woman."

Folke mutters to himself around the fat cigar in his mouth as he aims the crossbow through the bars. He closes one eye for aim, then lets an arrow fly.

It slams into a hay bale outside the gate.

"Damn, old man," I snort. "Your aim isn't as good as it was once—"

I have to swallow my words when a horse that had been foraging on the hay bale rears up, spooked, the whites of its eyes flashing. It tugs so hard on its lead rope that the threads snap. It skitters backward, dragging half a wooden rack with it.

Golden Sentinels rush over to capture the spooked horse.

"Gotta keep 'em distracted," Folke mutters. "And one more for good measure." He lets an arrow fly in the other direction, this one glinting off a sentinel's brass backplate.

The soldier whirls, sword drawn, which causes chaos as no one knows where the attack came from.

"Captain Fernsby!" Ferra shouts toward the castle. "Open the damn gates, we're coming in!"

The royal soldiers inside the courtyard call out to one another, rushing to roll back the gate just enough to let in our wagon. A dozen more soldiers draw swords, holding off the sentinels who try to push their way inside.

Exhaustion rolls off both warring armies, and I get the sense this is a daily occurrence.

"Basten," Sabine whispers, fast and urgent. "I could help—"

I can already see the fey lines breaking out at her fingertips, and I quickly grab her cloak to hide her fingers. "Not yet. We've got this."

"Easy as a whore with her legs up," Folke chuckles as he reaches through the bars and smashes the crossbow hilt on a soldier's helmet.

There's a collision of swords, a smash of metal, but then we're clear of the gates. Myst and Ranger crowd in behind us, and Captain Fernsby slams the gate shut. A few sentinels who are trapped inside are quickly dispatched, their blood rolling into the gaps between cobblestones.

A stableboy rushes up to take Myst and Ranger to the safety of the castle stables.

Sabine's eyes are big, her hand tightly gripping her knees.

"We're safe," I reassure her. "The horses, too."

"It isn't that." She flicks her fingers with the quiet confidence of someone fully aware that they could bring lightning down on any attacker's head. But her voice is rattled. "It's...so different here from Norhelm. Even from Duren."

"Welcome to a city at war, sweetheart," Folke says around his cigar. He swings open the rear door to usher her out.

She still looks shaky as she climbs out, but then Ferra is stomping toward us, tearing off her stiff armor with ample grumbles. She sweeps her hands over her male-soldier's face like washing away the dirt's grime, using her godkiss to reveal her true high cheekbones and lavender eyes. She combs her fingers through her disguise's tawny, ear-length hair, and it stretches out beneath her palms into glistening black locks to her waist.

Once she's herself again—save the armor that hangs clumsily on her—she throws her arms around Sabine.

"Sabby! Gods, woman, we missed you!"

Sabine grins, wide and sincere. "I missed you too, Ferra."

"This isn't teatime, ladies!" Folke gives Ferra's ass a hard grab as he herds her toward the castle. An arrow launches over the iron fence, which he dodges seamlessly. "Save the chitchat for when we aren't being actively shot at."

I wrap my arm around Sabine's back, sheltering her as we rush up the castle steps and through the grand entrance.

Shadows fall over us.

Gods, it feels like a lifetime since I was here last. Riding up at Rian's side. Ready to swear my life to him all over again.

The castle's entryway, Raven Hall, is blessedly cool, a still eddy carved from the chaos thrumming at the outer gates. Stone columns flank the foyer, their carved ravens staring down with stone eyes. Light spills in through high arched windows, glinting off the mosaic floors.

Sabine's shoulders drop a notch as her gaze drifts across

the room's symmetry, the hush of it. No shouting. No stench of the streets. Here, at least, there is still law. Still control.

"You're here, finally," a voice says. "We were about to send an army to see if you'd been run through by a monoceros horn."

Lord Kendan strides down the central staircase, his Lord of the Iron Banner's cloak billowing behind him. A white-haired general, old but tough as bricks, flanks his left side, and Lady Suri Darrow skips down at his right, her eyes full of bubbly joy at our arrival.

Kendan stops, his cloak coming to rest around his polished boots.

He's barely taken a breath before he kneels, bowing his head. "Rising King Basten. It is an honor."

I scratch my jaw, groaning.

This whole "king" thing is going to take some getting used to.

Now *this* pretty bastard? Kendan is exactly what a king should look like—practically stepped out of a damn gilded frame hanging in the royal archives.

Not my potato-hauling ass.

"Get up, Kendan, for gods' sakes," I grumble.

Kendan bristles against my lack of decorum, blinking hard, but then bows to Sabine.

"Lady Sabine. I'm Lord Kendan Valvere, at your service. As Lord of the Iron Banner, it's my duty to bridge the gap between the army and the king—or at least, it was, before the city fell apart."

Sabine recoils slightly at the surname. "Rian's brother."

Kendan grimaces. "His eldest, yes. Our middle brother, Lore, took to the Panopis Sea years ago."

"We can trust Lord Kendan," I begrudgingly inform

Sabine. "Despite his Valvere surname. Kendan hasn't double-crossed us, and gods know, he's had plenty of chances."

"It's true." Lady Suri bounces on her toes, clasping her hands at her chest. "Kendan is a...well, a highly honorable man. Oh, it's so good to see you, Sabine!"

She flounces herself into Sabine's arms. Sabine stiffens only for a second, her pulse still on edge—she's in more than one disguise, after all—before melting into a hug with Suri that ruffles my jealous edges.

I'm glad she has a friend, no question.

But my protective instincts are working overtime.

I glance between Suri and Kendan, quietly observing their stances. Hard not to notice that strange, almost formal pause Suri used when talking about him. When I left Old Coros, the two of them were practically engaged. Hell, I figured it was only a matter of time before their wedding announcement. The only thorn between them seemed to be Rian—who delighted so wickedly in teasing Suri.

What's gone stale between them?

"You feel chilled to the bone." Suri pulls back, frowning in concern at Sabine. "Are you well?"

"It's...just the journey," Sabine stutters. "I'm exhausted. And this old cloak doesn't hold much warmth."

Suri takes Sabine's hands, rubbing them in her own to warm them, but then squeaks in surprise. "This ring! Does it mean you're married?"

She looks between Sabine and me with wide eyes.

A genuine smile breaks out across Sabine's face. I can't help but puff up my chest a little, adjusting the potato sack on my shoulder.

"We are," Sabine says, smiling.

Suri squeaks with delight.

"Forgive me, then, Rising Queen Sabine." Kendan bows again. "And apologies for the cumbersome titles. Now that you're here, we'll ready everything for the coronation. In mere days, you two shall be King and Queen of Astagnon."

I shift from one foot to the other but can't manage to feel at ease.

"First things first," Ferra exclaims. "We have to change you out of this questionable attire! You need a bath, food, rest!" Ferra slips her arm in Sabine's, and Suri takes her by the opposite arm.

"And you must tell us everything about the wedding!" Suri chirps, practically dragging Sabine up the stairs. "Goodness, and I must know everything about your time in Norhelm. Are there really cloudfoxes? And where is Tòrr? What about the rumors about..."

As Suri chitters on, Sabine tosses me a look over her shoulder. I have to stop myself from taking a step after her, the shadow always in her wake.

You can't be at her side in every moment.

Once the women are gone, Folke abruptly drops his smile. He and Kendan exchange a loaded look.

"Come with us, you." Folke drags me unceremoniously by the arm into a storage vestibule filled with old wooden flagpole handles and rolled banners.

Kendan sweeps in behind us, closing the door.

"What the fuck is this?" I ask, flicking a banner's golden tassel. "Last time you abducted me, I ended up with a bruised rib."

"We have news," Folke says, ignoring me, eyes lighting up. He wets his lips, excited. "Lord Kendan has been working his connections. It turns out Beneveto wasn't the only person with sway inside the Red Church."

"Good," I mutter, suppressing a shiver, "because I watched his soul ooze out of his body."

This earns me cocked heads from both Folke and Kendan.

"His...soul?" Folke echoes.

I think briefly of what they'd do if they knew the God of Death walked among mortals. Or that he gets more looks from women than the three of us combined.

"Never mind," I grumble. "Something to tell you...later."

"Well," Kendan cuts in, "the Red Church's loyalists are caught between supporting Rian and supporting us, the opposition. We calculated that if we could win over their support, we'd have more than enough sway to defeat the Golden Sentinels. Even if Rian makes it to Duren, he won't have an army anymore."

I scrub a hand over the stubble on my jaw, nodding. "You can do it? Broker a deal with the Red Church?"

"It's already done." Kendan claps a triumphant hand on my shoulder. "For the past few weeks, I've been meeting secretly with the new head of the Red Church. She hasn't been officially named the new grand cleric, but that's only a technicality. Now, with Matron White on our side, we..."

His voice dies when he sees the blood drain from my face.

Folke grabs my shirt collar, pulling me close. "What is it? What's wrong?"

I think of the last time I saw Matron White, swallowed by a chasm.

"A...slight problem," I start, but then the vestibule door swings open.

I draw my knife on instinct, ready for a fight if needed…

…but a woman, not an attacking enemy, sidles in and closes the door behind her.

Her cold, pinched eyes meet mine.

She doesn't smell like brimfire smoke any more, but the backs of her hands and one side of her neck are bandaged.

It's fucking Matron White.

Definitely *not* dead.

CHAPTER 15
SABINE

Suri and Ferra continue to *ooh* and *ahh* over my ring with loud, girlish giggles as they lead me up the curving main staircase to the second floor. We pass a pair of royal guards, and the second they're out of earshot, the giggles die.

They pull me into a second-floor workroom overflowing with fabric, thread, and measuring tape. Ferra's full-length gilded mirror from Sorsha Hall stands in a corner, though I can only imagine how hard it was to convince Rian to transport it here.

Ferra slams the door shut and turns the key.

"We'll get to the whole bath, food, and rest part. But first, so much has happened we have to tell you about," she says, her lavender eyes a little wild. With a dramatic flourish, she stretches her arms out as though defending the door from an onslaught. "Finally, we can talk about it without those idiot men listening in."

I catch my reflection in the mirror and flinch—I've been practically dipped head to toe in mud. I start to untie the farmers' dirty cloak from over my hair. "Aren't you and Folke still together? He called you his jewel."

"Ugh, yes." She sees me struggling with the knot and comes over to help. "We're together. We're hopelessly in love. Don't you dare tell a soul—I'm sure I'll loathe him again tomorrow."

I look down to hide my smile. "I see not everything has changed."

Ferra seems, well...even more Ferra than usual.

Life in the capital city looks good on her. She was always Duren's most fashionable resident, but now that she has access to the best the kingdom has to offer, she shines like a silver piece. Her hair is swept back into an elaborate Immortal Crown, with glittering strands of silver filaments woven through. Her gown has ruffles upon ruffles ranging from midnight blue to a soft cerulean, mimicking the layers of the ocean. She smells like incense only a king could afford.

Looking at her, it's hard to believe there's a war outside.

"Ferra means no ill will against Lord Kendan or Folke," Suri pops in to explain, as she helps me untie the apron from around my back. She pulls the dirty apron over my head, sliding unsure looks to the door, and the hair lifts on my arms.

My heartbeat picks up. "Is it...Basten, then? You're worried about?"

"No!" Suri looks horrified. "No, we wouldn't go to these lengths to put Basten on the throne if we didn't completely believe in him. We're all leading the opposition together. Why, you should see how late Kendan toils into the night in the castle library, poring over old military strategy books. And Folke...well, his methods might be coarse, but they're effective. It's just that sometimes men have a way of overre-acting. You know? Starting wars over the smallest thing. Some decisions are best left to a woman's calmer judgement."

Ferra pauses. "Although...can Basten hear us? There's something about his godkiss that's always made me uneasy. Not about his intentions, just about how deep his power goes. As if he's hiding something more."

I pick dried mud flecks off my wool dress, keeping my eyes down. Ferra might as well be reading my biography from a history book.

Basten might not be hiding anything, but me? Check.

I pretend to smooth back my tangled hair while double-checking that my ear is curved.

I say breezily, "I'm sure Folke has poured so much whisky down Basten's throat by now that his senses are dull as a brick."

I mean it as a joke, but Ferra nods her agreement with a little too much certainty.

My gaze falls on a stack of old books on the mantelpiece, and I turn to Suri. "This isn't about the missing book, is it? The second volume of *The Last Return of the Fae*? Did you find it?"

My voice lifts with a touch of panic, but I cross my fingers that they interpret the tone as excitement.

Once, I was so desperate to find the second volume that I nearly tore apart Rian's library. I had reason to believe it contained the secret to putting the fae gods to sleep—possibly forever. And I still want to find it. Of course I do. Nothing would please me more than stopping Artain and Iyre from using the seven kingdoms as their game board, toying with human lives like game pieces.

It's just that now, that missing volume could be a weapon against *me*, too.

Suri's face falls. "No. I've looked for it everywhere. Rian assigned me the position of Castlekeep, so I have keys to nearly every door in Hekkelveld Castle. But it isn't in the library. Trust me, I've checked every shelf. Nor is it in any of the offices I have access to. I even scoured the attic." She squeezes my shoulders from behind and reassures me, "Don't worry, Sabby. We'll find it."

Suri and Ferra peel me out of the farmer's dress, then wrap me in a borrowed silk robe. Ferra sniffs my hair and mutters something about maybe tackling the "bath" part sooner rather than later, and Suri briefly disappears and returns with a bucket of bath water and a scrub brush. She gets a fire going in the room's small fireplace, then hangs the iron kettle so the water will warm.

"You say a lot has happened," I start, slowly working my hair loose from its simple braid.

It's still hard to meet their eyes. To say a lot has happened on my end, too, would be an understatement. Just being here in my human glamour feels like a lie. What am I supposed to do, break out in my pointed ears? Make that water boil with a blast of fey?

Instead, I clear my throat and try to lighten the mood. "Would that involve Rian's brother that I met downstairs? Basten mentioned some flirtation, at least on Kendan's side." I give Suri a sly smile. "He half expected you'd be engaged by now."

Suri shoots to her feet, the boiling water forgotten. "Lord Kendan?" Her voice rises about three octaves.

I nod.

Suri flashes a look to Ferra that fills me with a wrinkle of jealousy. Their close friendship is clear in their shared looks; the sentences they finish for one another. They've had months to become friends here. If Rian hadn't sold me out, and Immortal Iyre hadn't kidnapped me, then maybe I'd be laughing right along with them.

Now, I feel a step apart. Left behind.

And sad that the closest female friend I made in Volkany was a sweet, silly goldenclaw that died from Rian's poisoned river.

"Oh no," Suri says in a rush, toying anxiously with a thin gold chain around her neck. "Nothing like wedding bells. Lord Kendan is an esteemed colleague, nothing more."

Ferra clears her throat pointedly, and Suri puffs out an air of defeat before admitting, "Okay, maybe there was some initial attraction. He's a handsome man—he's a Valvere, after all. That family's morals might be bankrupt, but they're rich in looks." She sighs. "Kendan isn't like the rest of his family. He's honorable to a fault. There was...a fumble or two in a coat closet. I just couldn't force myself to be excited about the prospect. I find his respectability, well, dull. Is that wrong? I thought that's what I wanted after Charlin. Someone upstanding and consistent. But then I came here and met...other people...and realized I need a little spice in my life."

I raise an eyebrow. "Who is 'other people'?"

Her walnut cheeks pinken to a sunset sheen. She suddenly becomes very dedicated to tearing rose petals to throw in the warming bath water, shredding them to within an inch of their lives.

"Suri?" I draw out her name like a scolding mother. "Who is it?"

I glance at Ferra, who makes the gesture of sewing her

lips shut, but gives a pointed look toward her makeup stand, where a blue-ink stick of kohl rests.

"Oh, gods, you don't mean *Rian*?" I blurt out in horror.

"*Ofcoursenotthatscrazy!*" Suri vomits the phrase as though she's had it ready on her tongue, waiting for this accusation.

I lean back, stunned.

It *was* Rian.

"I'm…going to need a minute." I sink into the dressmaker's chair and pinch the bridge of my nose.

Suri flounces down at my knees, fretting with her dress sleeves as though she could tug them so far over her hands she'd disappear. Ferra quietly moves to unhook my bathwater and pour it into a large ceramic bowl.

"I'm not interested in Rian!" Suri vows, her face twisted up. "He's odious. In fact, he's the most odious man I've ever come across. That dreadful sense of humor. The ridiculous swipe of blue eyeliner. I'd sooner swoon over a goat!"

I blink, still struggling to catch up with everything that's happened in the last few minutes. There's such a thing as protesting too much…but Suri at least *seems* to believe her own words.

But her pink cheeks say differently.

"The men think he's halfway to Duren," Ferra says, deftly shifting the conversation as she dips a clean rag into the rose-scented water. "But Suri and I suspect he's closer. Still somewhere in Old Coros, hiding out."

I lean forward, resting my elbows on my knees. "Why?"

"There's nothing left for Rian in Duren," Ferra explains. "His father is dead. His cousin, Lady Runa, barely keeps Sorsha Hall running. Besides, some of the chambermaids overheard Rian telling some drinking buddy that now that he's got a toe in the capital, they'd have to tear him out." She leans in, giving the bathwater a stir. "I've quietly put out word throughout the city's brothels. Knowing him, if he is still in the city, it'll only be a matter of time before he dips into one. One of our informants will spot him."

She hands me the damp cloth, and I run it mechanically over my body, wiping away days of travel grime. I hope they don't see how my hands are shaking. The idea that Rian could be somewhere close sparks off too many things at once.

"Here," Ferra says, lifting the lid off a wooden box. "I think you'll find this more suitable attire for a future queen."

With reverence, she lifts out a delicate mauve gown. It has puffed sleeves at the shoulder, which cinch at the bicep and then tighten down to the wrist. The plunging neckline and side-lacing corset are embroidered with fae knots, and a long, golden, woven belt loops around the waist and plunges to the floor. The style is from another era. Not at all the modern rage.

I stare because it feels somehow familiar. As though, a thousand years ago, I wore dresses like this.

"It's beautiful," I say, quickly hiding my shock with practiced awe. "Too beautiful for a simple Tuesday. I'll save it for the coronation."

Ferra preens, plucking off a small fleck of dust on the neckline. "Nonsense. Of course you should look god-like every day of the week."

I flinch. *Too close to the truth.*

A bell chimes outside, and Ferra curses and gathers up the dress. "Quickly, now. We have something else to show you before they begin serving supper in the great hall, and everyone loses their minds. War breeds hunger, you know."

Between Ferra and Suri, we manage to scrub away most of the travel grime, and Suri washes my hair and weaves it into an Immortal Crown with her deft fingers. Ferra spends the time buttoning the hundreds of buttons on the dress's back.

"No wonder no one got anything done in ancient times," she mutters. "All they did was push buttons through button holes. There. Finished. Now—look at yourself."

She spins me toward the mirror with a proud tilt of her head, an artist admiring their work.

But as she stares into the mirror, her eyes narrow slightly. "Gods, Sabine, it looks like you just emerged from a soak in milk and honey, not days on the road. You don't have so much as a blemish. In all my days of beautysculpting, I've never come across a woman who doesn't need a single little tweak. You were always beautiful, but now...well, what have they been feeding you in Volkany?"

She lifts a teasing corner of her mouth, but her eyes don't jest, and I quickly look away from her reflection.

She can tell I'm different.

I smooth my hands down the long sleeves; grateful the dress hides most of my fey lines.

Just in case I slip and drop my glamour.

I clear my throat. "What was it you were so anxious to show me?"

"Oh!" Suri says. "Come. Quietly. We have it trapped in the Castlekeep's office."

"It..." I repeat. "...trapped?"

Ferra throws open the door, peering down the hallway before signaling to us. We pass a few guards, but they seem too distracted by the dinner bell to pay us much attention.

Suri leads the way through locked servant passages, her

official keyring jangling, and we climb a level and then come out on a higher floor. The word MERCY is inlaid in mosaic ceramic tiles in the floor.

"Like all the ancient fae castles," she explains, motioning to the mosaic, "Hekkelveld Castle is shaped like a star. The towers at each of the five points are named after human values. This is Mercy Tower. The others are Charity, Wisdom, Honor, and Faith. Though you'd be hard-pressed to find much of those values in Old Coros right now. At least, not beyond the castle gates, where the Sentinels are turning the streets to ruin."

"In Drahallen Hall..." I start, my throat tightening at the memory. "The five towers are named after ancient monoceroses, and they're built like long, thin wings that stretch out to form the star's points."

Suri throws me a concerned look over her shoulder. "It must have been so terrible for you there."

"Oh, actually—" I stop myself from contradicting her, from telling her about the beautiful gardens, the incredible fae wildlife, the sinfully decadent parties. Instead, I swallow back so much I want to say to them and nod.

We reach a stately wooden door that Suri unlocks with one of the jangling keys. She opens it into a small office, packed with boxes and overflowing stacks of papers. Books line one of the walls. Unruly stacks of papers and scrolls cover the desk.

"The previous Castlekeep kept terrible records." Suri indicates the piles. "It's been absolute chaos trying to sort it all out. But anyway, this is what we wanted to show you."

She stops at a wooden trunk that's secured with a heavy iron padlock. Suspicious air holes are drilled in the side.

My fey lines shiver beneath my skin, cold and insistent. I

clamp a hand over one velvet sleeve, tugging the cuffs further down.

Suri unlocks the trunk, one lip nervously pinned between her lips. She glances at Ferra. "Ready?"

To my surprise, Ferra has produced a butterfly net from somewhere and now brandishes it like a weapon. "Ready."

Everything is happening so fast that I can only sputter for them to wait, to explain everything to me first, but Suri's already opening the lid.

I brace myself against whatever's inside that trunk, thinking of Beneveto's terrible, hungry corpse staggering out of Tòrr's cage.

"Wait—" I start, too late, taking a step back as my heart shoots into my throat.

A puffy head pops out of the trunk.

Its fur is a glossy silver blue. Its purple tongue lolls to one side as it happily pants.

"Plume?" I cry in surprise. "Plume!"

Both Suri and Ferra whip around at my voice.

Yes it is Plume! Plume cries happily.

"Wait," Ferra says, still holding the net at the ready should the cloudfox try to escape. "Do you *know* this creature?"

"Yes! Her name is Plume. She..." I trail off. Oof, where do I start with my history with the mischievous cloudfox? I settle for a half-truth. "She's a friend I made in Volkany."

Suri slumps into a chair and rubs her temples. "Oh. This changes everything. Ferra and I found her snooping around the Reliquary Garden the day before yesterday. We thought she must be a spy, sent by your father."

"Hell of a hard time capturing her," Ferra adds, wrinkling her nose at the cloudfox, who pauses to wrinkle *her* snout back.

I drop to my knees and pet Plume's cloud-like fur, soft as cotton tuffs, with a dampness like fog. Something tightens in my chest. Not pain—just the pull of home.

Of Volkany.

"We didn't want Lord Kendan or the generals to know about her yet," Suri explains. "We were afraid they'd torture her, and we knew you were coming, so we thought we'd trap her and let you interrogate her instead."

Plume pants happily as she rubs against my palm, begging for pets.

I laugh. A real laugh, as I bury my face in her soft fur.

These are my friends, I tell Plume. ***I'm sorry about the trunk. They thought you were a spy.***

Yes! Plume yips excitedly. ***Yes, Plume is spy!***

My grin falls. ***Wait—you were sent here to spy on me?***

She yips again.

I run my hand over my Immortal Crown braid, needing the grounding drag of my nails against my scalp. To Ferra and Suri, I explain, "She says...well, I need to talk to her more. I'm confused."

Ferra and Suri watch in rapture. Ferra passes Suri a bag of roasted nuts.

I ask Plume, ***Tell me exactly why my father sent you to—***

The fae king did not send Plume! Plume chuckles as though I'm simple-minded. ***The fire horse told Plume to fly ahead to this castle and watch girlie.***

I nearly lose my balance and have to grip the edge of the trunk to hold myself steady. ***You mean...Tòrr? Tòrr sent you?***

She nods eagerly.

But why?

Plume leaps out of the trunk, spinning a restless corkscrew in the air, happy to stretch her furry legs.

Silly girlie. To spy, as Plume told you! To make sure girlie speaks for the quiet ones—the ones with fur and feathers. They can't hold weapons or trot into castles. They can only watch big boots start marching and wonder if anyone will think of them.

I slowly sink back on my heels.

It hits me, what she means, and why Tòrr sent her.

Gods, what an ass I've been.

I've been so focused on the throne—the clash between Rian and the opposition, the game of politics, of human loyalties. So caught up in the rising tension between the fae in Volkany and the humans in Astagnon. I keep telling myself I'm doing this to save lives.

But until now, that's only been *certain* lives.

Human lives.

In the fog of the Gloaming, I forgot who I'm meant to protect most of all. The natural world stands to lose everything, and I've let it slip from my mind. Me, Goddess of Nature, of creatures that creep and crawl. I've been training so hard to use my power to help the river valley refugees. The *humans* who are suffering. I've neglected the animals who call that same poisoned valley home.

Despite everything, I've still been looking at the world with human eyes.

Loving with a human heart.

Worrying about human problems.

I lift my head slowly and let out a deep exhale that stretches all the way to my belly.

Plume, I promise you, I won't forget the animals, I vow. ***Fae and mortal ones alike. Not the spiders. Not the snapping turtles. Not the earthworms. Tòrr didn't need to send a spy, but I'm glad he did. It reminded me of what's most important.***

Plume bounds from the gilded mirror to the windowsill, far more interested in exploring the furniture than my vow. ***Okay, whatever!***

But the vow sits heavy with me.

My back bows over beneath the weight of it all. Everything that pulls me in opposite directions.

Fae.

Humanity.

Animals—the ones I never should have forgotten about, the ones who have always stood at my back when humans failed me.

"What did she say?" Suri sees the tears in my eyes and drops down, wrapping an arm around my back.

Ferra looks in distaste at the cold, bare floor, but drags over a stool next to where I'm slumped and sits.

I blink hard, fighting back tears I'm afraid will come out silver.

I can't hold this in any longer.

"The rumors...about the risen fae...are true," I manage to choke out between sobs.

Ferra clutches her silver locket, sucking in a breath. "You mean Immortal Iyre?"

"Iyre, yes." I wipe at my eyes. "Basten wasn't lying about seeing her. But there are others in Volkany. Other fae."

Suri leans in, her lips trembling as she whispers, "You saw them?"

I nod, lips pressed tightly, afraid of the truth tumbling

out. "Samaur. Woudix. Artain—gods, he's an *asshole*. And Vale..." I sniffle, wiping my nose, and it comes away with a streak of silver. Luckily, I'm able to wipe it on a fold of my dress. "Vale is...King Rachillon."

A heavy silence follows, broken only by Plume's silly, rasping panting.

Ferra says slowly, "But King Rachillon is your father."

"Yes. Yes. Yes—that's right. You see, fae don't sleep for thousands of years in underground tombs, like we were led to believe. They lie dormant in bloodlines, waiting for the right generation to reawaken from their human hosts. Rachillon is Vale. And I'm—"

Their eyes widen, horror blooming.

I don't finish. I don't need to.

Instead, I turn my hand over, and the silver tears spill from my palm—slow, shimmering, unmistakable.

Fae.

CHAPTER 16

BASTEN

"**W**hat the *fuck* are you doing alive?" I bark at Matron White, all of us packed so tightly in the vestibule I can smell everyone's breakfast on their breath. "I watched you *die*."

Folke and Kendan both jolt in surprise. I don't know what Matron White told them about what happened in Bremcote, but apparently, she left out some key details.

Did she tell them Sabine is fae?

She pins her judgmental eyes on me as she touches the key emblem dangling from a gold chain around her neck.

"By the blessing of Immortal Iyre," she says. "I fell into the earth—right into our cellar, where my fall was broken by burlap apple sacks." Her lips purse. "I got my share of burns while getting out, but at least I *got* out. I cannot say the same for any of the others."

Kendan rests a hand on his forehead. "Anyone care to explain what you're talking about?"

Matron White slides me a smug smile. "Do you want to tell them, or shall I?"

I groan inwardly, shifting my weight from one foot to the other to buy time. After the shock of seeing the old bitch alive, my first concerns go to Sabine.

I heard her footsteps on the castle's second floor. Is she okay? What is she going to do when she learns of *this*?

"What did the Matron tell you?" I ask Kendan.

He exchanges a look with Folke, both of them wary. Slowly, Kendan explains, "She showed up here just a few hours before you did. She said there had been a fire at the Convent of Immortal Iyre."

"That's it?" I ask, keeping my eyes firmly on the Matron. "Nothing about Sabine?"

My heart slams behind my ribs. In a few words, the Matron could ruin everything. She knows how dangerous Sabine is. How unpredictable.

The Matron smiles thinly at me. "I've been eagerly looking forward to sharing the miraculous news."

I narrow my eyes, not trusting her for a second.

"Miraculous?" Folke echoes.

Her wrinkled cheeks pull into a wide smile as she lifts her hands toward the heavens in reverence. "Immortal Solene has risen, and it is my great honor to spread the joyous news. All this time, she slept within the convent's young ward, right under our roof!"

Folke chokes on a breath, coughing. He pulls out his flask and takes a sip. "Wait. Your ward? You mean *Sabine*?"

He whips his head around to me.

Slowly, still tense as an iron spring, I nod.

Folke spits his whisky back into the flask and fumbles to screw back on the lid. "Fuck!"

"Oh," Kendan says, looking stunned. "*Oh*."

"We weren't planning on telling everyone just yet," I mutter in Matron White's direction through clamped teeth.

I'm still waiting for her to reveal that Sabine burned the convent and killed every Sister inside.

Tried to kill the Matron, too.

But the old hag just keeps her hands raised in that annoying fucking reverential pose.

Lord Kendan hasn't said a word. I can't read how he's taking this news in his heart's beat. It's faster than usual, but not the rat-a-tat of fear. More like...intrigue.

I sigh. *I guess the jig is up.*

"There are six woken fae in Volkany," I explain. "King Rachillon is Vale. He stabbed Sabine with a knife, and she came back as Immortal Solene. But she's still Sabine," I snap defensively. "She's both. The goddess and the girl. She can glamour herself so she looks human. And she's the only one of the gods with any semblance of morality. Iyre included."

The Matron ignores my slander of her patron goddess as she clasps her key charm again.

Folke taps me on the shoulder, urgently, and jerks his head toward the corner.

I join him there, still wary to take my eyes off the Matron for a second.

"It's true?" he asks, voice hot and urgent.

I nod.

Folke's eyes go wide as he strokes his beard, muttering an unrepeatable word of awe. He leans in close and drops his voice. "What's it like, eh? In bed? Sleeping with a goddess? Hot as fuck?"

I groan, throwing him a look to see if he's serious that's the first place his brain went.

He wiggles his eyebrows insistently.

"Folke. You're an ass." I pause, drop my voice, too. "But yes."

He grins, white teeth gleaming, and slowly nods as though he knew it all along. He offers me a swig of the whisky, but I roll my eyes and head back to the others.

"This news," Kendan says in a measured, thoughtful voice. "Could be exactly what we need."

"What?" I snap.

Matron White nods eagerly, ignoring me. "Indeed, Lord Kendan. My thoughts went to the same place. We can use Solene's powers to retake the city from King Rian's forces. There are already rumors that the fae have risen. Thousands flock to our churches daily; we can easily whisper in a few ears that Sabine was loyal all along. That in fact, she is Solene, Guardian of Nature, sent to protect our kingdom with brimfire."

The thrill in her voice makes me finally understand why she isn't outing Sabine for murdering her own fellow nuns.

And why she's ready to praise the woman she once abused.

Matron White cares about power more than vengeance.

It turns my stomach, her gluttony for control dressed up as piety. But...at least I can trust her ambitions.

Kendan starts counting off on his fingers as though already making plans. "We'll meet with the rest of the opposition and strategize about how to use this news to our advantage. If we play our cards correctly, we can bring every priest, Sister, and congregant to bow at Sabine's feet."

"Whoa. Slow the fuck down." I throw out my hands like I'm herding cats. "Sabine's powers are still unpredictable." I give Matron White a pointed look. She should know the truth of that statement as much as anyone. "She's still learning. Better to introduce her true nature to the public gradually. A spotlight could stir her fey in dangerous ways."

Kendan nods. "We'll need to meet with her straightaway."

"Not this old bitch." I jab my thumb in Matron White's direction. Her right eye twitches with irritation, but she keeps her mouth shut. "Keep her the hell out of Sabine's sight. If Sabine knows she's in Old Coros, she might just bury the entire city. I'll figure out how and when to tell Sabine."

Matron White bows her head, obedient—for now.

But I see it in her eyes. She's already calculating her next move.

And I'm running out of time.

CHAPTER 17
SABINE

Midday sunlight spills through the bedroom window to light up the mauve folds of my coronation gown. The buttons are all fastened, all three hundred of them. My hair has been styled by the kingdom's finest beauticians. I've been scrubbed down to my toes.

We've barely been in Astagnon three days, and already, we're about to call ourselves its rulers.

The Valor Bell chimes in the distance, and I count the gongs.

"Eleven," I say as I turn to Basten. "One more hour as commoners."

Basten leans on our bedroom's large table, dressed in a shirt embroidered with deer antlers, as he fumbles with golden cufflinks. Without meeting my eyes, he murmurs, "Darling, there's never been anything common about you."

I take pity on him and help him with the cufflinks, then smooth my hands over his shirt's antler embroidery. Already, it's become the symbol of his reign. We have Ferra to thank for the inspiration; she latched onto the interlocking antler pattern immediately and promptly ordered new banners to be sewn, as well as for the symbol to be hastily stitched onto every royal soldier's shirt, and the emblem to be painted on the castle gates.

Basten plucks at his belt, unfastening and fastening it again.

"Are you well?" I ask, picking up on his uncharacteristic tics. "Don't tell me the bold Basten Bowborn, who faced down a goldenclaw, is nervous."

He combs his fingers through his hair, messing up the style Ferra spent an hour on, and frowns down at the table.

The surface is inked as a map of Astagnon, from the Mag Na Tir Forest to the Panopis Coast. An iconic table. One of a kind, transported here from Sorsha Hall at Rian's command.

For his new bedroom—our bedroom now.

It's strange, settling into a space where Rian once lived. The room bears all the marks of him everywhere we look. The enormous bed dressed in black silk sheets—Rian's favorite color. The heavy oak furnishings still bear the Valvere coin emblem. Even the sideboard is stocked with his favorite brand of whisky.

He was only here for a few months—but his ghost is everywhere. I swear that, at times, I can even smell his incense.

"Nervous?" Basten says, still not quite meeting my eyes. "No. I was nervous when we were married, afraid you'd turn me down. This is a piece of cake. You know I just bristle at all the decorum."

I give him a sympathetic smile. "You're going to have to get used to it. We both are."

I go to the window, peering down anxiously at the

courtyard. The castle gates are quiet now, but I know that the Golden Sentinels camped out on the other side might stage another attack at any moment.

"What are people in town saying about today?" I can't keep the squeak out of my voice.

He pauses, listening, and then clears his throat. "Nothing for you to worry about. Folke's been spreading rumors that all that talk about you being a traitor was spread by Rian. That Rian wanted to discredit you."

"And it's working?" I press. "People believe it?"

He hesitates. "Some do."

My meager bravery shrivels. There's something odd about the way he's holding back, only giving me partial truths.

"What aren't you telling me?" I ask.

Basten finally settles on a belt hole and secures it, saying breezily, "What? Nothing." Then, he glances at Rian's brass clock on the mantelpiece. "The guards will be here soon to get us—are you ready?"

I study him for a few moments, trying to figure out what's going through his head. There's something he isn't telling me. At the same time, I don't want to press too hard. Because it could open up the fact that *I'm* hiding something from *him*, too: Woudix's secret visit in the woods.

I turn back to the window, and a different type of fear spreads up my throat, bitter and tangy. "Today the people are going to crown me as their queen—and I'm lying to them. I'm not even one of them. Not human."

"Hey." Basten takes my hands, then steps back to take me in, wearing the coronation gown. His voice is low and steady. "Look at you. If there's a lie here, I can't find it. From where I stand, you are every bit a queen." His thumb brushes my knuckles. "Fae, human, all that matters is where your heart lies."

A swell of love for him—tangled up with my own hopes and insecurities—bubbles up around my heart. I squeeze his hands, looking down at my wedding ring.

"I can do this." My voice hitches at the same time that my fae blood burns, wanting release. "As long as you're at my side."

He leans in to kiss my forehead, and there isn't a trace of deception now. "Always."

We've barely broken apart before a knock comes at the door. We follow the royal guards through the castle and into the Reliquary Garden. Hekkelveld's layout is the inverse of the one at Drahallen Hall—the gardens here are within the main castle's star-like wings, not outside of them. Which means the gardens are smaller, more intimate, but today the Reliquary Garden is packed to within an inch of its life.

As far as I can tell, most of the attendees are castle staff and advisors, by necessity. The city is at war, so citizens of Old Coros can hardly stroll through the barricaded castle gates to witness the ceremony. But I spot heralds posted high atop the castle walls, ready with flags to alert the city to their new king and queen.

Basten holds my hand with a firm grip—sturdy as stone —as he leads me down the pathway toward a makeshift dais that has been erected by the Wall of Remembrance, where murals of the great kings are etched in white marble.

Maybe a graveyard isn't the most romantic place for a ceremony, but then again, this isn't our wedding. Our wedding was perfect in its simplicity: The birches. The forest mouse. The deer bowing before us.

This coronation? This is deserving of all the weight and gravity of centuries of rulers before us.

The attendees gathered between the headstones crane their necks, eager to see every second. This many eyes on me make me want to shrink into myself. Hide behind the heavy gown. Two elderly men in the front row—old generals—whisper among themselves, eyes locked distrustfully on me.

The crowd shifts and murmurs. I don't need Basten's hearing to pick up on my name whispered from one person to another, and it feels like a flock of crows takes off in my stomach. All fluttering wings, sharp caws.

Are they whispering that I'm a traitor?

Calling for my arrest?

Or have Folke's whispered rumors worked?

Out of the corner of my eye, I glance at Basten, searching his face, aching to know what his godkissed senses are picking up in the crowd's murmurs. His jaw is tight, his freshly shaven face grave—the weight of what this day means for him carved into every line.

After all, when the sun sets, he'll be a king.

Everything will change.

And yet—even standing beside his own crown—his eyes keep coming back to me like I'm the only thing that matters.

And, gods, nothing in this world could ever matter more to me than him.

Ahead of us, Kendan stands on the dais behind a podium that is draped in a banner with Basten's antler crest, looking official in his Lord of the Iron Banner chainmail sash. On two velvet pillows beside him rest the king and queen's crowns.

The larger of the two is forged black steel, intricately shaped like a wreath of raven feathers. The smaller—*mine*—

is a circlet made from a single, thin steel feather, dipped in gold at the tips.

I'm so fixated on the crowns that it takes me a moment to notice, from the corner of my eye, bright red robes among the crowd.

A dozen Red Church priests and Sisters stand on either of the dais's sides, like a gauntlet I'll have to pass through to earn my prize.

My feet stumble to a stop.

"What—what are they doing here?" I whisper in Basten's ear.

"We need the support of the Red Church," he reminds me, low and quick.

Basten might have a point, but the fae in me doesn't want to hear it. The silver energy beneath my skin pulses with anger, wanting to be let loose. Sure, these aren't the *same* Sisters who locked me in the convent's cellar for days on end with nothing but brackish water to drink. And yet these Sisters, here and now, wear the same familiar red robes, severe Immortal Crown braids, and deep frown lines edging their lips.

Are they really any different?

In fact, that last Sister on the left, the one with a bandage on her neck, could be the spitting image of Matron White.

In fact, it's unnerving, the similarities. Every step closer, I keep waiting to see a different chin, green eyes instead of blue.

When we're ten feet away, my feet stop dead.

It's...*her.*

It *is* Matron White.

I lurch backward, heart fumbling wildly in my chest. *She shouldn't be here. She shouldn't be more than ash!*

I gasp, clutching my chest, so stunned I feel frozen.

Basten suddenly curses under his breath, and turns sharply to face Kendan, voice a low growl. "She wasn't supposed to be here!"

Kendan shifts his weight, anxious not to ruffle feathers on such an important day. He mutters quietly, "It was a last-minute decision. We knew you wouldn't support it, but you'll see that her presence is necessary."

"Wait." I grab Basten's shoulders, fingers digging in like claws. "You *knew* Matron White was alive?"

He winces, turns to me with soft eyes and starts to explain, "Sabine—"

But Matron White steps forward, stealing the attention, and falls dramatically to her knees at my feet.

Her head bows, her hands reach up beseechingly, her eyes roll back in her head as though she's prophesizing. "I sense it...a change in the air...divinity itself walks amongst us...this woman, she is not mortal! She is greater even than a queen. She is fae! She is a goddess! She is...*Solene!*"

The crowd stirs, voices rising in confusion.

Basten tenses, his fingers coiling into a fist, and mutters low and angry, "You scheming bitch."

I look around me, disoriented. As confused as the audience. Only gradually do I realize what's happened. Kendan and the others have set me up. Thrust me on a stage and neglected to tell me I have the pivotal role.

The silver fey flares under my skin, demanding to be unleashed. To put this hateful woman in the grave for good this time.

"Show us!" Matron White beseeches. "Show us your power, O Immortal One!"

"You think I'll perform for you?" I hiss at her, as if we're the only people in the garden. "You locked me away. You made me beg for sunlight."

She suddenly starts shaking as if seized by a holy spirit—never mind that I've seen this act a thousand times. Every Sunday in the convent's nave, when she pretended to be moved by Iyre's favor.

It takes me straight back there.

A little girl.

All alone.

Beaten and neglected for years.

Fey stutters in my veins, pushing and urging, until I can't hold it back. I start to raise my hands.

"Sabine," Basten whispers a low warning, but I ignore him.

"You want everyone to see what I can do?" I hiss to Matron White. "I'll show them. I'll finish what I started."

My power aches to melt the smile from her face and reduce her, once and for all, to ashes.

Sparks crackle at my fingertips. The crowd gasps as my glamour falls away, revealing my shimmering fey lines.

"It's true!" someone cries.

"She's really her—look, she's Solene!" another person calls.

I aim my fury at Matron White, ready to make brimfire erupt from the hem of her robes, when movement in the crowd catches my eye.

A few rows behind Matron White, a young maid, barely even twelve years old, lifts her hands. Her fingers are folded into the symbol of the Winged Lady. Her wide eyes brim with hope.

My fey stutters.

All of a sudden, my rage falls away, and I realize I'm about to kill a woman in front of the very people who are meant to follow me.

My chest heaves—I can't kill her. Not here. Not like this. And, dammit, *she knows it.*

I force my attention off her smug hint of a smile and to the little maid. My rage softens at the edges, and I lift my hands skyward.

I shoot out fey toward the dark clouds. They part at my command, letting the sun pour down. From the trees come white doves, marigold petals clutched in their beaks. They scatter blossoms over the crowd like the day I got married.

The crowd gasps. Cheers swell.

My pulse hammers. I feel the weight of hundreds of eyes scrutinizing me, evaluating me, inspecting me, fearing me, adoring me.

This is exactly what I didn't want. *To lose control of my own story.*

Kendan motions to the low benches on the dais expectantly.

I only stare, still flooded by so much attention and conflicting feelings, until Basten gently takes my hand.

"Together," he whispers. "We'll get through this—I'm here for you, always."

I turn my wide eyes on him, clutch his arm harder, and finally let out a tight breath.

"Before gods and men," Kendan announces, lifting his hands heavenward. "Today marks the change from one reign to another. One Astagnon to another. We come together not in a time of peace, but peril. Our city bleeds. Its people tremble. And yet, a bold new hope for our future has risen!"

My face feels hot as I gather the antique gown's heavy skirt and, holding Basten's arm for support, lower to my knees on one of the low benches. He does the same, and side by side, we stare out at the crowd.

It feels so vulnerable, like this. On my knees. The cold late fall air on my bare neck. The truth about my fae nature revealed now to everyone.

Kendan continues, "We place upon you, Lord Basten, a crown of crow feathers, the ancient symbol of wisdom and justice. Not as a reward, but as a charge. To protect this great kingdom against all enemies, human and immortal."

Kendan signals to Matron White, who lifts the crow-feather crown from the velvet pillow and lowers it ceremonially over Basten's head.

Kendan pronounces, "From this day forth, you shall be known as King Basten Valvere of Astagnon."

Applause erupts throughout the Reliquary Garden with enough force to make the headstones tremble. Tears glisten in elderly maids' eyes as they clasp hands with one another. The heralds posted on the castle walls raise their flags.

For a moment, I forget to breathe—then Kendan lowers his hands to signal to the crowd to quiet.

In that silence, all my worry creeps back into me.

"And now, we place upon you, Lady Sabine, our Goddess of Nature, Immortal Solene, the crown of the feather of truth." Kendan signals to Matron White again, who holds the crown over my Immortal Crown braid. "Henceforth, may you shield this kingdom against its darkest enemies.

Let us crown our new regent, Queen Sabine Valvere of Astagnon."

Matron White lowers the crown on my head. Her movements are perfectly reverential, but I don't believe her act for a second—it's impossible to know if she supports me or not, if she sees me as a traitor or a true savior.

I hold my breath, staring out at the audience.

"The Winged Lady!" A young man cries.

The Winged Lady symbol spreads like wildfire, until I'm gazing out at dozens of lifted hands in my honor. My chest aches with relief, with gratitude.

Sure, not everyone in the audience seems pleased— there are the old generals still scowling, a troop of soldiers who remain stony-faced. But still. It's enough.

They accept me—as I truly am.

Basten takes my hand in his, his bright eyes more adoring than the stars themselves.

A sea of Winged Lady gestures flutters below me. I feel it —the weight of their trust in me.

And I think to myself: *I can do this.*

Matron White leans close to fasten the crown on my head with a brass pin, and whispers in my ear, "I still own you, girl. Fae or not."

I don't look at her. I look past her—to the young maid with the Winged Lady gesture marveling up at the falling petals.

I may be the one kneeling now—but soon enough, Matron White is going to bow to *me*.

CHAPTER 18
BASTEN

Gods, if Sabine could only hear what I can.

As Sabine and I make our way back through the Reliquary Garden, bowing and accepting adoring prayers to her, my ears fill with hushed, awe-filled whispers that stretch back all the way to the outer wall.

Word is spreading through town. *Immortal Solene has risen to save Old Coros from the Cold Coins.*

We reach a line of gray-haired advisors waiting to touch our foreheads in blessing. I have to grit my teeth and remind myself to wipe the impatient scowl off my face.

Kendan is going to hear an earful for this stunt. Forcing Sabine to reveal her fae nature is an asshole move—even though, I begrudgingly have to admit, it *worked*.

Still, Sabine's fey glows in uneven bursts—she's so damn overcome that I'm afraid she's going to break apart at the seams, burn every person's eyes with her silver light.

I'm desperate for a second alone together. I'm her acolyte—her protector. She's worried she's going to hurt me, but the need to check on *her* burns through me.

"Congratulations to our Queen and Goddess," a stiff advisor cuts in, eyes flashing like a fox's. "We are eager to discuss potential negotiations with your father, King Rachillon. If we were able to get our hands on that monoceros..."

"We will speak soon enough." She smiles tightly, cutting him off. It's more of a grimace, really, and I lay a protective hand on the small of her back.

I say, "Of course, Lord Blakely. We look forward to long, productive meetings with you...at another time."

More well-wishers press in, anxious to lay hands on us like we're blessed statues, and my own heartbeat starts to hammer.

Damn, these stiff clothes. *I* wasn't even the primary one thrust in the spotlight, but the seams poke at me in all the wrong places. I wish I could rip them off, go back to my loose hunting garb.

"We are graced with your presence, Lady Solene!" an elderly cook proclaims, stepping forward with the kitchen staff.

Sabine stiffens under the sudden attention.

I smile disarmingly while I lock hands with Sabine and form a barreling ram with my other arm to push us through the crowd as politely as I can.

"Yes, yes," I murmur through clenched molars. "Such an honor...she's a marvel...will work hard to serve the kingdom..."

Women surge toward Sabine, reaching to touch her gown like it's spun from legend. They press in so closely that I'm forced to tighten my grip on her hand just to keep her near.

On the other side, advisors close in around me, voices clashing, each trying to claim a piece of my attention.

Then, in a blink, the crowd shoves between us—my fingers slip—and she's gone.

Swallowed whole.

Her wide eyes find mine one last time through the crush, a silent plea hovering there—before the tide takes her.

"Enough," I grunt. "Fuck it."

I barrel my way through the crush of bodies like a beast. Gasps ripple as I reach her and, wordlessly, scoop her into my arms, lifting her right over my shoulder like a sack of flour.

Regal? No. Effective? Absolutely.

She yelps, but her arms loop around my neck on instinct.

Hell, let everyone gawk and stare. If they want her, they'll have to go through me, first.

"Basten!" Sabine cries, clamping a hand onto her crown to keep it from falling off. "What are you doing?"

"I'm getting you out of here, wildcat," I murmur, adjusting her on my shoulder.

I've shocked the crowd enough by manhandling a goddess that it's easy to push through now. Gaping sentries scramble to open the castle doors for us, and I stride right past shocked staff up the stairs and don't stop until I've plunked her down on the royal bed.

Gods—it reeks of sandalwood in here. Rian's signature scent. No doubt the maids wanted to ensure our marital bedroom was appealing, but they really shouldn't have.

If Sabine's between the covers, that's all I need.

"Your pulse was skyrocketing," I say. "I had to get you out of there before you opened the earth and swallowed everyone whole."

I tug at my stiff collar, practically growling at the uncomfortable fabric.

She bounces on the mattress, pupils blown, lips trembling, fey flaring across her temples. Her crown tumbles onto the black satin sheets.

"Basten," she breathes, as she runs her hands over her arms, throwing back up her human glamour. "Matron White...what was that?"

I sink next to her, immediately protective, and scrub my hands over my face. "I didn't know she'd be there—I swear it. The day we arrived, Kendan revealed to me that the Matron had survived the fire, and she convinced me that we need her to get the Red Church on our side. But I swear to you, I didn't want you to find out like this."

Sabine looks down at her hands, at the fey that is only now starting to steady. I'm afraid she'll claw me with harsh words for the lie—but then she seems to soften.

"You should have told me," she says, still looking down. "But I understand as well as anyone that there are..." she hesitates, "...reasons to keep secrets."

Secrets? Is she keeping some of her own?

But her look grows more contemplative as she runs her fingers over the silk sheets, and the moment shifts. "It's strange, isn't it? Being in Rian's bed?"

I groan, at least relieved to move on from the topic of Matron White. "That's the last thing I want to think about."

She frowns at how I'm plucking at my clothes, then pushes up to her knees on the bed. "Stop that, you're only going to rip out the buttons, and Ferra will scold you ceaselessly for it. Let me undo them for you."

I surrender to her small fingers, which deftly free me from the restrictive clothing. As soon as I can, I shrug out of the shirt and scratch all the places on my chest where it itched me nearly to death.

She smiles in amusement, unable to stop herself, which breaks the heaviness between us. "You're like an itchy old dog."

"Guilty," I bark.

She winces as she pulls a pin from her hair. "Men have no room to complain. You have no idea how uncomfortable women's clothing is. And this antique gown? It might as well have been cobbled together from granite and wood."

My voice drops. "Then, I guess we'd better strip you, too."

I reach for her sleeve, pushing my luck.

She sees the glint in my eye and shimmies away, slapping at my hand. "This gown is a thousand years old. Ferra will want to spend an hour carefully getting me out of it."

I rub my chin, not liking the sound of that. The day has been torture. Waiting, waiting, smiling, waiting.

"We have a fleet of seamstresses. They can mend it."

I grab the heavy brocade skirt and drag her to the foot of the bed. She feigns affront but can't hide her laughter. I spin her around, pressing her belly down into the mattress, as I tear at the buttons down the dress's back.

With every peek of creamy skin underneath, my blood runs hotter.

Gods, I need this.

So does she.

Once I shuck the gown off her, she's left in a thin slip that leaves little to the imagination. "Stay there," I order. "Don't move an inch. I want to fuck you in this crown."

I scoop up her circlet, climb onto the bed, and rest it back on her messy braid.

She looks back at me, over her shoulder, with sly eyes that do all kinds of wicked things to me. "I didn't think you cared about crowns."

"Riches are riches, little violet. And they look damn good on you."

She twists to be on her back, and I lean in to capture her lips with my own. She opens her mouth for me, soft lips teasing my own until I can feel my muscles stiffen with growing need. I fumble to get my belt off, shucking off my pants, and then crawl over to her. I bury my face in the crook of her neck.

"Damn," I growl. "Fucking incense is so thick I can't smell you."

I nuzzle against her shoulder, biting her skin lightly. I'm so used to perceiving her in every possible way. Sight, taste, touch. It kills me not to smell her scent beneath the sandalwood oil drenching every inch of furniture.

Something creaks in the big oak wardrobe, and I whip my head around, frowning—but Sabine pushes up to nibble on my jaw, and I forget day from night.

A moan rolls up my throat as I push her back down to the sheets. The crown slides off her head to clatter to the floor. She twists to pick it up, but I trap her wrist, guiding her back to the bed.

"You don't need it. You've always been a queen."

She gazes up at me with those ocean blue eyes, and with her braid worked halfway loose and wild, I think to myself that I could fuck her forever like this, damn the outside world.

"Not everyone was pleased today," she points out.

I grunt deep in my throat, dismissive. "A few old fossils who can't handle change and lack imagination. They'll grumble, but they won't stand in our way. I don't like how they went about it, but Kendan and Folke's plan worked. The tide's already turned toward you, little violet. All those people gazing at you as their savior."

She runs her finger down my jaw. "They were looking at *you*, too."

I look away. It's an uncomfortable truth, something I don't quite know what to do with. I've been so fixated on putting her on the pedestal she deserves that it feels really fucking strange to be up on one myself.

I capture her wrists and lift her arms over her head, interlacing our fingers, pinning her to the bed. Locking our gaze, I say in a low voice, "Together. Always."

She tilts her chin toward mine. "Together."

I claim another kiss, this one hungry and hot. I want to pour all my faith into her—because there's that small, nagging part of me that's worried we aren't in lockstep. That a crack between us is stretching more and more each day.

That we both have secrets.

Maybe if I kiss her hard enough, it will bridge the growing gap.

She moans, shifting her hips under me, and any worries about *gaps* vanishes. I roll my hips against her, so flush not a crack of daylight could shine between our bodies. Her breasts strain against her shift's thin fabric, teasing my chest.

Raw energy pulses beneath her skin, so cold it burns.

I break the kiss to drag my mouth down her long throat, licking and sucking along her buried fey line. "Let go, little violet. With me, you don't have to hide."

Her body shudders, and for a moment I think she'll show her true self to me again, but then she clenches her fists and shakes her head. "I want to do this together. As humans. Our first time as king and queen, like the first time we met."

I'm not sure how I feel about her holding back. How long she can pretend to be something she isn't. Especially now that the truth is out there.

Still, I slide her shift off her shoulder, replacing the fabric with my lips. Her skin is icy cold to the touch—the fey in her freezing both her veins and mine.

"Give me one minute," I say. "You're freezing."

She protests, but I climb off the bed and strike a match to light the massive fireplace, which the servants have already stacked with wood.

I get where she's coming from—a part of me wants to pretend, too. That we can be tethered forever, that the bond will never break.

As warmth rolls into the room from the growing fireplace, I climb back on top of her. I take a moment to stare down at her, so beautiful it hurts to look at, and gently move aside some of her tangled hair.

"My bride. My queen. My goddess."

She wraps a hand around the back of my neck, locking her gaze to mine. "My everything."

She leans up, and I lean in, and our lips crash together with a mix of warmth and cold, urgency and delicious patience. I reach down to slide her shift's hem up her hips, dragging my fingers over her bare thigh.

I murmur, "I want *your* scent."

Before she can protest, I move between her legs and pry her knees apart. She lets out a small, guttural cry, but we're far from the blushing virgin she once was. There will always be something innocent about her, but now that she knows her passion, has bent it to her will, my little violet can be wicked, too.

I bury my face in the warm core between her thighs and breathe in deeply.

Finally, I can smell the sweetness of her scent on her damp underwear. It's better than honey. Sweeter than violets. Like something I could lap at forever and never get my fill.

"Gods, you smell so much fucking better than incense," I groan.

I hook my fingers in her underwear and slide them down her knees, then shove them off her feet. Her quivering body is open to me, the shift shoved up around her waist. She's leaning up on her elbows, gazing at me with those hooded eyes that promise all kinds of tantalizing things.

"That's sacrilegious," she tuts, teasingly. "Incense is holy."

I grunt as I grip her ankles, wrenching her legs closer to me, and purr against her belly, "Then let the gods punish me. Starting with you."

I dive back in to devour her. I flick my tongue over her glistening clit, and when she gives the sweetest little buck in response, my muscles tighten in pride. I close my mouth over her hot center and suck gently, then reach around from behind and press a thumb into her core, teasing the outer folds while punishing her with my mouth.

"Basten," she gasps. "Oh, fuck. Don't stop."

I come up for air just long enough to murmur, "I had to get you to myself. All those damn diplomats vying for your attention, thinking they deserved a goddess—"

A muffled cough from the fireplace cuts off my words.

I freeze.

What. The. *Fuck.*

I whip my head around, my pulse suddenly pounding like a war hammer, brows pinned together.

I stare at the enormous fireplace; the ancient hearth with "VIRTUE" carved in the stone, the flames churning out a thin line of smoke.

Sabine sits up, sensing my alert, and blinks fast. "What is it?"

She didn't hear the cough.

I keep staring at the fireplace. Fuck, am I losing my mind? Or did I really hear a—

Hmph-kff!

It comes again. Undeniable this time. Something—or someone—shifts position in the fireplace, trying hard to be silent, but my huntsman instincts snap into place with razor-sharp precision.

"Don't move," I growl to Sabine.

I roll off the bed, bare-ass naked, reaching for the closest weapon I can lay a hand on—a wine bottle resting on the table. I grip it by the neck, ready to slam it into whatever person or animal has crawled in the fireplace.

My mind reels.

Could Kendan have double-crossed us, sent an assassin?

One of Rian's ever-loyal Golden Sentinels?

Or Vale?

"Basten." Sabine leans forward, a strange glow to her eyes. Once, she might have shied away from the hint of danger, pulled the cover up over her thin shift. But that girl has evolved. Now, she's the guardian of nature. More comfortable in her naked, natural body than in the most elegant gown. "What do you hear?"

I approach the fireplace in slow, measured steps. I hold a finger to my mouth, signaling for her to be quiet.

Yeah, it feels a bit ridiculous to be brandishing a bottle when she could burn our intruder with brimfire with a snap of her fingers—but blue ashes might be hard to explain to the maids.

I cock my head as I take another step closer. There's a rustle of fabric. Yep—something is in there. Hiding in the huge chimney. When I lit the fire, the smoke must have flushed it out.

I could wait for it to suffocate—but let's be real, patience isn't my greatest virtue.

I drop to my knees, reach into the fireplace, and latch my hand onto...a boot.

I give a sharp tug.

"Ow!" someone howls as they lose their grip on the inside chimney bricks and crash down. They fall in a jumble into the massive hearth, half in the fire and half out, a tangle of soot-stained clothes and flailing limbs.

I immediately grab them by wherever I can—the shoulder and thigh—and haul them bodily into the room.

"Ow, ow, ow!" the person wails. "I'm on fucking fire!"

I go still.

Gods, I know that voice.

I reel backward, letting go like I've been struck by lightning.

On the bed, Sabine claps a hand over her mouth to hold in her gasp.

Our intruder rolls back and forth on the rug to put out the fire chewing through his shirt sleeve, burning his flesh so that it smells like a fucking barbecue in here.

I don't help put out the flames.

I can't.

All I can do is stare...as Rian Valvere finally gets the fire extinguished, rolls over on his back, and looks up at me with a sheepish grin while a final wisp of smoke rises from his burned shirt and says, "Imagine the chances of us running into each other like this, Wolf."

CHAPTER 19
SABINE

I *must be dreaming.*

The past and present crash together in my head like a terrible orchestra with no sense of start or finish. This...this can't possibly be real. My breath jerks short. For a long, blinding moment, I don't know where I am. The bedroom, the flickering fire, the shape of our three figures—all of it blurs.

It's...him.

Rian.

Basten manages to shake off his surprise while I'm still gaping and speechless. Even though Basten is bare-ass naked, he towers over Rian and plants his bare foot heavily on Rian's chest, pinning him down.

"First of all," Basten growls, hunching forward to eclipse Rian. "It's Basten. *King* Basten. No one has dared to call me Wolf in months. And second of all, fuck you."

He raises the wine bottle in his hand to smash down on Rian's head, but Rian throws up his elbows to defend himself. His right arm is charred and weeping blood, the flesh oozing out wisps of smoke.

"Wait, dammit!" Rian cries. "Fuck, just let me explain!"

To his credit, Basten has the presence of mind to pause, the bottle held at the ready, but his rapidly rising and falling chest shows that his patience is strained. "What's there to explain? You've been hiding in our fireplace for gods-knows how long to kill us as soon as the crowns were on our heads."

Rian scoffs, trying to push up to his elbows, but then winces at the pain in his arm. "This was *my* bedroom long before it was yours." His face pales as his wounded arm oozes more blood, but he grits his molars and offers us both a scowl. "And secondly, kill you? With what, a piece of coal? Do I look like I have a crossbow shoved up my ass?"

Basten actually cranes his neck like there might very well be the backside of an arrow sticking out Rian's pants.

At Basten's silence, Rian huffs and twists around to face me. Two dice, carved from bone, roll out of his pocket.

"Sabine!" Rian begs, curled on his back like a helpless, wounded animal. "Songbird, tell him to be reasonable. It's all a misunderstanding. I thought it was best for you to be where you belonged."

I nearly laugh.

He can't be serious.

I bend down to pick up the dice.

Once a cheat, always a cheat, I think. I'm sure they're weighted, just like his Golath dime was.

I set the dice aside and head to the desk, where I snatch up Basten's hunting knife in its leather sheath.

"Use this." Now that I've found my voice, it's ruthless. I

toss the knife to Basten over the bed. "It'll hurt more than that bottle."

Basten catches it easily and flicks his thumb to pop open the snap to unsheathe it.

Rian's face pales another shade.

"Wait!" he cries, hands out defensively as he scrambles to slide away from Basten, but he can't roll onto his side with his damaged arm. "Fuck, Wolf— Basten, I mean— Are you really going to kill a man with your dick out?"

"Sure." Basten, unbothered, stalks toward him, but in that same instant, Rian's helpless act vanishes. Of course, it was always an act. There's never been anything helpless about Rian.

He manages to get his feet underneath him and shoves a knee in the air right into Basten's exposed groin.

Basten lets an ungodly curse rip as he drops the knife and doubles over, clutching his balls.

Rian rolls onto his left side and pushes to his feet, cradling his right arm to his chest, eyes flashing with that Valvere cunning.

He kicks the knife across the floor, out of Basten's reach.

While Basten is still doubled over, Rian and I both watch with held breaths to see where the knife stops—next to the map table.

We lock eyes.

I pull in a breath.

"Fuck," he says.

We both dive for the knife, scrambling across the room, but just as my fingers graze it, he kicks it under the bed. He drops to his knees, cursing at the pain in his burned arm, as he scrambles under the bed.

I reach to grab the knife, too, but Basten is by my side in a second, shaking his head.

"I've got this—I owe him a world of hurt." He grabs Rian's ankles and jerks him out from under the bed, while Rian twists and kicks like a tantruming toddler. Basten is barefoot but manages to get a solid kick to Rian's wounded side, and Rian yelps and curls inward.

"You gods-damned rat," Basten seethes. "We hear that you've fought your way nearly to Duren, but you've actually been holed up here the whole time? Hiding in your own damn bedroom fireplace?"

"You're king now…" Rian chokes out, eyes fluttering as he winces. "You'll see. They give you books of secrets…so many places to hide in the castle…"

Basten snatches him by the back of the collar and drags him to his feet, then throws him against the bed like a knap-sack. Rian collides with the edge of the mattress, gagging at the jolt of pain against his wound, but manages to catch himself and stagger to his feet.

I toss my hair back, holding my fists at my side.

"Coward," I spit, the word flung like a blade.

Rian turns toward me—fluid, practiced, almost theatri-cal. His eyes drag down the length of me, slow and deliber-ate, and for a breath I think it's just more of the same: that same insatiable look he always wore like a second skin. Cunning dressed up as lust.

But no.

This is different.

He isn't just looking. He's studying.

"Why?" he demands. "Because I stayed? Instead of turning tail and running?"

"The city is burning because of you!" Fury seizes me, and

I ball my fists, barely able to hold myself back from snatching up the nearest lantern and smashing it in his face.

Rian's head tilts, curiosity flickering in his eyes. His gaze darts—quick, precise—to my ears, then my brow. So fast, most wouldn't notice. But I do.

A spike of panic bolts through me. On impulse, I grab hold of the shell of my ear. Rounded. Human The glamour still holds.

And yet.

"Something's different about you, songbird." His voice is light, teasing—but his gaze pins me like an arrow. "Maybe being queen suits you."

It's the kind of line meant to disarm. But underneath the jest, there's calculation. I see the wheels turning behind his eyes.

Gods, he hasn't dulled an inch. He might even be *sharper* now. I'm speechless, struck by the powers of his perception. If I didn't know otherwise, I'd think he was godkissed. That he could see straight to my hidden self.

"Don't fucking look at her."

Basten's voice cracks like thunder, and before I can react, his fist is already halfway to Rian's face.

Rian ducks with a soldier's instinct, and then he charges at Basten, ramming his good shoulder into Basten's bare stomach.

It knocks the breath out of Basten, who staggers back a step before recovering and swiping for Rian, but he slips right by, as wily as ever.

Rian darts toward a heavy brass candlestick, but I track his intention and launch myself onto his back, wrapping my arms around his neck. I slide my arm flush to his throat, pulling as hard as I can to choke him from behind.

"Fuck, songbird." His strained voice wheezes as he tugs at my hands, trying to pry them off me. "There are better ways to say you missed me."

Something twists sharp and deep inside me—because damn him, *I did*. Miss him, I mean. Gods, is that crazy to think? Of course, I didn't miss the lies or the smirk or the thousand little manipulations. But I longed for some better version of him that might have existed, once.

Because there was a world where we could have been friends. Basten, Rian, and I. Gods, we were so close—right on the edge of something real.

And instead, he chose to play us both like a song.

I *hate* him for that.

So, I squeeze harder.

He wheels around and slams my back against the wall. Pain rockets through me. Dazed and aching, my limbs go slack. Rian slips out of my grasp, dancing backward to keep some space between us.

He massages his throat, rubbed red from my handprint, and spits out in a rasping voice, "If there's anyone you should hate, it's Basten. I gave you to him to protect. I trusted him. He fucking let us both down."

His words echo hard against the room's cold edges.

I can feel the energy in the room shift. Basten straightens, going deathly silent. The hair on my arms rise.

Rian, you idiot, I think.

With a cry, Basten hurtles into Rian, driving him backward into the map table. The sharp corner cracks against Rian's skull with a sickening thud. He shouts, dazed—but still fast. His knee shoots up toward Basten's groin. Basten twists just in time, catching the blow on his thigh.

Rian's hand flies to the table. He grabs a pewter tankard

and slams it into the side of Basten's head. It hits with a wet, hollow crack.

Basten collapses face-first to the floor, groaning as blood pours from the gash at his temple.

Rian stands over him, chest heaving, the tankard still clenched in his fist. His hair rises at sharp angles, eyes wide and glassy. His mouth twitches like he's about to laugh or scream—maybe both.

He looks feral. Half-starved. Completely unhinged.

Well, I understand why. He's been living in the walls, spying in silence for weeks—it's clearly scrambled something in him.

"I didn't want to do this, old friend," he mutters to Basten. "You're going to end up with a massive headache, but we both know you won't fucking stay down."

He starts to bring down the tankard again on Basten's head.

And my world stops.

Another part of me takes over.

The fey lines on my limbs blister open, spilling silver light across the dark bedroom. An otherworldly howl climbs out of my throat with enough force to make the chandelier quake. I feel my human glamour fall away like I've clawed through my skin, shed the lining. My sharpened incisors cut against my tongue.

That's what we gods are—*predators*.

Blinding light reflects in the mirrors, forcing Rian to shade his eyes. He's turned away, ragged breath shaking out of him, but manages to peek between his fingers.

"Oh. *Oh*. Well—this changes things," he murmurs in a daze.

I aim my palms toward his boots and blast out a bolt of fey.

His trouser cuffs catch with blue fire, which rapidly spreads up the fabric to lick at his already burned shirt. He scrambles backward, trying to pat out the brimfire with his one good hand.

He slams his back against the wall and rolls against the stones, but it does little to smother the flames.

A darkness rises in me. The predator closing in.

Suddenly, a wave of dark liquid splashes over Rian.

I blink, jolting out of my trance.

Basten pours the uncorked wine bottle over Rian's clothes, extinguishing the blue flames, soaking him in blood-red merlot.

Rian collapses against the wall, slumped and struggling for breath, looking barely human in his wrecked clothes and burned skin. I'm not sure how he's even still conscious.

He starts to sink to the floor slowly, but Basten grabs him by what's left of his shirt collar and jerks him up.

"You don't get the peace of a concussion," he growls.

Rian's eyes flutter, barely conscious. "Tell Sabine...that's a hell of a party trick."

As he coughs up phlegm, looking like a broken puppet with jumbled strings, the rage bleeds out of me.

My breath goes thin—I realize how close I came to killing him, and immediately throw my glamour back up, tugging on my ears until I feel them curve again.

My heart pounds hard, ashamed that I lost control. Then, I stumble over to where Basten has him up against the wall.

"What—what now?" I say breathlessly. "Do we kill him?"

"It's what he deserves," Basten vows, flashing his teeth. But then he lets out a long breath. "But we're king and queen now. We have to do this right. Let the tribunals rule on his heresy, first. *Then* we can laugh at the gallows."

I expect Rian to go white as limestone, but he only cackles instead. It turns into a cough. When he finally clears his throat, he cracks his eyes open—still some life in him.

"A fae?" Rian muses almost to himself, half-delirious. "I knew it. I mean...I didn't know it...but I *knew* it. Always knew there was more to you, songbird. Saw it the first time I laid eyes on you in that church nave. Let me guess... blue fire could be Thracia, but I'd bet my hand on Solene. No wonder the fucking birds worship you."

My throat goes tight as I shift from foot to foot, cold in only my shift.

Once again, Rian sees me better than anyone. In one look, he can read the most closed-off person in the room. So, it should be no surprise that he sees me—really *sees* me—in a way few others do.

"That's right," I say, holding my chin high. "And it wasn't wise for you, a mere human, to betray a goddess. You'd think a Valvere would know better."

"Ah, but I'm not a Valvere, isn't that the point?" He coughs again, wincing with every movement. "Basten wears the crown now. The kingdom has accepted him as their king. They've all turned their back on me—except the Golden Sentinels."

Delirious as he seems, his eyes shine with cunning.

Basten tightens his hold on Rian's collar, shoving him back harder against the wall. "Do your loyal Sentinels know you've been hiding here the whole time like a rat?"

Rian lifts one shoulder. "A rat, maybe, but one who could

end this city's war with a single word." His eyes shift to mine, a cocky grin sliding over his blood-stained face. "I've overheard all kinds of things the past few days, songbird. You don't want to work with Matron White? Fuck her. You *don't* need her. Let me go, and I'll call my generals off. Order a surrender. The city will be yours. All the devastation and bloodshed ended in a snap."

I stare at him, unblinking.

He's... He's... Gods, he's so cunning that I'd almost laugh if I didn't want to kill him so badly.

For a moment, the three of us, worn out, stare at one another, until finally, I turn away. "Let him go."

"What?" Basten's face twists.

"He's right," I mutter. "We need him."

Rian grins wider, and Basten groans so deep in his chest it sounds like distant thunder.

"Fine," Basten barks. "Here's our offer, asshole. You send a message through your little spy network to call your generals to surrender. No more Cold Coins pillaging the city. Once they're all arrested and the Sentinels have turned in their weapons, I won't break the neck off this wine bottle and stab it through your black heart."

Rian blinks, slow and unmoved. "That's touching, Basten. And my freedom?"

Basten tips back his head and laughs at Rian's gall. "Out of the question. You earn your life, not your freedom. Our offer won't last long. You have..." Basten glances at the mantelpiece clock. "...until midnight."

I don't need to look at the clock to know from the moon's light that Rian had better decide quickly.

As in, *really* quick.

In fact, in the next breath, the church clock outside chimes midnight.

Rian sighs, though it's broken by rattling coughs. "Fine," he relents. "Get me parchment and a quill."

Basten releases him and strides over to the desk.

Rian rubs his throat, eyes locking onto my wedding ring before snapping back up with a gleam, and murmurs wryly to me, "Basten swore a vow to me, too, you know. And look at us now."

CHAPTER 20
BASTEN

First order of business after discovering Rian Valvere is alive?

Get some damn pants on.

Second? Bind that asshole's hands behind his back, smiling in dark satisfaction when he chokes out a pained cry, and dragging his ass to the castle infirmary.

My preference would be to let his burns rot and fester—serves him right for being dumb enough to hide in a fucking chimney. But Sabine made the point that we can't let him succumb to his injuries before he's able to call off the Golden Sentinels.

We exchange some heated words over his fate late into the night, it's true. Hell, I even overheard the castle maids gossiping about us in the hallways. *All is not perfect between the king and queen*, they said.

Whatever. They don't fucking know us.

While I'm dragging Rian to the infirmary, Sabine goes to wake Kendan and summon the other opposition leaders to the meeting chamber, middle of the night be damned. She moves with certainty, purpose.

Me? I'm just trying not to show that my hands are shaking.

Seeing Rian again wrecked something in me. I hate him, sure, but it wasn't always that way. We were friends once. Almost brothers. We relied on each other in a brutal world that wanted to strip away our boyhood, forge us into unfeeling men.

He betrayed that trust...and yeah, I guess I betrayed his, too.

So now, with his weight slumped against my shoulder, I don't know what I want more: to punch him again, or to beg him to tell me why.

Most of all, I hate that he saw Sabine exposed like that. Not just in her gauze-thin nightgown: he's seen her far more bare than *that*. I mean the moment of raw vulnerability where she dropped her glamour.

A less cunning man would see a goddess in her full splendor and fall to his knees.

But Rian? I saw it in his eyes—he clocked her lack of control.

And I'm sure he's already figuring out how to use that to his advantage.

"Go," I bark, digging my knee into his ass to make him walk faster. "What's the matter, your legs weak from weeks of hiding in fucking walls?"

Rian stumbles as he shuffles down the hall, leaning against one wall for support. I can tell from his breath that he's aching down to his bones, but when he twists back toward me, he manages to flash a blood-stained smirk.

"You married her," he says.

"I did."

"You think she'll ever be happy with a mere mortal," he coughs, "when she could have a god?"

I glower back at him. "I've met the other gods. Trust me, they're no prize."

I shove him to keep him moving.

But the words lodge deep. He's not entirely wrong. I've watched carefully from the sidelines as Sabine has grown and changed. Her eyes lit up like never before while studying with Woudix, slowly unlocking her power. Around them, I felt like they were speaking a language I don't know.

At what point will I—flesh and blood—not be enough?

When there's no more blood in my veins to satiate her?

We reach the infirmary, where a godkissed healer gives Rian a sleeping dram that shuts him up for a good hour, thank the gods. While the healer and nurses tend to his wounds, I lurk in the hallway, keeping my ears open.

The news is already starting to slither through the corridors: *Rian Valvere was found hiding in the castle walls.*

It hasn't reached the masses yet, from what I can hear. Just a few night sentries whispering by torchlight. But come dawn? It'll be everywhere.

And when it is, panic will follow. The people taking shelter here—families, soldiers, servants—will wonder what it means. If the Golden Sentinels will storm the gates to get him back. If our fragile safety within these walls will soon shatter.

Someone really needs to take the lead here, send out a clear, steady message to keep people from panicking.

They'll look to Sabine. The savior of Old Coros. But I know my wildcat, and she isn't ready for that kind of pressure.

So, fuck it, I guess it's me.

I try drafting an announcement in my head as I pace the hallway. I've spent enough time with the Valvere family that I know how to speak like an elite, but I'm not sure that's the tone I want to send with my monarchy. Kings have royally fucked up this kingdom for centuries. I don't want the people of Astagnon to see me as distant, aloof.

Hell, I'm one of them. I come from the streets.

I've barely managed to string a few thoughts together when a nurse informs me Rian is awake.

Though the godkissed healer mended the worst of his injuries, he still looks a wreck in blood-and wine-stained clothes, with a busted left eye and a nasty bruise on his jaw.

"Couldn't have gotten the healer to fix this up?" Rian mutters, motioning with his shackled hands to his eye.

"My goal was to keep you alive, not make you pretty. Come on." I grab him by the cuff and shove him ahead of me down the hallway.

Two of my toughest sentries trail us to the upper level of Mercy Tower, just in case Rian has another card up his sleeve. Mercy Tower is where the financiers operate, though the rooms are empty now—during a citywide war, tax disputes are hardly a priority.

At the end of the hall, a narrow set of stairs spirals upward into the attic, where the sharply pitched roof houses a single dusty old cell.

"The *Coffin*?" Rian scoffs out the name of the ancient cell. "Come on, Basten. The Coffin hasn't been used for a hundred years, not since the High Quarter Uprising. At least lock me up in the city's dungeon—I won't be suffocated by cobwebs there."

"The dungeon is outside the castle gates, where your

sentinels still maintain power. You pushed our forces back here, so this is where you stay. Give me your hands."

I untie the rope binds, darkly satisfied that they leave ugly red welts on his skin.

I kick open the rusted cell door and shove him inside.

The low, angled ceiling forces him to hunch forward. He looks around the meager space, kicking at an old chain.

"Is it too much to ask for a shit bucket?"

I turn to the two guards and say quietly, "Bring a bucket of water and the most flea-ridden blanket you can find in the stables."

They leave us, and I busy myself by swinging the door shut, letting the *eeeeek* of the rusty hinges crawl up the back of his spine.

It shuts with a satisfying slam.

"The Castlekeep is bringing the key." I let my hand fall on the heavy iron lock. "And then we'll see if I leave you here to rot for all eternity, or if your gamble to save your skin pays off."

Suddenly, his hand falls on mine. I flinch, expecting an attack, but he leaves it there as his brown eyes sear into mine.

"I never wanted her harmed," he insists, low and urgent. I try to pull my hand away, but he tightens his hold briefly. "*Tamarac.*"

I jerk my hand back, stung by the word that used to bind us like brothers.

"Could have fooled me," I mutter.

"I knew King Rachillon was coming for her," he continues in a rush, his bandaged hand curling around the bars. "And yes, of course, I wanted the throne for myself. Would the kingdom have been better off with that ass,

Beneveto, on it? So, I struck a deal with Rachillon that I knew would benefit me—and *also* Sabine. I sold her out, yes, but only because I knew that if anyone could keep her safe, it was you."

"Me?" I whirl on him, more like an animal than a king. "You had a fucking army to protect her!"

He tips his chin up, bruised eye unflinching. "And you had her trust."

I stagger back like I'm slapped, turn away from Rian, and wipe a hand over my face. My heart can't seem to find a steady rhythm. It's fucked up, all of this. That I want him dead. That a part of me is glad he's alive. That...maybe I *could* have done more to protect Sabine.

Rian presses closer to the bars and whispers, low and intimate like we haven't become enemies, "What happened up there, north of the border? Did you get your memories back?"

A block of ice forms in my stomach, and I snap, "Trying to get intel, even now?"

He doesn't skip a beat. "Intel? Of course. Just as you always are, with those ears of yours that catch everything. I have a strong interest in saving my own ass, but I swear to you, I care about you and Sabine. I want to keep us all safe. The people of Astagnon, too."

I give a harsh laugh.

"I'm serious." He flashes his teeth, the lantern light catching on them. "Talk to me. I can help you. If the fae are truly awakened, then we have bigger problems. This messiness in Old Coros between my Sentinels and your royal soldiers? It's child's play. You know that the *real* war will be between the forces of fae and those of humanity. Who's going to advise you then, eh? Kendan?" He barks a laugh.

"He's good with strategy, as long as it's something he's studied in history books. But he lacks creativity."

I pace deeper into the shadows, rubbing the back of my neck.

Rian's always had a golden tongue. He knows exactly what to say, every damn time.

And the worst part?

Half the time, he's not even lying.

That's the thing about the Lord of Liars—something only I have ever really understood. He doesn't *need* to lie when he can wield the truth like a weapon.

A growl rumbles in my chest. This old shirt of Joruun's is so damn stiff—I seriously need to get Ferra to make me something I can move in. I might wear a crown, but the truth is, I feel like a royal ass.

I want Sabine to talk to—but she's been so distant. Not out of malice, just stretched thin. She has challenges bigger than anything I could ever deal with.

And dammit, I'm tired of feeling alone.

Rian's a dead man, right? I reason. *Who is he going to tell my confession to?*

I lean on the bars, letting my hair curtain my face. I give a gruff, "Fine," because I don't want him to see the loneliness in my eyes. "Give us a good strategy for dealing with the fae, and maybe you can earn yourself an upgraded shit bucket."

Rian's lips curl into a lopsided smile, marred by the dark bruise.

And just like that, it's suddenly ten years ago, and we're just two boys conspiring to break into Sorsha Hall's confectionery to steal honeycakes.

Slowly, I unburden the heaviness on my chest to him.

Cautiously. Carefully. Being incredibly fucking selective about what details I give him about Volkany and Vale and the fae, knowing full well he'll use them to his own advantage if he can.

The trick with Rian is, he'll always do what's best for himself. But if you can hitch yourself to his goal, then you can benefit from his self-preservation instinct.

The lantern flickers steadily over his wide eyes, hungry to drink in everything I have to say. And damn, if a part of this doesn't feel good. To be like this again. Even on opposite sides of the bars.

I've...missed him.

Fuck me, but it's true.

"So that's it," I say, letting out a heavy sigh. "Vale sent us here to win the throne and prepare Astagnon for the gods' arrival."

"That's *it*?" Rian throws his hands in the air. "What about Sabine? You left out the part where she's a fucking goddess!"

"I told you how it worked. Vale killed her human body, which awakened the goddess inside."

"I'm not talking about the fucking *logistics*. What does it mean for us—for the world—that she's one of those self-interested tyrants?"

The muscles along my back bristle. "Sabine is different."

"Do you hear yourself? She's fae. She isn't different at all."

"No." My voice hardens enough to make Rian flinch. He falls silent, waiting, watching. When we were boys, I never raised my voice to him. Always let him take the lead. But things have changed. "No, she's still Sabine and always will be. She cares about humanity. She wants to fight for us."

Rian busies himself brushing dust off the bars, waiting until I've stopped pacing.

He lifts an eyebrow. "You didn't grow up attending Red Church classes every Sunday, and it shows. Immortal Solene is the guardian of nature. That sounds positively bucolic, doesn't it? And sure, that includes dandelions and butterflies, but it's also fucking *lava*. It's earthquakes. It's monoceroses."

"It's humans, too," I snap.

He laughs, shaking his head. "You know how humans fit into nature? We destroy it."

I open my mouth to argue but snap it closed again. All I can think of is the murals in Drahallen Hall's basement. The ones painted over to hide the truth.

What Rian says...it hits too close to home.

My head jerks at a sound—footsteps on the floor beneath us. A jangling key ring.

We don't have long before we'll have company.

I grab a bar, leaning in. "What did your Red Church classes tell you about the fall of Calisyrune?"

Rian frowns, surprised by the question. "The ancient city? What do you want to know?"

"Why it fell."

Rian's mouth curves in a slow smile as he gently taps the bruise on his temple. "Ah. That information isn't shared with children in Red Church classes, but the Valveres have a lot of access to old information. I'll tell you all about what happened to Calisyrune—over a bottle of whisky."

I can't help but roll my eyes. It's just so fucking *Rian*. His life is on the line, the kingdom is in jeopardy, but he holds out for a drink.

"Let me guess," Rian says. "Sabine blinks those sweet

doe eyes and swears she's loyal to humanity, then blasts someone with brimfire the next moment?"

The words drip with smugness—but they also ring with truth.

I wince.

Basten, just walk away. Let Rian rot. The friendship is over.

But I find myself saying, "I can keep her under control." There's a forcefulness to my voice that pushes a little too hard.

Rian stares at me for the space of several breaths, then slowly shakes his head. He chuckles, which rolls into a full-bodied laugh, stoking my ire, until he doubles over in coughs.

That's a *little* satisfying.

The attic stairs groan under someone's soft footsteps, and soon, Lady Suri joins us in the narrow attic. She wears a dressing robe over her nightshift, belted tightly against the chill. Her face is unadorned, her hair wrapped in ribbons for tomorrow's curls.

She holds a lantern in one hand and her jangling key ring in the other.

"Basten? Sabine told me to come. It was all very mysterious. She said it couldn't wait until the morning. That you need the old attic cell key....oh!"

Her lantern swings wide as she steps into the corridor, the beam slicing through the shadows—

—and landing square on Rian's face.

Suri jumps. "What the *fuck*?" she blurts, then claps a ladylike hand over her mouth to banish the curse.

Rian moves instantly, rising from his crouch behind the bars with unsettling grace. Despite the bruises blotching his face, the split lip, and the swelling around one eye, his smile blooms.

"Well, well," he drawls. "Lady Suri. What an utter delight. I was worried they'd send some square-shouldered guard with bad breath. But instead..." He rests his bruised knuckles against the bars, eyes glittering. "I get you. Pretty and profane. I'm touched."

Suri flushes—not deep, just a bloom of heat over her brown cheeks. Her hand goes to her curls, patting down a flyaway ribbon almost unconsciously.

She recovers fast, though, jaw setting hard.

She strides right up to the bars and smacks his injured hand hard with the iron key.

Rian hisses through his teeth, jerking his hand back with a muttered curse. But his grin doesn't falter. If anything, it widens.

"You ass," Suri snaps. She shoves the key into the lock and twists, locking him in. "It will be my pleasure watching you wither behind these bars."

"Pleasure?" Rian says, dark and amused. "Careful. You'll get my hopes up."

Suri scoffs, disgusted, and turns away, lantern light throwing her shadow long across the stone as she strides back down the stairs.

"Basten," she calls over her shoulder, "I'm going to need a *serious* pay raise to deal with this."

CHAPTER 21
SABINE

A guard knocks on my bedroom door. "Queen Sabine, the prisoner has asked to speak with you again."

I'm cross-legged on the bed, bent over a stack of smooth gray pebbles on the quilt, trying to levitate them into a stack with fey alone.

At the interruption, they crash down.

I sigh.

"Not today," I call to the guard, loud enough to hear through the door. "Or *any* day—be sure to tell Rian I said that."

The guard hesitates. "Yes, Majesty."

I pick the pebbles up, weighing them in my palm.

Rian has been locked in the Coffin for a week. Brackish water to drink and a pile of hay to sleep in. Like everyone else, I thought he would have broken by now. We're talking about *Rian Valvere*, the privileged lord whose fine ass has rested on velvet pillows his whole life.

But he's made of tougher stuff than he lets on.

He asks for me daily. Begs for me to speak to him. Basten has gone to the Coffin a few times to press him for information, though I suspect he really just wants to curse him black and blue. And of course, I get reports from Suri on Rian's aggravating behavior behind bars.

But I can't bring myself to go.

To be honest, I'm...scared.

Rian was easy to hate when he was a kingdom away. Things couldn't have been clearer: he sold me out to my father in exchange for a crown. But his words still echo in my ears.

It was best for you to be where you belonged.

I can't help but wonder, in the secrecy of my own mind, if he understands the world—understands me—better than almost anyone.

But then again, even if it's true, does it matter? There is no world in which I would admit to Rian Valvere that he was right about *anything*.

I line up the pebbles and concentrate again, sparking fey to lift one a few inches—and the guard knocks again.

The pebble falls.

"*What?*" I growl, harsher than I intended.

The door opens, and it isn't the guard this time.

Basten raises his eyebrows, keeping his distance in the doorway. "I wanted to let you know that Rian agreed to order his forces to surrender. We're going to give the signal at first light tomorrow."

I sit straighter, pushing my hair back. "That's wonderful news."

Basten keeps his hand on the doorknob. "We'll have to

see how it plays out. Hopefully, the sentinels will turn over their weapons and vacate the city peacefully."

"But you suspect they won't?"

"Let's just say we need to be ready for anything." His eyes fall to the untouched tray of brown bread and butter at the foot of the bed, and he sighs. "You need to eat, Sabine."

Eat.

The fae hunger in me licks up with frenzied, sudden need. My eyes go to Basten's neck as my mouth waters.

Drink drink drink.

I quickly lower my eyes and lift a shoulder. "I'm fine."

His hand twists on the doorknob, as though he can't make up his mind between entering or exiting. "You're weak. Let me help you."

DRINK DRINK DRINK.

The thirst for his blood—his breath, his life, his everything—roars so violently between my ears that I drop the pebbles, suddenly breathless.

"*No*," I practically growl. "Leave me alone."

I see the sting of rejection in his eyes, but I don't have the strength to tell him the truth: that I'm afraid the next time I drink from him, I won't be able to stop.

He'll insist. It will turn into an argument, until we're both at each other's throats.

I sigh. "Sorry—I just...I'm trying to concentrate."

"Sure, wildcat." He doesn't meet my eyes as he leaves.

As soon as he's gone, I slump forward, rubbing my temples. I hate this—the distance between us. All I want is for it to be like it was before, the two of us against any challenge.

"Lady Sabine."

I jump a mile, hand flying to my chest to keep my lungs from exploding.

Woudix leans on the windowsill, toying with the fae needle in one gloved hand, with Hawk curled at his feet.

"Gods—you surprised me! How did you create a portal so quickly?"

My head whips back around toward the door, worried Basten might come back at any moment. Or that his nose will pick up on the fresh fae scent of iron and myrrh.

"I've had millennia to learn how to sew." He stows the needle in his leather vest. "If you're worried about privacy, I put up a shield. Like before, this visit remains between the two of us."

He holds a finger to his lips, and guilt burns through me. *I'm keeping secrets from my own husband.*

"I've been practicing," I start, motioning to the pebbles, but Woudix barely acknowledges my words.

His face is pinched, distracted.

"I didn't come for your training. I have news to report from Drahallen Hall. Captain Tatarin was successful in finding Immortal Thracia's resting place."

My spine pulls straight in surprise. "You mean, her human body?"

He nods. "Her soul slept within the bloodline of a minor royal family along the northeastern coast. The body of a young, godkissed countess. The captain's faction brought her to Immortal Vale, who awakened her."

The Northeastern coast? It rings a bell, but I press on.

"And her Gloaming?" My hands shake against my corset strings, remembering when I went through the same agonizing process.

"Samaur is helping her through it, as I helped you. She is adjusting rapidly."

Something twists in my stomach. Jealousy. That the transition is so much easier for the rest of the fae.

Woudix folds his arms tighter, the line between his brows deepening. His voice falls low. "Thracia woke from her slumber with a taste for war. She's trying to convince your father and the rest of the court to dismiss the plan for a peaceful welcome to Astagnon. To invade instead."

"What?" I climb off the bed and grip the bedpost for support. My heart slams in my chest. A dozen questions and protests fill my mouth, and I struggle to settle on one. "We had an agreement!

"Your father doubts your ability to bend public sentiment in time by the Blood Moon, and he grows impatient."

"We're making progress! The public has already embraced me. Look—" I snatch up the clay bird from the breakfast tray. "See? They give me offerings out of devotion, not fear."

Woudix walks slowly to the map table, dragging his fingers over the carved countryside in relief, along the raised border wall.

"It is not me you must convince. This possibility deeply troubles me—hence why I am here. That much death all at once goes against the world's balance."

I sputter, "He can't attack. Tell him...tell him the full fae court isn't awake yet! There's still Alyssantha. And Popelin. And Meric."

Woudix's fingers walk their way, feeling over the dips and rises, to the tiny model of Hekkelveld Castle. "Alyssantha and Popelin are not among the more powerful fae. Their affinities are love and pleasure; hardly necessary for war. Meric *is* powerful," he concedes, "but has always kept to himself. Traditionally, his resting place is the last found. It could take years more, and Vale grows impatient."

I press my fingertips to my temples, where the fey pounds beneath my skin.

"Look." I grab his wrist, squeezing tight. "This city is already in chaos. We have a plan to make the Golden Sentinels surrender, but even if we succeed, the people will be ravished, war-torn. They can't take more violence."

"Then what do you propose?" he says.

I release him, flexing my hand from where his fey chilled my own.

Then, I grab the kitchen maid's clay bird.

"Give my father this," I say urgently, pressing it into Woudix's hands. "Tell him that the maid who gave me this must have spent her last coin on the clay. That even tired and during a siege, she woke early to make it for me in the dark morning hours, by her last precious candlelight. That's the power of true devotion. Remind my father how much more sacrifice he'll get from mortals when they offer it freely."

"And if he still doubts you?"

I harden my jaw. "You can assure him that I'll have the public ready to eat out of his hand by the Blood Moon. Acolytes lined up around the block. Banners rolled out just for him. Events in their honor—games, theatrics, recreations of legends." I pause, seized by a crazy idea, and grab a handful of dirt out of a potted lily on the windowsill.

"I'll strike a fae bargain swearing it so."

Woudix's eyes flash in warning. "Sabine..."

But I'm already speaking the words. "A pinch of earth to

close the deal. What's given now, the ground will seal." I let the dirt fall between my fingers.

He taps his fingers on the table's edge, one by one, with excruciating patience. "That may just be enough to sway your father."

Then, he slips the clay bird into the inside of his coat and takes out a book instead.

"For your training." He holds it out to me. "You are ready for the next level."

I take the book. It feels old but is in good condition, wrapped in smooth calf leather—it feels practically alive in my hand.

He takes out the fae needle and moves his long fingers in the air, feeling for something unseen, and then stabs the needle into the fabric of space.

A beam of moonlight spills out—night has already fallen in the far north.

He pauses to look back at me. "I have my reasons for avoiding war—but I admit I am curious about your own. You're Goddess of Nature. You care that much about the humans here?"

"Of course." My throat tightens. "My husband is human. It's only natural that I care about his kingdom."

The silence stretches.

"*His* kingdom," Woudix points out. "Not yours."

My chest shrinks inward, suddenly starved for air. I force a few breaths, keeping my head high as Woudix finishes unstitching a portal, passes through, and seals it up.

Only then do I collapse against the table, slide to the floor, and hug the book to my chest to keep my hands from shaking.

I swore a fae bargain.

Which means I *can't* fail—and I only know one person with a mind devious enough to come up with a bombproof plan to make the public adore a court of fae who could snuff them out with a snap of their fingers.

It's time to pay Rian Valvere a midnight visit.

A secret one.

CHAPTER 22
BASTEN

The following morning, we stand on the rooftop of Honor Tower—me, Rian, and Kendan—looking out over the pillaged city of Old Coros. Smoke rises from burned-out husks of shops that careless sentinels torched, drunk on both whisky and power. The air is fetid with the stench of weeks-old rotting food scraps and animal shit.

A shiver ripples over my skin, pulling it tight with anger.

Old Coros isn't my hometown. Hell, I can count on one hand how many times I've been here. There was a time when the people here, the streets, the buildings meant nothing to me.

But now I wear the crown.

It *is* my home.

And nothing pisses me off more than someone making a mess of what's mine.

"Okay, you clever ass," I mutter to Rian from the corner of my mouth. "Now's your chance to prove you're worth more than those rusty shackles binding your hands."

Rian slides me a droll look as he raises his bound hands toward the row of parapets, rattling the very shackles in question. "The second, third, and sixth parapet. That's the signal."

I pierce him with a heavy look of doubt, unwilling to deal with any more of his lies.

"Don't trust me?" he says wryly.

I don't even dignify that with a response.

His lips curl in a raking smile. "How are things going with your wife, by the way?"

"Why the fuck do you care?"

Rian shrugs, flicking an imaginary speck of dust off his jacket with his bound hands. "Marriage is the art of hiding your secrets better," he quips. "At least, that's what my father used to say."

I narrow my eyes at him—he's just trying to get under my skin.

Begrudgingly, I take his word for it and signal to the soldiers to begin hanging sheets from the parapets that Rian indicated.

They're black sheets, Rian's signature color. He swears up and down that this is the plan he established with his generals, the Cold Coins. If he hangs black sheets from certain parapets, they're to call off the siege.

I run the fabric between my fingers as a soldier walks back carrying it, and grunt. "Shocked they aren't white. You'd be the spineless kind to use the color of surrender."

Rian scowls, Kendan flicks his gaze between the two of us like we're warring children.

"Can we get on with it, please?" Kendan mutters.

I signal to the soldiers, who bind the sheets with ropes and hang them from Honor Tower. It's a windless day, and the sheets hang heavy, like bodies at the gallows. Honor Tower stands high over the rest of the city, designed to be visible from every quarter, a shining beacon.

Which means the Cold Coins can't miss our message.

"Now," I say. "We wait and see if they still obey their master's call." I slap Rian on the shoulder.

It's tense as we stare down at the courtyard below, where our soldiers have barricaded the castle gates. At sight of the sheets, sentinels camped out on the opposite side rush to pick up their weapons, already on alert and ready should a fight break out.

But they're only infantrymen—it's the Cold Coins who will make the call.

"It's an old tradition, you know," Kendan says as we wait, motioning to the sheets. "To use hanging sheets in code to send a signal. They did it in King Byrne's reign."

"I know," Rian snaps, irritated. "Why else do you think I did it?"

Kendan raises an eyebrow. "You mean you were actually paying attention in our tutoring lessons? Could have fooled me. You and Lore spent more time snickering over drawings of naked ladies than the ancient texts."

Rian smirks, his eyes wistful. "Wonder if we still have those drawings."

I smack him on the back of his neck, sending him reeling forward. With his hands bound, his balance is off, and he nearly stumbles right off the roof before catching himself on a flagpole.

"Fuck, Basten!"

"March yourself to the stairs," I command, pointing to the courtyard, where a flurry of tense activity is breaking out. "I think your generals are about to pay us a visit."

I make Rian walk ahead of me, giving him a good jab in the ribs whenever he slows, as we make our way down to the courtyard. However, as soon as we step out into the sunlight, my jesting stops.

Now's the time to be a king—not Rian's tormenter.

Even if it's so damn fun to.

I pause at the entrance to Raven Hall for a squire to help me fasten my scabbard and shield—heavy, official weapons that are meant to blind my opponents with their riches. I shift uncomfortably under their weight.

"How about I trade you for that bow and arrows?" I say to the squire, pointing to a simple wooden bow in the weaponry stockpile.

Kendan leans in and murmurs heavily, "May I remind you that you're no longer hunting to put venison on the dinner table, King Basten."

I groan—I see why Rian was always so irritated with his older brother—but relent.

"Keep it on hand, eh?" I say quietly to the squire, who nods with big eyes.

I stride out into the courtyard, and here, at least, I feel like I belong. The stockpiles of weapons. The hastily erected tents, gaunt soldiers with sleepless eyes. I might as well be in an army encampment in Mag Na Tir Forest, not a palace.

At my appearance, the royal soldiers snap to attention. I have to give them credit—for as exhausted and malnourished as they are, they manage to present a semblance of order.

"King Basten," each one says, bowing his head as I pass.

There's commotion on the other side of the gate, where the Sentinels part to allow their three generals to approach.

I use the term "generals" loosely: Two are meathead

former swordsman-for-hire I know from the fighting ring. Mallik and Gaez. Brutes, despite their golden armor. The third is a mean, wiry little gray-haired spy named Boone.

The notorious Cold Coins.

I stride straight up to the gates, puffing up my chest like a charging wild boar, my hand showily resting on the heavy iron sword at my side.

I stop six feet from the gate, far enough to avoid a thrust blade. Kendan follows behind me, dragging a reluctant Rian along with him.

"Generals," I bare my teeth, hissing out the word. "Let me introduce myself, because it's been a while since we served together. Basten Valvere, King of Astagnon, though I believe you once knew me by a different name. Wolf Bowborn?"

Gaez leans forward to spit as his response. The man *reeks* of cheap brandy.

I smile inwardly, because he just made this a lot more fun.

I grab Rian by the shoulder and drag him, stumbling, to the gate. "Maybe you'll recognize him, then, eh? You were stupid enough to choose this ass for your leader, and now he's given you an order."

I point to the black sheets dangling from Honor Tower.

Gaez squints theatrically as he looks over Rian. "Can't tell who that is under all the bruises. Could be anyone."

"And those sheets?" Mallik cuts in. "Nah, don't remember any signal about sheets."

Rian's hunched posture explodes as he hurls himself against the bars, swiping a hand through to try to grab the general by the neck. "You lying bastards! You know it's me!"

The three of them step back in feigned surprise, holding

their hands out helplessly. "Rian? That really you?" Boone says.

Mallik shakes his head, breath heavy with booze. "Nah, can't be, rumor has it Rian fled to Duren."

Gods help us, Mallik is even drunker than the others.

Gaez grins wolfishly at the other two. "This is just a nobody."

Rian garbles a furious growl and lunges again, but this time, Kendan intercepts him, grabbing both shoulders and yanking him back hard enough to drag his boots through the dirt.

"You can't even control your own fucking temper, let alone command your so-called army!" Kendan snaps, his voice low but scalding. "The army that was supposedly *loyal* to you!"

They grapple—Rian twisting in his grip, Kendan holding fast.

"You think you can hold this city without me?" Rian spits at Gaez, breath ragged, straining against Kendan's grip. "You'll lose control in a week."

"Done plenty well without you so far," Gaez answers, casually picking dirt from his nails. "Figure, why not keep up the party? The Cold Coins are famous here. All the wine, cards, women we want."

"Because everyone's terrified of you," Rian blusters. "You've throttled them to within a few days of starvation!"

He manages to tear free of Kendan and grips the bars, pressing his busted face to the gap. In a low, poison voice I know all too well, he threatens, "I put you where you are. Gave you the keys to this city so you could safeguard it for my return, not pillage it. Do you know what happens to those who cross a Valvere? The last man who tried ended up on the sharp end of a—"

"Enough." I slam my iron shield against the bars, silencing him.

I spare a few moments to scowl at the generals, then direct my attention to the sentinels behind them.

"Golden Sentinels," I announce, loud and resounding. "Your disgraced leader, the erstwhile king—" I jerk my head in Rian's direction "—is done playing at wearing a crown. He's hung the black sheets, the signal to surrender. As your new king, I command you to lay down your arms, return control of the city back to me and my royal army, and kneel before me. Do so, and your treasonous actions will be pardoned. Refuse, and be strung up alongside those sheets, right next to the Cold Coins."

A few sentinels pitch their heads up to look at the high parapets of Honor Tower, probably imagining swinging there by their necks.

I have a modicum of sympathy for them. Once, I was a Golden Sentinel myself, so I know that half of them are just farmers who had a bad crop and needed coin.

There's a tense moment where no one quite seems to know what to do. One sentinel starts to shrug out of his bow strap, as if to surrender, but no sooner does he lift the strap over his head than General Mallik swipes a crossbow from a nearby fighter and aims it square at his chest.

He lets a bolt loose, killing the man.

At the same time, Rian lunges at the gate again, trying to get his bound hands through the bars to grab Gaez. Mallik acts fast, turning the crossbow on Rian.

Kendan dives forward to grab Rian by the scruff and haul him out of range. It all happens fast. To most people, it would be a blur, but my senses let me see everything in painstaking detail.

Mallik grins wickedly as his eyes dart from Rian to Kendan—then swings the crossbow to target the elder brother instead.

"Fuck!" I shout, slamming my elbow into Rian, which causes him to tumble sidewise into Kendan, knocking Kendan out of the crossbow's primary trajectory.

Instead of hitting his heart, it lodges in his right shoulder instead.

Kendan drops to one knee, clutching his arm, grimacing in pain—but he's a trained soldier, too. He knows how to take a hit. And he's smart enough not to lean against the gates for support, where he'd get a knife in his side.

"Kendan?" Rian's voice rises an octave. "Brother!" He drops to his knee.

"The Lord of the Iron Banner is injured!" one of our soldiers yells, and from one breath to the next, everyone has a weapon at the ready.

Fuuuuck, I think to myself. This was not supposed to go down like this.

"Hold!" I shout, lifting my hand to command the soldiers not to attack through the gate. Once fighting starts, I know, it won't stop until half of us are dead. "Hold, by order of your king! Archers, at the ready. Swordsman, get into position."

The soldiers stir at the command; it's been years since they had clear military leadership, if not decades, other than to march in parades.

But they quickly fall into step, taking up the positions.

Gods, they almost look...inspired.

"Now listen, you bastards." I draw my sword and thrust

it in the Cold Coins' direction. "I'll give you to the count of three to seriously rethink your plan going forward. Until now, you've been stray dogs loose in the city. But the fae have risen, and they'll be in our kingdom faster than you can fuck a whore. I'm here now, and I'm done playing games. Surrender."

The Cold Coins don't bat an eye to hear such language from a king. Gaez merely uses his short sword to scratch an itch on his chin as he belches out a bubble of cheap brandy. "I'll take my chances with the fae rather than bow a knee to the likes of Wolf Bowborn."

A silent groan rattles in my chest.

So, he wants to do this the hard way? Well, fuck it. When has it ever *not* been the hard way?

I mentally scan through my assets in the courtyard, from the number of soldiers to the weaponry to the horses, ready to give a formation command.

When...

"You bowed to *me*, asshole, under penalty of death. Remember that?" Rian's voice cuts like a knife. There's a layer of playfulness, the Valvere charm, but beneath it, all I hear is pure seething fury.

I know what happens when Rian uses that tone.

"Fuck," I bite out, whipping around toward where Rian crouches on the ground next to his wounded brother.

Rian is crouched, making himself look small, but I see the glint of metal in his fist.

It's the crossbow bolt from Kendan's shoulder.

I step forward to stop him from doing something stupid, but I'm not fast enough.

Rian raises his bound fists, the bolt hidden between his fingers, and throws it with perfect, calculated aim.

It zips through the bars to spear Boone so deep in his left eye that the man staggers back, garbles, and falls down.

Dead.

For a second, no one moves. This was...unexpected. Hell, I knew Rian's aim was good, but I didn't know it was *that* good.

Everyone else seems to process what happened at the same time I do, and chaos erupts.

The remaining two Cold Coins shout to their men to fire arrows at us. A few sentinels—those loyal to the Cold Coins—nock arrows and take aim, but most stand stunned, unmoving.

"You heard me, you bastards!" Mallik shouts. "Fire!"

Now, even the few loyal to them seem to have second thoughts.

That's all I need to see. I whip around to my own troops and give the order.

"Archers, hold! Guards, roll back the gates. Infantry, prepare to surround the traitors!"

To their credit, none of my troops hesitate at my command. They rush to roll back the gates and flood into the street with swords raised, shouting for the sentinels to surrender. It fills me with a feeling I don't know how to handle.

I've never led before—I've certainly never been *followed*.

The air crackles, ready to ignite, as the soldiers face one another. One wrong move, I know, and full-on war will erupt.

So, I raise my sword at the opposing army.

"Lay down your weapons! You will be pardoned. But if you choose to strike my men, there will be no mercy."

My soldiers form a tight circle around them, shields and

swords at the ready. They're exhausted, untested, but there's courage there. I can use that.

It seems to trigger something in the sentinels, too. An archer in the middle of the crowd tosses his quiver to the ground and takes a knee. A few murmurs of dissent spread through the others, but two more archers surrender. Then, the rest of them fall like a house of cards. Dropping weapons. Bending the knee to me.

"Cowards!" General Gaez spits at them. Sweat pours down his bald scalp, into the thick folds of his neck. With a grunt, he suddenly slams into one of my soldiers, knocking the man clean to the ground, and sprints off.

A few sentinels bolt too, fleeing along with him.

"Archers!" I shout. "Fire! Hunt them down!"

A team of my soldiers peels off to pursue the defectors. But they have a head start. Archers fire but miss, and Gaez darts around a corner.

My adrenaline is roaring, but my heartbeat is steady as stone. I snatch the squire's bow, nock a quick arrow, and set my aim at the back of General Mallik's fat head.

I let it fly.

It slams through his skull just as he rounds the corner. Blood sprays out of his mouth as he collapses to the ground. The other fleeing sentinels trample his body as they make their escape.

My chest heaves as I toss the bow back to the squire, who stares at me with wide eyes.

In fact, the entire battle zone falls so quiet all I hear is ragged breathing, as the prisoners and my men alike look to me, awaiting orders.

I wipe sweat off my brow with the back of my hand. "Round the prisoners up, get their names, and secure them in the city dungeon. And someone get Lord Kendan to a healer."

"I can walk," Kendan mutters. He pushes to his feet, clutching his arm, and gives me a nod. "Not a bad first act as king, Majesty."

As he limps off toward the castle, my men move quickly to collect the surrendered sentinels' weapons and line up the prisoners along the outer gate. From upper windows of the nearby shops and houses, I see citizens peeking out, as though afraid to dare believe the siege is at an end.

Dammit, it does something to me.

This feeling, is it...pride?

"Had to fucking steal my thunder, eh?" Rian's voice snaps me out of my modicum of happiness.

It's just me and him left on this side of the gate. I snort and punch him lightly in the shoulder. "Couldn't let it be said that Rian Valvere had better aim than Wolf Bowborn. I have a reputation to uphold."

Rian rolls his eyes, but there's a touch of amusement there. This exchange...it feels so familiar it aches. *Like old times.* Sparring and riling each other up. Before Sabine came into my life, these moments with Rian were the only thing that gave me a single damn light in the darkness.

"So," he says, holding up his bound hands. "Did I earn myself my freedom?"

"Hell no," I say, hard and fast, clapping a hand on his shoulder and turning him back toward the castle, where his attic cell awaits. "But you did earn yourself that whisky."

As I shove him forward, I can't miss his chuckle—like old times.

CHAPTER 23
SABINE

I pace back and forth in Hekkelveld Castle's library—housed on the second floor, with a balcony overlooking the city like a bird's perch. I clutch Woudix's ancient book to my chest with an iron grip.

It's been two days since Woudix came. Two days since I quietly went to visit Rian in the Coffin, to give him back his bone dice in exchange for a strategy that will win me the public's favor.

One day since Rian helped Basten end the siege on our city.

And it vexes me—how useful he's been to both of us. *How much we've needed him.*

The door groans open, and I spin around, holding the book tighter.

Basten steps in, dressed in a fresh black linen shirt with his antler symbol across the shoulders, his hair pulled back in a loose knot at his nape, and my body softens.

"Basten, thanks for coming." I step forward, a million words poised on my lips. Because of the siege's end, we've barely seen each other outside of a few glances in our comings and goings. He's been out in the streets, hour after hour, feeding the hungry, carting the injured to the castle infirmary, helping the royal army plan the arduous task of repairing the city. While I've been poring over Woudix's book, transfixed by every page. "I'm so glad you're here, I—"

A step behind him, Kendan strides into the room, followed by Suri, followed by Matron White.

My words cut off, strangled.

Other than the bandages covering the burn marks on her face and arms, she looks exactly like the woman who tormented me for twelve years, down to that damn self-righteous smirk.

Instantly, I go cold from my ears to my toes. It's followed by a wash of anger.

"What is *she* doing here?" I spin on Basten, my cheeks burning red, chest heaving so hard I can barely catch a breath.

Kendan sets a rolled map on the library table, clearing his throat as though that could break the stalemate between the Matron and me. "You called for all the leaders of the opposition."

"I'm not certain you understand who exactly I'm *opposed* to," I say between clenched teeth.

"*Goddess,*" Matron White interjects, and I can't help but bristle at the note of sarcasm in her tone, "May I note that, thanks to my priests' efforts, the city's opinion of you has drastically changed. Why, no one even remembers a time you were labeled a traitor. They blame Rian Valvere for spreading those slanderous rumors and praise you as the Winged Lady of legend, the Goddess of Nature, here to save our kingdom. Why, just this morning, every Red

Church in the city held a candlelight vigil for your salvation."

Gods—how this woman's face irritates me. The only small amount of satisfaction I get is knowing those burn marks will disfigure her forever, and every time she looks in a mirror, she'll think of me.

She goes on to say, "I am only here as a mouthpiece for the Red Church; a messenger of devotion, here to report on the church's ample efforts to aid in the city's clean up; *surely* you wish for us to continue our assistance to the hungry and needy?"

I stare daggers at her.

Basten folds his arms, looking no more pleased than me. He lets out a long exhale. "Sabine?"

"You don't have to work directly with the Matron," Suri suggests. "What if we ask her to leave for now, and I'll be a go-between?"

I bite back bitter anger. "It's fine. She can stay."

Kendan taps the map, hoping to bring us back to the plan. "Queen Sabine, I'm glad you called this meeting. Now, if you'll look at this map, you'll see that the High Quarter and Varn Row sustained the most damage from the siege. We're bringing in bricklayers from as far as Blackwater to help repair efforts. As far as the dissenters, I'm afraid at least two dozen sentinels fled, as well as one of the leaders of the Cold Coins. Folke is out now, leading a team to hunt them down, but progress is slow."

I glance out the window, where the top of Faith Tower is just visible. "Ask Rian, then."

Kendan starts, blinking hard. "Rian Valvere?"

Basten gives me an odd look, as though I might have bumped my head.

"I'm not suggesting we pardon him," I say flatly. "As far as I'm concerned, he should remain a prisoner indefinitely. But we also have to be practical. He's a *resource*. No one knows this city's safe houses like Rian does. He could lead you straight to their hiding places."

"Thay may be true," Kendan admits, "but it's risky to let him out into the city on his own, even with guards."

"I'll go with him," Basten says.

Both Kendan and Suri sputter at the same time. Suri then garbles, "Basten, you can't! You're the king!"

"Lady Suri has a point, Majesty," Kendan agrees. "You can't put yourself at risk hunting down criminals. Besides, your face is well known. Step into the Sin Streets, and you'll be swarmed with your subjects asking for your favor."

"I'll wear a mask," he says, his hard voice leaving no room for debate. "But if we're letting that cur out of his kennel, I'm damn sure holding his leash."

Kendan still looks like he has doubts, so I raise my hands.

"It's good to hear progress on recovery efforts," I say, "However, I called this meeting because I've become aware of a possible threat—the Fae Court was considering attacking Astagnon."

Suri jumps up, alarmed. "What?"

I quickly lift my hands higher for calm. "It's okay—I struck a fae bargain. I promised we would provide events worthy of the gods, that will stir the public's adoration. Now, we just have to make good on that bargain. And I think I know how."

Kendan and Suri exchange concerned looks. Matron White gnaws on the inside of her cheek, glancing out the window as if a bolt of Vale's fey will shoot down from the sky at any moment.

Only Basten keeps his eyes on me. "How?"

"Games," I say, my eyes lighting up. "We hold two days of Fae Games for the masses. We'll do a recreation of the Ride of Night and Day. Meric's Labyrinth in the Hedge Maze. Goldenclaw rides for children."

They stare at me, but I push forward.

"It's about ritual," I explain. "And repetition. Re-enacting legends of old, again and again, gives them power. That's what people love most about the fae. The stories. So, we'll bring the stories to life for them. Remind them why they should embrace the fae, not fear them."

I feel a little breathless as I gaze between their faces.

Certainty brims in my chest—I know this idea will work. Because it isn't my idea at all.

You need a reason to make the public care, Rian said when I went to see him in the Coffin. From the other side of the bars, his eyes lit up. *To make them forget their fear. Only their wonder.*

"I...think that could work," Suri says, her eyes lighting up. "In fact, that's brilliant! Just like the Theatrics we saw in Duren of the Night Hunt. I've never seen people so riveted."

"It's one thing," Kendan points out, "to entertain the masses with actors and pantomimes. But what happens when the real fae arrive, and it's no longer a game?"

My stomach curls. I wrap my fingers around the book's edges. "That's where this comes into play."

I set the book on the table. They all lean forward, curious. There's no title on the cover, so Suri carefully flips the parchment pages to the first one.

She gasps. "The *Last Return of the Fae*? The second volume? You found it! Where was it?"

I skirt her question and flip through more of the pages, showing them the handwritten text.

"It's only partially written in the Old Tongue. I've translated a few portions already. Once I can figure out the other language, I'll finish translating the final part, about how to put the fae back to sleep. Then, when my father and the court arrive, we'll give them the opportunity to do the right thing. There's a real chance that having their blessings could do great things for Astagnon, if they set their intentions toward it, instead of pure selfishness. If they don't, we'll have the threat of putting them back to sleep to keep them in line."

Suri doesn't look at me as she whispers, "But you *are* one of them, Sabby."

My eye twitches. "I care about the people of this kingdom."

"What I meant was," she presses, "won't it put you to sleep, too?"

The room falls silent, and the crackle of the fire feels almost deafening. I exchange a quick look with Basten—but I'm not sure what I read in his dark brown eyes.

"I'll do what I have to," I say quietly.

No one responds, and I can feel their doubts like moth-wings beating against my face. Basten must sense my isolation, because he purposefully comes around to my side of the table, flipping through the book.

"Where did you find it?" he asks. "And where did you get the information about the fae court?"

I fidget with a loose thread on my dress sleeve, not meeting his eyes. This is a secret I've already kept too close, too long. Anyway, there's no lie I could say that anyone would believe.

"It was given to me. By…Woudix."

"Woudix?" Suri echoes with a gasp. "You saw him?"

I look away and nod.

The room goes still enough that my breathing rasps like dry autumn leaves. I'm acutely aware of everyone's eyes on me, wavering with a million questions, but at the moment, the only person's thoughts I care about are Basten's.

I look up at him, my heart hammering, tugging so hard on the loose thread that I might unravel my whole sleeve. "I…should have told you. He's…he's visited me a few times."

Instantly, I flinch. Maybe I should have lied.

After all, Basten lied to me too about knowing Matron White was alive.

Basten's face is closed off to me, dark and cloudy like a night storm. The longer his silence stretches, the faster my pulse raps, setting off waves of panic that stab into my heart.

"You've been meeting secretly with *Woudix*?" He spits the last word with such vitriol that everyone in the room takes a step back.

"I only kept it secret because I knew it would upset you," I rush to explain. "There are some things you don't understand, that only fae can explain to other fae."

"How many times?" he demands, his voice rising.

From the corner of my eye, I see Matron White exchange a look with Kendan that says *"so much for wedded bliss"* without needing to say anything at all.

"Only twice," I blurt out, pulling harder at the thread. "He used the fae needle to come to me in the woods after our wedding, and—"

"After our wedding!" Basten throws his hands up, pacing tightly in the small room.

"—and again, to give me this book," I continue. "That's it! We did nothing but discuss how to handle the fae court's arrival. Woudix has as many doubts about my father as we do. He's invested—if war breaks out, so much death upsets the balance of his realm. He came to me because he wants peace, too. That's why he gave me the book. He risked everything to meet with me secretly."

Basten stops short, trying to marshal his feelings. His chest rises and falls quickly. He closes his eyes, but when he opens them, there's still the sting of betrayal there. "I accepted the role of your acolyte. Fully knowing that not a single acolyte has lived longer than a few months. If anyone bore a risk, it was me!"

"This is why I didn't tell you," I say, my own voice rising. "You don't understand! You stand here telling me I have to work with Matron White, yet you hate the fae so much you can't put it aside to see the benefit of working with *them*."

"No—that's different." He raises a finger.

"Is it? How? You're the human king, why am I more interested in protecting your people than you?" I jab my finger into his chest.

Suri makes a small squeak.

Basten falls back as though struck by a battering ram, blinking hard at me. I close my mouth quickly. *Did I go too far?*

Suri's gaze is glued to the carpet like a small child whose parents are fighting. Matron White is riveted, her arms folded as she stands by the fire and watches.

I shouldn't have raised my voice.

Basten and I are king and queen—we should be presenting a united front.

More than that—we should *be* a team.

The others' reaction seems to calm Basten's temper the same way it did mine, and he drops the tense set of his shoulders. He rakes back his hair, taming his unsteady breathing.

I swallow, searching his eyes for a tiny crack, a flicker of softness I can cling to and find my way back to him.

"Regardless of how the book was acquired," Kendan cuts in, his official tone smoothing over the last of my prickly edges. "The Fae Games are a strong idea."

I keep my eyes low, focused on the book, trying not to show how my hands are shaking—though I can't hide anything from Basten.

"I haven't said the best part yet. At the end of the Fae Games, bring the Cold Coins out to the gallows. Only, instead of hanging them, my father will pardon them. The ultimate show of peace. That the humans of this city can trust the fae."

I look eagerly between their faces, feeling slightly less confident than before.

That's an awful idea, Rian said when I proposed the pardon. *You want the public to embrace the fae? They want to see them burn, not be pardoned. Give the people what they want.*

The whole point, I tried to explain, *is to show the fae are peaceful.*

Is peace why the public adore fae tales? Do the Dramatics in pubs showcase their benevolence? Look—I know how the public thinks. I was raised in a family that catered to their base impulses. We made a fortune off gambling, whoring, fights for coin. No one worships a damn pacifist. You want people to love the fae? The Cold Coins terrorized the city—give them bloody, raw vengeance as only the fae can do.

The memory of Rian's words see-saw through me, make my nerves jangle. Yes, Rian *does* understand how the public thinks, what drives them to spend their few precious coins.

But we aren't appealing to people's base instincts. We're appealing to their highest ones. To the fae's, too. Trying to create a *better* world.

Lord Kendan nods slowly, his eyes growing more excited. "The new reign will be marked by peace, not vengeance. We won't set the prisoners free, of course, but life in the dungeon should both demonstrate mercy and appease the public's desire for justice." He starts rolling up the map. "If we are all in agreement, I'll have my staff begin preparations for the Fae Games, starting on the Blood Moon."

Basten nods a dismissal.

Matron White touches the key emblem on her robe—the gesture of homage to Immortal Iyre, which feels like a slap in my face—and primly strides from the room. Kendan finishes rolling the maps and leaves.

Then, it's Basten and me. And about six feet of air between us that crackles like heat lightning, charged with everything we've said and haven't said.

This tension can't possibly hang over us forever. At some point, it's going to have to break.

I glance his way and murmur, "You don't think it's a good idea, do you? You don't trust me."

He sighs, his voice softening. "I don't trust the fae."

I close my eyes, take a deep breath, and head for the door. Before leaving, I look back. "Exactly."

CHAPTER 24

BASTEN

I've missed the feel of a blunt object in my hand.

I'm dressed in one of Folke's old whisky-stained cloaks with the hood raised, a tattered cloth around my nose and mouth, so only my eyes are visible. The crown? Left in the Treasury Room on a velvet pillow. The king's sword? On its rack in the Royal Armory.

The best part of all is getting to wear a comfortable fucking shirt for once.

Ahead, Folke strides down the Sin Streets district, stepping gracefully over reeking puddles of piss and ale. Dim lanterns cast pools of murky light into the dark night, barely enough to read the signs for pubs and brothels.

Behind him, Rian skirts the puddles, shackles clatter lightly around his wrists, hidden under the cloak. "Dammit," he mutters. "I stepped in dog shit."

"You're lucky we let you out of the Coffin at all," I say, following him closely, in case he thinks he can bolt. "You have Sabine to thank for that—and the fact that you're the only one who can take us to the safe houses."

Folke stops and looks both ways down a street. "Speaking of..."

"Next street, take a left," Rian murmurs to Folke. "A tavern by the name of The Cracked Keg."

Folke jerks his head in a nod and follows the directions. I keep my head down, all too aware that the last thing I want is to be recognized. After all, I'm trying to mitigate my reputation for growing up a street rat, present myself as worthy of the crown. It wouldn't do to be caught sniffing around the Sin Streets with the likes of a spy and a traitor.

A bar fight breaks out across the street, and despite my better sense, I grin beneath the cloak's hood. Damn, but it feels good to be back on the streets. A little mud on my boots never bothered me. Blood on my knuckles, either.

Folke stops at the street corner and pulls a flask out of his vest. He takes a deep swig and passes it to me with a wink. "Need to look convincing."

"Well. In that case." I take a deep drink, then pass it back.

I'm here to help my kingdom, yeah. But even a king needs to let off some steam.

"Hey!" Rian argues. "Not so convincing if we *all* don't drink."

Folke tucks the flask in his pocket and pats it. "Sorry, friend, but you can't drink without revealing your shackles. You're here to identify faces, not *get* shit-faced."

He grabs Rian by the shoulder and hauls him down the street toward the Cracked Keg.

Inside, it's so crowded that we have to shuffle to even get in the door. It's a payday evening, so everyone with two cents to rub together is out drinking. And, it's a bit of a celebration, too. The city is finally liberated from the Golden

Sentinels' hold. Supplies and food are flowing through the gates once more. Finally, bellies are full.

I swallow, feeling a strange warmth in my chest. *Pride.* But then a customer suddenly shoves past me and vomits on the floor right next to my boots.

I grimace and wipe my boot on a stool leg.

"Okay," Folke says, leaning in close to me and Rian. "Where's this safe house?"

Rian jerks his head toward the bar. "Kitchen."

Folke's brow wrinkles. "What?"

"The kitchen," Rian hisses again, jerking his chin a second time at the bar. "Through that door. Behind the bar. It's a safe kitchen."

"Who the hell ever heard of a safe *kitchen*?" Folke hisses.

I groan, because I very well might be the world's biggest idiot to put my faith in Rian Valvere.

And yet, here we are.

Folke heads for the bar, but Rian grabs him, the shackles clattering softly in the folds of his cloak. "Wait—you can't just walk behind the counter. You'll be beaten over the head with a pewter tankard. There's a rear entrance. That way, by the latrines outside."

He indicates a small wooden door.

We push our way through the crowd as unobtrusively as possible. Not that anyone throws us looks, anyway. We're three men in a bar full of bastards just like us. Half of them are too drunk to even see their own noses, anyway.

Still, I keep careful tabs on the few individuals around the room who don't reek of ale. The sharp ones pretending to be drunker than they are. Sure, most just want to cheat at cards. But I catch a glimpse of the bartender sliding a thick pouch of coins under the napkin of an outgoing tray.

Safe kitchen. Well, fuck, maybe Rian knows what he's doing after all.

We exit to the narrow, muddy alley with a deep ditch by way of latrine, with a half dozen men pissing into it while singing old fae ditties. Rian points toward a wooden swinging door next to crates stacked up and a bucket of rotting potato peels.

Folke pauses to face us, pulling back his cloak a few inches to show the short sword in its scabbard. "Okay, here's how it will go down. We're going to pull the old Drunkard's Deceit. Basten, you'll have my back. Rian, you find a corner and post yourself there like a fucking broom, got it? Not a peep, not a move. Your only role is to not get in the way."

Rian sighs. "Fine."

My heart is thumping. My adrenaline is pumped. Thank fuck for the handkerchief that hides the smirk on my face, because I'm enjoying this far too much.

"Let's play," I say, cracking my knuckles.

In a snap, Folke transforms into a slobbering, cross-eyed drunk. He throws himself against the swinging door, stumbling into the kitchen, and Rian and I watch from the upper gap in the doorway.

"Bladder's about to explode!" he slurs as he blusters his way toward two young men cleaning tankards by a barrel of soapy water.

The youths jerk to attention, stumbling back to get out of Folke's way. I can hear from their heartbeats that they're on edge—they were even before we set foot inside. I can also hear the muffled breathing of another man—older, judging by the rasp in his throat—not visible, but somewhere nearby.

I sniff the air. *Cheap brandy.*

It's Gaez.

I grab Rian's arm and shove him inside. I'm not giving the bastard a second to slip away—I have to fucking fight *and* babysit.

We burst in, and I spot a gap behind the water barrel and shove Rian toward it. Then, in the same move, I puff myself up big and stomp loudly toward Folke.

"Jacko, you ass! Latrine is outside!" I shout.

Folke pinwheels toward me sloppily, taking the opportunity to stumble toward the only other door; a backroom with a suspicious number of locks.

"What, you blind? It's right here!" Folke slams his shoulder against the door, acting drunk, but it doesn't budge.

The young dishwashers jerk toward us, arms outstretched to herd us back toward the alley. The taller one grunts, "Hey, you pissers. Get the fuck out."

The shorter one quietly picks up a knife next to a pile of potatoes.

"Yeah, yeah," I say. "My ass of a friend here downed too much booze. Get over here, Jacko—"

I swipe for him, but Folke dodges my hand with a drunken giggle, and I slam my fist into the back room door instead.

Shit—it *still* doesn't break open.

At the same time, loud footsteps sound in the back room. The locks click on the other side, and the door swings open.

General Gaez's face, bruised and red-cheeked from drink, scowls back at me.

"What the fuck's going on out here, boys?" he snaps to the dishwashers.

I grin beneath my handkerchief as I shove my foot in the door so he can't shut it again. At my side, Folke drops his drunken act, smoothly drawing his sword.

I tug down my handkerchief and grin. "We meet again."

Gaez is well trained enough as a fighter to show only a flicker of surprise before grabbing for a meat cleaver just inside the back room, as he shouts to the dishwashers, "Kill them!"

I slam my elbow into his forearm, smashing the meat cleaver back into his own face. A cut bursts over his left temple. He falls backward but catches himself, blood dripping down into his eye.

"Folke, handle the boys," I call. "I've got Gaez."

Folke spins his knife around, grinning at the dishwashers. "Hello, there."

The shorter youth jabs the peeling knife at him, but Folke picks up a potato and catches the blade it in, twisting it out of the boy's hand and tossing it, knife and all, into the water barrel.

I slam my shoulder against the back room door, pushing my way in. It's barely more than a pantry. A cot on the floor, a small cache of weapons, plenty of booze. Gaez has been holed up here for a while.

Gaez lunges for me, a fist swinging toward my head, but I block it.

I sigh, because this is almost too easy.

Then, a shout comes from behind me, and I immediately swallow my words.

Sentinels flood into the kitchen from the alley. The dissidents who fled along with Gaez. One, two, three, four. They're all armed—I recognize the bartender among them and a few pub patrons. They're armed to the teeth with swords and crossbows.

The nearest one clocks me immediately and aims his crossbow.

Fuck.

Rian suddenly bursts out of the corner and slams into him, and the arrow the man lets loose zips by my head to lodge into the wall.

I come up, tossing back my hair, my chest fucking pounding. I glance at the arrow that nearly skewered me.

"You're welcome," Rian prompts, and then immediately launches himself at the next sentinel. His hands are bound, but he manages to use his body weight to knock the man to the floor. It's so tight in the kitchen that they slam into the water barrel. It topples over, sending suds everywhere, dirty tankards clattering all over the floor.

One of the dishwashers loses his balance and slams into the table corner with a sickening crack.

And then, all hell breaks loose.

Gaez comes at me with a sentinel's shield, slamming into my chest so hard my breath shoots from my lungs. I crumple forward, clutching my middle, and he raises the shield to slam the edge on my neck.

I shoot forward before he can, striking him in his gut, knocking him back.

We both collapse to the back room floor, grappling for the nearest weapon.

Behind me, Folke and Rian are taking the four sentinels in the kitchen. The other dishwasher is gone—probably ran out to get more reinforcements, which means the clock is ticking. We can take five men, maybe. But not a dozen.

"Folke, stop the fucking dishwasher, he's getting away!" I shout.

Folke slams his elbow into a sentinel's face, then disappears into the alley, the door swinging behind him.

"Brother, catch," Rian calls, and I look up in time to see a rolling pin hurtling my way.

I grab it and immediately bring it down on the back of Gaez's head.

He gags and slumps forward, stunned, but only for a second.

"Don't call me that," I snap at Rian, pushing to my feet and raising the pin again. Gaez pushes groggily to his knees, and I slam it down on his head again. "I'm not your fucking brother."

Rian, a knife between his shackled fists, swipes it down toward one of the sentinels as he scoffs, "I've called you that for years."

Gaez still struggles to get back to his knees, and I slam my boot on his back, knocking him prone on the kitchen floor, pinning him there with my weight while I toss the rolling pin aside and reach for a sword from his weapons cache.

I swing it in an arc as one of the sentinels rushes me, slicing him across the chest.

"Yeah, a brother you'd muzzle, right?" I say to Rian. "Chain like a hunting dog?"

Rian knees a sentinel in the gut, and when he straightens, gives me a quizzical look. "What the fuck are you on about?"

"That's what you said to Captain Tatarin," I spit, and bring down the blunt end of my sword on another sentinel's head, all the while Gaez struggling to get free under my boot. I shove him down harder, shaking with fury—but I realize it isn't for him.

It's for *Rian.*

"She warned me about you. Captain Tatarin. How you planned vengeance on the man you considered a brother. You said you'd muzzle me, wasn't that the word? Chain me? Break me like a dog?"

The truth slams into me.

This is why I've been so furious.

For what Rian did to Sabine, yes. But for what he did to me, too. The gut-punch that Rian had already stopped seeing me as his brother long before all this. That maybe he *never had.*

"Captain Tatarin...?" Rian stares at me in confusion, but it doesn't last long. A sentinel hurls a tankard at his head, and he ducks just in time, then grabs a bucket handle and swings the wooden bucket into the man's ear.

"You fucking idiot," he cries, eyes widening in realization. "I wasn't talking about *you!*"

The air halts in my lungs, and I have to forcefully drag in a breath. Gaez gets a hand free and slams a fist into my boot, but I bring down the sword next to his neck.

I can't kill him—we need him for the fae to pardon—but I'm getting tired of this dragged-out bullshit.

"For fuck's sake," I mutter to Gaez, "You want a choke collar out of bruises? Stop moving. I'm kind of in the middle of something."

He garbles curses at me, spit flying out of his mouth, but I ignore him and face Rian.

"What are *you* talking about?" I sputter.

"Kendan!" Rian explodes. "I was telling Captain Tatarin how much I wanted to throttle *Kendan.*"

"Kendan *is* your brother."

Rian pinches the bridge of his nose, muttering a curse under his own breath. "He isn't my brother, that's the whole point. I'm not a Valvere. I was angry—I wanted Kendan's damn iron sash ripped off him. I had a plan to frame him with a few whores, humiliate him." He looks up, a waver of hurt in his eyes. "You thought I was telling Tatarin that I was going to muzzle *you*? Why would I do that? You're the only damn person from hell and back who hasn't betrayed me."

My heart thumps hard, so hard I can't speak for a minute.

"I had sex with your bride."

He groans, exasperated with me, as he twists the knife deeper in the sentinel's neck. "Please. I told you, I got over that in a week."

He's lying. Of course he is. Sabine has a hold on every man, woman, and horse she crosses paths with, and Rian is no exception.

And yet, I know the sound of Rian's pulse when he lies, and I'm not sure he's lying. Not entirely.

For a heartbeat, I just stare at him.

Because if he's not lying...

If he truly let Sabine go when he gave her to me...

"Rian—" I start.

But I'm cut off by Folke, who crashes back into the kitchen with blood pouring down one shoulder, his cloak nowhere to be found.

"Gentleman," he says. "Time to go—*now*."

Rian and I exchange a look—something has changed here, between us, but I don't even begin to know how to put a fucking name to it.

A sentinel groans as he rolls over, trying to stand, but Rian clutches the knife between his bound hands and slams it into the man's chest, making clean work of it.

Then he and Folke climb over the other dead bodies and help me haul Gaez to his feet.

I focus on binding Gaez's hands behind his back to keep me from thinking too hard about this misunderstanding with Rian. I tug hard, so hard he curses.

For weeks, I've been seething at Rian. Stewing in it. Thinking he wanted to muzzle me like a dog, that I meant nothing to him. And now...fuck, I don't know how to feel.

More shouts sound from outside, and we hustle into the alley, dragging Gaez with us.

We shove Gaez into an empty wheelbarrow and push it forward into the shadows.

While Folke leads off any rogue sentinels that might be following us, Rian and I cart Gaez straight to the city dungeon, run again by the royal army since our forces retook the city.

The sentinels used the dungeon to house prisoners of war, and did a poor job of it; it still reeks of stale piss and dried blood. Our men have cleaned it out and laid straw, but it'll take a while to get it back into shape.

Not that I mind when it comes to Gaez.

He can rot down here, for all I care. As long as there's enough life in him by the Fae Games for Vale to make a big show of sparing his neck. *Life in prison.* Yeah...sure. We'll throw him back down here and let the rats do the rest—he won't survive long.

The dungeon tower, a square monolith with "JUSTICE" carved above the door, sits to the north of Valor Circle.

Now, Lady Suri paces in front of it, guards flanking her, her Castlekeep keyring jangling with every tight step, as she huddles beneath a heavy velvet cloak.

"Lady Suri. Thank you for coming." I nod, tugging down my mask. "You look about as out of place here as a rat on the dinner table."

Rian slaps me and chimes in, "Forgive him. He doesn't know how to speak to a lady. You'd be the most delectable rodent ever to be served on *my* table."

She gives him an exasperated look, though there's the slightest rush of pink to her cheeks.

"Believe me," she says, "It isn't my choice to be here. But the dungeon cells we have keys for are already full, so I have to unlock the secondary unit." She huffs in the cold, skirting her satin shoes around a muddy puddle. "I'm not about to let my keys be separated from me."

She slides the main gate key in the lock, and steps back for the soldiers to open the gate. We drag Gaez down the stairs, and she trails behind us, hunting for the keys that correspond with each cell.

"The previous Castlekeep didn't label anything," she explains. "One hundred keys on here, and for each door, I have to try them all."

My boots splash in puddles in the hallway. The first unit of cells are full; Folke's men have been doing a good job rounding up the remaining dissenters. A man cat calls as Suri passes, and Rian shoves his foot through the bars to kick over the man's piss bucket.

"Hey!" the man snaps.

"She's a fucking lady."

Suri rolls her eyes, but there's a slight tug at the corner of her mouth. "Here, I think this long iron key corresponds to the second unit..." She tests out two keys, and the third one opens the lock. She sighs with relief, stepping back as she tightens her shawl.

"I'll leave this key with the dungeon master until a new one can be forged. Now, my bed is calling, if you gentlemen don't mind—"

What happens next is so fast I can barely track it.

The dungeon guards are helping drag Gaez in, when suddenly, he shoots to his feet, fresh as sunrise, and shoves the two guards into the newly unlocked cell.

They slam into me, unintentionally pushing me back with them.

Gaez slams the cell shut and twists the key. He jerks it out of the lock a second before I reach it, then wraps his chained hands around Suri's neck, dragging her back to the wall.

She shrieks, clawing at his hands.

His beady eyes throw sparks as he spits, "Try anything and I choke her out."

I slam my hand against the bars, rattling them. My mind races. The two dungeon guards and I are locked in a cell. The only other guard is a floor above, unaware.

And fucking *Rian* is the only one free.

Suri keeps struggling to get free, but he has a hundred pounds on her. The more she struggles, the harder he pulls the chain against her neck.

"Rian Valvere." Gaez spits on the floor. "Here's your chance to escape. Consider it a final gift from your general. Don't say I never did anything for my short-reining *king*." He jerks his head toward the exit. "We separate, use the sewers to get out of the city. Meet up in the village where you lost that game of Hazard to the executioner."

He chuckles, thinking he's won.

And maybe he has.

My stomach falls to my feet. Rian could really fucking do it. Escape. Without me and Folke babysitting him, he could slip into the night. Hell, he knows every safe house in the city. Plenty of blacksmiths could be bribed to remove his shackles.

He could be on the road to Duren by the morning.

Fuck.

I grip the bars, squeezing so tight my knuckles blanch. "Don't you fucking do it, Rian."

Rian glances behind him at the hallway as though weighing the distance. His tongue darts out between his lips like a snake sampling the air.

How many times have I seen that cunning in his eyes, across the Basel table?

Rian slides a calculating look back at Gaez. He jerks his chin toward Suri. "What about her?"

Gaez sneers. "What the fuck do you care? She a good tumble between the sheets?"

Suri squeaks and kicks at him, but her little feet do as much damage as a kitten's paws.

Rian's face darkens. "That's a lady you're talking about."

Gaez guffaws, a fleck of spittle flying out to land on Suri's cheek. "Like that ever stopped the Lord of Liars."

An unreadable look comes over Rian's face, and for a second, I think he's going to throw himself at Gaez. But then, he breaks into a devilish grin. "Remember where I hid when I stole my money back from the executioner? The little cottage with that well-endowed washerwoman..."

Gaez barks a laugh, but it turns into a cough. "Right. I'll meet you there."

Rian laughs, rich and conspiratory. Then, his eyes light up as though an idea has just struck him. "Her keyring—toss it to me. I'll set the other prisoners lose behind you. The guards will be so busy trying to catch them, it'll buy us time."

Rian steps forward, holding out his hand for the keys. He slips so seamlessly into his commander's voice that Gaez obeys on instinct, fumbling in Suri's pocket for her keyring. She clasps harder at the chain around her neck, her eyes wide and spitting fire at Rian.

"Here."

Gaez tosses the keyring to Rian, but Rian misses, and it clatters on the floor.

Rian curses and stoops down for it—

And grabs Suri by the ankles, jerking her in one swift tug out from Gaez's grasp. She shrieks as she's ripped from the man's hands, his chain clattering as he swipes for her, but Rian already has her on the ground.

He drags her, kicking and screaming, by the feet down the hall.

"You bastard!" she screams. "Let me go!"

"I'm saving your damn life, Suri!"

Rian shoves her into a safe corner, then launches himself at Gaez. He feigns moving in for a bear-hug around Gaez's middle, but at the last second, pivots to the side, sliding on a skid of mud around Gaez's back.

Before Gaez can turn, Rian has his *own* shackles around the man's neck.

"Not a bad trick, thanks for the idea," he spits. He kicks

the keyring toward Suri as he strangles Gaez. "Quick. Unlock the cell."

Suri blinks, one hand still clutching her throat, eyes still wide and wild.

"It's okay, Suri," I say, holding out my hand. "The keys."

Suri crawls on her hands and knees to the keyring, her hand shaking, her throat rubbed raw.

She passes me the key with a shaking hand.

In seconds, I have the cell gate open. I tear out to where Rian has Gaez with his shackles around the man's throat. I don't hesitate for a second before slamming my fist into Gaez's gut.

The air rushes from his lungs.

I grab him by the shoulders. Rian lifts the shackles from his neck, and I throw him into the cell I've recently vacated. One of the dungeon guards takes over with the keys, locking him in, while the other runs to sound the alarm.

It's...done.

Suri breaths hard, still on hands and knees, her pretty dress soaked through with mud.

I whirl on Rian, who's slumped back against the wall, catching his breath.

"You could have escaped," I bluster, not understanding why he wouldn't. "You realize I'm going to just drag you back to the Coffin, right?"

"Oh, I know." He smiles between pants. "But then I'd miss having this beautiful woman owe me her life." He tilts his head toward Suri. "At the very least, a kiss."

Suri scoffs, one hand pressed protectively to her throat, staring at him—half appalled, half...not.

Rian smirks. "What? Gratitude comes in many forms."

Suri swallows hard. "I'll believe you're on our side," she

says warily, "when you risk something that costs more than a few bruises."

Rian's teasing fades. His eyes sharpen, turning grave in a way that makes the hairs on my arms lift.

He points to Gaez, unconscious in the cell. "You really should kill him. Sabine's plan? To have the fae pardon him? It won't work. She still believes people rise to hope. That's not a fae instinct—that's a human fantasy she's clinging to. The public doesn't crave forgiveness. They crave spectacle. Peace won't buy the fae a single fan that vengeance wouldn't win tenfold."

I stare at him, heartbeat loud in my ears, almost swayed by his conviction.

But then I grab him by the collar and drag him toward the stairs, where I'll lock him back in the Coffin despite the fact he just saved Suri's life.

"You act like you still call the shots," I say. "Sooner or later, you're going to have to learn your place."

CHAPTER 25
SABINE

I yawn, rub my bleary eyes, and turn another page.

I've lost track of how many days I've been hunched over a table in the castle's library, sun-up to sun-down, trying to make sense of the *Last Return of the Fae: Volume II*'s esoteric writings.

The language isn't entirely foreign. It's written in a blend of the Immortal Tongue, which was drilled into me at the convent, and an even more ancient fae language whose oddly sloped letters tickle the back of my head. It's a bit like staring at a landscape for hours, only to suddenly notice a deer that's been standing ten feet away the entire time.

If I run my eyes over the lines enough times, I don't know how to describe it, but the nonsense begins to make *sense.*

It's slow, yes.

Painstakingly so.

But not without a touch of thrill.

Every word I translate sings to the silver deep in my

blood. The more I remember of the ancient fae tongue, the greater a connection I feel to my past selves. While reading, I've gotten flashes of dream-like memories: Of speaking these ancient prophecies in the Garden of Ten Gods. Of raising a silver chalice at Drahallen Hall's Head Table. Of chasing cloudfoxes through iridescent ferns to a stream, where I called for water to rise into the air and form loops for the creatures to bound through.

I suddenly jolt, my head bobbing sharply.

I nodded off again.

I yawn and shift on the hard wooden chair, pulling my shawl tighter around my shoulders. I reach for a sip of water from a glass and pause, remembering my memory-dream.

Hesitantly, I dip my middle finger in the glass, then let a single drip fall back in. I swirl my finger in the air, concentrating on the water...

...and as though following the path I've carved for it, the water flows upward into the air, playfully spiraling around my finger.

I grin, laughing from the simple joy of it. Soon, I'll be strong enough to help feed the people in Old Coros still hungry from the siege. Maybe even restore the Lunden river valley.

But the laugh turns into a cough, and I hunch forward. The water splashes back into the glass.

"You're depleted." Basten's voice comes from the library door.

I turn, rubbing the exhaustion from my eyes, and glance at the clock. *It's after midnight.*

I ask, "How long have you been there?"

He drops his arms and saunters in, dragging out the

chair next to me. "Long enough to see you command water to do the impossible." He nods toward the water glass. "You're doing well."

His words are kind, but his tone is off—still distant. Like we just can't seem to hit the right note together.

My stomach suddenly groans painfully. I can't hide the ache, and I clutch my belly.

Basten's face falls serious. "You need to feed, Sabine. You've been here for days with that book, barely eating, not consuming so much as a prayer."

"I'm fine."

He leans back with a tense exhale, the chair groaning under his weight. "The Church of Immortal Solene in Old Coros is just a few blocks away, in the Quiet Ward. Since people learned of your Rise, its congregation has swelled from a dozen to over three thousand. They've petitioned to build an altar to you here in the castle's Queen's Walk, where your devotees can present offerings."

My mouth salivates at the mention of an altar, instinct and thirst mixing in a dangerous clash, but I squeeze my hands tight and shake my head.

I say, "The city's still recovering. The Cold Coins starved the people for weeks. They need every scrap of food and cloth and coin for themselves. I won't take that from them."

I drag my fingers through my hair—it feels dry, stiff, in dire need of washing—and slump forward over the book. "Anyway, this work is too important. The things I'm remembering..." I trail off, looking away.

A part of me is eager to tell him about my dream-memory. He's my person—I want to share everything with him. Yet at the same time, I'm keenly aware that it only pushes me further away from humanity.

From him.

I clear my throat. "The language is starting to make more sense. I can't stop now; my father will be here on the Blood Moon, and I have to translate how to put the fae to sleep before then."

He rests his hand on my chair back, his thumb rubbing circles on my upper back. Gently, he tilts his head back to expose his neck. "Drink from me."

The flash of tanned skin above his collar makes saliva pool in my mouth. Gods, have I ever been this ravenous?

Drink drink drink.

I can practically taste his blood on my tongue, but I drop my hands in my lap, under the table, and squeeze hard to resist the urge. "I'll drink wine."

"Wine isn't enough." His voice is stern, concerned. He rolls back his shirt sleeve and offers me his arm. "You need human sacrifice."

I turn away, my stomach twisting. "My father was right. The longer my fae self has been awake, the harder it is to stop once I start. I don't want to drain you anymore. What happened to Pax..."

His heel taps hard on the library's wooden floor. "You aren't Iyre. You'll stop in time—we've discussed this. We'll defy the odds."

Drink drink drink.

I look at my hands clasped in my lap. My voice comes out as barely a whisper, "You don't know that. *I* don't know that."

Basten leans forward, his brown eyes as soft and strong as a goldenclaw's. "If you won't drink from me, and you won't accept offerings, how will you maintain your strength?"

I rest my hand on his knee, quieting his anxious jitters. "All those new devotees you mentioned? They're praying to me—I can feel it. Prayers cost them no food from their table, and it gives me strength. Besides, according to this book, fae can get by for a long time on prayers alone. Once, Immortal Meric survived a decade from a single woman's daily morning worship."

Basten doesn't look convinced, but before he can press the issue again, something scratches at the library window.

We're on the second floor, high above the garden, so it's little surprise when I see Plume's lolling tongue fogging up the glass.

I unlatch the window for her, stepping back as she zips in and bounds from one table to the next, an endless ball of energy.

"Plume!" I call, waving for her to calm down. In my head, I say, **What happened?**

She bounds off a spinning globe and onto a bust of Old King Joruun perched on the fireplace.

She says, **She sent Plume to tell girlie! Said to hurry!**

I have to duck as Plume pirouettes off the bust and lopes across the tables, only to jump on Basten's shoulder and use it as a springboard to reach a high shelf.

He ducks and mutters a mild curse.

I ask quickly, **Who said that?**

Girlie's sunshine friend! she answers.

"What's gotten into her?" Basten asks, bracing one arm overhead to fend off Plume's next leap.

"She says Suri sent her to me," I say, worry drumming against my ribs as I whip back toward Plume. **Where is Suri?**

Plume jumps again and lands on a shelf high above my head, her tongue lolling, breath thick with the scent of pine needles. ***Coffin!***

I pull in a sharp breath, confused. Why would Suri be in the Coffin?

Basten is at my side in a second. "What?"

"The Coffin. The jail cell in the attic." The realization hits me as I meet his eyes. "Rian!"

He slams my book closed.

We bolt across the library, weaving past startled maids burdened with stacks of bed linens, and race up the tight, spiral stairs to the top of Mercy Tower. I seize the attic doorknob and twist—only to feel it stick.

A groan tears out of me. "It's locked!" I cup my hands around the keyhole and shout, "Suri? Are you in there?"

"Sabby?" a muffled voice replies.

"Stand back," Basten says. He grabs an iron candlestick from a wall sconce and uses the blunt end to slam against the lock. After a few strikes, the wood splinters, and Basten shoves his weight against it to break the final hold.

I spill into the narrow attic hallway, blinking to adjust to the low lighting of a single lantern on the far wall.

Basten draws his hunting knife, ready for anything.

"Sabby!" Suri reaches through the Coffin's bars.

I stop short, shocked to see her locked *inside* the cell, but rush forward to clasp her hand.

Her eyes are red from crying, but otherwise, she looks unharmed.

"Suri—what happened?" I breathe.

Basten patrols the corners of the attic, muscles set tense. "Suri, where is Rian?"

"Gods, I was such a fool!" Suri rasps, a hand on her throat. "I mean, he's the Lord of Liars—and I fell for one of his tricks, even though I knew better!"

"Slow down," I say, squeezing her hand for support. "Tell us exactly what happened."

Suri plucks at her lace collar, lips pursed together. "He's been hounding me for days to bring him something to read to pass the time. Well, yesterday he mentioned *Dancy's Forest Tales*. He could even quote whole sections. It was my favorite book as a girl. I had a copy with a broken spine and falling out pages from how much I pored through it. I don't know, something about him liking that book, too, was... charming? Unexpected? That's the thing about Rian, he's driving me mad one minute, making me laugh the next."

She sighs before continuing. "So, I gave in. I brought him the library's copy. We read the story of Hildy and Lord Vallen aloud, passing the book back and forth through the bars. It was just...innocent fun. Then we got to the part where Lord Vallen asks Hildy for a kiss as payment for her debts, and Rian said...he said...Gods, I can't! It's *humiliating*!"

Basten rests a hand on the bars. "Continue, Suri."

She huffs up toward the air, pacing, and finally explains in a shaking voice, "He reminded me that I 'owe him a kiss' from when he saved me from Gaez's attack. It was ridiculous. I assumed he was joking. But, I mean, you have to admit it, Sabby. Even a Sister would find Rian Valvere handsome...that's just a fact. And I haven't kissed anyone since Charlin..." She trails off, fumbling with her lace collar.

"Lady Suri," Basten prompts.

She hiccups. "He kissed me. Through the bars." Her eyes drift off, growing hazy, as if she can still feel the ghost of his mouth on hers. She licks her lips—a tiny, unconscious motion—like she's chasing the last of it. For a second, something bright flickers over her face—a kind of breathlessness.

Then it collapses.

Her shoulders fold in. She covers her face with both hands, voice muffled with shame. "I can't believe I fell for it. He was only distracting me so he could steal my keyring from my pocket and swap it out with a chunk of brick of the same weight. He ended the kiss, and I was so...so *overtaken*, that I barely realized he'd unlocked his cell. He pulled me in to take his place, then set himself free. He *did* come back briefly to bring me a basket of snacks and some extra blankets, in case I got cold."

She motions to a small pile of supplies: cinnamon cookies, a bottle of sherry, warm slippers.

"I called and called for help," she continues, "but this cell is four stories high. Plume finally came to that leak in the roof, and I managed to get a message across to her." She points to a damp spot on the ceiling where a board has rotted out.

Basten whips his head around to the door. "You're saying Rian *escaped*?"

Suri nods.

"Fuck!" Basten slams the handle of his knife against the bars, then takes a moment to steady himself, then races out of the attic.

His boots clomp heavy on the stairs.

For a moment, I'm so stunned I can't move. I still can't process Suri's story.

A kiss? Rian and Suri?

I don't even know how to begin to wrap my mind around that. I mean, yes, she's inexperienced, but she isn't a fool. She wouldn't have fallen for just anyone's pretty words. She must have actually *seen* something in Rian.

Didn't you, once, Sabine?

I go rigid. But underneath the shock is something bitter—the ache of a wound I should've seen coming. After all we've been through—taking him prisoner, stopping the bloodshed in the city, even daring to share wine with him again—he still turned on us.

On *me.*

Gods help me, that's what stings the most. A part of me wanted to forgive him—to trust him.

And he used that against us.

"I'll send guards to unlock the cell," I say to her in a rush, and then hurry after Basten, even as she's calling back to me.

But adrenaline pushes me forward. I feel my human glamour fall away, being left behind as the fey lines blister free. My incisors sharpen against my bottom lip, my hunger snapping in my throat.

Now, I'm on the hunt.

I catch up with Basten at the bottom of the stairs, where he's banging on doors to rouse the sleeping guards. "Up, soldiers! Swords at the ready, Rian Valvere is on the run!"

Night guards and sleepy-eyed maids all stop to stare at me as I race to the window; they aren't used to seeing me in my fae appearance.

My blood races through my veins, sending my silver glow pulsing, as I scour the courtyard below for any sign of Rian. Knowing him, this is no random seized opportunity. He's surely been planning this escape, possibly for a long time.

"Can we not have a crisis at midnight, for once?

What's wrong with noon?" Folke, still tugging on his pants, stumbles down the hallway as his jaw stretches in a yawn.

"Rian fucked us," Basten spits, as a guard hastens to help him strap a sword around his waist. "He escaped. Folke, get to the gates, make sure they're sealed—"

Commotion on the stairs makes us all turn to find the sentries from the castle entrance hustling up the stairs, out of breath in their clattering armor.

"About the gates, King Basten," one of them says, pausing to brace his hands on his knees. His face is corpse-white beneath his helmet. "And you, Queen Sabine." He glances at me, my silver sheen reflecting in his eyes, and he swallows hard. "You—you need to come see this for yourself, Majesties."

Basten and I share a look—the kind that carries a dozen memories of what Rian has already proven himself capable of.

And then we run.

I follow the soldiers down the stairs to the first floor, my pulse running hot. I don't feel like a princess now. Or a queen. I feel like a predator stalking the man who wounded her with far more than arrows.

We pass through Raven Hall and out into the front courtyard, shrouded by night, where a dozen soldiers are gathered with torches. They stand back from the gates, giving it a wide berth, almost stock-still.

"What are you doing?" I cry. "Your king gave the command, swords up!"

I grab Captain Fernsby, but as he turns toward me, I get a view of the gate. Of what they're all staring at.

And my own feet drift to a stop.

"Oh, Rian," I exclaim under my breath. "What have you done?"

There's no sign of Rian, but one of the fugitives is here. The leader of the Cold Coins, the dissident group of Golden Sentinels who refused to surrender at Rian's order.

The man is strung up outside the gates, his motionless arms splayed to the sides, hanging by ropes like a puppet. A large battle axe, the same kind that Immortal Vale carries, is cleft deep into his skull. Golden arrows stick out of his chest. The telltale black-purple mark of belladonna poison stains his lips. Smoke still rises from his hollowed-out eyes, burned to nothing but ashes. Ivy vines wind around his neck.

Basten steps forward, breathing hard, and the soldiers fall back to give him room. "How did...?"

Even with the question unfinished, we all know what he's asking, and no one has the answer.

"Look!" I grab Basten's arm and point to the stone pavers outside the gate, where someone has scrawled in chalk:

WE COME NOT TO HARM, BUT PROTECT.
WE BRING JUSTICE, NOT PAIN.
LAY DOWN OFFERINGS TO US, AND WE WILL LAY YOUR
ENEMIES AT YOUR FEET.
SOON, WE WILL ARRIVE.
THE GAMES WILL BEGIN.

Despite the late hour, a crowd of onlookers has already gathered on the other side of the gate. Nighttime workers, drunks from the pubs, bakers getting an early start on their bread dough.

They point to the body, hushed voices rising and falling in a mix of fear and awe.

"That's Gaez," a tavernkeeper calls. "The leader of the Cold Coins."

"It's the work of the fae!" a busker adds, his lute dangling from his shoulder. "Those are Artain's golden arrows! And Vale's axe. And look—Thracia's belladonna poison on his lips!" He suddenly locks eyes with me and starts. "Oh—Lady Solene! King Basten! Forgive me, I did not see you!"

Gasps ring out once they see us on the inside of the gate. One by one, everyone falls to their knee, head bowed.

"Is it true, Lady Solene?" a street sweeper asks, keeping his head lowered. "Did Vale himself bring Gaez to justice? Is this a fae miracle?"

An elderly lady bows before me. "Thank you, my lady, for this miracle! Our gratitude to all your kind!"

I gape, slowly looking between the ivy wrapped in a noose around Gaez's neck and at my own glowing fey lines.

"I—" I start. "I didn't—"

Basten jerks his head at me, a signal to stay quiet. I close my mouth. His jaw is rock-hard, anger simmering in his eyes, because he knows as well as I did that none of the fae had anything to do with this.

He steps close to me and murmurs low, "What's done is done—let them worship you." He pauses. "You need the strength."

"*Rian* did this," I hiss.

"I know."

Captain Fernsby turns to the soldiers and commands, "Cut down the body. Get these gates open!"

The soldiers finally snap to attention, though they look as shaken by the spectacle as the onlookers.

I spot one of them quietly making the maze gesture of Immortal Meric beneath his cloak.

Even the soldiers are believers in this so-called miracle. Well, why wouldn't they be? Rian gift-wrapped a perfect miracle for them as only Rian could: bloody, violent, full of vindictive glee.

Give the people what they want, he said.

"Soldiers," Captain Fernsby orders. "Scour the city for the fugitive, Rian Valvere!"

The royal soldiers pour through the gates and out into the dark streets, pushing through the rapidly growing crowd coming to stare at the fae miracle. It seems like more and more people appear by the second. Even at this late hour, word must be traveling lightning-quick through Old Coros.

A miracle?

No—call it by its real name. A *betrayal*.

I lurch toward the gates, fey already sparking at my fingertips, but Basten stops me with a touch on my wrist.

"Sabine, wait." He drops his voice. "No—he's here. He's still in the castle. I know how he thinks."

I pause. "He hid in the walls once, he wouldn't be stupid enough to do that again."

"He would," Basten insists, "precisely because no one would expect him to."

He jerks his head back toward the castle. In the chaos of soldiers rushing out the gates, the public growing in number by the minute to fawn all over the gods' "gift" of vengeance, and lamps switching on all over the city, I barely know what to do.

But even with the distance between us, Basten has always been my North Star—and he knows Rian almost as well as he knows himself.

I nod.

The two of us run away from the crowd of soldiers, rushing into the castle as everyone else is pouring out.

CHAPTER 26

BASTEN

As we sprint through Raven Hall, I unlatch my heavy sword and let it clatter to the ground. It's the weapon of a king, not a hunter. I need to be light on my feet. Lithe, fast. And lord knows I have enough knives strapped on me to skin a herd of deer.

Sabine heads for the grand staircase, but I stop in the center of the foyer, right on the raven mosaic, and tilt my head toward the high ceiling.

When she doesn't hear my footsteps beside her, she stops on the first step, one hand on the stone railing, and looks back.

"What is it?" she asks, following my gaze toward the ceiling.

"I need to listen." I drop to one knee, resting my head on my fist, and close my eyelids.

Hekkelveld Castle is surprisingly quiet at night. Not like Sorsha Hall, which was filled with the sounds of debauchery 'til dawn, or Drahallen Hall, where the fae hardly know day from night. Sure, it's a cavernous structure, filled with hundreds of people on any given night, so even at midnight, there are still sounds of night sentries pacing, maids and stewards cleaning, dozens of people snoring.

I'm listening for something specific.

I'm listening for...

There.

The unique clatter of the two bone dice in Rian's pocket.

"Third floor," I say as I explode to my feet. Sabine hoists her skirt, and together, we race up the stairs. Back and forth, back and forth. Six flights. She keeps pace with me, not a flicker of slowing down, but when we reach the third landing, she grips the railing to catch her breath.

Her silver glow dims, flickering like dying firelight. She's weakened. Malnourished, for a fae. And yet I'm struck by the absolute certainty that even diminished, she's the most beautiful, vicious creature to walk the earth in ten thousand years.

"You need rest," I say, cupping her chin to tilt her face to meet mine. "Stay here and guard the stairs in case he tries to come back down this way."

Her eyes, sunken and tired, flash with a defiant spark. "Like hell. *I'm* going after him."

I let out a sharp, growling exhale. "Then at least drink from me first." Moving fast, I start to roll up my sleeve.

She slaps my hand away, turning her head. "I said no— I'm not risking you."

"Sabine, you'll die like this!"

"I'm *immortal!*" She practically bares her teeth at me, still leaning heavily on the railing. "When will you understand that, Basten? At worst, my powers will fade to human level. *Your* level. Still strong enough."

I stalk in a tight, predatory circle. "I'm trying to help you.

You're too damn proud. You used to take what I offered with open hands, wide eyes. Used to *beg* me for it."

Her cheeks blaze pink. "That was before a kiss might accidentally drain you dry."

A whiff of sandalwood and saddle leather hits my nose, slamming into my lungs like a bolt of lightning, and the heat from our argument shifts to the thrill of the chase.

I whip my head around to the southern hallway, resting a hand on the hunting knife at my side.

"He's close," I say, then smell the air again. "Faith Tower."

Her eyes meet mine, full of fire. She doesn't ask permission. Hell, the opposite. There's practically a challenge burning in her expression as she sprints toward the Faith Tower.

My hand tightens on the knife hilt. I don't call her back —what would be the point? She's already half a world ahead of me, headed somewhere I can't follow.

I hate this. How we move more like clashing swords than husband and wife.

I watch her run, her silver glow flickering in the darkened halls. She's burning herself down to the wick.

I run after her, catching up fast, and we pass beneath the archway to Faith Tower like two competitors racing to the finish. She leans against the spiral stairs; a hand pressed to her belly as she fights to catch her breath.

All five towers in Hekkelveld Castle contain a narrow, steep spiral staircase winding up through its center. At each floor, the staircase opens onto a circular landing surrounded by a ring of doors—each door leading to rooms arranged around the outer edge of the tower.

On the third floor, six doors ring the perimeter. I think

back to the architectural maps Kendan tried to drill into my head, when I was more interested in scowling at the painting of Rian in the Council Room, barking for the servants to take the damn thing down and burn it.

Sabine starts to speak, but I hold up a finger. "I need to listen—he's close."

If memory serves, Faith Tower's second and third floors house the lower castle staff, six to a bunk room. The senior staff are on the fourth and fifth floors. Each of the rooms here are filled with sounds of rustling sheets, sleep-sighs, crackling fires.

I frown, concentrating, listening for the telltale clatter of Rian's bone dice. I step from one door to another, pressing my ear to the wood, frustration drumming against my ribs.

"He isn't in any of—" A soft clatter grabs my attention, and I jerk my head toward the wall between the fifth and sixth bunk rooms.

I approach softly, keeping my own noise to a minimum, and rest my fingers against the wall. It's a type of plaster; gypsum, I think. I knock, feeling for a hollow section between two wooden studs.

There—*again*. The clink-clink of bone dice in his pocket.

"He's in the walls," I mutter.

I pull back my fist and slam it straight into the wall. Plaster splinters, a crack giving way beneath my knuckles. Blood blooms across my hand, but I pull back and throw another punch.

A few confused cries come from the bunk rooms, where the noise has roused the maids. I ignore them, tuning my hearing to focus only on the sounds inside the wall.

It's a scuttling. Scrambling, like a rat.

A *big* fucking rat.

With a growl, I slam my fist into the plaster again. It shatters, chunks raining down and releasing a cloud of whitewash dust. I tear at the pieces, ripping through the wall to create an opening. The wooden beams on either side are barely more than a foot apart—this castle is old enough that they used oak, solid as steel.

I shove my shoulder between the beams, gritting my teeth as I strain to squeeze through to the gap on the other side into Rian's secret passageway.

The beams scrape at my clothes, digging splinters into my chest. I grimace, pushing harder, but I can barely fit my head through.

"Fuck!" I cry.

Sabine tugs on my arm, her face flushed, her heartbeat as vicious as my own. "I can fit through," she breathes. "I'll flush him out. You follow the sounds of our chase and be ready to catch him wherever he exits."

Gods, she might be weakened, but her appetite for vengeance is as sharp as ever.

I slide out of the gap, shaking chunks of plaster out of my sweat-soaked hair. Sabine hikes up her skirt and steps over the rubble, her small frame easily slipping between the narrow studs. She looks back at me, reaching out a hand.

I clasp hers, a strange, tender wallop in my chest. "Together, little violet."

My damn voice breaks.

She cocks her head. "I meant for you to give me one of your knives."

I blink, stung, but act fast, tugging a small blade from the holster in my boot and sliding the hilt into her palm.

She starts to duck into the wall gap, but pauses, and emerges again.

For a moment, I see the same deep love in her eyes as when she stood beneath a bower of branches and agreed to be my wife.

"Basten?" She clenches my hand, hard enough that nothing could tear us apart, and whispers, "Together. Always."

And my heart pounds again with hope.

Then, she's swallowed by the darkness.

I listen for her movements on the other side of the wall; her dress scrapes against the narrow passageway, splinters catching on velvet and lace. If *she* can barely fit, Rian must be packed in there like a sausage.

Good. It'll slow him down.

I bolt ahead, skirting around the backside of the spiral stairs, my senses sharp as blades as I pick up on any whiff of sandalwood, any clatter of bone dice.

The sounds of Sabine's movements move further and further away; the secret passage is taking her back through other rooms, where I can't easily follow.

"Shit." I try a bunkroom doorknob. Locked. So, I slam my shoulder against it and burst into a room with squealing young maids bolting upright in their beds.

"M—majesty!" one of them cries, clutching the blankets high over her nightgown. The others quickly move to bow as best they can in their beds.

I power through their room, only glancing at the beds to make sure Rian isn't hiding under one, and then slam through the door on the opposite side that leads to the servants' hallway. A steward carting a load of firewood drops his bundle in surprise as I storm past him.

My heart slams like a stallion as I run my fingers over the walls, feeling for vibrations, listening for the telltale scramble of someone moving inside. *There.* About a hundred feet ahead—I hear Sabine's skirt drag against brick. Then, another scuffle, about a hundred feet ahead of *her*. Someone substantially larger is struggling to fit through the passage.

"Got you, you bastard," I mutter from a clenched jaw. Now, I just have to figure out how to reach him. It's a damn maze between the servants' rooms, the main halls, the servants' halls, and the secret passages, which wind and twist to their own chaotic logic.

I hurl myself through a door, finding myself in the third-floor servants' sitting room. It's empty now, the benches tidily stacked to one side, a basket of wool ready for tomorrow's spinning.

Two doors lead to the rest of the castle, but fuck if I know where. I've never been in these sections before.

I pick the door on the left and shove through, stopping short when I come out in the formal hallway that overlooks the Reliquary Garden. Wind rattles the windowpanes, and I spare a glance down at the tombs looming in the moonlight, licking my lips to taste the air.

A woman's cry, muffled by walls, snags my attention.

Sabine.

Adrenaline rockets through my limbs as I hurtle forward, charging down the hallway and into the main portion of the castle. There's no sign of the guards who should be posted here—they must have followed Captain Fernsby's orders to scour the city for Rian.

"*Basten!*" Sabine calls, and I pivot sharply toward the sound, a moth to flame. I stampede past the grand stairs, only to pause. To listen.

Her voice...she's descending to the second floor.

I double back, leaping over the railing and taking the

stairs three at a time as I charge downward. At the landing, I stop, fighting to quiet my breath so I can hear.

She's still moving down. *First floor.*

I charge downward toward Raven Hall, and my eyes latch onto the entryway fireplace. It's enormous, tall enough for a man to stand upright, and wide enough for two men to lie flat. It's cold now—only lit in the harshest days of winter.

Soot tumbles down to the brick hearth.

"Really got a thing for chimneys, huh?" I mutter. More soot falls, along with the sound of scrambling. The jangle of his bone dice in his pocket.

Sure enough, Rian Valvere drops down, cursing and coughing out soot, dusting off his clothes.

He locks eyes with me.

"Oh, *fuck*," he says.

He bolts, and my adrenaline kicks up a notch. I'll never catch him like this, only halfway down the spiral stairs—so I leap over the stair railing, falling ten feet, and crash to my boots a stride behind him.

Pain splinters through my shins, but I lunge forward and swipe at his jacket.

He shrugs out of it, moving lithe like an animal as I fall to my knees, and I'm left clutching nothing but fabric as he sprints toward the throne room.

"Fuck!" I shout.

More soot falls in the chimney behind me, and a second later, Sabine crashes down. She's streaked with cobwebs and soot, but her eyes are on fire, hot as live coals. She spots me on my knees and staggers over, throwing her arms around me.

"Basten! Are you okay?"

"Don't worry about me." I push to my feet, gritting my

teeth against the pain in my legs. Hell, it's hardly my first time fighting with a sprained ankle. "Rian—he's headed for the throne room."

She takes off on feather-light feet, and I'm a step behind, shaking out the last stiffness from the fall.

We crash into the throne room a few paces behind Rian.

At night, it's deathly still. Cavernous and quiet. The floor so polished it reflects the moonlight. All furniture stacked to the sides except the king's throne on the dais.

Carved from a single block of blackened oak, reinforced with bronze braces, inlaid with intricately carved feathers along the armrests. It never moves—the thing must weigh as much as ten horses.

Rian skirts around the throne, headed for the rear door that leads to the Hedge Maze.

He glances at us over his shoulder, eyes sharp. Even now, hunted and almost cornered, he looks like the one doing the stalking. As though *he's* the hunter.

"Stop, Rian!" Sabine commands. He charges straight ahead, ignoring her, and she catches herself on the throne and pulls in a deep breath. "I said *stop*!"

She throws up a hand, and wind slams the door open, blowing him back across the polished floor.

He catches his balance, skids to a stop, and tosses up his head. "You have all kinds of tricks up your sleeve, don't you, songbird?"

"I'm just getting started." She swipes her hand right, and another burst of wind slams into him.

He scrambles away from the main force of the wind, but it puts him further from the exit.

I lurch forward to close off his other means of escape, back into Raven Hall. Sabine skirts the opposite way around the throne. It's a game of catch between the three of us: Rian keeping the throne between us and him, all of us lithe on our feet.

"Enough!" Sabine claps her hands together, and another blast of wind crashes into Rian as he's in front of the throne, knocking him into the seat. His head hits a brass decorative brace, and he hisses from pain.

I take the opportunity to rush forward, draw my hunting knife in one clean move, and press it against his throat, pinning him in the seat.

Sabine joins us, breathing so hard I'm afraid she'll collapse, her silver light dangerously depleted.

My eyes snag on her—she isn't looking good. Using her powers just now nearly wrecked her. I might have a knife at Rian's neck, but it's *her* well-being I'm worried about.

Sabine rests her hands on the throne's gilded armrests, and I shift to stand behind the throne, still with the knife against Rian's neck as insurance.

Sabine leans forward over him, her sooty hair hanging wild in her face, looking like a creature straight out of some dark, ancient story.

"Only a fool would betray a goddess," she seethes, flashing her incisors.

"Betray?" Rian clutches his head, trying to lean forward, but meeting the sharp side of my blade. He throws me an irritated look over his shoulder. His hands tense on the armrests, knuckles going white next to hers. "Sure, call it that if you like."

She laughs bitterly. "What would you call it?"

"Don't blame me for doing what neither of you had the spine to do!" His voice cuts through the air, sharp as my blade. "You were too cautious to do it yourselves. Too afraid.

But look at what my little stunt accomplished—exactly what you wanted. As we speak, the public is fawning all over your precious fae even before they set foot in our kingdom."

He shifts, pressing as far as he dares against my blade. "I had the courage to act. You should be bowing at my fucking feet, not holding a knife to my throat." He leans back, looking far too comfortable on the throne, with a grin like he owns the world. "You're fucking *welcome*."

With a growl, I lower the knife and lean over to grab him by the collar instead, shoving my face an inch from his. "You're trying to claim you escaped so you could help us? Bullshit."

"What choice did I have?" he spits back at me, matching my fervor. "Your stupid plan to have the fae pardon them would never have worked, and you were too dense to listen to me!"

I pull back, throat thick.

"So why run?" Sabine says after a beat. "If you were just *helping*."

His eyes shift to hers, simmering and moody.

He shifts his hips as he snakes out his tongue, wetting his lips. "Because you'd never believe me. Not even after I just fucking won you exactly what you wanted. And the best part? You didn't have to lift a finger. I did the dirty work. The murder. The violence. I *always* do the dirty work for you, songbird, can't you see that? I make the hard calls."

Sabine rears back, eyes wide and incredulous, a streak of soot down her cheek like a blackened tear. "Hard calls? What, as in handing me over to my father?"

"Yes!" He tries to lean forward, but I still have his collar in my fist, and I slam him back against the throne. He winces, writhing beneath my hold, eyes sparking hot on me, too, before shifting back to Sabine. "Admit it, Sabine. You know I did the right thing. For both of us. I got the throne, short-lived as my time on it was. You got a family—you got fucking *powers of a god.*"

A strange look crosses Sabine's face. She straightens, touching the point of her ear. She swallows hard, her throat bobbing around something hard and bitter.

Rian shifts his hips, getting *really* fucking comfortable on that throne, if you ask me.

"Sabine," I say. "He'll say anything—"

But Rian plows ahead, eyes fastened on Sabine. "I helped you when you wouldn't help yourself. You're held back by your humanity, both of you. But you, songbird...you're starting to wake up, aren't you? You're beginning to realize there's so much more for you out there." He bites his lip, shaking his head with a *tsk-tsk,* and mutters almost to himself, "Gods, we would have made one hell of a couple. If the two of you would only get your heads out of your asses, we could still be something. The three of us. Loyal to one another."

"Loyal?" I growl, fisting Rian's collar tighter, dragging him a few inches off the throne. "I lost my fucking memories because of your *hard call!*"

He pulls back his lips, meeting my anger with his own. "And what about me? Do I look like I came out ahead? You're on the throne. You have Sabine. Hell, you even have my family name! What more do you want from me, Basten? My blood on your knife? Fuck, go ahead, then. I'm so sick of your griping! Put us all out of our misery and just do it."

He tilts his head back, teeth still bared, fully exposing his long neck to me.

I freeze for half a breath, the knife trembling in my other hand. A flicker of regret—longing for a different outcome—flares in my chest. But I shove that feeling down deep.

And I press the blade to his throat anyway. "Gladly," I snarl, though my voice cracks at the edges.

"Wait!" Sabine holds out her hand, the fey line on her palm pulsing faintly. With her dress in tatters, her hair soot-streaked, she looks like she's just been through battle. "Wait, Basten."

"Wait?" My voice is hoarse. "You wanted this. His death."

"I did." She drags a hand through her hair, pacing in front of the throne, her own tongue darting out. "Part of me still does. But now, I...agree with Rian."

"*What?*" I explode, stepping back from the throne like it's on fire.

She clasps her hands, fingers wringing together. "I...I think we were wrong. About pardoning the traitors, I mean. And...maybe about more. Look, Rian is..." She huffs out a long burst of air, sliding Rian a side-eyed look. "Rian is a lot of things, plenty of them unspeakable, but you saw how the people reacted to his stunt. It *did* give us what we wanted."

I take a moment to breathe, to process what I'm hearing. Gods, I hate this. Being on opposite sides of a silent war with Sabine.

And worst of all? I hate that a part of me wonders if she's not entirely wrong about Rian.

He got his hands dirty tonight—dragging Gaez out of the dungeon, slitting his neck, burying a fucking axe in his head.

And nothing in it for him, this time.

The knife in my hand feels suddenly heavy. Slowly, I sheathe it, but leave the clasp open if I need to act fast.

My voice scrapes out low as I ask Sabine, "So now, what? Let him go? Give him a fucking title and satin sash?"

Sabine paces in front of the throne, her brows pulled in tight. I watch her closely, fighting to keep up a brave front. All of this—this gods-damned *mess*. I'm tired of it, down to my fucking bones. Dammit, I miss the way things used to be.

From the looks of it, she does, too.

She stops in front of the throne, and a change seems to come over her. It's small. Almost imperceivable, but I know her better than my own reflection.

A glint of wildness flashes in her eye. Her fey pulses brighter, just for a moment.

She cocks her head and asks in a deep, velvety rumble, "Are you loyal to me, Rian?"

Rian takes a second to clock her strategy, the gears turning behind his eyes. Then, he leans back, eyes hooded, half a smirk hanging on his lips.

"Always," he says. "Songbird, Sabine, Solene. Glory to all of you. Glory to whatever you fucking turn out to be next."

Sabine glances at me—a question or a reassurance, I'm not sure—and then holds out her hand to Rian, her wedding ring flashing in her own glowing silver light. She flashes her incisors. "Prove it."

Rian's breath catches, unsure, but only for a fraction of a moment. Then, he leans forward, taking his time now, head bowed to her. He wraps his fingers around her hand and kisses the ring, letting his lips linger on the cool bite of silver.

His fucking lips are on my woman.

I shift from foot to foot, muscles tight, heart hammering like a damn battering ram. Sabine comes around the throne and rests a soft, reassuring hand on my shoulder. Her soft eyes meet mine. "Trust me, Basten."

I bite back my jealousy, crack my neck, and let out a grunt.

She smiles softly, a mischievous twinkle in her eye, and dips down to slowly raise her skirt to mid-thigh. She toes off her right boot, then extends her beautiful foot, wiggling her perfect toes.

She clears her throat pointedly at Rian.

He doesn't move, his lips parted in a half-question, a touch of disbelief in the way his gaze flicks from Sabine to me.

A drip of sweat rolls down my temple. It isn't warm in the throne room, but my clothes feel tight. Restrictive. I can't quite seem to catch my breath.

"You want me to—" Rian starts.

"Are you loyal or not?" I slam my hand against the back of his head, pushing him off the throne onto his knees.

He winces but quickly recovers, the vexed look still dancing across his features. As though he expects me to wrap my hands around his throat at any moment and choke him out.

Gods be damned, I bet he'd *like* it.

He starts to lower to his hands, but he doesn't move fast enough for my liking, so I dig my boot onto his back until he's on all fours, prostrate before Sabine.

"I, well..." he chuckles, starts again, this time with his perpetual trace of irony. "I'm your servant, songbird."

But there's something different in the way his voice breaks at the end. As if, for once, he actually means it.

He lowers down and presses a kiss to her toes.

Still lowered, an inch from the floor, he tilts his head and murmurs, "Anywhere else you want me to kiss you, songbird?"

There's a challenge to his voice now. A slick confidence, like he's holding a shit hand at Basel but is ready to bluff his way to win the whole pot.

His eyes slide to mine, testing me, as he trails his lips over the arch of her foot to her ankle. He runs a reverent hand up her calf to her knee.

He murmurs, "I'll worship you anywhere."

I look toward the ceiling, roll back my shoulders, and fight the urge to kick his damn lips off her. My own skin is hot, pulling tight as my muscles tense. I'm not sure how much of this I can take.

Of course Rian is getting off on this. I've known him a long time—nothing could surprise me less. Hell, Rian would get off on the power play between a damn cat and mouse.

But it's not just him.

I'm acutely aware of Sabine in every moment—so attuned to her own needs that I know the thrum of her pulse better than my own. And something about having Rian grovel at her feet, the man who shamed her now kissing prayers along her skin...it's affecting her, too.

Her breath hitches. Her pupils dilate. Her pulse throbs.

I growl, territorial, but Sabine turns to me and rests a hand on my chest. There's something in her eyes. An openness that begs me to trust her. To stand by her side. To be with her—even through this.

Gods help me, I always will.

As the silence stretches, Rian's practically panting like a

dog, trailing his fingers along her bare thigh, ready and willing for everything.

Abruptly, she steps back, pulling her leg away from his touch. Her skirt falls to cover her skin.

Rian gives a small whimper of longing, but she clicks her other heel on the floor. Sharp. Commanding.

She's all business again as she jerks her chin toward me.

"Now show your loyalty to your king," she says.

I bristle, blinking fast. Glance at Sabine. Wait...*I'm* a part of this?

It's one thing for Sabine to assert her domination over the man who tormented her. She deserves to make him beg. I like to see his lips on her about as much as I'd like to be dipped in molten lead, but there *is* something, well, satisfying about seeing him on his knees before her.

The great High Lord of Duren, the former King of Astagnon, reduced to begging like a dog for a scrap of her mercy.

Rian sits back on his heels, his eyes wide and the smirk gone from his face. If he has a losing hand, he isn't trying to bluff now.

He looks between the two of us, as incredulous as a school boy, as if, at any moment, we'll all burst into laughter and call it all a jest.

Stab a knife into his heart.

But Sabine's face remains serious as fucking stone.

I swallow, shift my weight to the other foot. I could stop this. Just one word, and it would end.

But...I think I understand now what Sabine is doing.

Me? I prefer to work out my differences with Rian with our fists. But I guess there's more than one way to work out such bone-deep tension.

Rian looks to me, his brows pulling together, still unsure if I'm about to stab him in the ear. He starts to speak but then stops, wetting his dry lips, and raises an eyebrow. "Toes?"

"Fuck you, you ass," I growl. "Put your lips on *me*, and I'll kick you to the Panopis Sea. You can kiss my *boot*."

Rian's mouth quirks, almost a smile.

Truth be told, this—whatever *this* is—isn't entirely new. We were youths once. Neither of us strangers to the brothel *or* to the bottom of a tankard. Most nights, we sought our own pleasure, but there were a few times we ended up in some pub's backroom with a girl shared between us. My cock between her lips while Rian took her from behind. I can't count the number of times I've seen his bare ass pumping into some whore. But those times...they were different.

None of those girls meant much to either of us. As long as the girl was willing and we kept her moaning with pleasure, then I didn't think twice about sharing. Jealous? Hell, I was too drunk to hardly know where she ended and Rian began.

Now?

I haven't had a sip of ale. I'm not some gawky youth. I'm Sabine's fucking husband—and I've killed men for even looking at her the wrong way.

But...she's depleted.

It's clear in the hollows around her eyes, the dullness to her skin. She needs replenishment in a way no bread or bottle of wine can give her—not now. She's gone too far. She's too damn stubborn to drink my blood, so worried that she won't be able to stop.

She might not be wrong.

The truth I don't want to face is this: I don't think my blood alone can satisfy her. Not my prayers, not my cock. Which means *I* can't satisfy her. I'd lay down my life for her, let her drink me dry, but even then, she'd soon need more.

But with two of us...

Rian and me...

Together, we might be enough.

The thought cuts me like a blade, so wrong, but also necessary.

All this tears through my head as Rian slowly wipes the back of his hand over his mouth, then lowers, painstakingly keeping his eyes on me, to my boots.

A silent question.

A silent offering.

He touches his lips to the leather, all dirt and soot and damn, probably even horse shit.

He murmurs wryly, "Glory to King Basten."

I flinch, ready to grab him by the scruff and tell him to fuck off, but I stop myself.

There's a strange feeling in my chest—a hot, dark kind of pride. Maybe...I see what Sabine gets out of this. For all the times I've said Rian and I were like brothers, it isn't true. Not really.

He always had the money.

The title.

The power.

Until, well, *now*.

I glance at Sabine, and she meets my gaze with a question in her eyes. She steps forward, combing her fingers tenderly through my hair, her lips full as she murmurs, "You said you'd follow me anywhere, Basten. Will you follow me here? End this tension between the three of us, once and for all?"

My pulse slams.

She stares at me, and I stare back, at a loss for words.

Finally, I unclip my belt that holsters my knives, pull it off with a snap of leather.

Whatever is about to happen? Hell, it's going to be dangerous enough without blades.

I toss the belt and holster across the polished floor.

"He can touch you," I say to her, low and possessive. "Kiss you. Worship you. But only *I* fuck you."

CHAPTER 27
SABINE

At Basten's words, a ripple of pleasure tears through my body, catching me off guard, like a dash of water. My body reacts as if it belongs to a stranger: my thighs trembling, breath growing strained beyond my control.

It's the fae in me.

Hungry.

Lustful.

Needy.

I grip Basten's bicep, digging in my fingers. "I didn't mean... With Rian..."

I stop short, unsure what I'm trying to say.

Because I think I *did* mean it.

When I commanded Rian to show his loyalty to me by kissing my ring, then my toes, it was a simple test. To see if this all-powerful lord, who once held half the known world at his fingertips, would bow to the girl he once tried to dominate.

I meant to end the relentless power play between us—

all three of us—once and for all. To have Rian finally confess, with his lips on my toes, that *I'm* his god now, and Basten is his king.

If Rian wants our forgiveness, then he'll need to beg for it on hands and knees like the dog he is.

I didn't mean for this game of shifting power to play out like *this*.

And yet, maybe the fae in me knew exactly what I was doing.

"It's okay, little violet." Basten threads his fingers through my hair at my temple, gazing at me with adoring eyes. "You need this. You've refused my blood. Turned away offerings. Even sex...you're so depleted that I'm not sure I can satisfy you on my own." His throat tightens, his Adam's apple bobbing.

Gods, this must be so hard for him.

He leans close and whispers in my ear. "Let me do this for you."

A bolt of need shoots straight to my core, and I can't swallow back the moan that pushes to my lips. It's true. My muscles feel slack. My head foggy. Skin dry, pale. I've suffered for longer than I want to admit, and the hunger... damn, this hunger.

It *burns*.

But I force myself to breathe steadily. I splay my open hand on Basten's chest, licking my dry lips as I search his eyes for a clue as to how he really feels.

My voice breaks as I whisper, "I don't want to deepen the rift between us."

He cups my head in his big hands, and his embrace is so comforting, like coming home, like I finally feel safe, that I let my eyes sink closed.

He brushes his thumb over my cheek. "The past few weeks have killed me," he murmurs, "Being apart from you, feeling you slip from my reach. But this?" His hand slides to the back of my neck. "I think this could finally bring us together."

He leans in closer, breath ghosting across my lips, and continues, "It isn't about romance—not with Rian. It's a power play. Between the three of us. Always has been. So, let's end it right now. On this fucking throne. Strip ourselves bare—no more wondering, no second-guessing. Take what we need from him, put him in his place, and show him and the whole fucking world that you and I are *done* hiding our love."

My breath stalls in my lungs, as if I can't trust what I'm hearing.

Basten exhales, breaking the tension as he whispers in my ear. "You and me—we're the endgame. There will never be anyone else. It doesn't matter that you're a goddess, that I'm a king. We're Sabine and Basten, always. Equals. Bare to each other as..." he laughs, shaking his head, "...as you were on that damn naked ride."

A surprised laugh catches in my throat, too.

Basten's voice deepens. "Rian was right about that, too. He saw the true power in the tale of Solene's Ride, coming to one another as simply man and woman. And this—" he glances toward Rian, dominance sparking in his eyes, "—this is triumph. Claiming what's ours. Claiming *him* on our own terms."

Rian, on his knees beside us, shifts. His lips are parted slightly, showing a hint of white, straight teeth. His eyelids are at half-mast, thick with lust and the adrenaline still burning off him.

And something else…the bare, bright-eyed hope of a man who's been starved too long.

"If I could add—" Rian starts.

"Shut up," Basten growls.

Rian's mouth slams closed. There's no question he's game for whatever might happen. He's practically *panting* already. It strikes me in that moment that this is what he's always wanted. The three of us. Friends, lovers, confidants, whatever you want to call it. He doesn't care whose body leads or follows, whose hands command—so long as he's allowed a place in it.

My need burns straight down to my belly, leaving me flushed, but I fight to keep the hungry fae inside me at bay.

"Are you sure about this?" I whisper.

Basten tips my chin up. "Sometimes, we have to say fuck it and jump, not knowing what's on the other side."

He interlaces his fingers with mine. The bundle of fey nerves in my palm, the one that's always winter-cold?

For once, it warms.

Heat pours through me, dripping over my skin, pooling in my core. I can't seem to lick my lips enough to keep them moist.

I unlace our fingers and drag my hand, exploring, up Basten's arm. Goosebumps erupt wherever my fey sparks against his skin. I marvel at it, how his body reacts to my caress.

How in sync we are.

Finally.

"What do you want, goddess?" he says, low and wicked.

I drag in a rasping breath, looking between the two of them. "I want you, Basten. Your hands on me. Now."

"Praise be," Basten murmurs in a wicked voice that's anything but chaste.

He clutches me around the waist, his touch burning, his own fingers shaking with need. Gods, it feels good to know he wants this, too. This union between us.

He crushes his mouth to mine, nipping and biting and licking as though he's starved for me. His hand slides low on my hips, fingers tightening possessively in the fabric.

I tilt my head back and moan, "More. More adoration."

Rian sinks to his knees and buries his face in my skirt, breathing in my scent deeply, moaning in response.

I arch my back, breasts pushing against Basten's rock-hard chest, and a groan tears out of his throat. He pulls away, breathing so hard it rasps in his throat, and presses his forehead against mine.

"Fuck, little violet. The things you do to me."

He wraps his hand around the back of my neck, and I lean into his hold, panting against the cool, dark air. Keeping my eyes locked to Basten, I grab Rian by a fistful of his hair.

"You," I command. "On the throne."

Rian pushes to his feet, so eager to please he's stumbling, his hair mussed and messy, but for once he doesn't comb it back into place. He sinks into the throne and kicks out his legs, leaning back, eyes simmering.

I gather handfuls of my skirt, dragging the heavy fabric up to my thighs, and sink my ass into his lap. His hand falls around my waist, pulling me closer.

He wraps his hand around the length of my neck from behind, fingers pressing gently into my throat. I lean back against his chest, bunching my skirt around my hips, never once breaking eye contact with Basten.

Rian needs to learn his place. If he wants to be in our lives, it's either below or beside us—never above. He'll have to earn that place. Prove he can follow instead of stealing control.

"Pray to me," I order him.

Rian runs his lips against the side of my neck. "Let me serve you, songbird. Say the word, and I'll bare my throat, my heart, every damn piece of me."

A ripple of pleasure—of power—shudders up through me.

Rian pulls away, only to trail a kiss along my opposite jaw. "Tell me where to touch. Where to worship. How to please you until you're too weak to stand."

As he watches us, Basten's eyelids are heavy, his chest rising and falling in hard breaths. His hair's come loose from the tie at his nape, and strands hang over his eyes.

I reach out a hand to him.

He steps forward. Slow. Deliberate.

Then drops to his knees.

"Open for me, little violet," he commands.

Shivers of pleasure tear through me as I swallow a needy moan, unable to keep from bucking my hips like an animal.

Behind me, Rian's hold tightens around my throat and waist. He murmurs more sinful prayers against my skin as his lips trail down my bare neck.

Basten grabs my skirt in his fist, shoving it higher around my waist, and with one seamless move, wrenches my panties down to my knees. He slides them down the rest of my legs so slowly it aches. I whimper, gripping the throne's armrests with white knuckles.

I'm wet. Soaked enough to make a whore blush. But this

beast inside me, the fae, it's wanton. It doesn't know shame. Or restraint. It just *hungers*.

"Taste me," I moan to Basten, writhing in Rian's lap. Rian's hand tightens on my hips, fingers dipping down over the bunched-up folds of my dress.

Basten grips my thighs, holding them apart with such confidence as if they belong to him. He plants his lips to my inner knee, scorching a line of hot kisses along my thigh toward the glistening center demanding his attention.

"Gods, yes," I pant, arching back into Rian's chest.

"Fuck, songbird," Rian moans hotly against my neck. "I always knew you were secretly debauched."

"Rian," I pant, writhing in his lap. "You're just lucky I let you find out."

Basten's tongue finds my swollen heat, and I cry out. I reach back to grip the back of the throne, holding on for dear life. Basten tortures my pussy relentlessly. Sucking. Licking. Flicking his tongue over my clit until I start to see stars.

My body responds with a rush of hot energy. *This*—this is what I've needed. Better than food. Better than offerings. I need Basten and Rian served up on a platter, offering me every wild delight inside them.

Gods, it's so *fae* it makes my blood sing.

Basten pulls away, and I whimper in objection. I throw my leg around his shoulder, hooking him like a shepherd's crook, trying to drag him back.

He chuckles darkly as he wipes his mouth with the back of his hand. "Don't worry, wildcat. I've just started. You want worship? I can do more with my tongue than speak prayers."

He stands up, grabs me by the wrist and pulls me to my feet, guiding me by the chin to meet him in a kiss. I lean into him, sliding my tongue over the seam of his lips, asking for entrance.

He opens his lips for me, and I press my incisors against his bottom lip—not hard enough to break the skin, just enough to make him groan.

"Rian," Basten barks, sharp and commanding. "Get the fuck on your feet."

Rian jumps to his feet, trying—and failing—to hide how worked up he is. There's a hunger there I've never seen in him before. As if being told what to do—*finally*—is doing something to him.

As if the command itself lights him up.

Now that the throne is unoccupied, Basten guides me back into it, the hard oak cupping my ass, but then turns me so I'm draped across the armrests. The carved feathers press into my skin with a hint of pain that only stokes my need.

Basten jerks his head at Rian and says simply, "Like that time at the Velvet Vixen—only don't you *dare* try to cross any lines with her."

The reference means nothing to me but clearly does to Rian.

Rian kneels by my feet, eyes blown wide, and tugs off my remaining shoe. He caresses my foot like he's polishing gold, then kisses along the upper portion of my arch.

I gasp, toes curling.

Basten sinks to his knees on the other side of the throne. He takes my arm, nuzzles his face in my palm, and then drags his tongue down the length of my arm to my shoulder, sliding my dress strap down to free my breast, and capturing my bare nipple gently between his teeth.

A hiss wracks out of me as I writhe lengthwise on the throne, tormented by pleasure. Together, each from either end, Basten and Rian feast on me like a holiday buffet. Basten's mouth does wicked things to my breasts, until I'm arching my back and crying out for mercy.

At the other end, Rian wraps his hands around my hips, holding me steady as he kisses the inside of my calf.

The fey shivers in my veins, waking up from its slumber. Silver light spills out of my fey lines, casting an otherworldly glow over both men's faces as they devour my body.

Flashes of memory return to me. *Acolytes bent over my body, worshipping me with their mouths. I've done this before... thousands of times before.*

But it's never been like *this*.

I dig one hand in Basten's hair, winding my fingers across his scalp to hold on securely, and thrust the other hand in Rian's hair, feeling the movements of his talented mouth moving back and forth over my thigh, nipping and biting so wickedly.

I think I might burst from pleasure, pop like a corked champagne bottle.

"I..." I start, my voice turning into a growl. "I want *more*."

Basten comes up for air, lips swollen and eyes aflame. He takes a moment to look me over, draped across the throne from head to toes, and the look in his eyes says everything I need to know.

A chasm between us?

No—not anymore. Like this, we know exactly who each other is.

He fists his hand in Rian's collar, dragging Rian to his feet. Rian pants, his eyes glassy and unfocused from the thrill of it all.

"More, little violet?" Basten repeats. The half-grin is gone from his face as he rests his hand on his belt. He's all business now, his cock straining at his pants, the pinprick focus of a hunter in his eyes, ready to claim his prize.

I sit up on the throne, suddenly breathless. "*Please.*" I'm not sure I trust my own voice not to break with need.

"Goddesses don't beg," he says, approaching slowly and taking my chin in his big palm. "I swore to serve *you.*"

The fey beneath my skin throbs, surging hotter and faster. I whimper slightly, licking my lips again, eyes pinned to his jugular.

A fear suddenly seizes me. "Basten, if we take this too far—"

He presses his thumb to my lips, sealing in my protests.

Slowly, he shakes his head. "Let me take care of you, goddess. You won't hurt me. Not with Rian taking on half your need. Now be a good girl and sit in Rian's lap."

A flush of warmth spreads through my core, and I have to squeeze my thighs together to keep from shaking. Rian is more than happy to trade places with me on the throne, spreading his knees, bucking his hips in anticipation.

I start to sit on his lap, but Basten grabs me. "No—like this."

He spins me around to straddle Rian's hips.

I'm facing Rian, who leans back, hands on the armrests, not touching me in a way that's somehow even more intimate than when he had his hands all over me.

From behind, Basten nuzzles his lips over my ear, biting down gently on the earlobe, and at the same time, fists Rian's hair to crane his neck back.

He commands to me, "Drink from him."

My breath rushes in and out. I stare, wide-eyed, at Rian's exposed neck. The vein throbbing there, in time with my own demanding pulse.

My mouth pools with saliva, appetite roaring to life almost uncontrollably.

Drink drink drink.

"Rian?" I ask hoarsely.

He shifts his hips, rocking his erection against my hips. "Don't ask permission. Fucking *drink*."

A yawning need clenches me, and suddenly, my mouth is all over his neck. I break the skin, letting his warm blood flood my mouth. Spicy, metallic, a trace of alcohol that goes straight to my head.

A shiver of pleasure thrums through me as I lap at his blood.

"That's it," Basten says, as he slowly winds my hair into a rope, then wraps it around his fist. He stands behind me, bunching my skirt up around my hips. "Take what you need."

Almost immediately, I'm drunk and dazed. From the alcohol in Rian's blood. From the prayers he whispered against my skin. From the pleasure aching down to my bones.

"I want you, Basten," I moan, barely knowing which way is up.

"As my goddess wishes." He pushes my skirt over my bare ass, grabbing a handful of flesh and kneading it as he frees his massive cock.

I feel him line himself up with my entrance. He rubs the tip of his cock over my slick center, teasing me. Throbbing and tingling sensations ripple up and down my core until I'm pushing back, demanding him.

"That's a good goddess."

He slides into me slowly, torturously. He knows exactly what he's doing. Filling me inch by delicious inch.

A moan tears out of me as I tip my head back, arching my spine. I roll my chest against Rian, bare breasts rubbing against his silk shirt.

Basten grabs my hips to hold me in place, sinking fully into me. I gasp from the fullness, barely able to catch my breath. He reaches around and strokes my clit with his thumb, flicking lazy circles that have me grinding my hips back against him.

"Right there," I cry. "Right there—that's what I need!"

Rian shudders at the sound, forehead pressed to my shoulder. Basten's grip tightens. The three of us move in the same frantic pull—want, power, submission all tangled together.

The pressure crests.

Basten speeds up, working my clit in time to his thrusts, and I feel energy build until it's impossible to build any more. His cock throbs inside me, so close to exploding. He thrusts once more, hitting me achingly deep, and I come undone.

Silver stars burst across my vision. I shudder, muscles twitching uncontrollably. All thoughts vanish. I quiver, I spiral, I burst.

The room explodes in light, and it's only dimly that I realize the light is coming from *me*.

I'm glowing bright as the moon. Lighting up every shadowed corner.

Basten's cock throbs a final time, shooting hot cum inside me. An exhale rips out of me as I collapse against Rian's chest, burying my face in his shoulder, hands twisted tight enough in his shirt that my fingernails shred the fabric.

Together—

The three of us break.

I'm shaking. Spent, and yet somehow full.

With a groan, Basten pulls out of me. I slide off Rian's lap and sink backward onto the floor, needing the steadying feeling of stone beneath me. I lay flat, gazing up at the ceiling. My muscles are jelly. My thoughts...poof. Gone.

Rian, looking dazed, crawls onto the floor beside me, lying back to stretch himself out on the floor.

Basten sinks to his knees, too, bracing himself before leaning over and burying his face in the crook of my neck.

For a silver-tinged moment, the three of us simply *are*.

"By Popelin's last fucking coin," Rian mutters, wiping a hand down his sweat-soaked face. "When I escaped, freed a prisoner, and turned around to murder him this morning, I can safely assure you, I had no idea what the outcome would be. But *this* was not it."

He draws a thin metal flask from his pocket, unscrews it, then tips it back.

Basten huffs a laugh, exasperated, but there's no real malice behind it.

He says to Rian, "This doesn't mean we trust you. You have a long way to go to earn back anything resembling honor. But..." He tips his head back, resting it on the throne's seat. His eyes sink closed, a battle fought and over. "It's a fresh start."

"Just, please, no more Coffin," Rian mumbles.

I touch my lips, hyper-sensitive and swollen, as I play back what just happened, my skin still snapping from the overwhelming sensations.

"House arrest." My voice is barely a rasp, but it's confident. I look at Basten. "He doesn't leave Hekkelveld Castle without our permission. Two guards shadow him at all times. We give him a bedroom—he can sleep, go to the bathroom, eat in the dining hall." I stretch out my leg, kicking Rian's foot with my own. "If you mess this up, I'll kill you for real."

Rian grins up at the ceiling, eyes glassy and unfocused. "I've never had this." He motions to the three of us with one tipsy finger. "Friends."

"We aren't friends," I say, hard. "I *still* might kill you."

But his smile doesn't dim. He looks boyish. Almost… innocent, in a way I don't think Rian Valvere has been a day in his life.

And it strikes me that maybe Rian only sought power because he was taught to want it. Cunning was beat into him by a cold-hearted father bent on domination. That maybe, what he wanted this entire time was simply *acceptance*.

He takes another drink from his flask, sighing contentedly.

CHAPTER 28
BASTEN

The sun rises and falls over the city skyline, and word arrives that Immortal Vale is marching across the Astagnonian border.

I search for Sabine to give her the news, and find her on the balcony overlooking the Queen's Walk, gazing north toward the distant Darmarnach Mountains.

A dove coos beside her, as she pets its snow-white feathers softly.

I stop at the open balcony door. She hasn't noticed me yet. I lean in the doorway, letting my eyes drift over her.

Gods...she's beautiful. There's a quiet radiance humming under her skin. Her power is back—calm, coiled, sure—and the air around her vibrates with it. For the first time in too long, I feel perfectly in sync with her.

Is it wrong that a tryst between me, her, and Rian brought the two of us together? Maybe. It probably should have pushed us apart, driven the wedge further.

But ours was never the kind of love written in clean lines.

My boot scrapes the floor, and she looks over her shoulder.

A smile breaks across her face, broad and full-lipped. "Basten." But then it falters. She looks down at her hands. "About what happened. The throne room—"

"Hey. We said no second-guessing." I catch her chin to steal a kiss before leaning against the stone railing. "You're fae. Things are different now. *You're* different. Your needs have...evolved. I'm sure as hell not going to let you go, so I guess I have to evolve with you. Open up to...things I wouldn't have done before."

She looks up at me, daring to hope.

"Doesn't mean I'm eager for it to happen again," I clarify, dropping my voice. "Can't pretend I don't want only *my* hands on you." I pause. "Unless you need—"

"No," she says softly, quickly. "Yours are the only hands I want on me, too. I don't need another tryst." She cocks a half-grin. "His blood, though? I don't have qualms about draining that on occasion."

My heartstrings pull taut. This was all I needed—this reassurance that it's only me and her. Together, always.

I draw her into a kiss, then when we break, I pull a messenger's letter out of my jacket pocket. "This arrived at dawn. Your father departed Norhelm with the fae court in tow three days ago. Apparently, it's quite the procession. They have Tòrr with them. Saddled goldenclaws. An army of devotees and acolytes praying the whole damn way. If they manage to keep to the schedule, they'll be here tomorrow."

Sabine sinks back against the railing next to me, leaning into my side. *Gods, we fit so well together.*

"Will the city be ready?" she asks.

I comb back my hair. "Kendan and Rian assure me they have it under control."

She snorts. "I can't believe they haven't killed one another yet. Brothers raised in the Valvere household, under Lord Berolt's tyrannical parentage."

I wrap an arm around her back to pull her close. "Rian knows full well his actions must be pristine as a fucking saint if he wants to keep the shackles off. For his part, Kendan will do what is best for the kingdom, regardless of what irritating bastards he has to tolerate. Even his brother. *Especially* his brother."

She smiles as she picks up the dove in her cradling palm, stroking its back.

"I have to admit that Rian's stunt has been more effective than I could have ever imagined," I say. "Everyone is talking about Vale's miraculous message—that he'll slaughter any of the public's enemies. And of course, they credit you with making it all possible, as savior of Old Coros. For the Fae Games, we've brought in extra troops from the southern villages to aid in crowd control. Additional food and supplies for the pilgrims we anticipate, too. As far as the festival grounds, they've overseen the construction of several stages throughout the city. Ferra's helped design the decorations at the royal arena. I hear it's over the top. Gold and silver, to honor both you and Vale. Hundred-foot-tall banners, living willows, painted dancers."

Sabine holds out the dove, which takes flight into the blue sky. "The fae will love that."

Despite her words, there's a hitch of worry in her tone, and my protective instincts crop up. I run my hands down her arms. "You fear the Games will not go as planned?"

She looks down, chewing on the inside of her cheek.

"Actually, it's the opposite. I'm...gods, well, I'm *hopeful*. That's a strange feeling, of late." Her gaze shifts downward. "A dangerous one."

She gives a self-conscious laugh.

Gods, when she looks at me with those round, soulful eyes, I feel like I could die right here in her arms. Of all the things I love about her, this is the truest. Her complexity. How she can be my hopeful little violet at the same time as a blistering force of nature who sends gods to their knees.

I interlace my fingers with hers, silently drawing her closer. It's times like these I wish we were still just two nobodies in a clearing in the woods, a campfire between us, nothing to answer to except our own dreams.

"I'm nervous, Basten," she confesses. I wrap an arm around her back, fighting the urge to hold her so tight no one can ever pry us apart. She continues, "I've bet everything on this gamble. That I can keep my father and the other fae in check. That we can maintain harmony with humans in this Return. Am I a fool?"

I place a kiss on the crown of her head, wishing I could show her that hope is never foolish, never when it's hers. "You're fae. You care. You prove it's possible every damn day."

She lets out a held breath, but her fingers pluck anxiously at the satin ribbon around her waist.

I take her hands, stilling her nervous fidgeting, and guide her eyes to meet mine.

"You and me, Sabine. We'll face the whole damn world and make them bow, men and gods alike."

～

Something jolts me out of slumber.

I'm tangled up with Sabine in silk sheets, sprawled in the enormous royal bed, wishing I had Captain Tatarin's godkiss to stop time and stay like this forever. Sabine's soft breasts form tempting hills beneath the sheet. Her hair streaked across her pillow. Her legs intertwined with mine.

DA-DUUMM!

A trumpet blares again from the city gates, and this time, I can't pretend I didn't hear it.

Fuck.

I drag a hand down my face, rubbing away the last of my dreams, and then sit up. I pause, turning to gaze at Sabine.

She's sound asleep—the trumpet was a mile away, too far for her ears to catch. Her lips are parted, full. Her face wrinkled from the pillow.

She suddenly rakes in an ear-splitting snore.

A smile cracks my face.

Gods, I love this woman.

But as I get dressed, my good humor sinks into something harder. That trumpet means that Vale's cavalcade must have been spotted on the road into Old Coros.

The fae are coming. *Gods help me—am I ready?*

I wait as long as I dare before waking Sabine with a gentle kiss on those perfect, pouty lips of hers. She jolts mid-snore, blinking awake in adorable confusion.

"B—Basten?" She heaves a few breaths, looking around the bedroom, then sinks back to the pillow. "Gods, I was dreaming of the Games. I was back in The Night Hunt, only this time, all nine gods had bows, not just Artain."

I sink onto the mattress beside her and nuzzle my lips over her temple. "I'd bury them all under rock. All nine."

Her moan tilts toward pleasure as she leans up to meet my lips. Then, she blinks up at me with a frown.

Her voice flattens. "My father's here, isn't he?"

"The trumpets sounded," I admit.

She sighs, rubbing her face, then swings her legs out of bed and begins to dress for the day. "You have your speech?"

I nod.

She shucks off her loose chemise, giving me a glorious, greedily long look at her naked body, while she deliberates in front of her wardrobe.

"I thought Lord Kendan picked the golden dress for you," I observe, leaning back on the bed to admire the view.

"He did." Sabine holds up the gold filigree dress, running her fingers down the metallic laces that span the sides. "Gold is my father's color. Kendan and I agreed it would be an indication of welcome. Of solidarity. Of—peace."

My heartbeat kicks up, and I fidget with the caribou pelt blanket. "But now?"

She hangs the golden dress up, then reaches for another, hesitating a beat before selecting it. She takes it out, holding it over her frame, and turns to me for my opinion.

Tawny brown with a white sash—the color of fawns. Rising over each shoulder, intricately embroidered pine-green antlers mirror one another, meeting around behind her back. On the hem, embroidery of the Innis River.

It's simple yet complex. It's pure nature in thread and cotton.

It's...*her*.

"Ferra brought me this last night," Sabine admits. "She and the seamstresses have been stitching it secretly for weeks. She called it a luck charm...for when I need good fortune."

I stand up, walking behind her, looking at her with the dress held up in the mirror. I brush aside her hair and kiss her neck. "And that's today?"

"No." Sabine's answer is swift, certain. She runs her hands over the river embroidery. "Immortal Popelin deals in luck. I trade in harder currency. Water. Wings. Brimfire."

My lips curve in a smile. "Wear it."

We dress—both in our antlered attire, the symbol of our reign—and are ready when the guards alert us that Vale's parade has reached the gate.

Already, I can hear the city's excitement. The festivities don't officially begin until midday, and yet, footsteps fill every street. Children's joyous calls echo in the arena's waiting line. The smell of sugared, roasted almonds hangs in every breeze.

We find Kendan and Rian impatiently waiting for us in Raven Hall. Kendan is the spitting image of decorum, in his freshly polished Lord of the Iron Banner chainmail sash, his neck shaved within an inch of its life.

Rian, on the other hand, sips from his whisky flask while he sings an old fae ballad under his breath, his bone dice clattering sinfully in his pocket as he paces, his eyes freshly lined in blue kohl.

I roll my eyes. I can't believe I let such a fool put his hands all over Sabine. It won't happen again—but the one time?

It was a wrong that somehow righted us.

"Majesties." Kendan bows his head. "The fae court has reached Old Coros, and with your blessing, our guards gave passage through the gate. They'll now make their way to the royal arena."

I grumble under my breath.

Sabine squeezes my arms, a scold with no real teeth. "We'll be ready to receive them there."

A line of carriages waits in the front courtyard. Lord Kendan takes the first, along with a fleet of our highest-ranking soldiers. Then, it's the royal advisors, and the next few carriages are all taken by minor lords and ladies. Lady Suri climbs into one pulled by dappled gray mares, and Rian attempts to casually slide in beside her—but she shuts the door in his face, then shuts the window, too.

I have no idea what's going on between the two of them. A few days ago, he had his lips all over Sabine, so I'd be hard pressed to believe he has any real intentions with Lady Suri.

On the other hand, it felt clear in that tussle on the throne that Rian might have once desired Sabine, even fancied himself in love with her—but it wasn't real love. Not as I love her.

And I think Rian understands that now, too.

He chuckles, intrigued by Suri's challenge, before getting in the next carriage with Folke and Ferra.

Sabine and I are shuffled into the royal carriage at the end, pulled by Ranger and a matching chestnut gelding.

Sabine slides her hand into mine but is silent as we roll through the city.

We stare fixedly out of either window at the lines of citizens waving and calling to us, carrying children on their shoulders to witness this monumental day.

"A day one thousand years in the making," I murmur under my breath, heavy with irony, as I wave my hand in the air like a showman. "The Third Return."

Sabine rolls her eyes good-naturedly at my dramatics. "Does it count as an official Return if only seven out of the ten have risen?"

I shrug. "Who's counting when it's gods?"

We both smile, but it doesn't quite reach our eyes. I can hear in the hammer of her heart how nervous she is. To say a lot is riding on these Fae Games is an understatement. The whole damn *world* is in the balance.

"At least I get to see Tòrr," she muses with a fond smile.

I groan. "Oh, great. The murder horse."

She bumps her shoulder into mine.

We reach the royal arena too soon for comfort. I climb out, helping Sabine down, and we paste on smiles and wave to the crowds who have been waiting in lines overnight.

We're funneled into the stands, already packed with crowds who have been there since dawn to snag the best seats, and then we're ushered by a thick battalion of soldiers to the Immortal Box.

I sweep in, shading my eyes against the direct sun, and am immediately greeted with a champagne glass thrust in my face.

"Compliments of Folke." Ferra presses the glass into my hand, then another into Sabine's. She jerks her head toward the arena, where I spot Folke speaking with the announcer and a fleet of arena guards. "He figured you'd both need a drink."

"Only one?" Sabine jests, though her nerves betray her as her hand shakes.

Despite being the kingdom's official race grounds, Old Coros's Royal Arena is actually smaller in size than Duren's arena—but not by much. It's also a perfect circle, compared to Duren's oval shape. The greatest difference, though, isn't the architecture—it has similar statues to the ten gods, stadium seating, and columned breezeways.

The difference is tradition—and it's striking.

In Duren Arena, the sand is raked clean after every match. Not a drop of blood is left to dry. The moment a blade is lowered, crews sweep in—restoring the floor to a pristine, unblemished gleam. The audience demand it. They come for spectacle, not the stain of consequence.

But the royal arena?

Here, blood is left to rot.

This is no place for sport—it is a pit of judgment. Trials are ended here. Executions carried out. And the sand carries that history. Layers of death soaked into the sand, until the arena floor sheens a deep, rusted red.

"I need to go backstage and find my father and the other fae," Sabine says.

I clutch her hand, suddenly not wanting to let go. She looks at me a little mournfully as she slides her fingers from mine.

She isn't gone long before Rian sidles up, swirling a pewter goblet. "Well, well. How long before Vale sweeps in and takes credit for *my* dirty work? Let's put some coin on it. I say ten minutes."

I lean on the railing, rubbing my hands together. "If you didn't want him taking credit for your supposed miracle, you shouldn't have staged it that way."

He only stares at me, and I sigh.

"Twenty minutes," I wager.

This earns me a grin.

Slowly, I give a pointed glance back toward the women on the other side of the Immortal Box. "Did your so-called miracle have to involve kissing Lady Suri?"

Rian snorts before taking a deep sip of wine. "Merely a trick to escape."

"I may not be as trained in tactics as you," I say slyly,

"but surely there were easier ways to steal the keys from her. You have seventy pounds of muscle on her—you could have overpowered her with your pinkie."

He *tsks* as though I've suggested something outlandish. "She was merely a means to an end."

"You risked your freedom to return to deliver snacks to her. You stuck around to make sure she'd be comfortable. You left her *cinnamon cookies*."

"Don't forget the sherry. An excellent vintage. Imported from Clarana." This earns the ghost of a rakish grin. "I'm not a *monster*." He finishes his wine in one swig and sets down the goblet, cutting a long look toward Lady Suri. His tone is softer when he says, "She's much too good for me."

"You have that right."

He slams a fist into my shoulder, and I grunt darkly to know I hit close to home.

"Really," he says, serious now, lowering his eyelids as he observes her. "She sees the good in even the vilest creatures. I could never abide that—if she started to see some good in *me*. Then our little game would be no fun at all."

I slap him on his back. "Don't worry, little risk of her finding much good in you any time soon."

This earns me another punch.

Just then, trumpets blare to announce the start of the procession. The mirth vanishes from my face, and apprehension licks up my spine. I swing by the refreshment table to throw back my own steadying glass of wine.

"King Basten," Kendan prompts. "They're ready to begin."

I choke back another glass for good measure, wincing at the sweetness, then draw myself up to my full height. Squires approach with my cloak, crown, and king's sword, moving in an efficient dance as they dress me to play the part of the ruler.

When, let's be real, everyone knows a mortal king is only a figurehead against a fae one.

Still, damn if I'm going to let that show on my face.

Gripping the king's sword hilt, I stride over the burgundy rug to the front of the Immortal Box, where the announcer bows with his loudspeaker in hand.

The trumpets finish with a flourish, and after a long stretch of applause, the crowd falls silent.

The announcer puffs out his chest, raises his loud-speaker, and cries, "Citizens of Astagnon, those dwelling in Old Coros and arriving from towns far and wide, I present to you on this auspicious day, King Basten Valvere of Astagnon!"

I'm not entirely prepared for the roar that swells from the stadium. Even after all this time, I can't get used to the fact that I—*me*, Basten the Bastard—deserve so much as a pauper's devotion.

But as soon as those thoughts rise, they fall away.

Royal blood flows in my veins. Yeah, that's never meant much to me, but more so, I have the love of the most powerful woman in the known world.

And *that*? That makes me feel like I could fucking fly.

I draw the king's sword, thrusting it up toward Vale's blue sky. "Astagnonians!" I cry. No loudspeaker. No heralds. Just the grit of my voice on the wind. "You welcomed me as your king. You welcomed my bride, Queen Sabine of Brem-cote, not only as your queen, but as a symbol of unity between the mortal and immortal worlds. Today, I bid you welcome the Fae Court of Old, King Vale the Immortal, and his Immortal Brethren!"

Trumpets blare, drums beat their triumphant thunder, and the fae enter in a procession.

The first through the gilded arena arch are Samaur and Thracia. God of Day, Goddess of Night. They ride in twin chariots pulled by palomino steeds, hands clasped as they wave to the adoring crowds.

Next to me, Rian sidles up and murmurs, "Thracia's been awake, what, three days? And already parade-ready?"

"Fae are born parade-ready," I mutter back.

I have to admit, Thracia isn't entirely what I expected. All the illustrations of her in the Book of the Immortals vary, based on the particular edition, but most show her as a hardened woman with thick black braids. *This* Thracia has the braids, yes—but she looks like she's about sixteen years old. Her warm brown skin is spotless, not so much as a wrinkle, plump as a babe's.

I'd almost feel a soft spot for her, a paternal protectiveness—if I didn't see that four-thousand-year cunning in her eyes.

And Samaur? That grinning bastard looks like he's won the fucking lottery, holding such a nubile beauty on his arm.

The trumpet blares again.

Immortal Irye and Immortal Woudix ride in next, on gilded chariots, though they don't clasp hands. I have to silence a growl at the sight of the God of Death, who dared to prowl around Sabine without my knowledge.

Directly behind them comes Immortal Artain, riding on the back of a sleek bay stallion, shooting cotton-ball-tipped arrows into the crowd with gifts of rose petal pouches affixed to the ends. Women swoon, elbowing one another in the closest rows to catch one of his prize arrows.

I'm far enough from the crowd that I can safely roll my eyes.

In any other Return, Immortal Solene—Sabine—would be riding in a chariot right by his side, hands interlaced just like Samaur and Thracia, fated lovers time and time again.

Today, that motherfucker rides alone.

The satisfaction positively *burns*.

Once Artain has shot the last of his prize arrows, Captain Tatarin rides in with the goldenclaw procession, and then, a drum roll begins. The crowd gradually dies down, sensing a shift in the air, though excitement still snaps like a lit sparkler.

The silver-and-gold drapes draw back over the archway, and two riders emerge.

Sabine and Vale.

They're together, riding tandem, on Tòrr's back. The monoceros is so massive that he can easily carry the weight of the God of Fae in his heavy golden regalia armor, as well as Sabine, who's light as a feather on her own, but at the present moment, is laden down by more creatures than any one person could count.

A tabby cat clutched in one arm.

A bare-headed vulture perched on her other one.

A badger with its paws on her shoulders.

A turtle balanced on one thigh.

A newt in the crook of her elbow.

A cloud of luna moths flutter around her head like a living crown.

Plume, the cloudfox, bounds through the air at Tòrr's massive rump.

Oh, and the forest mouse is clutching Sabine's hair with

one paw, holding a clover blossom in the other, though I might be the only one who can see the little furball.

You'd have thought the stars had broken through the sunlit sky by the way the crowd cheers. The deafening roar rolls through the stadium like thunder, rivaling even Vale's earth-shaking fey power.

Sabine pulls Tòrr to a halt where the rest of the fae have gathered in their chariots. She kisses each one of her animal friends on the head, then passes them off to waiting servants, and gracefully dismounts the hulking fae horse.

Vale descends next, taking her hand and bowing deeply to her.

"We fae are honored to enter my daughter's kingdom," he announces in a voice that needs no amplification. "She is known by many names. Queen Sabine. Solene the Immortal. The Winged Lady. This much is true: she has always represented the balance between humanity and fae. She unites us not just today, but across the ages!"

He lifts her arm high in triumph, and she presses a hand to her face to quell her happy tears. Just then, a perfectly-timed goldfinch lands on their clasped hands. All smiles for the crowd, she makes a show of being overcome by emotion.

The audience *oohs* as Vale gently pets the bird.

I'm not sure if anyone else catches how he gives Sabine's homespun gown the briefest disapproving look—but I sure as hell clock it.

The bird flies off, and Sabine takes up the loudspeaker.

"My beloved people," she calls in a honeyed voice, "To put it simply, we've...been through a lot together, haven't we?"

The crowd laughs good-naturedly, and people throw handfuls of fresh flowers on the bloody sand at her feet.

She wipes away happy tears and continues, "There was a time when you doubted me. No, no—do not deny it. I do not intend to start my reign as your queen on a bed of lies. It's true: I was born in Volkany, the kingdom that has historically been our enemy. Does that make me a traitor?" She falls silent, letting the silence stretch, before sighing theatrically and raising the loudspeaker.

"Or does it make me," she continues, "a bridge? A means to bypass war, to find harmony? I am a daughter of Astagnon just as much as I am of Volkany. A child of humanity as well as fae. I bring together the woken fae today because I believe, just as much as I believe in miracles, that we can be stronger together."

Her heartfelt speech is met with tears from the adoring audience. More bouquets of flowers fall upon the sand. The badger lopes back across the arena and wraps his thick little arms around her leg, and she kneels down and cuddles him.

Something thick lodges in my throat.

Sabine and I went over this plan a thousand times. Every step has been orchestrated to elicit maximum sympathy from the audience, from the goldfinch down to that irritable damn badger.

Fucking hell, though—she makes me believe it isn't an act. She makes me *want* to believe in something more.

She whispers something in the badger's ear, then picks him up and drapes him like a stole over her shoulders. She goes to stand beside her father, looking around at the other fae, and shouts, "My husband, King Basten, has given you his welcome. As queen of Astagnon, let me formally declare the Fae Games open for celebration!"

A servant runs out, struggling under the weight of a

hefty metal bell. There is no clapper or hammer, but Sabine raises her hands to the sky again.

Her human glamour falls like silk to the ground. In its place, silver light erupts across her skin—her fey lines igniting with a brilliance so pure it hurts to look at. The glow surges outward, refracting across the arena's crimson sand, scattering shards of silver light like blessings tossed from the hands of gods.

Behind her, Vale raises his arms as his own glamour melts away.

One by one, the others follow, shining in their full glory.

"Immortal Woudix, God of Death!" Sabine announces, presenting him.

"Immortal Iyre, Goddess of Chastity!"

"Immortal Artain, God of the Hunt!"

"Immortal Samaur, God of Day, and the newly awakened Immortal Thracia, Goddess of Night!"

Each one releases a dazzling bolt of their multi-colored fey into the air.

While the crowd is marveling over the theatrics, Sabine raises her hands again.

A bolt of lightning tears down from the impossibly blue sky, striking the arena bell with a chime that rings not like war, but like a celebration.

"Let the games begin!" she shouts.

The crowd rises to their feet, stomping and clapping, bouncing on their toes.

For a heartbeat, both fae and human stand united.

Awed.

Hopeful.

It's almost enough to make even a sinner like me want to

fall to my knees—except for the fact that I distrust every one of those preening gods next to my wife with a strength that could burn kingdoms.

The first day of the Fae Games passes like a dream.

After the opening ceremony, Artain performs a trick arrow show where he lands bullseyes on a series of wooden stag dummies while blindfolded and riding backward on a galloping stallion.

Then, whitewashed wooden beams are laid over the crimson sand, and dancers in flowing silk robes perform a graceful rendition of the heartwarming love story between Aria and Aron.

A portion of the old treasury has been converted into an exhibit hall for fae artifacts of lore: the fae needle, Saph's horseshoe, the immortal lasso.

In the Glassmarket District, Samaur and Thracia show off her fabled Midnight Vase of legend, carefully swaddled in silks in an oaken chest. Samaur uses his molten fey to shape handfuls of sand into pint-sized glass copies of the vase for the crowd to take as party favors.

Captain Tatarin spends the afternoon leading goldenclaw rides for children around Valor Circle. The gargantuan fae bears aren't dressed for battle today—instead, they wear colorful saddles with fanciful ruffles, and braided ribbons as reins for the children to hold onto. Tati herself wears a dark purple robe over loose trousers, and whimsical pink hearts painted on her cheeks—you'd never know she was one of the most elite soldiers of the Volkish army.

As sunset approaches, I change into a gauzy gown with draping silks in every shade of orange, pink, and yellow. Then, I make my way back to the arena for the final event of the day.

I step into the cool shade beneath the archway, in the staging area.

Myst is already saddled. Ferra stands beside her, working her godkissed magic on her mane, weaving sunset pink and orange streaks into her white strands, then using her deft fingers to wind them into the most intricate immortal braids I've ever seen—on a person *or* a horse.

"That's gorgeous," I breathe, overcome.

Ferra pauses to point a long fingernail into the shadows. "*That* one wouldn't let me near him."

There's a snort from the shadows, and a cloud of steam rolls across the sand.

"Tòrr!" I throw my arms around his massive neck, breathing in his iron-and-wine scent, the line of black scales that runs down his neck smooth and solid as leather against my cheek.

He stomps his foot. ***I refuse to carry the Fae King again —he weighs more than an ox.***

"What's wrong with Tòrr?" Basten enters the staging area, dressed now in charcoal gray riding gear with forest-green antler embroidery on his shoulders. "Too proud to have his mane braided?"

"That's what I said!" Ferra tosses her hands in the air.

"Basten." I stumble toward him, burying my face against his chest. Our duties have kept us apart nearly all day, and now, my heart sighs at the sight of him.

Gods, the irony. That it took Rian—his hands, his mouth, his twisted desires—to bring Basten and me back into alignment.

He cups my jaw, tilts my face to his, our foreheads touching. "Little violet."

The announcer calls something from the stadium, and the crowd begins to chant in anticipation.

"Are you ready, Queen Sabine?" Lord Kendan asks as he strides into the staging area, studying the distant horizon. "The sun is very nearly down."

I nod softly, my forehead still pressed to Basten's.

"Ready," I whisper.

I draw in a final breath before we break away, grinning at one another for strength. Basten mounts Myst in one graceful swoop, patting her neck in a show of affection.

Myst slides her eyes to me. ***Tell him to stop messing up my hair.***

I laugh and relay the message.

"Pardon me, crazy mare," Basten says dramatically, holding up his hands. "I wouldn't *dream* of ruining your hair."

Myst snorts and nods, satisfied.

A squire brings out a wooden block for me to climb on Tòrr's massive back. I settle on him, arranging the billowing drapes of my silken skirt with the help of the servants.

Then, Basten and I ride the horses to the edge of the staging area.

The last rays of day fan out over the cloudless sky. I have every confidence in the world—err, *mostly*—that Tòrr wouldn't use his solarium horn to channel sunlight and blast the stadium apart, but for the sake of putting the public at ease, we saved this performance for night.

The announcer calls from the Immortal Box, "For the day's closing event, I present your beloved new monarchs. King Basten and Immortal Solene, recreating the fabled Race of Sun and Moon!"

The energy in the stands feels on fire—voices rising, feet pounding, the whole stadium vibrating in anticipation. In my heart, the same blaze catches.

Basten reaches his hand out, and I take it.

"Together," I say softly.

He winks. "Always."

The drumroll unspools throughout the arena, the crimson sand itself vibrating, and I feel the beat spread up through my toes.

Beneath me, Tòrr paws the ground, sensing it too. Feeding off the raw energy.

Soon, I assure him.

The Race of Sun and Moon appears in Immortal Vale's chapter of the Book of the Immortals. It's one of the most well-known fae tales, recited to children at bedtime for generations.

Long ago, two rival kings waged war across the Near World, each seeking Immortal Vale's favor for a victory. But Vale offered no favor—only a race.

Each king was to ride from opposite ends of the realm,

one in the direction of the rising sun, the other in the direction of the rising moon, crossing blazing deserts, cliff-carved coasts, and darkened woodlands, until they reached the gates of ancient Calisyrune.

Weeks passed. Hunger hollowed the riders. Sun and wind flayed them bare. Yet both endured—and arrived within moments of each other.

But they no longer craved conquest.

The journey had burned away their pride, leaving men who now saw beyond borders and crowns.

Neither king won. Neither lost, either. They dismounted together and laid their swords at Vale's feet.

Wisdom does not sit on a throne, Immortal Vale famously pronounced. *It rides the common road, as you have just done.*

I glance over my shoulder at the Immortal Box, where six thrones have been brought out. One for each of the woken gods. They sit stiffly, watching with unreadable expressions, as if they actually care about the outcome of this recreation.

A trumpet blares, and a servant lowers the starting flag.

And I can't think any more about the fae.

"Go!" I dig my heels into Tòrr's side, but he doesn't need the cue. He's already tearing at the arena, pawing the sand, foaming at the mouth.

Beside me, Basten spurs Myst in the opposite direction. Half the arena waves flags with the sun emblem, while the other half thrusts their moon flags high.

Tòrr and I race through sets constructed of wood and paint. First, we roar through the ancient nameless deserts that would later become the kingdom of Kravada. Then, we pass through a forest where actors dressed as ancient warriors throw dull-tipped spears at us.

I lean forward, thighs pressing in to hold myself steady, gloved fingers woven in Tòrr's razor-sharp mane. The wind makes my eyes water, but I wouldn't trade this thrill for anything.

Circling in the opposite direction, Basten and Myst bound toward us. Myst is no competition for Tòrr as far as speed, of course—but this is simply a show. There are no winners or losers tonight.

We cross paths in the middle of a set made to look like the shallow shores of the Panopis Sea, complete with workers tossing buckets of water at us to mimic the surf.

Our eyes meet.

For that brief moment, I feel as if everything in the world has clicked into place.

It's working.

By tomorrow night, at the grand closing ceremony, all our efforts will have paid off—fae and mortals will be at peace. I know it. I *feel* it.

Tòrr and I weave between wooden pillars painted to look like villages, buying time for Basten and Myst to catch up in their direction.

Then, once we're equidistant from the finish line, a trumpet blares. We race to the final set in the center of the arena, where wooden pillars are painted to look like the arched gates of ancient Calisyrune.

We tear through the silken ribbon together. Me and Tòrr. Basten and Myst. We pull the horses to a stop, their bodies aligned head to tail, and Basten and I lean across the space between us to kiss.

The arena erupts.

The crowd throws flowers and offerings to the sand. Ribbons. Charms. Paper ornaments. The cheers swell into a roar that shakes the very bones of the place, our names chanted again and again.

In the Immortal Box, Vale strides to the announcer's balcony, lifting his hands.

"Good people of Astagnon," he thunders, "Let this be a lesson to all of us. In the game of war, no one wins if we do not stand together. Wisdom does not sit on a throne—it rides the common road. Your road!"

Flags wave enthusiastically, as tears glisten in people's eyes.

"Tomorrow," Vale continues, "The second and final day of the Fae Games commences at dawn with—"

"Brother, if I may!" Artain suddenly staggers to Vale's side, his cheeks stained telltale red, his voice slightly slurred. "In fact, we have one final surprise to close off the first night of games!"

A warning threads its way between my heartbeat.

Basten nudges Myst closer to me and says quietly, "Did you know about this?"

I shake my head hard.

Basten curses under his breath. "Artain looks drunk off his ass. And Vale looks about ready to murder him."

My heart thumps faster, my gloved hands twisting knots in Tòrr's mane. The energy in the crowd shifts—it's sharper now, and Artain isn't the only one who's been drinking. Half the audience is already swaying, singing old fae ballads half-slurred.

"Mortals!" Artain calls, pushing forward onto the balcony, holding out a hand toward the set in the arena's center. "Behold the gates of ancient Calisyrune. A final gift from us to you—and for you, King of Fae!" He turns to Iyre. "Sister, if you will do the honors."

Iyre steps forward, her red fey sparking at her palms. She weaves her fingers in the air, and a half dozen figures suddenly rise from the sand. Sitting upright in strange, jerky movements.

I gasp, tightening my thighs around Tòrr. "What trickery is this?"

Basten is silent at my side, on alert. He quietly feels for the hunting knife sheathed in the hidden holster at his side.

Garbled cries of surprise ring out from the crowd. The figures—people, though I'm hesitant to call them that—stand up and move jerkily toward the wooden set. Iyre twists her fingers again, and ropes fall from the upper portion of the set.

The figures slide their hands and feet into loops at the end of each rope.

Basten hisses at my side. "Those figures reek of rot—they're fucking dead bodies."

Tòrr stomps his feet beneath me, dancing nervously, as unnerved as I am.

"That's impossible," I say.

Basten throws an angry look toward the Immortal Box. "Not if Woudix is behind it."

My throat tightens. "He wouldn't do this."

"Who else can unearth the buried dead and make them walk?" Basten snaps back, though his anger isn't aimed at me.

"There are...godkissed Deathraisers," I stutter, but even my own logic begins to fall apart at the seams. Deathraisers can bring back the dead, yes—but they can't pilot them like puppets.

The crowd catches on that the figures are dead bodies,

and someone suddenly calls out, "It's them! The Cold Coins!"

I whip my head around, squinting into the gloaming light at the walking cadavers. Sure enough—there's no mistaking the deep gash in Gaez's skull where Rian buried an axe. I spy the generals named Boone and Mallik, too.

The crowd's mood shifts, uncertain and bordering unease.

Artain lifts his hands higher, quick to reassure everyone. "Mortals, this is for you! Do not fear, there is no danger! If you liked our first show of vengeance, when we slaughtered General Gaez, who had so wronged you, you'll *love* this. Behold, what happens to your enemies!"

Iyre moves her hands more, and the cadavers of all the fallen Cold Coins—Boone, Mallik, Gaez, and their other commanders—begin to dance a grotesque show.

It's a puppet show, I realize. *With the dead.*

I lift a shaking hand to my brow, trying to quell my panic and disgust. "Was Rian behind this supposed miracle, too?"

Basten immediately shakes his head. "He's not dumb enough for *this*. Rian understands what the public wants. When it wants vengeance, when it wants entertainment. Safety. *This* is a drunk couple of asshole fae who are about to ruin everything we've achieved today."

I narrow my eyes, glaring at Artain in the Immortal Box, and murmur, "Not if I can help it."

I spur on Tòrr, who leaps forward. We head straight for the lower rung of seating in the stadium. There's a fifteen-foot wall around the arena, too high even for Tòrr to clear, but I steer him toward a tall wooden crate painted to look like a barn.

He leaps onto the crate, then bounds into the stands.

The public scrambles out of our way, already jittery and restless from Artain's twisted human puppet show.

Tòrr and I stampede up the steps as people dart out of our way, straight to the Immortal Box. Tòrr tears through the space with wild abandon, gleefully stamping on broken champagne flutes and china plates as his massive rump knocks over the tables of offerings.

I dismount swiftly and barrel toward the announcer's balcony, grabbing my father's cape.

"Father—you have to stop this!" I throw out a hand toward Artain's puppet show. "It's going to ruin everything!"

"I never agreed to this," Vale snarls, his anger aimed at Artain and Iyre, not me. "These idiots decided to put on a show behind my back."

"What's the problem?" Artain sputters with a hiccup, as though it's all just a lark. "These naive sheep swallowed the first lie without choking—that we supposedly avenged them, hunted down their great tormentor. Why not feed them another?"

"Because there's a difference between vengeance and brutality!" I yell. I spin on Woudix, my breath catching. "And you? Are you a part of this, too?"

He shakes his head, slow and calm. "A Deathraiser—it had to be. It was not me."

"You asses!" Vale roars.

An argument erupts between the fae, while Samaur and Thracia drunkenly make out at the other side of the box, oblivious to anything but their own wanton lust.

Was I wrong about the fae? To think they wouldn't mess everything up?

"Listen closely." Rian suddenly appears at my side, and

for once, he doesn't seem as drunk as the others. "This was a bone-headed move by Artain, but even shit can be made to look like gold with enough paint. Get every fiddler in this city into the streets. Pay heralds to retell the day's successes at all hours—the Aron and Aria performance, the golden-claw rides. Open the royal meadery. Pass around enough gratis booze that even the children are too sloshed to remember this last part of the evening. Or care. They'll only talk about the good parts."

I pause, working my gloves between my fingers.

Vale looks at me. "Daughter, what say you to this plan?"

I meet Rian's eyes, then nod.

Vale snaps into action. With a flick of his hand, guards scatter, and within seconds, the spotlights shining on the grotesque puppet stage vanish.

In their place, the dancers from earlier, hastily dressed in their Aron and Aria costumes, flit back onto the stage, cheeks dotted with painted hearts, smiles a little too wide.

The trumpets strike up a sprightly tune, cheerful and false.

"Sabine—" Basten's voice cuts through the din as he bursts up the stairs to the Immortal Box, finally catching up to me. He stops beside me, breathless, eyes sweeping the arena. Servants are already rolling barrels of ale into the stands, passing tin cups to cheering patrons like nothing ever happened.

But Basten's gaze snaps to Artain, and I feel his body stiffen.

Artain is laughing—head tilted back, murmuring something into Iyre's ear. Whatever it is makes her smile like none of this matters.

I rest a hand on Basten's arm. "It's okay," I murmur,

swallowing back a dry lump. "Disaster averted—thanks to Rian's quick thinking."

But even as the words leave my lips, they taste wrong.

Like I missed something.

Something...slippery.

Something that can't be stopped now, even if I wanted to.

CHAPTER 30
BASTEN

I don't give a fuck about the fae, and I definitely don't give a fuck about drinking with them.

Still, appearances matter. That's the thorn in my side ever since taking up the crown; I can't just saunter off after my royal duties are done for the day and kick my feet up next to a roaring fire. Royal duties are *never* done.

Especially when the *gods* are pouring you wine.

So, Sabine and I smile into the late evening on the Immortal Box, pretending Artain didn't just put up one fucked-up show. Suri returns to the castle to catch up on her Castlekeep duties, but Rian, Ferra, and Folke have never left a party early in their lives.

"You rode well, King Basten." Captain Tatarin tips her silver goblet to me. The painted hearts on her cheeks are smeared, but she's one of the rare sober ones gathered in the box—her goblet holds only water. "Not every man would go up against a monoceros with a goddess on his back."

I wrap an arm around Sabine's back. "Myst nearly threw

me when we hit that forest set. The one with the actors. Guess we forgot to tell her the spears weren't real."

Tatarin and Ferra, beside her, laugh.

Vale catches the last bit of the conversation and joins in. "You might be interested to learn that in the true Race of Sun and Moon, both kings were slaughtered long before they ever reached Calisyrune. One by warring pirates, and the other succumbed to an infection."

Vale blinks pleasantly, as if he's just told a highly entertaining anecdote.

Ferra's eyes widen to show the whites, but she quickly clears her throat. "Right...if you'll excuse me." She goes off in search of Folke.

Captain Tatarin waits a beat before pasting on a smile. She raises her glass again. "Here's to the old scribes who turned tragedy into stories."

Sabine and I exchange a quick, wary look before weakly raising our glasses.

The Valor Bell chimes in the distance from Valor Circle. I count the chimes. Ten, eleven, twelve. *Midnight.*

Out of the corner of my eye, I spot Artain snake his arm around Woudix's neck and tip his head up to whisper in the God of Death's ear. He doesn't speak in the Common Tongue —it's some language I don't know. Samaur comes over to join them, rubbing his hands together.

Trouble practically *sparks* in his golden eyes.

The three of them set down their goblets and quietly leave the box.

I squeeze Sabine's hip, hard, like a signal. "Excuse me— the latrine calls, if you'll allow me leave."

An indulgent smile curls her mouth, but the shrewdness

in her eyes tells me that she knows perfectly well I'd never ask her permission to go piss.

"Granted." She mockingly bows, a genie granting a wish, and everyone laughs again. She lifts an eyebrow. "I'll meet you later in our chambers."

I signal to Rian. "Come with me—hold my cloak while I piss."

As we leave, Captain Tatarin starts retelling a bawdy story about two of her soldiers she caught in the woods in a compromised position, and thankfully, no one watches us too closely.

"So where are we actually going?" Rian whispers as soon as we're in the arena's breezeway, out of earshot from the others.

I drop my pretense of good humor and mutter darkly, "We're following the Blades. Artain, Woudix, Samaur. I don't trust those bastards."

Rian's mouth curls in a grim smile. "Kendan didn't think it necessary to have spies on hand tonight, but I knew better. I quietly tapped a few old connections. They stocked some weapons caches in all the usual places—like we talked about."

A pulse of relief goes through me. *Just like old times.* "Good. Here—trade cloaks with me."

We reach the latrines and squeeze into one of the stone chambers. I quickly swap cloaks with him, unbutton my royal shirt, turn it inside out, then tie a cloth around my face.

As we exit the arena into a cobblestone square, if one so much as glances at us, we'll look just like two more commoners in the festive crowd.

I close my eyes and smell the air for a trace of iron—the

underlying scent of any fae.

"This way." I tap Rian's shoulder and head toward Varn Row, the market district, which is all but a ghost town at this time of night.

Rian's footfalls fall in step with mine. To any passersby, we might look like twins. Brothers, at least. We know one another so well that we barely need words as we navigate the streets with just a look or a small gesture.

"Basten," he says eventually, breaking the quiet. His voice hitches. "I just want to say. Gods, not to be overly emotional or anything, but you and Sabine accepting me, sins and all. Bringing me into the fold. It means, well—"

"Shut the fuck up," I mutter.

He laughs softly, then gives me a grateful nod.

"There. They turned left at the corner." I head for a dirt road up ahead.

"What do you think they're up to?" he asks.

"Hell if I know, but nothing good. They went behind Vale's back with that deadman's puppet show. That was bold. There's no telling what stunt they might pull next."

Rian stops, grabbing my cloak. The light from the moon reflects on the shimmering eyeliner lining his upper lashes. "They didn't go behind Vale's back."

I wipe a hand over my face, looking left and right down the lane, anxious to follow that fae scent. Offhand, I mutter, "Yes, they did. Vale said it himself."

"I don't care what he *said*," Rian emphasizes, his voice a low hiss. "I know a lie when I see one. I've bluffed my way through Basel since I was five years old. Vale might have claimed he wasn't aware, but I assure you, he fully knew."

A wrinkle of unease turns over in my gut as I stop and

fully face Rian. "Why would Vale pretend not to know? Even act angry about it, if he condoned it?"

Rian rubs his own jaw, staring into the middle distance. "Maybe he wanted plausible deniability...I don't know. But I'm telling you, that man *knew*."

A spike of dread shoots through me. There's something wrong here that goes beyond Artain's drunken antics.

But before I can follow that uneasy line of thought, I catch a whiff of iron again.

We follow it through the Glassmarket and along the curving lane of High Quarter, following the city wall as it turns south, winding down grid-like alleyways—

—Until we come out right in the courtyard of Hekkelveld Castle.

Where guards are admiring their brand-new spears, freshly delivered from the blacksmith.

Spears that reek so strongly of iron, I couldn't scent a fae within ten paces if I tried.

I drift to a stop. "Fuck."

Rian cranes his neck. "What?"

I shake my head, sighing. "We lost them. Maybe they knew we were trailing them." I start for the entrance, lowering the cloth around my face so the soldiers will recognize me. "Come on. Promise to behave yourself, and we can check on Sabine."

We've just started up the central stairs when we nearly collide with Suri, coming down.

"Basten! Rian!" she says, startled to see us.

"Lady Suri?" Rian asks. "What are you doing up at this hour? Shouldn't you be getting your beauty sleep?"

She doesn't even bother to roll her eyes—too intent on

the stack of books she's carrying, her arms trembling under their weight. She pointedly ignores Rian and looks at me. "My assistant just brought me these books. When we locked Rian in the Coffin, he said he was bored out of his mind and asked me to fetch a book he'd been reading in the secret passages. I forgot to call off the order, and my stewards just finished unearthing all the old books hidden in the passages and wiping off the cobwebs."

Rian perks up, stepping forward to take them. "Better late than never. I was halfway through the history of the Panopis corsair fleet—"

"You don't get them anymore," she snaps, pulling back the stack. "You don't deserve them." She pauses—something bright, almost feverish, igniting in her eyes. "But that's not what matters. Look."

She lifts the topmost book as though it's fragile glass, not paper and leather.

"This," she whispers, "is the one Sabine has been searching for. The second volume of *The Last Return of the Fae*. I knew it had to be somewhere in these castle walls!"

A slow, electric tingle crawls up my spine. "*The Last Return of the Fae*?" I turn sharply to Rian. "You knew about this?"

He shrugs, open-palmed and infuriatingly casual. And gods help me—he looks truly baffled. "Never heard of it. I told you, I was reading about the great corsair sea battles."

I study him closely.

No twitch. No sweat. No shift of the eyes.

He isn't lying.

I hold out my hand for the book. "I'll take it to her. She'll be grateful, but there was no need to get this to us tonight.

Sabine already has a copy of the book. Woudix gave it to her."

Suri hesitates before carefully passing me the volume. "Yes, I was aware of that." There's a hitch in her voice. "I've seen it. That one has no illustrations, only text. They...aren't the same book."

A chill tears into me, because Sabine has been putting all her trust into Woudix's book. For fuck's sake, it's even supposed to contain the secret to putting the fae to sleep.

Immediately, I crack open the book.

It reeks of mustiness, the pages nearly disintegrating beneath my fingers. I've flipped through the volume that Woudix gave Sabine, too, and at first glance, they looked identical. This one is also written in a forgotten language, with only a few words of the Immortal Tongue here and there. But come to think of it, I don't recall any illustrations in that version.

I flip the page and freeze.

It's an illustration—one I've seen before. One definitely not in the copy Woudix gave Sabine.

"Lady Suri, get some sleep," I say, my voice suddenly hollow. "I'll make sure Sabine gets this."

She wrings her hands, blinking hard in the low lantern light, but nods.

"You, too, Rian," I snap as soon as she's gone.

"What?" His retort is sharp, wounded. He scoffs as he motions to the direction of the castle entrance behind us. "What about the Blades?"

I slam the book closed, shoving it under my arm. "We'll put tails on them in the morning. I'll have Folke stick so close to Artain he'll wonder if his shadow has come to life."

Rian paces, rubbing the back of his neck, looking like he's working through about a hundred possible lies in his mind.

"Rian, go," I bark.

He stops. His hand falls away, and for once, he obeys.

The castle is eerily quiet. Many of the residents are still out enjoying the festivities, which will stretch until dawn. Even now, I can hear music playing as far off as the border to the Silent Ward. But there are guards at the entrance to Raven Hall, and kitchen servants preparing for tomorrow's full day of banquets.

Their movements clatter against my ears—even their breathing deafens me now.

I climb the narrow stairs to the second floor, where a tiny contemplation room, a place for prayer and meditation, is set unobtrusively at the hallway's end.

I close the door behind me.

My heart thrums as I drop to the kneeling bench—worn smooth from centuries of use—and set the book on the low prayer altar. A shelf built into the wall holds a single candle and a box of matches beside it.

It's pitch-black in here. Normally, that wouldn't matter —my night vision's good enough. But that's what tricked me last time when it came to this specific illustration.

I brace one hand on the edge of the altar, the other fumbling for the matchbox. My fingers shake as I strike a match, the flame flaring to life.

Warm light spills across the parchment.

Blood-red ink gleams in its glow—the color my night vision can't pick up on.

Slowly, I flip through the book. As I suspected, it's the

same series of illustrations that I stumbled across on the lowest level of Drahallen Hall: The ten fae seated around a stone table. Meric with his maze. Alyssantha in the throes of passion with two maids.

I flip through the pages slowly, dread pooling in my gut with every turn. These illustrations are vibrant, nearly untouched by time—more vivid and detailed than the faded murals buried in Drahallen's crumbling plaster.

I stop on the image of Immortal Solene standing before the ancient, smoke-filled city of Calisyrune. She practically pulses on the page—her hair writhing like it might slither off the parchment.

I close my eyes for a breath, swallowing down the bitter taste rising in my throat, then force myself to turn the page.

As expected, it's the matching image, the same one I saw in Drahallen Hall's basement: Solene unleashing brimfire, the city swallowed in ruin as trees bloom and the raging Ramvik River runs clean.

Nature triumphant.

This was the image that first seeded a fear I couldn't shake—that Sabine, deep down, might do the same. That she might choose nature over humanity, the way Solene did.

But everything's changed now. I trust her, body and soul. Not that she wouldn't consider righting the balance between nature and civilization—but that she wouldn't decide alone.

She'd tell me.

We'd face it together.

Together, always.

I take a deep breath before I flip the next page.

The next illustration is the one I glimpsed when Suri

handed me the book. It was that moment when it all clicked like a fucking lock.

I flip to the next page and stagger back like I've seen a ghost, elbow knocking something over behind me.

No. No fucking way. It can't be.

"That backstabbing motherfucker," I growl, hands tightening on the edges of the altar until the wood nearly splinters. I stagger back, slamming my fist into the stone wall. "Fuck!"

My lungs feel too small, too empty. I pace, rubbing my sternum, trying to fight for air. My mind can't snag on a single thought.

Finally, I get my shit together.

I lean over the altar, hands still clenched like I'm trying to bend the wood in two, and force myself to keep flipping through the pages.

At first, I thought these illustrations were just records. Like the pictograms in Drahallen Hall. Thought they were showing me what already happened.

But no.

These aren't history.

They're a *blueprint for the future.*

A gods-damned prophecy laid out in ink and blood—how the fae intend to dominate the world, piece by piece, until there's nothing left to worship but them.

"Sabine," I whisper, and slam the book shut.

I sprint up the stairs to the royal bedroom in a daze, shoving past soldiers, nearly careening into the wall. I must look drunk—hell, I feel it—my head spinning so hard I can barely see straight.

I shove the door open hard enough to rattle it in its hinges—

—to find Sabine is already on her feet.

Her human glamour's half-fallen, silver light flaring at her palms like a weapon. Her eyes are wide, wild, searching the room until they land on me.

She exhales, hard. "Basten."

I'm breathless. "You're awake?"

"I had a dream," she says quickly, stepping toward me, voice tight with urgency. "No—not a dream. A memory, like before. I was coming to find you."

Our eyes meet, both of us shaken.

And I realize how in sync we really are now.

I drop the book at the foot of the bed beside her, where it falls like a brick.

There's a beat where she only stares at it, as if she knows what this means.

"*The Last Return of the Fae*?" she finally states, her voice distant.

"Suri found it." My voice is hoarse, choked.

Sabine's fingers hover over it, as if she's afraid it will bite if she touches it.

My ribs feel too damn tight as I pace, needing to move, my hand flexing in and out of a fist. "The copy Woudix gave you was a fake. He set you up, Sabine. Poured promises of peace in your ear and gave you a book filled with puzzles to distract you. Tonight? That fucked-up puppet show? Vale knew it was going to happen. Rian clocked it immediately—said Vale's anger was just an act. Sabine, this entire *thing* is an act. The Fae Games. It's all a trick. It was a means for Vale to take Old Coros by force, easy entry to the city. And I can prove it."

I expect her to deny it. To defend her father once more. Or maybe not—maybe just to show shock at his betrayal.

The last thing I expect is for her calm, still silence.

I flip open the book to the page where the murals in Drahallen Hall's basement left off, and jab my finger on it. "*This* is their plan. That bastard Woudix was behind it all along. And the puppet show today was part of the plan. To shock the public once with the resurrected dead, so that when it happens again, panic won't immediately set in. They'll think it's just Artain's buffoonery again. And when they realize it's an attack, it will be too late."

I flip through the illustrations:

A life-sized puppet show with human prisoners.

Dead bodies, brought back to their feet, terrorizing a city.

The fae court seated on thrones forged out of the rubble and violence.

She barely glances at the illustrations—the blueprint that lays it all bare, that shows us exactly what's coming.

"I..." She swallows, voice catching in her throat. Then, more firmly, "I already know, Basten."

A muscle twitches beneath my eye. I breathe deep, try to keep my voice level. "What do you mean, you know?"

She hesitates, then grabs my hand and pulls me toward the window. "That's what I wanted to tell you. I had another dream. Only—like before—it wasn't a dream. It was a memory. A recovered one from a Return long ago. I heard them speak about this plan. When I woke, I looked outside... That light? That's fey. It's a *portal*. Look."

A cold dread coils up my spine as I follow her gaze to the dark city skyline. Sabine points toward Valor Circle, where the Valor Bell tower rises over the rooftops. Where a flicker —bright and wrong—shimmers at its peak.

Fey light.

A portal.

Open.

And then I hear it.

The scrape of desiccated flesh and bone against stone. I know that sound because, unfortunately, I've heard it before.

It's the dry rasp of the walking dead.

CHAPTER 31

SABINE

The streets of Old Coros are so packed with midnight revelers that Basten and I can barely push our way through. Even without disguises, no one stops their merriment to bat an eye at their king and queen breathlessly stumbling toward Valor Belltower.

Except—

"Hey!" A cloaked beggar on the street corner, crutch at his side, suddenly shoves to his feet, moving toward us without a trace of a limp.

Rian shoves his hood back, darting glances at the crowd. "What the fuck are you two doing out here?"

"Rian?" I say.

"I told you to go to bed," Basten growls, shoving Rian in the chest.

Rian catches his balance, combing his fingers back through his hair. "Are you my mother now, Basten? Of course, I'm not going to heed your orders—not when those Blades are prowling around, suspicious as fuck." He tosses his hands in the air. "And gods, don't arrest me again! I'm so fucking tired of shackles. So, I slipped my guards again... you'd have done the same."

I crane my neck sharply at Basten, eyebrows knit together. "The Blades? What's he talking about?"

Basten pinches the bridge of his nose, muttering under his breath. "We were following the Blades earlier...it doesn't matter now. Rian, you should get back to Hekkelveld Castle and lock yourself in."

Rian stands taller, instantly intrigued. "Why? What are those fae bastards up to?" He reconsiders and gives me a sheepish grin. "Present company excluded, songbird."

I narrow my eyes at him. "What do you know, Rian?"

"Only that rumors are spilling out of the Silent Ward that Artain restarted his twisted puppet show again."

I step back, closing my eyes as my fey pushes hard beneath my skin. "We need to get to the belltower, now."

We charge ahead, sprinting as best we can through the crowd that's clogging the streets. I don't have the will to tell Rian to leave us to it—and to be honest, I'm not sure I want to.

He's proven himself helpful.

More than helpful.

Gods help me, he's almost *trustworthy* these days.

Finally, we break free of the throngs as we enter the circular road around the Valor Bell tower. It's an orderly section of the city, bordering the Silent Ward to the southeast. Nearby are churches to the ten gods, a few monasteries and convents, and parks with walking paths for contemplation.

Immediately, I skid to a halt.

At the base of the belltower, a blindingly bright portal cuts a hole through the fabric of space. My heart tightens, the memory still too fresh of Iyre pulling me through a portal just like this, tearing me away from Basten.

This time, however, no one is trying to steal me away.

Instead, bodies flow *from* the Volkish side into ours. They stagger. Their broken and bloody limbs hang limp. Their eyes are glazed over.

I press my palm to my mouth to catch my gasp. "Their chins, Basten. They all bear the spiral tattoo. It's...it's the river folk. The dead from the Lunden Valley. The ones who weren't as fortunate as the refugees."

The three of us stare in horror as wave after wave of resurrected bodies stagger through the portal, dragging behind them fishing nets and tattered burlap sacks.

I whirl on Rian, smashing my fist against his chest, and then blast a spark of fey, threatening. "This is *your* doing! I knew it was too good to be true—your newfound loyalty."

He holds out his hands. "*Me?* What are you on about? What do I have to do with the risen dead?"

"*You* killed them when you poisoned their river valley!" I cry.

His head cocks oddly, true bafflement on his face. "What...?" His eyebrows then rise faintly. "Oh, the north-western coastlands, by the border wall? I remember hearing a report about poisoned fields. What do *I* have to do with that?"

To my horror, a reanimated corpse—once a fisherman, by the look of his salt-stiffened rags—sets its jerking, unholy focus on a couple passionately kissing in front of a brothel. Its slack jaw snaps beneath the remains of a weather-worn cloak, teeth clicking with hunger. The lovers are too lost in each other to notice it drawing near.

"We'll finish this later, Rian," I growl.

A drunk suddenly stumbles into the corpse's path, laughing, and gives its shoulder a hearty shove. "Easy on the ale, friend!"

The corpse turns, teeth bared.

The drunk's companion stumbles to a halt, sober enough to yank his friend backward. "Trint—look! It's one of those puppet things that Immortal Artain dragged back from the grave!"

Trint recoils with a sound of disgust. "The fae are nothing if not dramatic, am I right?"

They laugh as if it's all a joke and wander off toward the nearest tavern.

Behind them, the corpse lunges.

Its teeth sink into the back of Trint's neck. He cries out, voice pitched somewhere between agony and horror.

But no one looks too closely, too consumed with their own merriment.

All I can think of is Grand Cleric Beneveto, staggering down from the jail carriage with that same feral hunger.

Now, it really hits home why his chains were necessary.

"When the dead return," I whisper, "They're...hungry. For mortal flesh."

Basten doesn't have a religious bone in his body, but I swear I see him silently mouth a prayer.

Rian turns toward a group of young men singing bawdy fae ballads as they stagger drunkenly down the street. "You! Get out of here. You're in danger!"

The youths laugh and push right past him.

"They won't listen to you," I say breathlessly. "We have to stop this at the source. Come on!"

I race down the street, heart rattling off-kilter, with Rian and Basten close at my heels. The crowd parts around us as we dart between carriages and carts, sprinting toward Valor Belltower.

When we reach the edge of the circular road, I come to a staggering halt.

Above us, a searing column of fey light pierces the clouds, shining like a blade into the heavens. The ground thrums with its energy. The bottom of the tower—once an unassuming archway leading to the stairs to the top of the tower—has become something else entirely.

A portal.

The arch now seethes with raw magic, a portal torn wide open to Volkany. From its depths, the dead spill forth in droves—staggering, snarling, lifeless things full of feverish need.

To the right of the portal, Iyre stands poised, graceful as ever, the fey needle in hand. Her fingers work delicately, widening the portal with careful skill.

Revulsion rises thick in my throat, but my gaze shifts— and locks.

Opposite her stands Woudix, shadowed in flickering black fey. Sparks crackle from his hands as he raises corpse after corpse, each one twitching to unnatural life.

My rage ignites.

"Woudix!" I shout, storming forward, my fey shattering through my human glamour like glass. "You traitor!"

I throw my hands up and unleash a bolt of silver fey, bright as lightning—but he pivots with inhuman grace, his own magic slamming into mine and dispersing it in a flash of sparks.

"I trusted you!" I cry, voice raw.

He turns toward me, unshaken. Hawk stands beside him, decayed and snarling.

"Lady Sabine," he says, smooth as polished stone, "I suggest you return to your bedchamber. You'd already chosen your side when you bound yourself to that mortal. It's the same side you choose every time. The *wrong* one."

My hands tremble so hard that my fey fails.

So, I step forward—and slap Woudix instead. *Hard.*

"You liar," I hiss. "You made me believe you were with me. All this time, you were just another pawn for my father!"

He doesn't flinch.

"I'm the God of Death," he says, voice low and dark, almost tender. "Why would I want peace, when I can have the world on its knees, endless bodies to fill my underrealm?"

From across the portal, Iyre lifts her chin and sneers. "How does it feel, Sabine?" she coos. "To finally see what was always coming?"

Basten snarls behind me—no words, just fury. His blade is out in one smooth motion, and he charges.

Iyre doesn't move. She doesn't have to.

With a flick of her fingers, one of the dead lunges at him.

But Rian is faster.

He launches forward, onto the corpse's back, and with a savage twist, snaps its neck, sending the thing crumpling to the cobblestones.

"Stop them, Sabine!" Rian shouts, wiping jelly-thick remnants of corpse flesh hastily on his trousers. "Use your godkiss like you did with the tigers in Duren Arena!"

For a breath, I hesitate, staring down at my glowing hands, where silver light pulses beneath the skin, soft and steady like a heartbeat. The memory of the tigers—how I reached into their minds, how they couldn't help but obey —returns to me.

I turn toward Hawk, Woudix's snarling companion, hoping, praying, that I can reach her the same way.

But as I try to project into her, I feel nothing. Not a mind. Not a soul. Just a dead, echoing void. When I direct my godkiss to the walking corpses, it's just as silent.

"I... I can't," I whisper, horror lacing every word as the truth sets in. "The tigers were alive. I can only control the living. These things—they're already gone."

The realization lands in my chest like a weight dropped from a great height. Even now, with all this power thrumming beneath my skin, I'm still bound by my godkiss's laws.

Basten's voice slices through my rising panic. "Brimfire."

When I look at him, his expression is calm, resolute. And I understand. *This is the only path left.*

I inhale, grounding myself.

Drawing the magic upward from my core, I feel the burn of brimfire gather in my chest, a blistering heat building behind my ribs until it surges through my arms and bursts from my palms in a sweeping arc.

The blue flame rushes across the stone in a brilliant wave, incinerating the corpses that stagger from the portal before they can take more than a few steps into the city.

But brimfire is not a gentle magic, nor easily controlled. As I learned with what happened at the convent. The flames leap—onto carts, onto banners, onto the wooden shutters of the belltower itself.

Panic stirs in the crowd as screams rise.

My heart clenches as I realize what I've done.

These aren't just monsters. They were people once. Men

who carved boats, women who sang to their children at night, lovers who kissed on darkened docks.

They should be in Volkany with the refugees, or safe in their villages, not here—twisted into weapons.

But I don't get to dwell on what they *should* be.

This is what they are now.

The bell tower chimes five tolls, each one echoing between my ears. *Dawn comes at six*, I think.

If it's too risky to burn the hungry dead with brimfire, and I can't command them with my godkiss...

Then maybe I can tap a different kind of strength.

I close my eyes, extending my sense of connection with the natural world beyond the city walls, to the sleepy lake Basten and I passed when we first arrived.

But I frown, sensing a barrier.

"Something's in the way," I say, gripping Basten's arm. "The city gate is closed—I need you and Rian to open it."

Basten holds my gaze, his eyes fierce with love. He nods without question.

Then I turn, gathering my skirts, and plunge back into the crowd.

The city still pulses with half-drunk celebrations, but the Royal Arena lies quieter now, the chaos of the day's events scrubbed clean. Even the workers have cleared out, the props and banners have been hauled away, leaving the great structure silent.

I slip through a side entrance, the guards at the gate catching the glow of my fae-lit eyes.

They drop to their knees instantly, heads bowed. "Majesty."

I say nothing as I pass, my gown sweeping behind me like a shadow.

Down, down—into the dark, echoing underbelly of the stadium, where old stone stairs lead into the backstage corridors. The holding stables lie just beyond.

And there—exactly where I hoped—stand Tòrr and Myst.

They're housed in a makeshift iron stall, Tòrr munches lazily on alfalfa hay. Myst flicks her tail beside him, alert but calm.

The stable attendant jolts upright at my approach, scrambling to cover the fact that he'd been dozing. He mutters something about not expecting visitors.

I wave him off with a flick of my wrist. "Go."

He bows, eyes wide with reverence, and scurries off, whispering prayers.

I take a moment to greet Myst with a scratch on her forelock. Then, I turn to Tòrr, my heart aching in a way I hadn't expected.

You were right, I whisper, stepping closer, my voice thick with something more than power. *You sent Plume to watch me. Not because you didn't trust me, but because you were afraid I'd forget what matters.*

Tòrr lifts his head, those ageless eyes meeting mine, full of understanding.

And maybe I did forget, I admit, resting my hand on his powerful withers. *For a while. I got so caught up in the human world, crowns and battles and thrones, that I forgot to look up—at the birds. And down—at the mice.*

The words tremble out of me, but I keep going.

But I'm looking now. I remember. The forests, the rivers, everything with wings or teeth or tails. I haven't forgotten who I am. I pause. *And I need your help, friend.*

Tòrr shifts forward, the stall's gate creaking under his weight, as if already answering.

I unfasten the gate's latch.

Let's make it right together, I say.

Tòrr gleefully paws his massive hoof in the straw bedding. His eyes flash with a ring of red, and a thick cloud of steam rises from his dripping nostrils.

I throw open the gate. There's no mounting block, but he lifts his front foot for me, giving me his massive hoof as a boost. I swing onto his back, licking my lips against the bite of iron in the air.

For once, I feel as fierce as him.

Feel his ambition as my own.

His drive.

You want to safeguard the natural realm? I say, leaning forward, knitting my bare hands in his mane, realizing the sting of pain from his razorwire hair doesn't hurt me anymore. **We'll show the gods that their power is nothing against nature.**

I squeeze my legs, and he takes off. We thunder up the ramp to street level, hooves striking sparks off stone, bursting into the night like a storm let loose.

In the short time that I was below ground, something on the city's surface shifted. The air no longer rings with jeering jokes about Artain's puppet show. Laughter has been replaced by screams—high, shattering wails of genuine terror.

Around the corner, a legion of the dead lurches into view. Filthy, bloated things with outstretched arms, vacant eyes, mouths agape. They fall upon citizens still drunk from celebration who are too slow or stunned to flee.

Then comes the tearing of flesh. The sharp, wet sound of

teeth sinking into muscle. The splash of blood on cobblestone alleyways.

I shift my hips on Tòrr's back, guiding him with my weight, aiming him like a living battering ram straight at the horde.

Behind me, the first golden threads of dawn stretch across the rooftops.

The sunlit rays shine just to the left of the Valor Bell—not quite reaching it.

Tòrr lets out a fierce snort, muscles coiling beneath my thighs with gleeful rage.

"Now!" I cry, digging in my heels.

He charges.

My hand shoots up, silver magic already thrumming. I hurl a blast of fey at the Valor Bell, causing it to swing to the left as its clapper rings out a deep, ground-shaking *gong*.

The bell's copper surface hits the ray of dawn's light, reflecting it and funneling it down the street into a glowing beam.

Tòrr lifts his spiraled horn into the glow, the light striking it and bursting into a cascade of iridescent color that dances across the early morning darkness.

Not just color.

An explosion of light that knocks down the dead, clearing our path.

CHAPTER 32
BASTEN

The streets are thick with the risen dead.

As Rian and I race down the Strand toward the city gates, no one's dismissing the bodies anymore as leftovers from Artain's little puppet show. People scream as they flee corpses, who shuffle their rasping way through the city streets like a virus, cornering and biting any warm body they can manage to trap.

"Lock yourselves in your homes!" I shout, pausing to help a woman who tripped over her cloak. "A church, a business—get anywhere but out on the streets!"

Woudix's risen dead are relentless, but they're also seemingly mindless. It doesn't take long to study them and observe that they take the path of least resistance. The widest streets. Any roads that are flat, downhill. Easy to traverse.

So, Rian and I steer clear.

If Rian knows anything, it's the back alleys of the Sin Streets district. He guides me away from the main thoroughfares, along catwalks and across rooftop shortcuts, until we reach a small tavern called The First Stop that serves as a resting point and wayfinding center for travelers entering Old Coros.

The resurrected dead haven't made it this far yet, but their growls reverberate just a few blocks away. *We don't have much time.*

Rian finds an old, coiled rope, left behind from a roofer, and ties it to a chimney. We use it to scale down the front of The First Stop, drop down onto its front benches.

My heart slams as I toss my hair back, turning to face the city gates.

And that's when I see them.

The dead aren't here yet, but we *aren't* alone.

Immortal Samaur and Immortal Thracia stand before the closed gate's wooden beam barricade. The beam is reinforced with iron caps and studs, and Samaur is currently using his sunlit fey to melt the iron, effectively creating a seal on the gates that no amount of manpower could ever open.

"Hey!" I shout. "Why don't you fucking stick to making party favors, eh?"

They're in their human glamour, both of them. Yet as they whip around, eyes flashing the whites, looking as vicious as animals, it's never been clearer that they aren't human.

"Lord Basten." Samaur's smile spreads, all teeth and no warmth. "Or is it King Basten now? You mortals live such short lives that I tend to forget what roles you currently play in your silly little games of pretend." He aims his contemptful smile at Rian. "And the Lord of Liars. Shame you never joined us in Volkany—you would have done well in Norhelm."

"Beneveto sided with you," Rian says, casually plucking at a wrinkle on his shirt. "How did that work out for him?"

Samaur's lips curl back, more like a predator now.

"Thracia." I step forward, ignoring the God of Sun, and appeal to the round-faced girl instead who looks barely old enough to be out of church school. "We don't know one another, but I've spent more time with Vale's court than you have. The rest of your fae brethren put on a good show of being benign, hiding behind their revelries. But now, they've shown their true motives." I pause, taking a deep breath. "There's another way. Sabine—Solene—isn't like the others. You don't have to repeat the past. Just because you always form an alliance with Samaur doesn't mean you have to this Return. You could ally with humanity instead. We could use your help."

At the same time that I'm entreating to her, I'm quietly scanning the city gates. Looking for any weakness in Samaur's barricade that we can exploit to get the gates open.

Rian gives Thracia a sweeping bow. "Rian Valvere—big fan, o Immortal One. If I'm not mistaken, your affinity is healing, no? There are a hell of a lot of people in this city who could use your favor."

To punctuate his point, a scream rings out from a few blocks away.

Thracia blinks her big, painfully innocent eyes. Her hair cascades to her waist in thin braids, held back by a midnight blue ribbon. She toys with the ends of her hair, looking between Samaur and me, biting down on her pillowy bottom lip.

And then she and Samaur burst into cruel laughter at the same time.

She clutches her narrow waist, doubling over, as more laughter bubbles on her lips. When she looks up, it's with that same wolfish smile as Samaur.

"Healing?" she sneers. "Yes, that is my affinity. Or better stated, that's one side of it. The other side is poison. It was my godkiss when I was confined to a human body."

"Your godkiss was poisonwork?" I ask, my voice leveling flat. I slide a look to Rian. "And you lived along the Northwestern coast, near the border wall?"

She looks me up and down with disdain. "Yes, poisonwork. *Bit* more powerful than your wife's ability to talk to mice."

I feel the blood rush between my ears. Because now, everything clicks into place. Why Rian so forcefully denied having anything to do with poisoning the Lunden Valley, in the Northwest. Why Vale made up that lie in the first place.

Thracia poisoned the river valley when she was still mortal.

"Mortals have done nothing to you!" I burst out, unable to bite back my temper. "Not the people in Lunden Valley, and not the people here. Old Coros has embraced you with welcome arms, showered you with gifts!"

"Yes, it was a lovely welcome," she says, admiring her midnight-blue, angled fingernails. "I bear no rancor against the people here. They simply need to be taught a lesson. Shock and awe. So they do not mistake our rule for weakness. This Return, there will be no question as to where power lies." She sighs, listening to the distant sounds of screams. "As far as what happened in the Lunden Valley, that was an accident—I was testing the strength of my godkiss and things got a little out of control." She smirks. "Maybe that should have been a sign I was fae."

Her casual dismissal of thousands of dead bodies chills me to the bone.

"The more people you kill," Rian says, shifting his stance, subtly falling back into the fighting position we used in the sparring ring, "the fewer there will be to worship you."

"Humans are like ants," she says, waving her fingers dismissively. "There are always more. You're constantly reproducing. Waiting a few generations for a larger population means nothing to immortals." She grins. "Besides, the ones we spare will pray to us twice as hard, after they've seen what we're capable of."

An explosion of light suddenly ricochets throughout the central district, near Valor Circle. The earth trembles from the aftershocks, clay tiles sliding off the tavern roof and crashing to the street.

Samaur and Thracia immediately shift into their fae appearances, fey crackling at their fingertips.

"It's the monoceros," Samaur says, narrowing his golden eyes to slits of light. "Come on."

He starts toward the explosion at a jog. Thracia hangs back, still focused on Rian and me, purple fey snaking up her arms, which already bear the scent of pestilence and rot.

"They're nothing," Samaur urges her. "The gate's sealed. No one is escaping Woudix's risen army. We did our work, and now Vale is going to need us if Tòrr is loose. Come on!"

His tone is sharp enough to jolt her, and she wrinkles her nose at us one final time before running after Samaur.

The instant they're gone, Rian doubles over, bracing himself on his knees, and lets out a long exhale. "Fuck me in the ass—they're annoying as hell, aren't they? They can all rot—Sabine excluded."

I immediately begin inspecting the iron seal Samaur welded into the gate's barricade. "We don't know about the others. Popelin. Meric. Alyssantha. There could be another good one in the court. Hell, at this point I'd settle for one who just doesn't want the world to burn."

Rian grabs a broken flagpole and uses the end to test out the gate, looking for any weak or rotten boards we could possibly break through.

When his attempts come up empty, he tosses aside the pole, impatient. "That Sun God really fucked us."

Another blast of light from the central district rocks the ground, and I duck beneath the gate's archway as loose stones tumble down.

"Sabine and that monoceros can do a lot of damage," I mutter. "But she's never gone up against the entire fae court before."

We spare what little time we can to continue testing the barricade, but nothing works.

Then, suddenly, Rian claps me on the shoulder. "Remember that pub in Blackwater? The Lazy Otter?"

My brow furrows. There have been a lot of pubs. A lot of long, whisky-soaked nights with Rian in Blackwater. Most of them blur together in an amber haze.

"The broom closet!" he says, slapping me again to jog my memory. "We couldn't pay—I'd lost my coin purse. The owner locked us in. To get out, we—"

My eyebrows shoot up. "The hinges."

He grins. "Exactly."

We dash to the gate's massive hinges—great iron brackets as thick as my fist. Samaur didn't bother to weld them shut. Which means they could be removed.

Rian grabs the broken flagpole and jams the end

beneath the first hinge pin, then starts battering it loose. It's slow work, metal groaning with every strike, but one by one —two on each side—we work the pins free.

"Stand back!" Rian shouts.

We race toward the safety of The First Stop's entryway.

The gate, still barricaded through the center, groans— then crashes forward in a roar of splintered wood and dust.

A thick cloud billows out. We both stumble back, coughing, eyes stinging.

But when it clears, the path ahead is wide open.

"Quick." I shove his shoulder, urging him toward the central district. "Back to Sabine."

It doesn't take a genius to figure out Sabine's location. I barely need to use my godkissed senses. All we need to do is follow the explosions of light that rock outward like lit powder kegs.

All around us, the resurrected army lurches down alleyways, weaseling into any open door or window they can squeeze through. Every once in a while, I catch sight of a fishline tangled around a cadaver's leg. A child in rubber clamming boots. A locket dangling around a mangled neck.

These things were *people* once.

Peaceful, just trying to eke out a living before Thracia poisoned their lands.

And then, we skid out into the Glassmarket. Or rather, what's left of it.

Once, it was a large, open square paved with stone, where glassblowers set up their workshops, smoke pumping out of fires all day, the repetitive clink of hammers on anvils.

Now, shattered glass litters the earth. Half the surrounding buildings are razed, and the other half is on fire. Walking corpses lurch through the wreckage after the wounded victims who can't get to their feet in time to get away.

"The dead didn't do *that*," Rian mutters under his breath, nodding at a toppled municipal building.

As though on cue, Tòrr suddenly tears into the center of the square, letting out an ear-splitting shriek as his hooves paw through glass shards.

Sabine rides him, strong and true. She's a sight in her fae appearance, her fey lines blazing silver at her temples, almost blindingly so.

"Sabine!" I climb onto the wreckage of a glassblower's forge and wave my hands to get her attention. "The southern gate—it's open!"

She looks my way, but there's something off about her eyes. It's like she's both here and not here. And then, I see the silver blood pouring down her hands. She's clenching Tòrr's razorwire mane so hard it's shredding her palms.

"I can barely control him!" she shouts. The monoceros dances sideways beneath her, steam blasting out of his nostrils, his eyes wide and wild. "He's gone mad from the violence. The more he destroys, the more he wants to tear apart!"

I feel like I've been kicked in the gut. *Fuck, when are we going to get a break?*

"I know a thing or two about monoceroses," Rian says, wiping soot from his forehead with the back of his sleeve. "Especially *that* one."

"You kept him locked in an iron cell for a year without a glimpse of sunlight," I point out.

"Exactly," he says. "At their heart, they're the wildest thing in the world. Sabine controls nature, but fae creatures are a different set. They're as untamed as the gods themselves. It doesn't matter how fond he is of Sabine. That she gave him his power, his name. She can't control him—not like before."

"So, what?" I bark. "He's just a loose cannon with pure violent delight?"

Rian looks grim. "Yes."

"*Fuck.*"

"Basten!" Someone calls my name from the opposite side of the square. I catch sight of a few figures who have taken refuge on one of the few intact rooftops, a guildhall with a water tank on its roof. Lady Suri waves her arms, her face pinched and bruised. Ferra is beside her, clinging to a narrow iron spire, her silk dress in tatters. Folke guards the stairs with a broken spire as a makeshift spear, shoving it at any of the walking dead who attempt to climb the precariously balanced ladder.

I smack Rian, jerking my head toward the others.

We jog across the square, smashing moving corpses in our wake, until we reach the bottom of the guildhall.

"The castle is overrun by the dead," Suri calls down, clutching her shoulder like it's dislocated. "Folke got us out. We were fleeing toward the southern gate, but the dead were too many."

"Stay there!" I shout.

And then I turn around. Look over the chaos. Once, none of this would have been my responsibility. I would have happily swiped a gin bottle from a burning pub and strolled out into a forest, worried about nobody's hide but my own.

Everything's different now.

People rely on me.

Dammit—I rely on them, too.

Tòrr rears up in the center of the Glassmarket, shrieking

toward the sky. He catches a beam of sunlight in his horn and sends its blasting across the square, where it shatters a nearby church spire. More screams sound as rubble falls.

But then—a different scream.

"Sabine!" I cry.

I turn just in time to see a blast of grave-black fey crackle over her; she tumbles off Tòrr's back and slams hard onto the broken stones.

I whip around. *Motherfucker.*

It's that bastard, Immortal Woudix.

He strides out of a throng of his undead corpses, moving with sickening calmness as they snap their jaws at every-thing that moves—except him.

Their god.

Sabine shoves herself upright, bracing on blood-slicked hands. Silver pours from a gash on her temple, trailing down her jaw—but she doesn't falter. Her teeth bare in a feral snarl as she throws one hand into the air.

Power ignites at her fingertips.

Her fey crackles—hot, wild, electric—and the ground beneath Woudix shudders. With a roar, roots explode upward, thick and gnarled, lashing like serpents to ensnare him.

But Woudix barely lifts his chin. One whispered word, no louder than breath—and the roots wither midair, shriv-eling black, collapsing to ash before they can strike.

Sabine's fingers twist sharply again, undaunted.

This time, wind whips in a rising spiral, faster and faster, until a razor-edged cyclone forms in the heart of the Glass-market, made of dust, debris, and shards of shattered glass.

The whirlwind tears through his armor. Shards of glass slash his leather and draw blood—but Woudix doesn't flinch. He leans into the wind like it's no more than a breeze, his eyes locked on Sabine.

Then he raises his hand.

And the dead answer.

A wall of his undead soldiers lurches forward in formation, groaning with hunger.

I start to charge, sword already high—but Rian grips my arm.

"Don't," he hisses. "They can't hurt her—she's immortal. But they can kill *you*."

Sabine doesn't hesitate. She slams her hands together.

A pulse of silver fey explodes outward like a shockwave, knocking the nearest undead back into the street.

Still, more press in. Dozens. *Too many.*

Sabine falters, breath ragged.

But then, a bell clangs loudly from the direction of the castle, and Woudix whips around.

He narrows his eyes. "I'm being summoned—but this is far from over."

He strides back through his dead army, torn cloak whipping behind him.

"Rian," I bark. "Go to her."

He bolts toward Sabine, reaching her just as she stumbles to her knees.

I don't wait.

I wrench a sword from a fallen soldier, strap his shield onto my arm, and begin to push forward—straight through the shambling wall of dead.

"Hey!" I slam the sword's blade against the shield to get their attention. "Over here. *I'll* give you a fight."

I'll be honest—this doesn't look good.

In fact, it's fucking *bleak*.

Sabine is weakened. The city is on fire. Risen corpses shuffle out of the smoke to attack anyone in sight.

And Tòrr? That murder horse is going berserk. He stampedes toward the guildhall, too crazed to stop now even if he could, and I can see what's going to happen a second before it does.

He's going to smash into the only pillar left standing. The guildhall is going to collapse—with Suri, Ferra, and Folke falling with it.

"No!" I cry.

Suri and Ferra scream, hurling down clay roof tiles, but the projectiles only smash against the horse's iron sides and shatter.

I meet Folke's eyes—at the same time, we both look at the water tank.

He swings his sword at the tank's nearest wooden support, hacking through the wood to weaken it. Then, he shoves his weight against the opposite side. His face turns red from exertion, sweat beading on his brow. He pushes harder, his one good leg trembling from the effort...

...and the water tank tips.

Falls.

The water tank crashes down, smashing into Tòrr just as he's mere feet from colliding with the guildhall's remaining pillar. The wooden tank shatters over the monoceros's powerful head and neck, and thousands of gallons of frigid water splash over his body.

Only...Folke falls, too.

He tries to catch himself at the last moment with his one good leg, but he's already off-balance, limbs strained from the effort.

He pitches forward, pinwheeling his arms.

Ferra screams.

Folke crashes to the ground, his head connecting hard with a broken board.

"Folke!" Ferra cries, gripping onto the rooftop railing as she holds a hand out, as if she can go back in time and stop him from losing his balance.

For a second, I can only stare.

I've been trained for this—for the unexpected. I'm a soldier. A hunter. A street fighter. I've seen so many accidents and deaths that by now, they all blur together.

But this?

This fucking *breaks* me. It feels like someone reached into my chest, smashed through my ribs, and ripped out my beating heart.

"No!" I surge forward, leaping over rubble and around the lumbering dead, and fall to my knees at Folke's side.

He's breathing. But it's strained. Wracked with choking sounds.

Blood stains the front of his shirt like a poppy flower blooming.

"For...fuck's...sake...Basten," he chokes out. "Leave this... old...man. Get...the...*gods*."

My eyes go wide. I clasp his hand, unwilling to let go. I can't tell from here how bad his injuries are. It doesn't look good, but with care, there's a chance he could make it.

Only, how the fuck is he supposed to get to a healer in the middle of a siege?

"Tòrr!" Sabine's weak voice croaks from the wrecked square. Weakly, she reaches out a hand toward the monoceros. "Tòrr, come!"

I realize three things at the same time:

One, Tòrr's no longer rampaging. Folke's stunt with the water tank shocked him out of his craze.

Two, the falling water tank broke his solarium horn, which hangs now by a small shard.

And three, Sabine isn't using her inner voice. The one she's always used to communicate with animals, especially Tòrr.

I look around at the wreckage.

It's...not good.

Be a king, Basten.

Tòrr nuzzles Folke's shoulder, firm and urgent, as if demanding the man get up. Gods help me, I could swear that bloodthirsty beast, who has never cared about any mortal in its thousands of years, feels *guilty.*

Sabine calls to him again, and Tòrr swings his head around, and after giving Folke one more look, rears up on his hind legs and charges down a side alley.

Gone.

"Hang in there, old man." I squeeze Folke's shoulder, then stagger toward Sabine, lifting my sword to block a walking cadaver who lunges at me. I slice him clean through, leaving two steaming halves on the broken cobblestones.

Rian leans over Sabine, picking glass shards out of her bare skin. Silver blood pools beneath her, but her wounds are already healing.

It's wrong, somehow. That within seconds, my perfect goddess, my warrior queen who has been to hell and back, doesn't have a scratch on her.

In seconds, her skin is once more smooth, flawless.

Cheeks perfectly flushed.

Lips so full they glisten.

She grabs my shoulder and pulls me into a tight hug. "Basten, I can't—can't use my fey. There's nothing left."

She lifts a trembling hand, but her fey lines are faded to a ghost of themselves, barely pulsing beneath her skin.

Without hesitation, I tilt her close to my jugular, my arms tightening around her weakened body. "Drink. That's an order. Every gods-damned drop."

Her sob catches in my shirt, ragged and raw, and it shatters something in me. She shakes her head, still pressed against the seam of my shoulder. "It'll take all of you."

"No. It won't." Rian drops beside us, kneeling on the blood-slicked stone. He rolls back his sleeve, revealing a gash already weeping red. "Not with both of us."

Sabine looks between us, her eyes impossibly wide, and then she makes her choice. She grips Rian's arm, where blood already flows, and drinks.

Deep. Desperate. Hungry.

Rian leans back, his breath hissing through clenched teeth—pain and something darker, sharper, humming beneath the surface.

Slowly, his face pales. His eyes sink.

Still, she drinks, and I see it—that fever in her eyes. The same reckless fire that nearly consumed Tòrr when the wildness took him.

"Enough!" I pull her off Rian and twist her toward me, pressing her face to my neck, to the spot where my pulse hammers. "Now me."

She struggles at first, but only briefly.

Then she sinks in.

Her lips part, her teeth find the artery, and the pain flares before it fades to something else entirely. Something electric. Her breath shudders against my throat, and the world tilts sideways. It's intoxicating, transcendent.

But I can feel it—how much she's taking.

Too much.

A heavy hand latches onto my shoulder, and I'm roughly pulled away from Sabine. She growls, angry and still hungry, eyes flashing, and starts to lunge toward me again.

But Rian presses a hand against her chest. "Sabine, you're going to kill him!"

She sways on hands and knees, hair blood-soaked and streaked around her, blinking hard to try to center herself. She licks a trace of my blood from her lips.

Her fey lines throb, but they aren't as bright as they need to be to defeat the entire fae court.

She knows it, too. "*More.*"

I don't hesitate. I yank open my shirt, baring my chest to her. If she needs more, she can take all of me. When I swore I'd sacrifice myself for her, I meant every gods-damned word.

But Rian steps in, scowling, and shoves me backward. "You're the king. People need you. Let me."

He starts to unfasten his shirt.

I stop him—grab his hands, steady and firm. My breath shakes, but my voice doesn't. "It's *because* I'm king that I have to do this. This is what a true king does."

Rian looks at me with wide, confused eyes.

"It's not about the throne," I continue. "It's this—sacrifices no one will remember but matter more than anything." My throat tightens as my gaze shifts to Sabine. "There was a time I didn't care about kingdoms. About anyone, really. But you changed that, Sabine. You made me care."

Sabine's eyes flicker with a brief flash of understanding, breaking her hunger.

Then we hear them.

Hoofbeats thunder down the alley—sharp, rhythmic, determined.

I spin just in time to see him.

Tòrr.

He charges through the chaos like a comet. He crashes his battered body through the ranks of the dead, sweeping them aside with bone-snapping grace. Silver blood streams down his sides from claw marks and bite wounds. His solarium horn, once flawless, is cracked, splintered in half, barely hanging on.

Still, he comes.

Skidding to a halt, Tòrr lowers his head. His massive frame shakes with effort, breath hitching with every ragged inhale. Wounds bloom across his flanks. He's broken, bleeding.

Silent and reverent, he kneels.

And the truth slams into me: He's giving himself to her as a final offering.

My blood, Rian's blood...it isn't enough for what Sabine is going to have to face. So Tòrr is making up the difference.

Sabine throws herself on his prostrate body, running her hands over his thick fur, the broken black scales slick with blood.

"Tòrr...no," she whispers, then her voice rises, fracturing. "Please. Please, no. I can't lose you, too. My heart—" She presses her forehead to his neck, choking. "It won't survive another goodbye."

For a moment, he is still.

Then, with what little strength remains, he lifts his head.

His eyes find hers.

They're already dimming, the red fire in them dying, but when they meet Sabine's gaze, something ancient stirs. I don't know if her godkiss has returned, but something passes between them. A moment, I think, not meant for mortals.

A thousand unsaid thank-yous.

A meeting of minds.

A dirge for what could have been.

And then, her sob breaks free. Raw. Seismic. She shakes her head, tears spilling down her cheeks. "I won't...I can't..."

But he presses his brow against hers, like a priest giving a benediction.

Like an *order*.

Sobbing harder, she bends and drinks from the wound. Her shoulders shake, her breath hitching with every swallow. For a second, she tries to pull back, but her body betrays her, clinging desperately to his offering.

She drinks deeply.

"I love you," she whispers, finally pulling her lips free. "I will honor your loss. I'll...I'll never let the world forget you. What you did for us."

Tòrr exhales one final time.

Sabine screams into his fur, the sound fracturing against my ears, full of bitter pain that she is only strong because he gave her his dying power.

Around us, chaos rages. Rian pushes back to his feet, slicing through corpses. Ferra and Suri appear from the smoke, wielding makeshift weapons, pushing back the horde inch by inch.

Seconds pass—but they feel like a lifetime.

Tòrr's eyes, once full of starlight, go cloudy.

No blink. No breath.

His heart—all six great ventricles—falls silent.

And then—

Sabine gasps.

She rises, shining like a fallen star, eyes burning with silver light, hair billowing as though caught in a whirlwind.

Alive. Glorious. Unstoppable.

Tòrr is gone, yes—but through her, he gallops still.

SABINE

I remember.

That's the first thought that enters my mind when I rise from the glass-strewn rubble, in a shredded and mud-stained gown, with the still-steaming body of a monoceros at my feet.

I remember...everything. Meeting Tòrr in another life, when he was nothing but a knock-kneed colt with a horn too heavy for his head. I met him a thousand years ago, and a thousand years before *that*. In fact, I remember *all* the monoceroses of old. Saph. Sunflare. Aurora. Hailstrom. Cloudveil. Stormwatch.

I remember the monoceroses because I remember every day of my former lives. The human bodies I've inhabited before, stretching back to the very first, a wizened woman with a beautiful lattice of wrinkles, wild white hair untamed and knotted around her shoulders.

I remember the First Awakening—the hot kiss of Vale's knife blade against my throat.

The Second Awakening, too, when his same damn knife slashed my belly.

I remember my nine fae brethren in painstaking detail, all the debauched midnight reveries, the games of fate with human lives in the balance, the long line of drained and discarded acolytes they've left behind without a care in the world.

Maybe, though, what I remember most isn't a memory at all—but a feeling.

Love. It hits me like a gut punch. Love for the eastern wind. For the first snow of December. For the tiny yawn of a mouse.

For Tòrr.

It's a love that is stained with his loss, that weighs me down like a boulder in my stomach. The kind of love that can tear down kingdoms with its bittersweet pain, that will live in me like a splinter for the rest of my life.

I understand now why my father tried so hard to hide the truth of my identity from me when I first arrived in Norhelm. In every single Return, I've chosen the side of nature over the fae. In some cases, it's taken me longer to arrive to that conclusion. Once, centuries passed before I realized the fae's rotten core and picked the wilderness instead of their gilded court.

And this Return? The Third?

It must be a record, because I've barely been awake as fae for weeks, and I already understand *exactly* what they are.

"Basten," I rasp, my voice somehow here and not here, like it rides the wind. I run to him, still choking on my sobs. "Tòrr..."

He holds me fiercely, and I swear I can hear a hitch of a

sob in his own throat. "He was a legend. Too fierce for this world. He burned too bright, too hot—and he didn't want you to do the same. To be ruled by his fury."

"He gave me everything. Blood. Memories. Power. I—I don't know how to break it to Myst," I choke out. "I'm afraid she isn't strong enough to take it. She's old, Basten. Tòrr was her final mate."

Basten pulls back to gaze into my eyes. "You tell Myst that we'll honor him. We'll make the most of everything he sacrificed to save the city, and we'll mourn his loss with all the respect due to a monoceros of his strength."

I nod, swallowing back sobs. I can feel Tòrr, deep in my veins. Urging me to stop crying. To make his sacrifice worth it—before it's too late.

I take a deep breath. "Get Folke to safety—there's still some life in him."

Basten cups his palms at my elbows, supporting me. "I will."

"I—I have to get to Hekkelveld Castle." I force myself to keep my eyes on Basten, to not look at Tòrr's broken body. "That's where Woudix went—that's where they all will gather. They're drawn to it. It's an ancient structure, built for them thousands of years ago." I pause, sucking in air, leaning my forehead against his chest. Then, I continue, "I'll face them there—but first, I have to stop their plague on the city."

"Let me help you," he says.

I swallow, touching my hand to his beautiful face. "Tell them—Suri, Ferra, Rian—to spread word through as much of the city as you can. Tell the citizens to climb to the highest floors of their houses. Rooftops, bridges. And to *wait*."

He nods. He can see the change in me. I know it. His eyes

are reverent as he looks over me, like I'm a living star. "I'll tell the others. But I'm not leaving your side."

"You have to." I rest a hand on his shirt, fingers twisting in the fabric. "I need you to get something for me."

I lean in close, whispering in his ear.

He pulls back, hesitant to agree because it means leaving my side, but he nods.

As he turns to give our friends the orders, my heart clenches—I love him so fiercely it feels like it might kill me.

Not in any of my past lives, not once, have I known a love like this. Basten is the only person who ever touched my soul and left his mark.

I'm fae, yes. But I'm also human. Somehow, that's the conclusion I always come back to in every Return. It's what my brother and sister fae forget:

That we're *of* them, not *above* them.

Suri and Ferra dig a broken door out of the rubble, and cart it over to where Folke lies. Together, Basten and Rian lift Folke's bleeding body onto it. Basten exchanges a few words with them, and then Ferra and Rian grip the door's edges, ready to carry the makeshift stretcher toward help.

But Suri spares a second to look over her shoulder at me.

Quickly, so fast I almost don't see it, she makes the Winged Lady gesture with her hands.

Then Ferra calls to her, and she reaches down to help lift the stretcher.

Tears flow harder down my face as I smile.

Friends. In thousands of years, I never had those, either.

The animated corpse of a fisherman, fish knife still dangling from his belt, stumbles over broken glass toward me.

Basten catches sight of him and peels off to move

toward him confidently, sword raised. With one clean swipe, he severs the man's head, then disappears around the corner.

I push to my feet, slowly becoming aware of how many of Woudix's dead are flooding into the Glassmarket.

It unnerves me, how I can't control them. How, when I reach into their souls, only a hollow chill answers.

There's only one god they answer to, and it isn't me.

Hunting for my breath, I press a hand against my chest, forcing myself to assess the situation.

All around me, the swelling tide of the dead terrorize any citizens who haven't managed to take shelter. They climb through broken storefront windows. Claw at locked doors. Screams of the living echo throughout the city in a deafening chorus.

I move instead toward the tallest heap of broken stone and splintered timber, and climb up the rubble until I stand above the chaos, above the screams, above the stench of death and blood and rot.

The air around me crackles, alive.

I draw in a slow breath, and with it I pull in everything they have given me—Basten's raw, stubborn devotion, Rian's cunning and strength, Tòrr's sacred sacrifice—until my heart feels too full for my body to contain.

Their blood burns like starlight in my veins.

I lift my hands to the sky.

My fingers knit gracefully through the air, each motion deliberate. My fey lines ignite like constellations across my skin, silver blazing outward, pulsing with a power that finally feels *right*.

The earth shudders underfoot.

Beyond the southern gate, the lake answers my call,

rising from its bed in a slow, majestic swell. I can feel its movements almost like it's a part of me. Water coils upward, shimmering and translucent, before surging forward in a roaring wall of force, pouring over hills, through valleys, straight to the city gate.

It blasts through, flooding the streets with unyielding power.

The wall of water crashes into the undead horde, sweeping them from their feet, dragging them under, breaking their brittle bodies apart, and carrying their now powerless corpses back to a final resting place at the lake's bottom.

And I stand there, hair whipping around my face, the floodwaters rising to my ankles. I slowly lift my hands skyward, reveling in the wind on my face, and feel it again— the sense that far from succumbing to the rising waters, I could simply take wing and soar away.

Eventually, the floodwaters drain. The water level sinks, revealing the broken city again, yet now, the flood has carried most of the broken boards, stone dust, and blood stains with it.

There's rebuilding to be done, yes. But it feels like a starting point.

The public peers apprehensively out of upper windows, too fearful to leave their hiding places. So, I summon the animals of the city and surrounding forests to enter first, to show them that all is safe now.

A herd of deer gracefully sweeps through the Glassmarket. A pair of hawks fly down to land on Valor Belltower.

Cats by the hundreds prowl through the streets, hunting any flopping fish the lake might have left behind.

Slowly, people emerge from their safe spots. Ladders are lowered. Helpers come in to assist those down from broken upper windows. Once they're back on the ground, people fall to their knees, sobbing out both their devastation for what was lost at the same time as their prayers for my salvation.

Every prayer, every bent knee—it builds strength in my bones.

Though I didn't call her, Myst races across the Glass-market—drawn to me, to my need, even without my summons.

Her dainty hooves are still painted sunset colors from yesterday's Ride of Sun and Moon show, though her pink-and-orange dyed mane is tangled now.

She skids to a halt before me.

She takes me in at once—my trembling hands, my bent back, the absence beside me where Tòrr should be. His body is gone, now. Swept away by the receding lake waters, carried to rest somewhere beyond the city walls, in nature—where he belongs.

But his broken-off horn remains lodged between two fallen bricks.

Slowly, I bend down to pick it up—what's left of it. I cradle the beautiful, deadly solarium spire in my arm as I approach Myst.

Her ears flatten. A broken whinny tears from her nostrils.

She knows what it means.

A living monoceros would never leave its horn behind.

Myst, I say. **My brave girl. My fierce friend. We...we lost him.**

She stamps her hooves, snorting loud. Trying to deny it. Willing me to take the words back.

I'm so sorry, I say, reaching for her head.

She jerks upright, breathing hard. Then, acceptance breaks, and she tosses her head up, letting out a sound somewhere between a howl and a cry that rattles through the city with the weight of her grief.

I know. I hold in my own grief as I fold forward and nuzzle her neck. *I know. I loved him, too*.

We stay like that, girl and horse, while our mourning finds a mirror in one another's pain.

Then, holding his horn, I swing onto her bare back, legs fitting around her like a well-worn pair of trousers. **He wouldn't want us to cry. He'd want us to fight.**

I click my heels. She hesitates, but then strides forward. Solid and sure.

A tribute to him.

As we ride through the broken city, people take a knee, lowering their heads to me. Bakers and soldiers. Children and tavernkeepers. Mothers and prostitutes.

But not only them: The street dogs stop and stretch their front paws in a bow. Chickadees swarm on every lamp post, tipping down their beaks. Every carriage horse lowers its head in honor.

I keep my chin high, bolstered by their devotion, which shines on me like the first rays of dawn, warm and welcoming and so full of love I could burst.

The fence surrounding Hekkelveld Castle is all but gone —either destroyed in one of Tòrr's solarium blasts or from my raging flood. Myst strides straight into the courtyard, where puddles still hold flopping fish.

No guards stop us.

No gates stand in our way.

I dismount and briefly press my forehead to hers, Tòrr's broken horn clutched tightly in my hands.

His sacrifice made it all possible, my pretty girl, I whisper in my head. ***He won't be forgotten.***

She bows her head.

We're two souls who have lost someone.

A girl and her horse.

Best friends.

I draw in a long, fortifying breath, tuck his horn into my belt, then step through the shattered archway into Raven Hall.

They're waiting for me.

Six of them—my so-called brothers and sisters. My *father*. The gods of the known world, seated on thrones they've used their powers to forge from the wreckage: bones and twisted metal.

Vale nods, his smile heavy and mirthless. "Daughter."

"Father." My voice is deep, almost as if the earth itself is speaking.

I focus on Woudix instead, slouched in the farthest throne on the right. Hawk is curled obediently against his shin, as always.

My gaze catches on the hound, and something cracks inside me. If it had been me tasked with her care, I would've given her a peaceful end beneath the roots of an old tree, her soul returned gently to the earth. Not this. Not an eternity prowling half-rotted and enslaved to a god's will.

Woudix sits too still as he gazes steadily back at me—but I catch the twitch of his right eye.

He's afraid.

I walk toward him slowly, deliberately, the light beneath my skin pulsing with new brilliance.

"Monoceros blood," I say, raising my arms so they can all see the fey glow through my veins. "I'm the first fae ever to drink it, isn't that right? I don't recall any monoceroses dying for any of *you*."

Artain's mouth curls into a sneer, an insult poised on his lips, but Woudix answers instead.

With violence.

Black fey explodes from his palms, a cloud of ash and soot surging toward me.

I raise my hand, my own fey bursting outward in a wave of silver so bright it cuts through the dark like a sunburst.

I leap aside just in time as a blade whistles past me—Thracia's glass-edged dagger, thrown with inhuman precision.

It shatters against the pillar behind me into a spray of mirrored shards.

Then, an arrow zooms at me from Artain's bow, but I twist out of the way in time, ducking and it only grazes my arm. I look down at the already-healing wound.

With Basten's strength in my bones, Rian's devotion burning in my blood, and Tòrr's final heartbeat alive in my chest, I rise to face them again.

"You thought you could tame me," I tell Woudix, my voice barbed. "With lies. With mimicry of friendship."

He leans forward, hands tented, and then slowly tilts his head toward Iyre beside him. "It was Iyre's idea. She saw Basten's memories before she consumed them—she realized how much true companionship meant to you. That friendship would hold more power than threats."

Iyre smiles cruelly, drumming her long nails on her throne. "You were *so* easy to manipulate."

"But Basten saw through you," I say steadily, looking between them. "Through both of you." I hesitate, regret lacing my voice. "Even when I couldn't."

Vale's thundering voice commands all our attention. "I take it your memories are back, daughter."

I turn to him and nod, slow and vicious. "They are. And there's one in particular I recall in blistering detail." I point a long finger at Woudix. "I remember how he can open any door and have it lead to the underrealm. Woudix, I advise you to open it now."

Then I raise my arms, head tipped back.

The earth trembles.

A deep groan splits the mosaic tiles of Raven Hall as the floor beneath the gods fractures. Cracks spread outward, glowing blue from beneath. Brimfire magma boils up from the chasms, burning a sapphire glow.

I call to it.

Guide it.

Shape it with the fluid movements of my fingers.

With a sweep of my arms, I forge the lava-like brimfire into columns—massive coils around the six gods in the shape of a cage.

Before the cage seals, Woudix shoots to his feet in an attempt to flee, but the brimfire strikes him, driving him back.

Vale lifts a hand, blasting his fey against the brimfire— but volcanic stone absorbs energy.

Artain draws another arrow, but the brimfire columns are too tight for him to pull back his arrow.

They're trapped.

The cage closes, its bars cooling into shimmering blue-black obsidian, but still hot enough to sizzle against immortal flesh.

Woudix grips the bars, silver blood hissing as it drips from his palms. "You think you can cage gods?"

"No," I say softly. "Not forever. But I *can* delay you."

"I'll call my resurrected bodies to come break the bars."

I pause, meeting each of their eyes in turn, before continuing. "It will take time for your dead puppets to free you. Hours, maybe. And we all know there's a simpler way out."

I step back, gaze sweeping over their trapped forms. With deliberate movements, I pick up the broken vestibule door, forgotten on the wrecked foyer floor, and drag it over. I shove it between the bars.

Iyre and Thracia have to scramble out if it's way as it clatters to the floor.

I point to the door on the floor.

"Banish yourselves to the underrealm," I say. "Or burn."

I grab Tòrr's horn from my leather belt and thrust it high, into the beam of sunlight from the broken ceiling.

Solarium—maybe the only thing that I've seen the fae afraid of. While it might not deal them a deathblow, it will wound them. Maybe even in ways they can never recover from.

And I *know* them.

They'd rather surrender with their pretty faces intact than risk a permanent scar.

Artain scowls but crouches down, reaching for the door-knob. "Woudix, brother. Open the fucking door. We can continue this *discussion* with our sister at a later date."

I smile at Artain in mock sweetness. "You always were the most vain."

"Woudix!" Artain prompts.

The God of Death's lip curls back over his incisors, refusing to budge.

"Do it," Vale hisses, low and impatient. "We'll play my daughter's little game, for now."

Woudix's jaw tenses, but he doesn't dare disobey a direct order. He crouches next to Artain, whispering low in an ancient language, and the edges of the door begin to glow with black iridescent light.

Artain gives me one final scowl. "Be seeing you again soon, darling," he hisses as he twists the doorknob. "Banishment to the underrealm is hardly a life sentence."

He jerks the door open. Instead of broken floor tiles beneath, it's a yawning portal now, earthen stairs descending into a darkened realm.

I stare him down, unblinking, the solarium horn high in my fist.

He descends the stairs into the wavering portal, which is windless, dark, cold as a grave.

Woudix stands next, leaning close to the bars. "One day," he purrs, "You'll join me in my underrealm. Maybe not for a thousand years—but you will."

He takes a step down but stops when he realizes Hawk is not at his side. Instead, she's looking at me. Torn ears raised. Big eyes wavering. My heart clenches for her—but he taps his thigh, and she turns to descend with him.

One by one, they leave.

Samaur, grinning ghoulishly, says before leaving "Remember—this is far from over. You struck a bargain to provide us with games, theatrics, and recreations of legends worthy of our stature. Your Fae Games ended halfway through, but don't fear. We'll plan something *truly* memorable for the conclusion—a new game. Something no one's ever seen before. Something to be written about in the history books for ages."

Thracia follows him through the door, looking my tattered gown up and down, unimpressed.

Iyre follows.

Finally, it's only Vale. He stands tall behind the brimfire bars, towering over me, and I swear I see a cold vein of pride in his eyes.

Almost...the thrill of a challenge.

"Enjoy your peace, daughter," he says. "While you have it."

He joins the others, taking slow, heavy steps like the clatter of a funeral bell—and then the underrealm door smashes closed.

I'm alone in the cavernous Raven Hall. The glow beneath the door cuts out, and now it's just a splintered old door sitting on top of tiles.

My legs give out.

I crash to the broken tiles, which were once such a beautiful tribute to humanity's virtues, and cradle Tòrr's horn against my chest.

I don't rest like that long before I hear heavy boots on the castle steps.

"Sabine!"

I whirl around to see Basten charging into Raven Hall. He pulls me to my feet, wrapping his arms around me so fiercely I can barely breathe, but I don't care. I squeeze him back just as viciously, sobbing against his shoulder.

"Basten. You're okay."

He kisses the top of my head, messy, desperate caresses like he's afraid someone is going to tear me away from him. He takes my cheeks between his hands, tilting my head to look at him.

"Are you hurt?" he asks.

I shake my head. Physically, I'm in prime condition. My fae blood has healed every tiny scratch, repaired my bruises, and restored the strength in my muscles.

But my heart aches as I clutch Tòrr's horn.

"One final thing," I whisper, and stagger to the tall doorway of Raven Hall, with the twin carvings of the words BRAVERY and VIRTUE still standing—one of the few unbroken parts of the castle.

I glance back at Basten. "You have the fae needle?"

He takes it out of his pocket, carefully wrapped in a blood-stained handkerchief. "Stolen from the exhibit hall, as you asked."

I set to work stitching apart the fabric of space along the stone edges of the castle's entry. I don't rush, remembering all the times I've used this tool before, and exactly how to set the portal's opening point to the exact place I wish to reach.

When I've finished, the view through the archway—the broken castle courtyard with the destroyed fence—falls away.

In its place, Basten and I stare at a river valley.

This one, however, holds no glistening lake, no leafy trees.

It's a shell of what it once was.

Bones and rot.

I set Tòrr's horn down carefully at my feet and press my hands together. I draw in a breath, letting the ancient knowledge his monoceros blood awakened in me settle into my core.

Slowly, my silver fey spreads from my feet, along the broken mosaic tiles, bleeding through the portal into the poisoned Lunden Valley.

As my fey crackles over the wrecked earth, grass sprouts in its wake. The barren lake gleams once more with blue shimmering waves, as a trout jumps with a splash. Leaves burst to life on the skeletal tree branches, welcoming the birds that sweep in to settle there.

I turn to Basten, leaning into his steadying weight, with tears in my eyes.

"I can't bring back those who died," I whisper. "The cursed souls Woudix manipulated into terrorizing the city. But it's a thriving, living valley again for everyone who lost their homes. Not just the refugees in Norhelm. The birds who lost their nests. The animals who had to flee their dens."

He cups my cheek in his hand, gazing into my eyes with awe and love—and a touch of unease. "The Fae Court isn't going to let this go. They're going to come back at us with every army they can gather, fae and mortal alike."

I let out a long breath. "I know. I'd hoped for peace. For a balance between fae and the mortal world. But now I see that I have to choose—and I'll choose this every time. Humanity. Nature. Animals." I look into his eyes. "*You.*"

He presses a kiss to my forehead and lets it linger, flooding me with something more than his devotion.

With love, always.

"I choose you, too," he says. "Together. Always. Against any damn storm coming our way."

EPILOGUE

SABINE

Through Basten's love, I feel a change.

No—a new phase. Like a caterpillar shedding its old form, again and again, until a moth lifts itself for the first time into the night.

It's something that's always been there, I think. Something I could call forth when needed, but I was too deafened by the mortal world to hear it.

My bones shift and slide along my back in a way that isn't painful so much as it's *powerful*. My fey lines flare and blister along the sharp curve of my shoulder blades.

I drop to my knees, tearing at my gown. Shove the neckline down over one shoulder until my bare back is exposed. I clutch the scraps of fabric to my chest as I heave a breath.

Basten kneels beside me, his touch sure and grounding.

"It's okay, Sabine. Let them come."

And they come. They break free. Delicate, powdery soft as a moth's, the same stone-white color as Myst's fur—unfurling into the beam of sunlight that shines like a spotlight down on my *wings*.

END OF BOOK FOUR

∼

One final book remains! Gods and mortals will come to a reckoning in book five, *Dark Gods Bright Dawn*!

∼

P.S. Join my mailing list to be first to hear news about *Dark Gods Bright Dawn's* release date, as well as to get access to a gallery of artwork of Sabine, Basten, and Rian!

A Note from Evie

Dark Hearts,

I hope this book gave you everything you dreamed it would: swoons, laughs, tears, and maybe even a few raised eyebrows. (Hello, Chapter 27!) Before you know it, the final book will be here, and Sabine and Basten's love story will conclude with godkissed fireworks.

Let the world know what you think by rating the series!

Rate White Horse Black Nights
Rate Silver Wings Golden Games
Rate Steel Heart Iron Claws
Rate Cold Stars Midnight Glow

xo, Evie